Charles Hastings Collette

The Life, Times, and Writings of Thomas Cranmer, D. D.

The first reforming archbishop of Canterbury

Charles Hastings Collette

The Life, Times, and Writings of Thomas Cranmer, D. D.
The first reforming archbishop of Canterbury

ISBN/EAN: 9783337295714

Printed in Europe, USA, Canada, Australia, Japan

Cover: Foto ©Raphael Reischuk / pixelio.de

More available books at **www.hansebooks.com**

THE

LIFE, TIMES, AND WRITINGS

OF

THOMAS CRANMER, D.D.,

THE FIRST REFORMING ARCHBISHOP OF CANTERBURY.

BY

CHARLES HASTINGS COLLETTE.
II

Omnes Homines—qui de rebus dubiis consultant, ab odio, amicitiâ, ira, atque misericordia
vacuos esse decet.—*Cæsar ap. Sallust.*

LONDON:
GEORGE REDWAY, YORK STREET, COVENT GARDEN.
1887.

To

THE MOST REV. EDWARD WHITE,

NINETY-THIRD ARCHBISHOP OF CANTERBURY,

AND PRIMATE OF ALL ENGLAND,

This Work is respectfully Dedicated,

BY

A SINCERE AND DEVOTED SON OF THE
CHURCH OF THE REFORMATION.

PREFACE.

"IT will be admitted by all who are in any degree acquainted with it, that there is no period of our history which is more interesting than that of the Reformation. And this is not merely considered in an Ecclesiastical, but in a Political and Philosophical point of view : and as bearing on our constitution, our laws, habits, modes of thought and action, on the whole history of our country since that time, and our own state and circumstances at the present day." Such was the utterance of the REV. DR MAITLAND. The name of CRANMER, as our first Reforming Archbishop, is necessarily connected with the history of that period. Whatever his personal merits or demerits may have been, we are mainly indebted to him for laying the foundation of that Reformation which entirely revolutionised the Ecclesiastical, Political, and Social position of this country. The "Life and Times of Cranmer," therefore, whatever individual opinions may be—whether for good or evil— must be of vital interest to every Englishman; but from the very nature of the subject, opinions will differ ; especially where theological questions are involved.

CRANMER stands the most prominent character in the history of the Reformation in this country, and has in consequence been equally the object of virulent attacks and of fulsome praise. To undertake the Biography of such a character, and to be entirely impartial, is difficult. It was Descartes who said that "the prime condition for discovering the truth is to be free from all prejudices." But every writer on such a subject,—be he a member of the Reformed or the Unreformed Church—will naturally have his own peculiar views and prejudices. How is he, then, to hold an even balance between opposite opinions ? Such, however, is the task upon which I have ventured. It is not an easy one. This protestation will of course be taken for what it is worth, coming from an avowed member of the Reformed Church of England ; and I do not hesitate to appropriate the sentiment of DEAN HOOK, who said, in his Preface to the "Life of Archbishop Cranmer", "I have no inclination to vindicate the character of Cranmer, for in his conduct there was much which was indefensible; but it is my duty as an historian to guard against the distortion of facts, while as Christians, we are bound to make due allowance for a person who, in a position not sought for by him, was surrounded with peculiar and unusual difficulties."

The number of "Lives" and "Biographical Sketches" that have been already published, renders the task more embarrassing from the diametrically opposite views taken of CRANMER'S actions and motives. Again, with so many details before us, a further difficulty presents itself, the fear of wearying the reader : — "Opere in longo fas est obrepere somnum," as Horace truly remarked — by a recapitulation of well-known historical facts. Under these circumstances I have not considered it necessary to trace Cranmer's life step by step, in all its details, which would be but a compilation, culled from the works of many excellent biographers such as Strype, Todd, Le Bas, Gilpin, and Dean Hook. I have therefore determined, if possible, to mark out a new line of proceeding, by taking the more prominent incidents of the Life and Times of Cranmer, viewed with the surrounding circumstances wherein he has been both censured and commended, and I have endeavoured to arrive at an equal and just judgment between, what may be described as, the two extremes.

Cranmer has bequeathed to us Writings which speak for themselves. These I have endeavoured to analyse; and the reader will, I trust, have a fair estimate of his labours, and appreciate the great work, which appears to have been the object of his life to accomplish.

I have endeavoured to avoid controversy; and the many opponents of Cranmer will find that I have not omitted to blame him where blame is deserved. He lived in cruel and most exceptional times, when corruption in the Church was at its height, and persecutions for conscience' sake were fiercely enforced; but it is a fact that all the charges brought against Cranmer relate to acts done by him while a Roman Catholic in doctrine, in strict accordance with the principles of that Church, and participated in by all his Episcopal contemporaries.

Our earliest notice of Cranmer's life and ultimate fall we derive from Fox's "Book of Martyrs," which may not inaptly be described as "the red-rag" of "Ritualists" and "Papists," at whose hands Fox has received severe castigation, being accused of wilful perversion of facts, and even of mutilating documents. I have, therefore, considered it not out of place to add, in an Appendix, a few observations on the Life and Writings of the Martyrologist, but I have limited my observations principally to testimonies of that writer's truthfulness,—a virtue in which he is accused of being lamentably deficient as an historian.

A Biography can scarcely be said to be complete without the writer giving an estimate, according to his view, of the character of the person whose life is reproduced. To come to a just conclusion, we ought to place ourselves, so far as may be possible, in the same situation, and under

the same circumstances, and consider both the times and
the surroundings of the period. We are too ready to form
an opinion, judging from our own present stand-point, and
according to our own present accepted notions of morality.
Having perused many different " Lives " and " Historical
Sketches " of CRANMER, and observed the diametrically opposite views and opinions arrived at by different
writers, I feel that any individual expression-of opinion on
my part might have, perhaps, even less weight, than that
expressed by others. In order, however, that a member of
the Unreformed Church may arrive at a proper estimate
of his character, and judge of his motives and actions,
he must take into consideration that every act of the
Primate, for which he has been condemned, was in strict
accordance with the principles and practice of his Church,
or shared in by his clerical and lay contemporaries, all
members of the same Unreformed Church, even if he
be charged with *Schism*. *Apostacy*, the result of honest
conviction, cannot be fairly deemed a crime, so long
as each party seeks to make converts to his creed. What
one sect calls *conversion*, the opposite sect calls *perversion*. From a Protestant point of view, it might be
said that every single act of CRANMER brought in judgment against him, having been perpetrated while a
member of the Unreformed Church, and in accordance with
Papal laws and customs in which he had been brought up,
must be condemned, but with a rider to the verdict, of
" extenuating circumstances." Members of the Reformed
Church, on the other hand, glory in Cranmer's alleged
apostacy. They esteem him for his work's sake, and point
to his Martyrdom as a practical vindication of the truth of
his doctrines.

CRANMER commends himself to us as a Churchman, as

the founder, and "great Master Builder," of our Reformed Church of England ; and, whatever his frailties and short-comings may have otherwise been, his Writings, which he has bequeathed to us, we prize as a lasting monument of his greatness. To borrow the eloquent words of his biographer, Strype :—

"The name of this Reverend Prelate deserves to stand upon eternal record, having been the first Reforming Archbishop of this kingdom, and the greatest instrument, under God, of the happy Reformation of this Church of England, in whose piety, learning, wisdom, conduct, and blood, the foundation of it was laid."

C. H. COLLETTE.

April 1887.

CONTENTS.

CHAPTER VIII.

CHAPTER IX.

CHAPTER X.

CHAPTER XI.

CHAPTER XII.

APPENDIX.

LIFE AND TIMES OF CRANMER.

CHAPTER I.

INTRODUCTORY.

> " To write History truly is an office little less than sacred. To indite justly the records of the bygone is a duty upon which honour and honesty impose the inevitable responsibility of faith and truthfulness."—S. HUBERT BURKE.

TWO notable characters stand forth prominently in the history of the REFORMATION of the sixteenth century, on whom unmeasured abuse and equally fulsome praise have been bestowed. These two characters are LUTHER and CRANMER. The truth would possibly lie equi-distant from the two extremes. At present, we are only concerned with Cranmer. Party spirit, enhanced by theological animosities, has gone far to embitter the controversy. A late biographer of Cranmer, Dean Hook, observed that, "the fault is not so much in misstatement of facts, but the inferences drawn from them." Would that such were the case! It is far otherwise. Human failings are, on the one hand, dwelt upon and even exaggerated by the opponents of the Reformation. Every act of the reforming Archbishop's life has been closely scrutinised, dwelt upon, and advanced as a cogent reason for condemning even the Reformation itself, which Cranmer was one of the principal instruments in effecting in this country. Where Cranmer

A

cannot be made personally responsible, he is made so indirectly, by associating him with others with whom he is
alleged to have been in close relation or friendship. Every
questionable act of which the King and his Parliament are
charged, and the several persecutions and confiscations,
are laid at the door of Cranmer, as the King's principal
adviser, and also his ready tool in all his questionable and
alleged nefarious transactions.[1] While it must be admitted
that some of the charges brought against Cranmer can be
substantiated, the cause of the Reformation does not require us to justify the failings of our Reformers. The
ready reply has been, that—

"The Reformation in England is founded upon *doctrines* which
revert back to the fountain-head—CHRIST—as revealed to us in the
New Testament ; and if that doctrine be true, it cannot be overthrown
by railing accusations against our Reformers, the teachers of these
doctrines, nor even by the exposure of their infirmities and sins.
Yet, unhappily, such has been the course taken by many who have
resorted to that line of argument to shake our faith in the justice and
desirability of such a reformation to which we, in England, are mainly
indebted to Cranmer."[2]

This is the view maintained by members of the reformed
Churches, who confidently challenge their opponents to
point out one single doctrine embraced in the three accepted
Creeds of the Christian Church, or maintained by the first
four General Councils, which was rejected by the Reformers.

"Cranmer's fate has been peculiarly hard. Living in evil days, and
exposed, after his death, to the malice of evil tongues, he has suffered
in almost every part of his reputation. 'Papists' have impeached the
sincerity, while Protestants have doubted the steadfastness of his principles ; and a too general idea seems to prevail that his opinions were
ever fluctuating, or at least were so flexible as to have rendered him
little better than a weak instrument in the hands of those who pos-

[1] See S. Hubert Burke's "Historical Portraits of the Tudor Dynasty."
London, 1883.   Vol. ii. p. 4 ; vol. iii. pp. 32 *et seq.*
[2] Todd's "Vindication of Cranmer." London, 1826. P. 14.

sessed more talent and more consistency.   But, if we are to be guided by the result of his ministration, the fact was far otherwise.   He was, in truth, the chief promoter and ablest advocate for the Reformation, planning it with the discretion of a prudent, and the zeal of a good man, and carrying it on towards perfection with a firmness, a wisdom, and liberality which obtained for him (by those who value the result of his labours) no less credit for the endowments of his head, than for the impressions of his heart."[1]

Occupying a more distinguished position, as Archbishop of Canterbury, than his contemporaries, Cranmer's actions become, as it were, public property, and, therefore, legitimate subjects for criticism.   But it must ever be borne in mind that the acts of Cranmer, which have been brought in accusation against him, were equally shared by a vast majority of the ecclesiastics and nobles of the land, who were all members of the unreformed Church, and professed to hold the *doctrines* and *practices* of that Church.   If persecution for heresy is laid to his charge, the practice was in strict accordance with the Canon Law of his Church.   If a reputed sorcerer or witch was to be burnt, it would be in strict conformity with the statute law enacted in times essentially under Church rule.   If schism be laid to his charge, it was equally shared by the leading clerical and lay members of the King's Council and Convocation. In fact, nothing can be more disastrous to the cause of the then dominant Church and religion than the ruthless attacks, justly or unjustly, made on Cranmer and his contemporaries in office, by their modern assailants, members of the same unreformed Church.   Such an argument, it must be admitted, could only be advanced in "controversy," but not as a justification where censure is justly due, and where censure is due, let each bear his fair share ; but let the judgment be a righteous judgment.

[1] Richard Lawrence, LL.D., "Bampton Lectures," pp. 23, 24 (A.D. 1804). Third edition.   Oxford, 1838.

While nothing new can now be advanced on the more than "thrice told tale" of the "Life and Times of Cranmer," there is still room left for criticism on the merits and demerits—the virtues and failings of a man, who, after LUTHER, has perhaps occupied more consideration, as well from the opponents as the advocates of the Reformation, than any other of the Reformers.

CHAPTER II.

LITTLE is known or recorded of THOMAS CRANMER'S[1] early history. He was born, 2d July 1489, at Aslacton, Northamptonshire. He was the second son of Thomas Cranmer, who is said to have been a descendant of ancestors who had for many centuries resided in the same county. CRANMER, the subject of this biography, was placed by his parents under the tutelage of a harsh preceptor, "a rude parish-clerk," from whom "he learned little, and had to suffer much." When relieved from the supervision of this task-master, Cranmer's father encouraged his son in the pursuit of field sports, with hawk and hounds. He became a good marksman, and a bold and skilful horseman. These accomplishments he seems to have retained even after he had risen to the highest office in the Church as Archbishop. His father died when Cranmer was about fourteen years old. He was then [A.D. 1503] placed in the University of Cambridge, and entered Jesus College, with the ultimate view, according to his mother's wish, of becoming a priest. His inclination, however, did not seem to turn in that direction, for he gave himself up to the dry study of logic, and scholastic philosophy of the day, and to Civil Law. These studies seem to have occupied his time until he arrived at the age of twenty-

[1] In the Letter which stands first in the list of "Cranmer's Remains," by Jenkyns (p. 6, vol. i., Oxford, 1833), the name appears at foot as Cranmar, and is noted by the editor as being the only exception.

two. He also made the Canon Law a special branch of his studies. He obtained a "Fellowship" of Jesus College in 1511. His attention was then turned to the study of Latin, Greek, and Hebrew, in all of which he became proficient. One of his favourite authors was the eminent Dutch priest ERASMUS, at that time a resident at the University of Cambridge. On these subjects he was occupied for four or five years, taking such full notes and copious extracts from his books of study as were worth preserving. When the writings of Luther began to excite public attention, these also engaged Cranmer's close examination, which first led him to enquire into the great controversies of the day, for he then, as Strype relates :—

"Considered what great controversy there was in matters of religion, not in trifles, but on the chiefest articles of our salvation, and bent himself to try out the truth therein. And forasmuch as he perceived he could not rightly judge in such weighty matters without the knowledge of the Holy Scriptures, before he was influenced with any man's opinions or errors, he applied his whole study for three years therein. After this he gave his mind to good writers, both new and old ; not rashly running over them ; for he was a slow reader but a diligent marker of whatsoever he read, seldom reading without pen in hand. And whatsoever made either for the one part or the other, of things in controversy, he wrote it out if it were short, or at least noted the author and the place, that he might write it out at leisure, which was a great help to him in debating matters ever after."

Such was Cranmer's course of study.

In his twenty-seventh year (A.D. 1516), while still a "Fellow" of his college, he married the daughter of a respectable farmer of a neighbouring county, a niece of the hostess of the "Dolphin" Inn. There is nothing on record to show that there was any impropriety either in this alliance or leading to it ; nor was the marriage, as sometimes alleged, a secret, for he did not attempt to conceal the fact. He resigned his Fellowship on his marriage, in pursuance of the college regulation.[1] The lady was not, as frequently asserted, a bar-maid. She was of respectable parentage, on a visit to her aunt at the time of her marriage. The visits of Cranmer at the "hostelry" could not have been considered derogatory, since it is admitted that the tavern was much frequented by the *alumni* of the University. Stephen Gardyner was amongst the students who dined and supped at this hostelry; and Bonner and Edward Foxe lodged there at times. In those days such establishments were owned or kept by men of position, and respected. The lady, in derision, has been called "Black Joan" from the fact of her having dark eyes and black hair, a "nick-name" perpetuated by Cranmer's assailants to the present day. So great, however, was the estimation in which Cranmer was held for his learning in the University, that although he had forfeited his Fellowship he was appointed Lecturer at Buckingham (afterwards Magdalen) College, his wife still residing at the "Dolphin" with her aunt until her death in child-birth, which took place within a year of her marriage.

On this subject two specific charges are brought against Cranmer—first, that he committed perjury in marrying while a Fellow of his college for breaking his vow of chastity. And second, that he was in consequence "expelled" from his college.[2] In the first place, at this period monks and friars alone were required to take vows of chastity, no

[1] The Rev. Dr Littledale, "Priest of the Church of England," in his Lecture on "Ritualistic Innovation," p. 37, London, 1868, thus comments on this marriage : "Cranmer's first appearance is his detection after he had privately married 'Black Joan,' the bar-maid of a pot-house in Cambridge, at a time when he was Fellow of Jesus College, and of course pledged to celibacy. He thus showed himself as a *liar*, by holding his fellowship under false pretences, and as a *thief*, by cheating his lawful successor to the vacancy." The italics are the Doctor's.

[2] Burke's "Tudor Dynasties, &c.," vol. ii. p. 4. 1880.

priest on taking Orders was so required. Cranmer was not a monk, and at this time was not a priest ; and further, a Fellow of a college is not required to take any such *vow*. The penalty, then, as now, was simply *forfeiture*. Celibacy of the priesthood, even at the present day, in the Church of Rome is accounted a matter of discipline, and not of doctrine, and may be changed as circumstances might require.[1]

Fuller, an admitted authority, in his History of the University of Cambridge, says, " Thomas Cranmer was *ousted* of his Fellowship in Jesus College for being married." [2]

The subject is referred to in Cooper's valuable " Athenæ Cantabrigiensis " [3] :—" He was elected fellow of Jesus College, but soon *vacated* his fellowship by marriage."

Le Bas, in his life of Cranmer,[4] thus alludes to the subject :—" The marriage of Cranmer was, of course, attended with the *forfeiture* of his fellowship. It did not, however, disqualify him from his office of a college Teacher and Lecturer."

Dr Hook, Dean of Chichester, makes the following observations on this marriage in his " Lives of the Archbishops" [5] :—" Cranmer's marriage was not regarded as disreputable, for although, as a matter of course, he *forfeited* his fellowship, he found at once an income to support his wife by accepting the appointment of Reader or Lecturer at Buckingham Hall."

---

[1] See "Faith of Catholics." London, 1846. Vol. iii. p. 228.

[2] New edition, 1840, pp. 150, 151. Fuller continues to observe on this subject—" His wife was kinsman to the hostess at the ' Dolphin,' which, causing his frequent repair thither, gave the occasion to that impudent lie of ignorant Papists, that he was an ostler.   Indeed, with his learned Lectures, he rubbed the galled backs and curried the lazy hides of many an idle, ignorant friar, being now made Divinity reader in Buckingham College.   But soon after, his wife dying within the year, being a widower, he was *re-elected* into Jesus College."

[3] Vol. i. p. 145.   London, 1858.   [4] Vol. i. p. 29.   London, 1833.

[5] Vol. vi. p. 433.   Edit. 1868.

On the death of his wife, Cranmer was re-appointed a Fellow of his College ; and here again it is asserted that it was on the presentation of " a penitential petition." I can find no authority for any such assertion. Such was the reputation which Cranmer had gained at the University, that Cardinal Wolsey, who had established a new foundation at Oxford, and had induced some of the more eminent scholars of Cambridge to remove to his new establishment, nominated Cranmer as one of them ; but though this appointment would have proved more advantageous in a pecuniary point of view, Cranmer declined to abandon his own College.

On what apparently trifling circumstances great events hang ! Had Cranmer accepted this tempting offer, he would have been removed from the atmosphere of the plague, which drove him to Waltham Abbey, where he met the King's two secretaries, which led to his engagement as the King's advocate for the divorce, then in active agitation, and his subsequent elevation to the See of Canterbury. He would have been spared the odium of any participation in the King's intervening marriage complications, and perhaps his ultimate martyrdom at the stake !

Cranmer now resolved to pursue his studies in Divinity with a view to enter the priesthood. He was, as before stated, re-elected a Fellow of his College and appointed Examiner in Divinity. He was ordained Priest, and took the degree of Doctor of Divinity in his fortieth year (A.D. 1523), and was appointed Public Examiner in Theology. Strype informs us that he became a " model of propriety, goodness, and piety to those who were placed under his charge." We are further informed that in the capacity of Examiner in Divinity,—

" He did much good, for he used to question the candidates out of the Scriptures, and by no means wou'd he let pass if he found they were unskilled therein, or unacquainted with the history of the Bible. The Friars, whose study lay only in school authors, especially were so, whom therefore he sometimes turned back as insufficient, advising them to study the Scriptures for some years longer, before they came for their degree, it being a shame for a professor in Divinity to be unskilled in the book wherein the knowledge of God and the grounds of divinity lay. Whereby he made himself from the beginning hated by the Friars ; yet some of the more ingenuous afterwards rendered him great thanks for refusing them, whereby, being put upon the study of God's Word, they attained to more sound knowledge of religion."

From this time until the incidents we are about to relate, which brought Cranmer into public notice, he appears to have passed an uneventful life at the University, principally acting as tutor, and, according to all accounts, with satisfaction to his superiors and credit to himself.

And here I may be permitted to borrow an extract from Mr Burke's late work, " Historical Portraits of the Tudor Dynasty," which he purports to give from a Letter of one John Alcock, a student and contemporary of Cranmer, and a chess-player at the " Dolphin," " abbreviated and modernised as to diction." If genuine, we may take it as an interesting description of Dr Cranmer at this period :—

" At this time Father Cranmer looked oldish ; he was of dark complexion, with a long beard, half grey ; part of his head had no hair ; he spoke little ; his amusement at times was chess. He was accounted an admirable hand at that game, which he enjoyed very much. His habits were temperate, and he frequently admonished young gentlemen 'for indulging in the use of strong liquors'—a vice then making progress amongst the students of Cambridge. Father Cranmer was reckoned a good horseman, and, like most early risers, was much given to walking on a summer morning ; his manners were cold and disdainful, unless to those to whom he considered it his interest to be the reverse. He seems to have had no desire for the society of educated women. I must state, however, that he had no opportunity of meeting them. ' Black Joan,' as his wife was styled from her hair and complexion, was a woman of no education—a peasant girl from a neighbouring farm. During the long years Thomas Cranmer was attached to Cambridge, he had many acquaintances, but was never known to have formed what might be called a friendship for any fellow-student."

Such, then, was Cranmer when he was unexpectedly and unwillingly called upon to enter upon more public duties. It was Cranmer's misfortune that his lot in life should have fallen on unhappy and troubled times, and to serve under a monarch represented to be—though not without considerable exaggeration—cruel, tyrannical, and lascivious.

It was justly remarked by the late Rev. Joseph Mend- ham, that, with the vindication of Henry VIII., we, as members of the Reformed Church, have little concern. Our opponents, with whom he, as little as ourselves, is a favourite, would gladly impose on us the necessity of his defence. But in one respect—his effectual renunciation of the usurped authority of the Papal See and its Bishops— *that* which constitutes his main if not *only* offence in the eyes of Romanists, we do and always will defend him ; for the rest he is more their client than ours. He wanted to establish a royal Papacy as absolute and persecuting as the purely ecclesiastical one which he was rejecting; but he was in reality making loopholes for liberty, and laid the foundation on which the Reformation was erected.

CHAPTER III.

THE PROCEEDINGS LEADING TO THE DIVORCE OF HENRY VIII. FROM CATHERINE.

WE are now come to the period of Dr Cranmer's first appearance, in 1529, as a public character. It was in connexion with the complicated circumstances " which were destined to occupy a prominent place in the history of this country," attending the marriage of Henry VIII. with his brother's widow, Catherine, the daughter of King Ferdinand of Spain and Isabella of Castile, his wife— Henry's divorce and his second marriage with Anne Boleyn, the daughter of Sir Thomas Boleyn, afterwards created Earl of Ormond and Wiltshire. The part taken by Cranmer in these events has furnished fruitful subjects of censure both of the King and Cranmer.

There is no action of Cranmer's life which has been so much under contention, to his disparagement, as his participation in these transactions ; nor have any events in the history of our Kings been so misunderstood, indeed misrepresented. Considering the important results which followed, we need scarcely express any surprise.

In order to make this clear, it will be necessary—as perhaps the most eventful period of Cranmer's life—that we should enter into a minute examination of all the facts and circumstances connected with those transactions, and the part which Cranmer took, in order, as is alleged, to further Henry's cruel and lascivious propensities.

The popular version is shortly as follows: We are told that Henry was a monster in his appetites and passions. After some eighteen or twenty years of married life, with Catherine, who had ever been to him a virtuous and affectionate wife, Henry *suddenly* fell in love, and carried on an illicit intercourse with Anne Boleyn, the Queen's maid of honour. Some have gone so far as to insinuate, the scandal boldly proclaimed by Sanders, a secular priest, that Anne was Henry's daughter—that Henry applied to the Pope of Rome to grant him a divorce on the plea of religious scruples—that the Pope *peremptorily refused* his sanction— that Henry could not restrain his passions, but with the aid of Cranmer obtained, in England, a declaration of divorce, on the pretence of having *suddenly* discovered that his first marriage was contrary to the Divine law according to the Scriptures—that Cranmer aided and abetted the King in these views, and took upon himself to pronounce the decree of divorce; whereupon the King married Anne Boleyn, whom he had previously " taken under his protection "— that the King rewarded Cranmer for his services by making him Archbishop of Canterbury—that Henry thus forfeited Pontifical favour, and turned Protestant, threw off the supreme sway of the Pope, proclaiming himself to be the head of the Church in England, and thus, with the further aid of Cranmer, introduced the Reformation, and founded the Church of England, " which " (according to Cobbett) " he cherished and maintained by plunder, devastation, and by rivers of innocent blood,"—and that the Pope issued his Bull of " excommunication and damnation against the *heretic* Henry, as a punishment for his past disobedience, and as an expression of his virtuous indignation."

Cobbett adds: " The tyrant, now both Pope and King, made Cranmer Archbishop of Canterbury, a dignity just then vacant ;" and the same writer throws on Cranmer the whole responsibility of the divorce and of the second marriage. The moral of the tale is thus curtly and elegantly summed up by Cobbett : " The Reformation, as it is called, was engendered in beastly lust, brought forth in hypocrisy, and cherished and fed by plunder, devastation, and by rivers of innocent blood." [1]

Such is the *popular* statement of the case which it is proposed to consider in the sequel. We have to encounter popular tradition, popular prejudice, popular romancers ; and more than all, an instinctive and honest repugnance to an alleged cruel persecutor, universally represented as having been abandoned to sensual gratification. If it be true that Cranmer aided and abetted Henry in any such nefarious transaction as thus popularly represented, he would deserve all that has been said of him in his condemnation. It will be a difficult task, in the face of such allegations

[1] See Ince's " Outlines of English History." This little work was re-edited by a member of the Roman Church, formerly a clergyman of the Church of England, and published by Gilbert, a Roman Catholic, 1856. The emendations relating to Henry VIII. and Cranmer in the original edition are found in pp. 62, 64. This book was adopted by the Society of Arts as a text-book for examinations, and was withdrawn on the falsifications being exposed.

Dr Milner's " End of Religious Controversy," Letter viii. p. 106, and Letter xlvi. p. 445. Derby stereotyped edition.

" La Chrétienne de nos jours," pp. 15, 16. Paris, 1861.

" Father Paul Maclachlin " in his controversy with R. W. Kennard, Esq. Letter xiv. p. 202. London, 1855.

Keenan's " Controversial Catechism," 12th edition, p. 23.

Cobbett's " History of the Protestant Reformation," Letter ii. sec. 60, 61, and " Introduction," Letter i. sec. iv.

" The Church and the Sovereign Pontiff." Dublin and London, 1879. This work is issued under the patronage and recommendation of two archbishops and twenty-one bishops of the Roman Church in Ireland. We are told on page 60 : " The cause of this ever-deplorable schism was the *refusal* of Clement VII. to declare null the marriage of Henry VIII. with Catherine of Aragon, his true and lawful spouse, and to grant that Monarch liberty to marry Anne Boleyn. The means he afterwards employed to destroy religion in England, were imposture, calumny, violence, robbery, and punishments the most terrible." There is not a word of truth in these assertions.

confidently put forward, to unravel historical facts, without
appearing to be an apologist for Henry VIII. and his
alleged "chief adviser," Cranmer. But, however tedious
minute details may be—and dates are of the utmost importance—it seems necessary, in relating the history of
" The Life and Times of Cranmer," that this first episode
in his public career should be clearly understood and
thoroughly sifted out, and more particularly as this divorce
led to the final rupture with the Pope, and the separation
and independence of the Church in England.

There can be no doubt that the acts in which Henry
was involved resulted, first, in casting off the jurisdiction of
the Bishop of Rome, which made way for the Reformation
in religion which followed. It would be, however, perfectly futile to shut our eyes to the antecedent facts,
and the character of the several agents in this historical
drama. But happily the cause of the Reformation does
not impose on us the necessity of vindicating, or even
palliating, the vices that too often intruded themselves in
the work. The Reformation is perpetually reproached
with the alleged vile agency by which the change was
brought about. That which, they assert, was engendered
in sin cannot be of God, or receive His blessing. But
supposing all to be true, as related of Henry, of Cranmer,
and of the other prelates and statesmen of those days, will
such facts disprove the necessity of a Reformation, such as
subsequently was effected, under which we have enjoyed
complete civil and religious liberty, liberty of conscience,
and an emancipation from various acknowledged superstitions, in worship and in practice, which darkened the
pre-Reformation era in this country ? Further, is it to be
believed that this country, but for these acts which transpired in Henry's reign, would have continued under the

subjection of a foreign priest, and that the eyes and under-standing of the people would not have been opened to the "more sure way" of the primitive simplicity of the Gospel, rather than placing reliance on a complicated sacramental sacerdotal system, in which the priest practically supple-ments the office of a "Saviour," and the Virgin and saints that of "Intercessors"?   It is impossible to conceive that the overruling tyranny of the court of Rome, fully described in a subsequent chapter, could have much longer existed.

Not even the cruel extermination of the helpless peasants of the south of France and Piedmont, and of the massacre of the Protestants in the Netherlands, or on St Bartholo-mew's day, could have arrested the progress of the Refor-mation, though thousands of Protestants were extirpated.

It is proposed to consider the circumstances connected with Henry's first marriage with Catherine of Aragon, the widow of his brother Arthur ; his divorce and second mar-riage with Anne Boleyn; and the parts which the Pope and Cranmer respectively took in these transactions.

At the period preceding that on which we are engaged, namely, the latter end of the fifteenth and beginning of the sixteenth century, Spain held a prominent position among the nations of Europe, being governed by Ferdinand, too well known in history to need further mention in these pages.

Catherine of Aragon was the fourth daughter of King Ferdinand and Queen Isabella of Castile.   She was the aunt of Charles, afterwards Emperor Charles V., who played a conspicuous part in the history of those times.

Henry VII. was the reigning King of England.   He had two sons, Arthur and Henry (afterwards King Henry VIII.). An alliance between Spain and England was considered to be to the mutual advantage of both nations, by the marriage of Arthur with Catherine—Arthur as heir presumptive to the throne of England, Catherine as endowed with the proverbial riches of an heiress of Spain. There can be no doubt that these considerations were the motives which actuated the respective monarchs. Catherine was to be sacrificed, for no affection for her future husband could possibly have existed. The marriage of Arthur and Catherine took place in England on the 14th November 1501, with great pomp and splendour. Bishop Warham is said to have performed the marriage ceremony. The marriage settlement is supposed to have secured a handsome dowry, the gift of Catherine's parents, but which, it appears, was never realised.

Catherine was then in her sixteenth year; Arthur, born 20th September 1486, was therefore fifteen years and two months old. The marriage was received with universal joy and approbation both in England and Spain, and Queen Isabella wrote a most cheering and affectionate letter to the King of England on the occasion. After the marriage the royal couple took up their abode at Ludlow Castle. It is stated that Catherine had great misgivings as to this union. In a letter she wrote to a friend she expressed her doubts of her future happiness, and a wish that she had never seen the shores of England. Neither of them could speak the other's language. Within a fortnight after this marriage, Arthur, in a weak state of health, readily succumbed to the plague, which had then set in. Catherine was thus left a widow.

Questions now ensued between Henry VII. and King Ferdinand as to the dowry of the Princess. Henry was naturally most anxious to retain this prize ; and, guided by this mercenary consideration, further projects of a continued union between the two houses were set on foot. Henry VII., then a widower, even proposed himself to marry his son's widow; but this was strenuously opposed by her parents. The next scheme set on foot was to effect a marriage between Catherine and the King's second son, Henry, who was then twelve years old, Catherine being eighteen. The Court of Spain was eventually induced to accede to the proposal, provided the dispensation of the Pope could be obtained—a union with a brother's widow being forbidden by Canon Law of the Church, and, as was considered, equally forbidden by Divine law. The same difficulties were raised to the proposed union in England by the leading members of Convocation and by the King's Council, the principal opponent being Warham, then Bishop of London, afterwards Archbishop of Canterbury. The union, however, was strenuously advocated by Cardinal Wolsey, Foxe, afterwards Bishop of Hereford, and by Gardyner, afterwards Bishop of Winchester. On the assumption of a consummation of the marriage of Arthur and Catherine during that fortnight's residence at Ludlow Castle, the Pope's dispensation was necessary.[1]

It must be understood that the Pope claimed, and still continues to claim, the absolute right of declaring not only divorce between husband and wife—even where no legal grounds are assigned, as sanctioned by our present laws— but of dispensing with prohibited degrees of affinity in sanctioning marriages. Several notable examples may be cited, to say nothing of private licences of no public interest. The King of Saxony received a dispensation from the Pope (but of which he did not avail himself) to marry again, during the lifetime of his wife, an Austrian archduchess.

[1] See Pocock's edition of Burnet's "History of the Reformation," vol. iv. pp. 545-6. Oxford, 1865.

Pope Stephen withdrew his anathema and sanctioned the divorce of the French monarch, Charles, from his then wife, to marry Bertha, Princess of Lombardy ; and when the same Prince divorced Bertha to make room for another, this act also was sanctioned by the French Bishops, and was not condemned by Pope Adrian. Innocent IV., in 1243, authorised the divorce of Alphonsus of Portugal from his Queen, to marry Beatrice. Again, we have the notorious case of Don Alphonsus II., King of Portugal. This monarch opposed the Jesuits ; they first induced his wife, Dona Maria, to abandon him ; the Parliament, then still under the influence of the Jesuits, decreed the deposition of the King on the ground of his being imbecile and impotent, and promised that his brother should be proclaimed King under the title of Don Pedro II. During his deposed brother's lifetime, Pedro married his brother's wife, after Pope Clement IX. had granted the necessary dispensation ; he bestowed his blessing on the new marriage. Alexander VI., in his Brief dated 8th June 1501 (the very year of the marriage of Arthur and Catherine), authorised Alexander, Duke of Lithuania, and afterwards King of Poland, to put away his wife to marry Ann de Foix, on the ground that she belonged to the Eastern Church, in direct violation of his solemn oath, given when wedding her, that he would never subject her to any compulsion on account of their religious differences. For thirty thousand ducats the same Pope allowed Louis XI. of France to dissolve his marriage with the Princess Jane, and to marry Anne of Brittany. We shall have presently to record a similar dispensation granted to Henry VIII. to marry again, " even within the prohibited degree of affinity," during Catherine's lifetime, and the Pope's repeated offer to recognise the legitimacy of Elizabeth, the issue of the second marriage.

Again, Cassimir the Great, of Poland, had married Ann, daughter of the Duke of Lithuania, and on her death married Adelaide of Hesse, who, in 1356, returned to her father, being indignant at her husband's infidelities. Cassimir then became enamoured of his cousin, daughter of Henry, Duke of. Lagin, whom he married, although Adelaide was still living. Urban V., by Brief, licensed this second marriage.

These are a few well-known facts in history. How many private dispensations have been given we have no public record ; we do know, however, of a dispensation recently granted to the Prince of Monaco to be divorced from Lady Mary Hamilton, though there was issue of their marriage. There was no *legitimate* cause assigned. She was allowed to marry again.[1]

We might also record several cases in which the Pope has exercised his assumed dispensing powers of permitting persons to marry within the prohibited degrees of affinity. For instance, we have the well-known case of Philip II. of Spain marrying his own niece under Papal dispensation. The Duke of Bouillon paid to the Pope one hundred thousand crowns to enable him to marry the widow of the Duke his brother. Scipio de Ricci, the pious and amiable Bishop of Pistoia, in his " Memoires,"[2] gives a description of the lax conduct of Rome in marriage dispensations within the prohibited degrees, for money considerations, which he designated an " infamous traffic ! "

It will, perhaps, startle the uninitiated reader, to be told that the question, whether the Pope may allow a marriage between *brother* and *sister*, has been gravely discussed.

---

[1] " Le marriage religieux à été annulé par le cour de Rome le 3 Jan. 1880."— " Almanac de Gotha," 1883, p. 53, title " Monaco."

[2] Tom. ii. cap. 33.   Paris 1826.

The Jesuit writer Escabor, in his notorious work, " Liber
Theolog. Moralis," published in Brussels, 1651, proposes
and answers the question ; and we may note that up to
that date, the work appeared in thirty-two editions in
Spain, and three in France, and has never been condemned by the Pope, or placed in either the " Prohibi-
tory " or " Expurgatory " Indexes.

The question is gravely asked :—

" Can the Pope give a dispensation for a marriage between a
brother and sister ? "—" *Answer*. Prapositus denies that he can,
because it is first degree of relationship, forbidden by the law of
nations.   But Hurtador affirms that such a marriage is valid by the
law of nations, and may, on just grounds, be allowed by the Pope,
e.g., if the king of Spain could not form an equal foreign match unless
with a heretic, or one suspected of heresy."—" If, however, the Pope
were to reply that he could not give a dispensation within the degrees
prohibited by law of God ? "—" You would have to explain that he
means he ought not to do so without a considerable reason."

It will be thus seen that the Pope of Rome arrogated
to himself a power, not only of granting divorces, but
also of dispensing with the laws of affinity, permitting
marriages within the prohibited degrees.   This assumed
dispensing power becomes important in our present
history.

In England, opinions appear to have been divided as to
the extent of the power of Popes.   Some maintained that
the Pope had no power of dispensation contrary to Divine
law.   If the marriage of Arthur had been consummated,
the Pope, they maintained, had no jurisdiction ; if otherwise, the previous marriage was deemed no marriage, but
only a contract, put an end to by the death of one of the
parties, and in that case the dispensation would operate ;
or indeed, it would seem not to be required.   Prince
Henry, in December 1503, was formally betrothed to the
widow, Catherine, and a formal contract and settlement

were entered into between the parties. This formal act was, according to law, deemed a *legal marriage*, and would have been a plea for annulment on the occasion of any subsequent alliance of the lady with any other person, in the lifetime of the other betrothed. For this betrothal the Pope's dispensation appears to have been obtained in March 1504, and as Le Bas curtly remarks, "Little did the Pope imagine that, by this tortuous policy, he was charging a mine, the explosion of which was eventually to rend the English Empire from his spiritual dominion."

This betrothal, or second marriage, was opposed by many Cardinals and divines as illegal according to the Canon Law. Notwithstanding, Julius II. granted to Prince Henry a dispensation by "Brief" to marry his brother's widow. This document[1] was reluctantly granted by the Pope, and still more reluctantly accepted by the English clergy. The document "dispensed with the impediment of their affinity, notwithstanding any apostolic constitution to the contrary." The Pope permitted them to marry, or, if they were already married, he confirmed it, requiring their confessor "to enjoin some healthy penance for their having married before the dispensation was obtained." It was on this authority that Prince Henry married Catherine when under age. He was then only twelve years old. Collier observes on this subject :—

" In these instructions the impediments of affinity, the objections of Catherine's cohabitation with Arthur, the supposition of her being already married to Prince Henry, are all overruled and dispensed with. For though there was no matter of fact to rest the last case upon, yet the Court of Rome was resolved to make all sure."[2]

Modern apologists have sought to exculpate or excuse the Pope by declaring that Catherine's first marriage was

---

[1] Minute of a Brief of Julius II., dated 13th March 1504.
[2] Collier's " Eccles. Hist.," vol. ii. pt. ii. bk. i.   London, 1714.

not consummated, and that, therefore, the Pope acted as if no lawful prior marriage existed. This is a fallacy. But the fact either way does not affect the question in the light they desire to place it, to shield the Pope. The Pope was not influenced by any such consideration one way or the other, for, in his Brief of License, he actually refers to the fact as probable.[1]

The fact seems to have been known to the parents of the parties. This is evident from the marriage contract itself, executed in June 1503, which has recently come to light, and has been published in the Kimbolton collection, which is given in the Duke of Manchester's book as follows[2]:—" Ferdinand and Isabel, as well as Henry VII., promise to employ all their influence with the Court of Rome, in order to obtain the dispensation of the Pope, necessary for the marriage of the Princess Catherine with Henry, Prince of Wales. The Papal dispensation is required because the said Princess Catherine had on a former occasion contracted a marriage with the late Prince Arthur, brother of the present Prince of Wales, whereby she became related to Henry, Prince of Wales, in the first degree of affinity, and because the marriage with Prince Arthur was solemnised according to the rites of the Catholic Church, *and afterwards consummated.*"

On comparing this document with the Pope's license for the second marriage, and his subsequent written consent to their separation, as we shall have to notice pre-

[1] " Carnali copulâ *forsam* consumma vissetis, Dominus Arthurus prole ex hujusmodi matrimonio non suscepta decessit." Cott. Lib., Vitel. b. xii., cited by Burnet, " Hist. of the Reformation." Records, b. ii. vol. iv. p. 5. Nare's edit. London, 1830. The authority of this document has been questioned. See *Quarterly Review*, January 1877 ; and see Mr Friedman's " Anne Boleyn," vol. ii., Appendix, *note* C., p. 328 *et seqq.* London, 1884.

[2] " Court and Society, from Elizabeth to Anne." Edited from the papers at Kimbolton. London, 1864, pp. 60 and 62.

sently, it is very probable that all the circumstances of the result of the first marriage with Arthur were fully made known to the Pope. The circumstance is mentioned as a fact in the Statute 28 Henry VIII. c. vii.

If the marriage was in itself contrary to law and morality, how could it be made legal and just by the act of the Pope? The marriage was believed to be contrary to the law of God; certainly contrary to the Canon Law, the law of the Romish Church established by decrees of Councils. The law of the Church seems to have been fully established, following the law of Moses, which forbade marriages with the widow of a deceased brother.[1] The marriage of a brother's widow was forbidden by the Emperor Constantine, and the children of those who were thus married declared illegitimate.[2] This law was confirmed by Theodosius the Younger.[3] By the canons of the Church (of which Henry was not only a professed member, but afterwards styled " Defender of the Faith ") such marriages were condemned as incestuous, and the contracting parties were obliged to undergo public penance. Thus, in the year 314, the Council of Neo-Cesarea, in Pontus, excommunicated any woman who married two brothers in succession, and she was not permitted to partake of the sacrament except on condition that she dissolved her marriage, and submitted to public penance.[4] So, likewise the Council at Rome, under Pope Zachary, A.D. 743, anathematised any one who should marry his brother's wife, founding the prohibition expressly on the law of Moses, which the Council declared to be binding on all Christians ; and they forbade

---

[1] Leviticus xviii. 16 ; xx. 21.   But see Deut. xxv. 5-10.
[2] Cod. Theod., lib. iii. tit. 12.   " De Incest. Nup.," Leg. 2.
[3] *Ibid.*, Leg. 4.
[4] Labb. et Coss.   " Concil. Conc. Neo-Cesarencis," can. 2, tom. i. col. 1480.   Paris, 1671.

the clergy to administer to such the sacraments of the Church, unless they consented to break the tie and do public penance, and to which the whole assembly of Bishops thrice chimed in—" Let him be anathematised." [1] And the same prohibition was confirmed by the Popes Eugenius II. and Leo IV., and taught by the early Christian writers, now called the " Fathers " of the Church. In confirmation of this opinion, we need only refer to Basil's 194th Epistle to Diodorus Tarsensis, wherein he argues against such marriages as incestuous and void.

Thus, then, the union of Henry with Catherine was contrary to the law of the Church of Rome, and accounted equally contrary to the law of God ; but the Bishop of Rome, in the plenitude of his assumed apostolic power, set aside both, for the interest, as he then supposed, of the Church, which was paramount.   The result proved a just retribution on the Pope.   This illegal marriage, and the subsequent divorce, were the original causes of the complications which ultimately led to a separation of the Church in England from the dominion of Rome, and with it the suppression of the Pope's spiritual jurisdiction in this country.

The betrothal of Prince Henry and the widow of Arthur was completed 24th June 1504, in the presence of the Bishop of Salisbury.   It is stated that Catherine was much taken by the handsome figure of Prince Henry, and fell desperately in love with him.

Henry VII. was subsequently persuaded by Warham, then Archbishop of Canterbury, that the marriage of Prince Henry with Catherine was contrary to the law of God.

---

[1] Labb. et Coss., tom. vi. col. 1546, and " Edit. Mansi," tom. xii. col. 383. Florent., 1766 ; and see *ibid.*, Eugenius II., ann. 824.   Leonis IV., ann. 847, referred to in the margin of the last cited place.

He also foresaw and pointed out to the King the troubles
that would ensue on a controverted title to the thrc .1e, as
the issue of such a marriage, it was represented, could not
succeed to the Crown ; a very serious consideration.   Accordingly Prince Henry, on coming of age (27th January
1505), that is, at the age of fourteen, by his father's command,
declared before a public notary, " That, whereas, being
under age, he was married to the Princess Catherine, now,
on coming of age, he protested against the marriage as
illegal, and annulled it,"[1] and accordingly the two separated to meet only as friends.   Prince Henry is further
said to have acted, in taking this step, on the advice of his
confessor, Longland.   It will be thus seen that Henry's first
separation from Catherine was effected on the same grounds
as were advanced on his ultimate divorce, full a quarter
of a century before Cranmer was consulted on the subject.

Henry VII. died 22d April 1509, when he was succeeded by his son, under the title of Henry VIII.

The question now began to be seriously discussed as to
the importance of continuing an intimate alliance with the
House of Aragon.   The Council of Henry VIII., therefore, prevailed on him to re-marry Catherine (then still remaining in England), which he did about six weeks after
his accession to the throne, 11th June 1509.   This marriage
took place at Greenwich privately, but there appears to be
no record of the event, nor is it ascertained who were
present.   It is not probable that Warham performed the
ceremony, as suggested by Dr Lingard, for Warham, we
know, strenuously opposed the marriage.

Of this marriage a son was born in January 1511, who
died the following month.   Another son was born, and

---

[1] This document is in the Cotton Library, Vitel., b. xii., and is cited in full
by Burnet, in his " History of the Reformation."   Records, b. ii., vol. iv. p. 5.
Nare's edition, 1830.

died in November 1514. The queen had many miscarriages; thus seeming to fulfil the prediction, according to Levitical law, that if a man took his brother's wife, he should die childless.

Our attention is now drawn to the appearance on the scene of another important character,—ANNE BOLEYN, the daughter of Sir Thomas Boleyn (Viscount Rochfort), and of Lady Elizabeth, his wife. The date of birth of Anne Boleyn is variously given as 1501, 1502, 1507, and 1511. Lady Elizabeth died 14th December 1512. In order to throw discredit on every thing connected with Henry VIII. and Queen Elizabeth, the daughter of Anne Boleyn, Sanders, a renegade secular priest, impudently put forth the infamous libel that Anne Boleyn was the King's bastard daughter by the good Lady Elizabeth.[1] The statement of Sanders was subsequently taken up by Phillips, a Canon of Tangers, in his " Life of Cardinal Pole," then repeated by Bayley, and subsequently perpetuated by the priest T. Bradly, in his " Sure way to find out the true Religion,"[2] a work embellished with extravagant abuse heaped on Cranmer.

The following earnest protest against this slander is from the pen of Mr S. H. Burke, himself a member of the Roman Church :—

"I must now enter upon an investigation of the shocking narrative put forward by Sanders against the stainless character of Lady Elizabeth Boleyn [mother of Anne Boleyn]. The writer, whose reputation for truth is on a par with that of John Foxe,[3] alleges that Lady Elizabeth Boleyn made a confession to her husband that she had ' criminal intercourse with King Henry ; and that the monarch was the father of her daughter Anna.' The allegations of Sanders have been added by Campion, Throckmorton, Allen, and other violent partisans on the

[1] "Sand. de Schism. Anglic.," p. 14, edit. 1628.
[2] Manchester, 1823. Third Edit., p. 29.
[3] "John Foxe." See Appendix at the end of the present volume.

[Roman] Catholic side.   Truth, however, must not be concealed, for
it triumphs in the long run.   Justice should be measured out to all
parties with an even and firm hand.   Dr Lingard gave much consideration to this shocking story, and pronounced the statement to
have no foundation in fact.   The question, he contends, is abundantly
disproved by Racine.   Dates, however, form the most important key
to *facts*.   Anna Boleyn was born about the close of 1501 ; Camden
contends that it was in 1507 ; Lord Herbert states expressly that
Anna was twenty years old when she returned from France in 1521 ;
so that she must have been born in 1501.   The researches of Miss
Strickland arrive at the same conclusion.   Mr˜ Hepworth Dixon
approaches the subject with a chivalrous indignation, and states that
the 'whole edifice of slander rests on a false date.'   He argues the
question with the ability and enthusiasm which characterises his mode
of defence.

   "' It was not,' writes Miss Strickland, ' till long after the grave had
closed over Lady Boleyn that the indignant spirit of party attempted
to fling aṇ absurd scandal on her memory, by pretending that Anna
Boleyn was the offspring of her amours with the King during the
absence of Sir Thomas Boleyn on an embassy to France.   But, independently of the fact that Sir Thomas Boleyn was *not* ambassador to
France till many years *after* the birth of all his children, Henry VIII.
was a boy under the care of his tutors at the period of Anna's birth,
even if that event took place in the year 1507, the date given by
Sanders.'   Henry, Duke of York, who appeared at the wedding of the
Infanta and Prince Arthur in November 1501, was at that period in
his tenth year.   Is it not then quite manifest that Sanders has put forward an untrue statement, in order to add intensity to sectarian
feeling—a sentiment that should be avoided in historical relations ?
Sanders has impeached the character of Anna Boleyn whilst connecṭed
with the French court.   At the time Anna left the convent at Brie her
character was without ' spot or stain ; the tongue of slander did not
touch her.'   Such were the words of one of her beloved school-fellows,
who was in after years an abbess. . . . The young English ladies
fondly called Anna ' Sister Nan.'   When at last a ' command came
from Hever Castle for her return, all the little maidens, the stately
dames of quality, and the various domestics, fell a-weeping.'   This
was the time and the place Sanders and other untruthful writers
describe Anna Boleyn as ' leading an impure life.' " [1]

---

[1] " Historical Portraits of the Tudor Dynasty and the Reformation Period,"
2nd edit., vol. i. pp. 92-94 ; and see Pocock's Edit. of Burnet's " History of
the Protestant Reformation," vol. iv. pp. 556-551.   Oxford, 1865.   The
calumny is of greater consequence than at first sight appears, for it brings in
question the legitimacy of ELIZABETH, the daughter of Anne, and indirectly

It is a lamentable fact to find such writers as Charles Butler, Esq., and Dr Lingard giving an indirect countenance to this slander; the latter refers to "an attempt" to refute it, "of its being problematical," and a "probability of its being in favour of the accused."[1] Mr Butler refers to "the powerful arguments of Le Grand," and the strong assertions of Sanders.[2]

To continue our narrative :—

Mary (subsequently Queen) was born 19th February 1516, who alone, of all the children of this marriage, lived to attain a mature age.

It should be here noted that Catherine's nephew, CHARLES, became King of Spain in 1516, and Emperor under the title of Charles V., in 1519.

We now come to the real cause of the second separation from Catherine; and it will be seen that it had nothing whatever to do with Henry's affection for Anne Boleyn, or of Cranmer's suggestions or interference. Roman Catholic prelates alone were responsible for the act, long before Cranmer was ever consulted. It was the custom in those days to betroth princesses at an early age. When Mary was about eleven years old (April 1527), she was to be betrothed to one of the sons of the King of France. The treaty of marriage had already been drawn up, on the 24th December previously (1526), but the Bishop of Tarbes, the French king's Ambassador in this country, denied the legality of Henry's marriage with Catherine, as being contrary to divine precept, with which no human authority could dispense; as also being contrary to the law of the

---

would support the atrocious attack made by Wm. Cobbett, that the Reformation was engendered by "beastly lust."

[1] Lingard's "History of England," vol. vi. p. 153.   London, 1848.

[2] "Book of the Roman Catholic Church," p. 191.   1825.

Church ; and he therefore denied the legitimacy of Mary, and pointed out that she could not legally succeed to the crown of England.¹ This put an end to the proposed marriage. In consequence of this startling objection, revived in this solemn and practical manner, the King's scruples were again roused. His sincerity at this time has never been questioned, on any reliable authority. Acting under the advice of Cardinal Wolsey, and Longland his confessor, who declared the union sinful, Henry was induced by these considerations to examine into the legality of the marriage ; and let it be noted that Anne Boleyn had not then been heard of at court. This ought to have some weight in the consideration of Henry's motives. Indeed, there is evidence that the King, for three years before this, had abstained from all intercourse with the Queen.² He considered the death of his children in succession as a curse from God for his unlawful marriage. He consulted the canonists and divines of the day, who testified against the legality of the union ; he consulted also his favourite author, Thomas Aquinas, and here, again, he found the opinion deliberately recorded that the laws laid down in Leviticus, with reference to the forbidden degrees of marriage, were moral and eternal, and binding on all Christians ; and that the Pope could only dispense with the laws of the Church, but not with the laws of God. The interests of the kingdom, it was urged upon the King, were involved in the question, which required that there should be no doubt as to the succession to the crown. If Mary were illegitimate, there was no immediate successor.

¹ It has been asserted by some modern writers of the unreformed Church, that this was a concocted plan between Henry and the French Ambassador, but there is no evidence of this.

² See the Letter to Bucer, referred to by Burnet in his "History of the Reformation," pt. i. b. ii. p. 60. Vol. i., edit. 1830.

The horrors of a civil war, such as had raged between the Houses of York and Lancaster, buried with his father, might be revived in another channel after his death. James of Scotland, the enemy of England, would be the next heir to the English throne.   Henry, by leaving no legitimate heir to the throne, would be bequeathing to his country a contested succession, and probably a civil war between rival claimants.   He accordingly longed for a son and heir to succeed him.   The want of such an heir was a bitter disappointment to him.   There was no hope of such heir by Catherine.   The entire nation was interested in the question ; opinions were freely expressed. Henry's subjects—that is, those who could appreciate the position—desired him to marry again, that there might be a legitimate heir to the throne.   The necessities of the times required this.   The urgency of the case was felt, and the importance of setting at rest the question of succession was pressed on the King.[1]

Thus doubts and difficulties were raised, commenced even from the King's accession, and now revived in a most practical manner.   To suggest that Henry was now moved by conscientious scruples would be at once to create an incredulous smile, so prejudiced are all our conceptions of Henry's character.   But we shall presently see that the Pope's own Legates gave him credit for sincerity in his motives, and it is a fact that he was still guided and advised by Archbishop Warham, and by his Confessor Longland, in all he did.   All the English Bishops except Fisher, Bishop

---

[1] There is no desire so justify or palliate an act, if in itself immoral or illegal, merely on political grounds, to meet a temporary difficulty ; but if example may be pleaded in justification, such an emergency, in the Roman Church, has been deemed sufficient for the interference of the Pope. Napoleon did not hesitate to set aside Josephine, without even the excuse of an illegal union, to marry another, with the sole view of perpetuating the succession, and this act was sanctioned by the French bishops.

of Rochester—all of the unreformed Church—concurred in
declaring, in the most solemn manner, that the marriage
with Catherine was illegal. The opinion advanced by the
bishops was endorsed by all the leading nobles of the land,
including the united bench of the jurisprudence of the
country, who were agreed on the subject, save, perhaps, Sir
Thomas More, but of this we have no evidence. He strenuously opposed, with Fisher, the supplanting of the Pope's
jurisdiction in this country. Both Fisher and More, there
is no doubt, would have readily acquiesced in the general
opinion but for the original dispensation of Julius II. The
Pope with them, right or wrong, in his decrees, was
supreme, and his decision, with them, was accounted above
the law. It was not, in fact, the *divorce* they would oppose,
but the questioning the legality of the original act, consecrated, as it had been, by the sanction of the Pope, and the
acting in an ecclesiastical matter without his permission.
Cardinal Wolsey, a politician as well as a divine, differed
in opinion, insomuch that in July 1527 he personally undertook to procure from the Court of Rome a decree for a
divorce, and for this purpose armed himself with the safest
passport, £240,000, to negotiate with ; but the existing
Bull presented a difficulty of which the Court of Rome
availed itself as a temporary excuse. Many subtle points
of law were raised on the validity or sufficiency of the dispensation ; and these points were argued with a vigour and
apparent earnestness as if important questions of interna-
tional law had been in dispute. The Cardinal did not
despair of success in getting the required consent. A fee
of 4000 crowns was paid to the Cardinal Sanctorum
Quatuor (sometimes called Santi Quattro) at Rome. In
a letter of advice to Gregory Cassalis, the King's Ambassador at Rome, Wolsey, cunning and worldly in all his

acts, expressed a great sense of the service rendered to the King by this Cardinal, bade Cassalis inquire "what were the things in which he delighted most — whether furniture, gold, plate, or horses—that they might make him acceptable presents, and assure him that the King would contribute largely towards carrying on the building of St Peter's Church." Cardinal Wolsey's negotiation, in that quarter at least, proved successful, as the Sanctorum Quatuor now found the King's demand most reasonable. This he freely expressed to Cassalis.

These negotiations, nevertheless, were allowed to linger ; for it must be remembered that the Pope at this time was a close prisoner in the Castle of St Angelo, placed there by Catherine's own nephew, the Emperor Charles V. The Emperor had defeated the army of Francis I., King of France. The Pope had aided Francis. This had greatly offended Charles, who charged the Pope with ingratitude and perfidy. He besieged Rome, and in May 1527, after the battle of Pavia, took the Pope prisoner, and detained him for about six months. The Pope, who had formed the Clementine League between the various European Powers against the Emperor, and had absolved the King of France from the oath which he had previously taken at Madrid, to enable him to join this League, was now punished for his perfidy and duplicity.

In December 1527 the King sent a deputation to the Pope, of which Dr Knight was one. They found him still a prisoner in the Castle of St Angelo, at the hands of Charles V. They got admission to him by bribing his guards. The King's demands to obtain a divorce were made known to the Pope, who promised under his hand to grant the dispensation required—namely, for a divorce—and further promised that the Bull should follow in due course. The

C

Pope's consent for a divorce was thus obtained in December 1527. He was actuated in this again solely by motives of expediency, hoping to secure the assistance of Henry in his troubles. It appears by a letter from Dr Oritz to the Emperor Charles, that the Pope was informed by Dr Knight of the King's intention to marry again, and what was the exact nature of the impediment.[1] It appears, however, that Dr Knight was outwitted, ᐧfor it was discovered that Santi Quattro, the able lawyer and canonist above named, introduced into the two documents executed by the Pope some changes which made them of no force. On this being discovered, a second mission was undertaken by Foxe and Gardyner. The Pope had in the meantime escaped to Orrieto ; and in this second mission the Pope was induced to sign two documents without any equivocation.

The popular statement is, that Henry " vainly attempted to obtain from the Pope his consent to a divorce from Catherine." In answer to this assertion we cannot do better than quote the authority of Dr Lingard, a priest of the Roman Church, and who is accepted by members of that Church as a good and reliable authority. He writes :—

" The Pope signed two instruments presented to him by the envoys of King Henry, the one authorising Cardinal Wolsey to decide the question of divorce in England, as the Papal Legate, granting to Henry a dispensation to marry, in the place of Catherine, *any other woman whomsoever, even if she were already promised to another, or related to him in the first degree of affinity*."[2]

[1] See Letter of Oritz, 7th February 1533, British Museum MSS., vol. 28,585, fol. 217. Quoted by Friedman, "Anne Boleyn," vol. i. p. 65. 1884.

[2] Dr Lingard gives the date January 1528. "History of England," vol. vi. pp. 128-9. Edit. 1848. It has been suggested that the words in italics were purposely inserted by the envoys of Henry to meet the alleged case of his supposed illicit intercourse with Mary, Anne Boleyn's sister, which, if it happened, would render void his marriage with Anne Boleyn, as being within the decrees of prohibited affinity according to the law of the Roman Church. But this is only supposition.

According to the same authority (Dr Lingard) the Pope further expressed his opinion in these unmistakable terms:—

"If the King be convinced, as he affirms, that his present marriage is null, he might marry again. This would enable me or the Legate to decide the question at once. Otherwise it is plain, that by appeals, exceptions, and adjournments, the case must be protracted for many years."

Such being the case, we cannot account for the strange inconsistency which condemns Henry for eventually following the Pope's own advice!

Here, then, we have the solemn promise of the Pope given to sanction the divorce, with the unholy permission to marry again, even within the degrees of prohibited affinity, before Cranmer appeared on the scene of action. There can be no doubt that had the Pope been a free agent in his Vatican Palace, and not under fear of the Emperor, the Bull itself would have been forthwith issued. The Pope, however, repudiated his promise!

On the 17th May (previous), 1527, both Cardinal Wolsey and Archbishop Warham, at a secret court at Westminster, held that the marriage with Catherine was incestuous. Bishop Fisher, on the other hand, held that such a marriage, *with the Pope's dispensation*, would be valid.[1]

Here we must draw attention to a most notable perversion of this part of our history, advanced by the Rev. G. R. Gleig, M.A., late "Chaplain-General to the Forces," and "Prebendary of St Paul's," and "Instructor-General of Military Schools," all of which titles are paraded on the face of his "History of England—School Series" (a manual still in use). Of this circumstance he says[2]:—

[1] "Letters and Papers." Brewer, vol. iv. pp. 1426-1429 and 1434.
[2] "First Book of History of England, in two parts." Part i. p. 97. New Edition. Longman & Co. 1866.

"A.D. 1527. Henry never liked his marriage with the widow of his brother. As the thing was done, however, he did not try to undo it, and for eighteen years he and his consort lived on good terms. She bore him children, one of whom, the Princess Mary, lived to reach mature years. But at the end of this term the Queen took into her household a young lady of great beauty, by name Anne Boleyn, whom the King tried for a whole year to corrupt, and when he failed, he cast about for some plan by which he might wed her. His old doubts on the head of marriage with a brother's wife began to revive. He spoke to Wolsey about them, and was advised to write.to the Pope for a divorce. He took that advice, and wrote to the Pope, who put the case into the hands of Wolsey and the Archbishop of Canterbury. Henry now thought that all would go smooth with him : but he was wrong." [1]

It is a lamentable circumstance that a person who puts forth a book of education—" to remedy a defect in school literature " (as stated in the Preface)—should scramble together popular fallacies, without bestowing the most ordinary pains to collate his statements with authentic sources. It is not in this passage only that Mr Gleig has allowed himself to be misled in this part of our history, as we shall have again occasion to note.

The Pope's promise having been thus obtained, the King, in February 1528, sent his representatives to .Rome to prosecute his suit, and obtain the formal Bull from the same Pope, Clement VIII. But alas ! the Pope was only a fallible man—a weak, impotent priest ! He found himself, as he himself quaintly observed, " like a red-hot piece of iron between the hammer and the anvil." If he issued the promised Bull of divorce, he would risk the renewed persecution of his old oppressor, Charles, the nephew of Catherine, from whom he had just escaped ; indeed, he feared for his own title to the " Chair of Peter," which was invalid by reason of his being the bastard son of Julian de Medicis, and

---

[1] The reader is referred to the several citations from popular works given in the note to p. 14, *ante*.

having obtained his seat by notorious simony, which invalidated his election. These objections might have been raised by the Emperor. Accordingly the Pope began to temporise, and delays were purposely interposed.

What could the poor old man do? He did not act on principle; it was a question of expediency with him. It was at this period that the French and English combined had defeated the Imperialists in the north of Italy; and when ultimate success seemed probable against his oppressor Charles, the Pope took heart, and told Sir Gregory Cassalis, then still Henry's Ambassador at Rome, that, if the French would only approach near enough to enable him to plead compulsion, he would grant a commission to Wolsey, with plenary power to conclude the cause.[1]

If the original documents, which are stubborn witnesses, were not in existence to prove these facts, one would scarcely believe that a professed Christian bishop, arrogating to himself the title of CHRIST'S VICAR ON EARTH, could have acted with such duplicity, and that such a clatter should be made of the Pope's alleged refusal "to consent to such a violation of Gospel morality!" The Pope, in his perplexity, communicated his wishes to, and consulted the Cardinals Sancti Quattro, and Simmeta; the result of this conference was a proposal from the Pope to Gregory Cassalis (which was communicated by the latter to the King on the 13th January 1528), to the effect that:—

"If the king found the matter clear in his own conscience (on which the Pope said no doctor in the world could solve the matter better than the King himself), he should, without more noise, make judgment be given (either by virtue of the commission the secretary had obtained, or by the legatine power that was lodged with the Cardinal of York), and presently marry another wife, and then send for a Legate to confirm the matter; for it would be easier to ratify all when

[1] See Froude's "History of England," vol. i. p. 126.   London, 1856, and the authorities cited by him.

it was done, than to go on in a process from Rome. Otherwise the Queen would enter a protest, whereupon, in the course of law, the Pope must grant an inhibition while the suit at law was pending, and require the cause to be heard at Rome. But if the thing went on in England, and the King had once married another wife, the Pope would then find a very good reason to justify the confirming a thing that was gone so far ; and thereupon promised to send any Cardinal whom they should name."[1]

This message the Pope desired Cassalis would convey to the King as coming from the two Cardinals, but he himself was not to be implicated or compromised in the matter. The affair, however, was not to be so easily settled ; other influences were put in action. The Pope was pressed by those who represented the Emperor Charles for an inhibition, which he refused on the technical ground of no suit pending.

Let us proceed in the history of these exceptional events. The Pope escaped from the Castle of St Angelo and fled to Orvieto, his escape being connived at, it is supposed, by Charles himself, where he signed the two documents referred to by Dr Lingard, but unknown to the Emperor. In May 1528, the Pope sent his Legate, Cardinal Campeggio, with a decretal Bull, to England, empowering the Legates, of whom Wolsey was one, to decree in the matter publicly, as an earnest of his proposal to Cassalis ; but in real fact this was only for delay. He had his private as well as his public instructions. The wily Cardinal first sought to solve the difficulty by endeavouring to persuade Catherine to retire to a convent. There she would be dead to the world ; but nothing could induce her to lay aside her character as a wife of Henry, or to admit the invalidity of her marriage. The Queen, backed by the Emperor Charles V., who undertook to maintain

---

[1] "Cotton Lib. Vitel.," b. x.   Quoted by Burnet, "Records," vi. b. ii. vol. iv., edit. 1830.

her title, adhered to her rights. The Legatine Court was opened to consider the matter on 31st May 1528. Diplomacy ensued, delays again were interposed. Had Catherine been unsupported by the Emperor, all this delay would have been needless. She would have found no sympathy with the Pope. Indeed, it is supposed that Campeggio brought with him the formal Bull of confirmation, to be used as circumstances might dictate, and that it had been shown to Wolsey ; but there is no direct proof of this. The alleged existing copy is supposed to be spurious. Campeggio's baggage was searched at Dover on his return home, but the document was not found.

Further pretences for delay were raised by Campeggio, and, when in July, nothing remained to be done but for the Legates to give their decision, they unexpectedly adjourned the Court until October, alleging that the vacation of the Law Courts at Rome had commenced : and on the 4th August an injunction was received, forbidding any further proceedings, as the Pope would himself try the Cause at Rome, where the King and Queen were cited to appear.

Thus matters remained until October 1528. This date is selected because it was in this month that the King is said to have first given any evidence of his affection for Anne Boleyn. Dr Lingard puts this date at 1526, but without sufficient authority.

Anne Boleyn went at an early age to France, and lived with the French King's sister, A.D. 1514. On the King's death, the Queen Dowager returned to England; but Anne was so much liked at the French Court that the wife of King Francis I. kept her in her service for some years, and after this Queen's death the Duchess of Alençon kept her in her Court while she was in France. These facts at least refute the calumny as to Anne's levity, if not direct im-

morality, while she was in the French Court, as these royal
personages were celebrated for their virtues. It is supposed
that Anne returned to England in the spring of the year
1527, and entered the service of the Court as maid of
honour. She was then young, beautiful, sprightly, and
accomplished. It was not until the end of the following
year that the first symptoms of affection were shown by the
King for Anne Boleyn—nearly two years after the public
protest by the Bishops of Tarbes as to Princess Mary's illegitimacy, and nearly five years after Henry's virtual separation from the Queen, if the letter to Bucer, before alluded
to, is to be admitted as evidence. The facts as above
related, in connexion with dates, clearly show that the
King's affection for Anne had nothing whatever to do with
his separation from Catherine. There is no record of
evidence that the Queen had any complaint against Anne's
conduct at that time, and so little was a marriage with the
King contemplated that there were other suitors for her
hand; and one of the charges subsequently brought against
her at her trial was a previous betrothal to another, which
in those days appears to have been a ground of objection
to her subsequent marriage.

The assertion that Anne was Henry's mistress before
their marriage is a cruel slander. Dr Lingard writes :—
"When Henry ventured to disclose to Anne his real object,
she indignantly replied, that though she might be happy
to be his wife, she would never consent to be his mistress."

[1] " History of England," vol. vii. p. 155. London, 1823. It has been long
asserted that Mary Boleyn, Anne's sister, was the mistress of Henry VIII. Mr
Froude opposes this assertion as unproved, while Mr Friedman, in his recent
work, "Anne Boleyn," 1885, Appendix B, vol. ii., seems to establish
this as a fact, though he admits that Crumwell publicly denied it at the
time (p. 326). The Act of 1536 (28 Henry VIII., c. vii.) has been repeatedly
quoted as having been passed specially to meet the case of Henry's alleged
intercourse with Mary, Anne Boleyn's sister, declaring such a marriage on that

And here we must again draw attention to the same writer, as to Henry's motives and Anne Boleyn's character.[1] "It had been intimated to Pope Clement that the real object of the King was to gratify the ambition of a woman who had sacrificed her honour to his passion on condition that he should raise her to the throne. But after the perusal of a letter from Wolsey, the Pontiff believed, or at least professed to believe, that Anne Boleyn was a lady of unimpeachable character, and that the suit of Henry proceeded from sincere scruples." Mr Froude, who has given this part of the subject a deep and impartial consideration, with reference to Henry's motives for a divorce, says :—

"The King's scruples were not originally, I am persuaded, occasioned by any latent inclination on the part of the King for another woman ; they had arisen to their worst dimensions before he had even seen Anne Boleyn, and were produced by causes of a wholly different kind."[2]

account invalid, and is therefore cited to prove that Mary Boleyn was Henry's mistress.   In a review of Friedman's book in the *Guardian* newspaper of 11th February 1885, we are told "That Parliament passed an Act (28 Henry VIII. c. vii.) ordering every man who had married the sister of a former mistress to separate from her, and forbidding such marriages in future." I think this inference is scarcely fair, in the manner this Act of Parliament is cited. True, the Act declares that the marriage was void from the beginning. But it deals with several other circumstances.   In section vii., a long list of degrees of affinity in which marriage is prohibited, every possible relationship is mentioned, among others, "brother and sister."   The Act then proceeds :— "That if chance any may to know carnally any woman, that then all and singular any persons being in any degree of consanguinity or affiancy (as is above written) to any of the parties so carnally offending, shall be deemed and adjudged to be within the cases of the prohibitions of marriage." As the Act itself annulled the marriage, there could be no necessity for this underhand and doubtful way of going to work. If the King notoriously had had intercourse with Anne's sister, why should they go through the farce of reciting a long list of consanguinity in this surreptitious manner, and intend the clause to apply to the King's special case. And, further, the Act was not *retrospective.* I consider it therefore unfair broadly to cite this Act to establish the accusation against Mary Boleyn.

[1] " History of England," vol. vii., p. 155, London, 1823, and see vol. v. p. 137.   Edition 1848.

[2] Froude's " History of England," vol. i. p. 106.   London, 1856.

This opinion is confirmed by Dean Hook, who said : " The idea of a divorce did not *originate* in the King's passion for Anne Boleyn." [1]

The Pope's own Legates bear out this view, who wrote to their master in May 1529 :—

"It was mere madness to suppose that the King would act as he was doing merely out of dislike to the Queen, or out of inclination for another. He was not a man whom harsh manners and an unpleasant disposition could so far provoke ; nor can any sane man believe him to be so infirm of character that sensual allurements would have led him to dissolve a connexion *in which he has passed the flower of his youth without stain or blemish,* and in which he has borne himself in his present trial so reverently and honourably." [2]

This was the sober opinion uttered by the Pope's own representatives, who could have had no motive in view to mislead or deceive their master : on the contrary, they were fully aware of his critical position; they were ecclesiastics of high station, sent here by the Pope himself to conduct this delicate and difficult matter. Gardyner himself maintained that the motives of the King were " most conscientious and virtuous."

Those who defend the conduct of the Pope for refusing the suit of Henry on the grounds of the sacredness of matrimony, and of Henry's alleged licentious demands, would do well to remember that at this very time the Pope gave his ready sanction to the most impudent request for a divorce ever presented to a court of justice—namely, the divorce of Queen Margaret of Scotland from the Earl of Angus, who thereupon forthwith married the worthless Methuen. This was a scandal and a disgrace to the Papal Court ; but we hear nothing of this, because, forsooth, no great results followed affecting the Papal power. [3]

[1] " Lives of the Archbishops," vol. vii. p. 358.
[2] Quoted by Froude as above ; and see Burnet's " Records," b. ii. n. xxiv.
[3] Froude's " History of England," vol. iv. p. 32. London, 1858.

When King Henry was informed of the limited authority held by Campeggio, and of his tergiversation,[1] he took the matter into his own hands, and sent Sir Francis Brian to the Pope publicly to announce to him that, if the formal consent were not forthwith given, he would act independently of the Pope, and lay the cause before his own Parliament, to be settled by the laws of his own country.

The Pope's difficulties increased ; the Emperor Charles, in January 1529, publicly interposed, and conveyed his threats in strong terms.   The affrighted Pope repented him of his promises to Henry ; and, while he declared to the Emperor that he would not confirm the sentence, he continued to " feed the King with high promises and encouragements," temporising with both, afraid to offend either ; and as Strype has it, " the Pope said and unsaid, sighed, sobbed, beat his breast, shuffled, implored, threatened."[2]   At the dictation of the Emperor he proposed to excommunicate Henry, while, at the same time, he communicated with the Bishop of Tarbes (still the ambassador of France in England) that he would be happy to hear that the King had got married without consulting him,— in fact, on the King's own responsibility,—so that he, the Pope, was not committed by the act.[3]

The Pope still instructed his Legates to procrastinate,

---

[1] Campeggio was leading a debauched life in England, and spent his time in hunting and gaming. His illegitimate son was knighted by the king. See " Dictionnaire Historique," art. Campeggio (Laurant).

[2] " Memorials," Appendix iv., No. 61, p. 100, folio edition.

[3] " A ce qu'il m'en a déclaré des fois plus de trois en secret il seroit content que ledit mariage fust jà faiet, ou par dispense du Legat d'Angleterre ou outrement ; mais que ce ne fust par son autorité, ni aussi diminuant sa puissance quant aux dispenses et limitation de droict divin."—*Déchiffrement des Lettres de M. de Tarbes*. Legrand, vol. iii. p. 408 ; quoted by Froude, "History of England," vol. i. p. 241. London, 1856.

who, in May 1529, wrote to their master urging him to grant a Bull of divorce. This document is extant, and is important.[1]   They told the Pope :—

" It pitied them to see the rack and torments of conscience under which the King had smarted for so many years ; and that the disputes of Divines and the decrees of Fathers had so disquieted him, that for clearing a matter thus perplexed there was not only need of learning, but of more singular piety and illumination. To *this were to be added the desire of issue*, the settlement of the kingdom, with many other reasons ; that as the matter did not admit of delay, so there was not anything in the opposite scale to balance these considerations."

These reflections are important as evidence, delivered at the time, of the opinion entertained by the Pope's own representatives :—" There were false suggestions surmised abroad, as if the hatred of the Queen or the desire of another wife were the true cause of the suit. But though the Queen [Catherine] was of a rough temper and an unpleasant conversation, and was passed all hopes of children, yet who could imagine that the King, who had spent his most youthful days with her so kindly, would now, in the decline of his age, be at all this trouble to be rid of her, if he had no other motives ? But they, by searching his sore, found there was rooted in his heart both an awe of God and a respect to law and order ; so that, though all his people pressed him to drive the matter to an issue, yet he would still wait for the decision of the Apostolic See." They, however, urged on the Pope to give a speedy decision, " considering this a fit case to relax the rigour of the law ;" and they significantly added, that if the dispensation were not granted, " other remedies would be found out, to the vast prejudice of the ecclesiastical authority, to which many about the King advised him ; there was reason to

---

[1] It is given in Burnet's " Hist. of the Reformation," in full, vol. i. pt. i. b. ii. p. 110 ; and vol. iv., " Records," No. 28. Nare's edition, 1830.

fear that they not only lose a king of England, but a Defender of the Faith."

It was evident that the Pope was acting the part of a cunning, though short-sighted politician, looking after his own temporal ends ; it is only surprising that the King, who is represented as being a very vehement and impetuous tyrant, bore with him so long and patiently.   It was necessary to do something.   Accordingly, a court was held in England, on the subject of the divorce, in June 1529, in the presence of the Legates, when Campeggio declared, in his official capacity, that the King and Queen Catherine were living in adultery, or rather incest ; but, nevertheless, no Bull was issued.   It was at this court (18th June 1529) that the King declared :—" That in the treaty for the marriage of his daughter with the Duke of Orleans, it was excepted that she was illegitimate ; on this he was resolved to try the lawfulness of his marriage, as well as to quiet his own conscience, as for clearing the succession to the throne.   If the marriage were found lawful, he would be well satisfied to live with the Queen.   He was first advised ·in the matter by the Bishop of Lincoln, and at his desire the Archbishop of Canterbury [Warham] had obtained the opinions of all the Bishops."   The court was adjourned, and on the 25th the Queen, with the concurrence of Campeggio, appealed to Rome, and thereupon, and to create further delay, in August 1529, the Pope, on the appeal of Catherine and the Emperor Charles V. (with whom the Pope had now entered into an alliance), issued an inhibition from proceeding with the divorce in England, and cited the King and Queen to appear at Rome, in person or by proxy, menacing spiritual censures, which were, however, subsequently withdrawn.   The King of England very properly refused to obey the summons, or to humour the Pope's whims and schemes. This was the first act towards questioning the Pope's authority in England. Henry then proposed to the Queen to remit the case to any four prelates and four secular men for decision, but she refused the offer.

At the Queen's request a second inhibition was issued in 1529-30, in stronger language, but which was equally impotent of purpose.

Cardinal Wolsey, then Prime Minister, went so far as to threaten the Pope, in a letter dated July 1529, addressed to Cassalis, at Rome, that if the question was not settled in England, and his Highness should come at any time to the Court of Rome, he would do so with an armed force.[1] In fact, he took an active part in forwarding the King's views for a divorce; indeed, according to Cardinal Pole, the idea originated with him. It appears, further, in a previous despatch from Wolsey to Gregory Cassalis, dated 5th December 1527, that the King had already consulted learned divines and canonists in England and abroad for the purpose of ascertaining whether the Pope's dispensation could give validity to his marriage with Catherine. But Wolsey's scheme had no reference to Anne Boleyn. He entertained the idea of a marriage between Henry and Renée, the daughter of Louis XII. of France. He is said to have afterwards gone on his knees—a daring act under the circumstances—to persuade the King to give up Anne. Motives of an unworthy character have been attributed to Wolsey in bringing about the divorce from Catherine. He aspired to the Papal chair, in which he was thwarted by Catherine's nephew, Charles V., in breach of promises given in that behalf. He was also offended with the Queen for having rebuked him for his luxuriousness and

---

[1] " State Papers," vol. iii. p. 193.

lax life. By this advocacy of the divorce he sought to humiliate the two.   It is difficult, at this distant period, to speculate on motives in the absence of precise evidence. It is, nevertheless, the fact that Wolsey's secret, compromising correspondence with the Pope, was discovered, which exasperated the King against the Cardinal.

Archbishop Warham ultimately decided in favour of the ·King's divorce.   He said that "truth and judgment of law must be followed."[1]

We now hear for the first time of the appearance of Dr CRANMER on the scene, which will form the subject of another Chapter.

[1] " State Papers," vol. i. pp. 195, 196.

CHAPTER IV.

CRANMER'S PARTICIPATION IN THE PROCEEDINGS OF THE DIVORCE OF HENRY VIII. FROM CATHERINE.

WE left Dr Cranmer acting as Lecturer on Divinity and Tutor at the University of Cambridge.

In September 1529 a plague, known as the "sweating sickness," broke out with great violence, especially at Cambridge. Dr Cranmer had then under his charge two of the sons of Mr Cressy, who was in some way related to his wife. Mr Cressy was living at Waltham Abbey, in Essex. To avoid the contagion, Dr Cranmer went on a visit with his two pupils to Mr Cressy.

By chance—but as Bishop Hall said, "God lays these small accidents for the ground of greater designs"—the King, on his journey northwards, or as some assert, to avoid the plague-stricken districts, passed through Waltham Cross, where he remained for the night. The King's secretary, Stephen Gardyner, afterwards Bishop of Winchester, and Foxe, the royal almoner, afterwards Bishop of Hereford, were also the guests of Mr Cressy while Dr Cranmer was there. At supper, the King's matrimonial position and the protracted negotiations with Rome for a divorce were naturally the subjects of conversation, when Cranmer expressed his opinions freely, that it was contrary to Scripture to marry a brother's widow, and recommended that, instead of a long and fruitless negotiation with Rome, it were better to consult all the learned men of the universities of Europe ; for, if they declared the marriage illegal, then the Pope must needs give judgment, or, otherwise, the original Bull being void, the marriage would be found sinful, notwithstanding the Pope's dispensation.   This advice was communicated to the King, who eventually commanded that Cranmer should commit his opinion to writing.   Cranmer was placed, at the request of the King, under the care and hospitality of Sir Thomas Boleyn, with leisure to prosecute his work.   Sir Thomas was then as well a friend, as also a prominent character in the Court, of the King.   This circumstance has given occasion to the charge that Cranmer was made a creature of that family, introduced by Henry to promote his own erotic views. Dr Lingard, without the slightest evidence, asserts that "Cranmer was a dependent on the family of the King's mistress."   If this be applied to Anne Boleyn, it is a most dastardly libel on the fair fame of Sir Thomas Boleyn and of his virtuous wife, suggesting that they could be parties to such a base transaction as is here insinuated.   Sir Thomas Boleyn was a man "most honourably distinguished for his piety, intelligence, and learning."   His friend Erasmus describes him not only as an accomplished Peer (then Earl of Wiltshire), but as a person of quiet and unambitious habits, and above all suspicion of having instigated the divorce.[1]

While a guest of Sir Thomas Boleyn, Cranmer drew up a treatise, maintaining that the marriage of Henry with his brother's widow was condemned by the authority of the Scriptures, Councils, and Fathers, and by the Canon Law; and he further denied that the dispensing power of the Pope could give validity to an union expressly prohibited by the Word of God ; and he declared his readiness to defend his opinion before the Pope himself if the King

[1] Erasmus.   "Ep." 1253.   Vol. iii. col. 1472.   Edit. Lug. Batav. 1703.

D

desired it.   This work is said to have been executed with
great ability, and excited much attention.   It was laid before the Universities of Oxford and Cambridge and the
House of Commons.   Notwithstanding this wide publicity,
not a copy now exists.[1]

The King availed himself of Cranmer's suggestion, and
accordingly sent him to Rome, where he, with a deputation
of English divines, after presenting the ˴Pope with a copy
of his book, offered to contend with him the two propositions: "That no man *jure divino* could or ought to marry
his brother's widow," and " That the Bishop of Rome ought
by no means to dispense to the contrary."   The Pope was
interested so far only as his personal safety was concerned.
His position was embarrassing for the reasons before
alleged, and he wearied out the embassy by delays, refusing permission that Cranmer should maintain his opinions
in public ; but, in order to reward Cranmer, or conciliate
him, the Pope conferred on him the title of the " King's
Supreme Penitentiary of England."

In 1530 Dr Cranmer proceeded to seek the opinions of
the Universities.   The judgment of the English bishops
(except Fisher, Bishop of Rochester) had been obtained
4th April 1530, declaring the nullity of the King's marriage with Catherine.   This decision was approved of,
ratified, and confirmed by—

The Universities of Oxford and Cambridge.—8th April
1530.

The University of Orleans.—7th April 1530.

[1] I may here mention that Cranmer is accused of having advocated the
divorce and second marriage, with a full knowledge of the King's alleged illicit
intercourse with one or other of Sir Thomas Boleyn's daughters, Mary or
Anne, and this is attempted to be established on the authority of a manuscript
in the British Museum, attributed to Cranmer.   Not to interrupt the narrative, I have placed my objections to this document in an Appendix to the
present chapter.

The Faculty of the Civil and Canon Law at Angers.—
7th May 1530.

The Faculty of Divines at Bruges.—10th June 1530.

The Divines of Bologna.—10th June 1530.

The University of Padua.—10th July 1530.

The celebrated Faculty of Sorbonne at Paris.[1]—2nd July
1530.   •

The Divines of Ferrara.—29th September 1530.

The University of Toulouse.—1st October 1530.

By the most famous Jewish Rabbis, and by a large
number of the Canonists in Venice, in Rome itself, and
many other places.

Many of the Cardinals at Rome sided with the King.
Even Cardinal Pole at one time warmly espoused Henry's
divorce.[2]

It is important to note, to the credit of the Reformers,
that Luther, Melancthon, and others, gave their opinion
that the marriage was void; but they maintained that the
King should not marry again during Catherine's lifetime.[3]

It is asserted, and perhaps on good grounds, that the
two English Universities were coerced in giving their judgment. But when it is also asserted that the Continental
Universities were bribed to give their decision in favour of
the divorce, such a statement, if true, must leave us to
arrive at the unpleasant conclusion that the entire Roman
Catholic community on the Continent was devoid of every
principle of justice and honour; an admission most damag-

---

[1] The Faculty declared "that the marriage of the King of England was
unlawful, and that the Pope had no power to dispense on it;" and to this they
attached their common seal.

[2] See Pocock's edit. of Burnet's "History of the Reformation," Preface, p.
xxx. Oxford, 1865.

[3] See "Colloquia Mensallia" [or Table Talk]. Bell's 2d Edit., folio,
1791, pp. 398-9.

ing to the cause of the unreformed Church, and to that of the detractors of Cranmer.

On the 13th July 1530 the King caused a Memorial to be prepared, to be submitted to the Pope, to which Archbishop Warham, Cardinal Wolsey, four other bishops, forty noblemen, and eleven commoners, put their signatures, representing the justness of the King's cause, the concurrence of the English and foreign Universities, the unwarrantable delays interposed ; and, in fact, they threatened other remedies if further difficulties / were interposed.

The matter was then referred to the House of Commons and to Convocation, both of which bodies decided the marriage to be illegal.

It appears that Sir Thomas More at first considered the marriage with Catherine illegal, and indeed " approved of the divorce, and had great hopes of success in it, as long as it was prosecuted at Rome, and founded on the defects in the Bull" of Pope Julius. When the opinions of the Universities were brought to England against the marriage, he took them down to the House of Commons and had them read there, and requested them to convey the information to their several constituents, " and then all men would openly perceive that the King had not attempted this matter of his will and pleasure, but only for the discharge of his conscience. More was a man of greater integrity than to have said this, if he had thought the marriage valid ; so that he had either afterwards changed his mind, or did at this time dissemble too artificially with the King."[1] Burnet points out the fact that Henry would scarcely have raised More to the Chancellor-

---

[1] See Pocock's edition of Burnet's " History of the Protestant Reformation," vol. iv. p. 552. Oxford, 1865.

ship had he opposed the divorce by maintaining the validity of the first marriage.

Can any one be surprised that the King of England now entertained a supreme contempt for the Bishop of Rome, for his vacillating and time-serving conduct? Accordingly, in September 1530, the King's Ambassadors at Rome were commanded, in the King's name, to refuse to pay submission to the Pope, or to appear to a citation before the Court of Rome.

Lord Herbert of Cherbury, in his history of "The Life and Reign of Henry VIII.," gives the text of a letter, under date 17th September 1530, written to Henry by Gregory Cassalis, his agent at the Court of Rome, the original of which he declares to have himself examined. In this letter Cassalis informs the King that Pope Clement VII., admitting the importance of the matter, had proposed to concede to his Majesty the permission even of having two wives,[1] under the supposition, perhaps, of being unable to revoke the act of his predecessor, Julius II., by granting a divorce from a marriage sanctioned by a Papal Bull, but that he might exercise his assumed prerogative by granting additional privileges without running counter to existing impediments.

On the 1st June 1531 a deputation, consisting of the Duke of Norfolk, the Earls of Shrewsbury, Northumberland, and Wiltshire, with several other Peers, the Bishops of Lincoln and London, Drs. Lee, Sampson, and Gardyner, waited on the King, supporting the divorce.

---

[1] "Superioribus diebus, Pontifex secreto, veluti rem magni fecerit, mihi proposuit conditionem hujusmodi, concedi posse vestræ Majestati, et duas uxores habeas."—Herbert's "Life and Reign of Henry VIII." p. 130. London, 1683. Pope Clement's Bull, issued in 1528, authorised Wolsey, jointly with Warham, or any other Bishop, to give sentence, and to grant the King and Queen permission to marry again.

It may here be noted that Cardinal Wolsey died on the 27th November 1530, which accounts for the fact of his name not appearing in these transactions after that date.

On the 14th July 1531, the King publicly and finally separated from Catherine ; having practically, and to all intents and purposes, done so previously in 1527, if not before.

7th February 1532, the Cardinal of Ravenna was bribed to advocate the King's suit ; and the Cardinals of Ancona and Monte (the latter afterwards Pope Julius III.) sided with the King.

We would now ask any reasoning man, why Dr Cranmer should be singled out and stigmatised for holding an opinion, which was supported by such a phalanx of prelates and divines, indeed by the learned of universal Christendom ?

Warham, Archbishop of Canterbury, died 22d August 1532.

On the 25th January 1533, the King married Anne Boleyn, six years after his virtual separation from Catherine ; and this took place while Dr Cranmer was abroad. We would urge the reader to weigh well all the events of the intervening period : the Pope's conduct, the want of a legitimate heir to the throne, the anxiety of the King's subjects on this head, and the ominous fulfilment, as it appeared, of Scripture, by the successive deaths of the issue of this first marriage. To all intents and purposes the King was, according to Roman Canon Law, legally severed from Catherine. The Pope's sanction had been virtually pledged, and all that was wanting, according to the then accepted notions, was the formal Bull of Divorce, which was withheld, not from motives of religion, or for conscience' sake—nothing of the kind—but from fear of the Emperor Charles.   An appeal to the court of Rome would only, as the Pope himself suggested, have complicated matters.   Was not, therefore, the King of England fully justified (even if no other considerations led to the important step) in passing—not all of a sudden, as untruthfully alleged — the Act prohibiting appeals to Rome ? It was not until November 1534 that the Act (26 Henry VIII. c. 1) was passed, declaring the King of England the Supreme Head on Earth of the Church in this country. And here again attention is drawn to the Rev. W. Gleig's version, in the School Series before referred to, as a further illustration of the fact, that our prejudices are influenced by early training, and that the popular elementary histories of the present day perpetuate known fallacies. Mr Gleig makes the declaration of Henry as being " Head of the Church of England," previous to January 1533, the date of the marriage with Anne Boleyn, whereas the Act, as stated, was passed in the year 1534 (26 Henry VIII. c. 1), Wolsey having died 1530.   Mr Gleig's version is as follows (p. 99) :—

"The death of Wolsey seemed to cut away the King's last tie to Rome. *He at once threw off* the primacy of the Pope. He declared himself to be head of the Church in England, and passed sharp laws against such as should dare to deny that he was so. In regard to the marriage, he acted as if the point were settled. In January 1533 he took Anne Boleyn to wife, and in April of the same year he had her treated as Queen ; and then, but not till then, he caused Cranmer, now raised to the See of Canterbury, to give sentence[1] that this marriage with Catherine had been against law from the first. An Act of Parliament confirmed this decree, and Catherine, with her daughter, withdrew from public life."

We now come to another important fact; namely, that on the 21st February 1533 the Pope of Rome himself

[1] The "sentence" attributed to Cranmer was given on the 23d May. Anne was not crowned till 1st June 1533.

signed the Bull of Cranmer's consecration as Archbishop of Canterbury. It was sent on the 2d March, and Cranmer was consecrated on the 30th March, 1533. The fact that the Pope himself thus approved and ratified Henry's selection of Cranmer, must be somewhat embarrassing to those who boldly assert that Henry made the selection of one he considered he could easily use as a pliant instrument to carry out his divorce scheme in opposition to the Pope's sanction. The Pope was perfectly aware of the part Cranmer was taking in the matter. At this time Cranmer held the appointment of Archdeacon of Taunton, and was also one of the King's chaplains. It is true he received the emoluments of his archdeaconry without doing the duties, but that was a recognised abuse in those days, extensively patronised by the Pope himself. Leo X. held a benefice when he was seven years old, and he subsequently held thirty different preferments in the Church! Pluralities of livings was one of the great abuses while the Pope held rule in England. It is, however, a fact that Cranmer refused to accept the Pope's Bull for his consecration, but delivered it over to the King, as he did not consider this form necessary to the validity of his appointment; and on taking the oath of fidelity to the Pope, before his consecration, which was the custom of the day, he accompanied it with a public protest: "That he did not admit the Pope's authority any further than it agreed with the express Word of God; and that it might be lawful for him at all times to speak against him, and to impugn his errors when there should be occasion." This he thrice repeated in the presence of official witnesses.[1]

In April 1533 the Upper and Lower Houses of Convo-

---

[1] This oath to the Pope, and a like oath to the King, will be the subject for consideration in a separate chapter.

cation declared the nullity of the first marriage, and it was on the 10th March 1533 that the bishops and archbishops held a consistory, over which Cranmer, *in his official capacity as Primate*, presided. " Though he pronounced sentence, he was but the mouthpiece of the rest, and they were all as deep as he."[1]   And on the 23d they came to a unanimous decision, declaring that the first marriage was void *de facto et de jure*.   Those who sided with Cranmer in the decision were (among others): Gardyner, Stokesly, Clerk, and Longland ; and the Bishops of Winchester, London, Bath, and Lincoln.[2]

It is this solemn decision of the united bench of archbishops and bishops in council which has been erroneously set down as " Cranmer's sentence," and the Convocation itself "a sort of tribunal"!   It was the sentence of the entire court, the highest ecclesiastical court in this country, confirming the previous decision of universal Christendom.   Cranmer did nothing more than *proclaim* or *record* the decision of the court over which he presided by virtue of his office as Archbishop of Canterbury, or Primate of all England.   Could the court have arrived at any other result ? or could its President have recorded any other decision ?   Cranmer's detractors seem to overlook this ; as also that the judgment was according to the rule then, as well as now, almost unanimously received and acknowledged—namely, that the marriage with a brother's widow was accounted incestuous, and forbidden as well by the law of God as by the law of nature ; a moral precept insisted on more particularly by that very class of persons who are most vehement against Cranmer—mem-

---

[1] Strype's " Life of Cranmer," b. i. c. iv. p. 21 (folio edit.).
[2] See Pocock's edit. of " Burnet's History of the Protestant Reformation," vol. iv. pp. 561-2.   Oxford, 1865.

bers of the Roman Communion. It is, therefore, an act
of injustice to impute to this Council or to Cranmer, who
only endorsed the opinion of the divines and learned men
of Europe, any motive other than an honest conviction in
the justice of their decision. They seem to forget that if
Cranmer "aided and abetted" Henry VIII. in an unholy
cause, and that Henry pursued this course without any
just ground, and only to gratify an inordinate passion,[1] the
bishops, cardinals, divines, universities, canonists, and
even the Pope himself, were guilty as his accomplices!
All were members, most of them priests, of the unreformed
Church of Rome. The Reformation in this country did
not actually commence until the succeeding reign.

After such a unanimous and solemn decision of universal
Christendom, what virtue could there be in a Bull of confirmation by a Pope,—in a Bull already promised, but withheld only from fear and from worldly motives?

In the month following, viz., 1st June 1533, Anne was
crowned Queen. The ceremony was attended by bishops,
monks, and abbots, among whom the Bishop of Bayonne
took a conspicuous part; they joined in the procession,
and the Bishops of London and Winchester bore the
lappets of her robe, thus giving this marriage their moral
support and sanction. Cranmer in one of his letters mentions the Bishops of York, London, Winchester, Lincoln,
Bath, and St Asaph as taking part in it.

On the 12th May 1533 the Pope cited Henry to appear at
Rome, being urged on by the Emperor to proceed to excommunication; but the Pope hesitated, and waited the result of
the proposed interview with Francis I. on the subject, which

---

[1] " Nothing," says Dr Milner, "than the King's inordinate passion, and not
the Word of God, was the rule followed in this *first important change of
our national religion.*"—" End of Religious Controversy," Letter viii.

it was hoped would bring about a reconciliation. On the 29th June the King appealed from the Pope to a General Council. On the news of the King's marriage arriving at Rome, the Pope was so exasperated, that in a fit of passion he threatened to boil Bonner, the King's messenger, in molten lead, or burn him alive. But he considered it more prudent to reserve his wrath ; and he postponed his judgment on the case to the 11th July, when he issued a Brief reversing the sentence of Convocation, and commanded Henry to cancel the process ; and if he failed to obey, he was to be declared excommunicated ; but he still suspended his formal censures.[1]   Henry refused to retract.

Elizabeth, afterwards queen, was born 7th September 1533, that is, ten months after the King's marriage with Anne Boleyn—namely (according to Sanders), the 14th November previous. After that date the King was never publicly *married* to the Queen, as alleged ; what Sanders calls a public marriage was only the King's open introduction of the Queen in public.[2] It was on this day, 7th September, that the Pope, on the interference of Francis I., King of France, promised to give his sanction in favour of the divorce, *provided the King submitted to his* (the Pope's) *jurisdiction*. Francis urged upon the Pope the necessity of complying with Henry's demand. The Pope, on this occasion, said to Francis—and which the King of France communicated to Henry by letter[3]—that he, the Pope, *was*

---

[1] "State Papers," vol. viii. p. 481. I am now citing these facts in chronological order, more especially in answer to the popular version put forth, referred to in the several writers cited in note, p. 14, *ante*. I shall have again to refer to some of these events, more particularly affecting Cranmer and the part he took in them.

[2] See Pocock's edit. of "Burnet's Hist. of the Prot. Reformation," vol. iv. p. 563. Oxford, 1865.

[3] See Froude's "History of England," vol. ii. p. 151, 1858, and "State Papers," vol. i. p. 421.

satisfied that the King of England was right, that his cause was good, and that he had only to acknowledge the Papal jurisdiction by some formal act to find sentence immediately given in his favour; a single act of recognition was all the Pope required. The French monarch was commissioned to offer a league offensive and defensive between England, France, and the Papacy. These were to be the terms of proposed concession! Henry VIII., however, replied with calm dignity befitting the high position he held in Europe, and as King of England. He rejected the proposal with temperate forbearance, and sent for reply:—

"That all his acts, from the commencement of his reign, proved that he was well disposed to the Pope; but, as matters stood, he would make no conditions. It would," he said, "redound much to the Pope's dishonour, if he should seem to pact and covenant for the administration of that thing which, in his conscience, he had adjudged to be rightful. It was not to be doubted that, if he had determined to give sentence for the nullity of the first marriage, he had established in his own conscience a firm persuasion that he ought to do so; and therefore, he should do his duty *simpliciter et gratis,* without worldly respect, or for the preservation of his pretended power or authority." . . .
"To see him," continued Henry, "to have this opinion, and yet refuse to give judgment in our behalf, unless we shall be content, for his benefit and pleasure *cedere juri suo;* and to do something prejudicial to our subjects and contrary to our honour, it is easy to be foreseen what the world and posterity shall judge of so base a prostitution of justice."

Henry declined to barter his dignity and the welfare and credit of his country for a second wife!

That the Pope of Rome was not actuated by any principle of religion or morality in refusing to confirm the original consent given for the divorce, becomes more apparent when we find that Pope Pius V.—the same Pope who afterwards excommunicated Elizabeth—so late even as the year 1566, thirty-three years after the birth of Elizabeth, offered to remove the impediment of her supposed

illegitimacy, and "reverse the sentence of his predecessor."
Yes, "and that he was extremely anxious to do so" on
condition, of course, that Elizabeth should "submit to
his rule"![1] The Spanish ambassador, De Silva, assured
Queen Elizabeth that—" She had only to express a desire
to that effect, and the Pope would immediately remove the
difficulty."[2]

If Henry, as is alleged, was actuated by " inordinate passion," the Pope was most certainly moved by an inordinate
love of power. But we cannot admit that the Pope was
" conscientiously inflexible," or that the " creed of the Protestants " was " more accommodating than the " (so-called)
" old religion which could not tolerate such a scandal," or
that Henry "was baffled by the incorruptible virtue of
Rome, " as alleged by Dr Milner ; the fact being that the
Pope had fixed his price for his consent, but it was
Henry, as also Elizabeth, and not the Pope, who were
" incorruptible."

Henry and his Parliament acted with becoming dignity
and without haste. The interview above alluded to
occurred early in September 1533. The King's answer was
returned in November following, and it was not until the
30th March 1534, after the Pope had refused Henry's appeal
to a General Council, and that his sentence had come into
force by reason of Henry's non-compliance with the order
of 12th July 1533, that the English Parliament passed
the Act abolishing the Pope's jurisdiction in England ; but
the Commons, by the Act 25 Henry VIII. c. 21, expressly
declared that a separation from the Pope was not a separation from the unity of the Church. The Pope, having no-

---

! Calling her his " dear daughter in Christ."
² See De Silva's letter to Philip II., dated December 1566, quoted by
Froude *in extenso* in his " History of England ; the reign of Elizabeth," vol.
viii. pp. 329, 330. London, 1863.

thing better to fall back upon, on the 23d March 1534
confirmed the sentence against the divorce; not in consequence, however, of this Act—they came almost together
—but probably in consequence of Henry's letter, backed by
the promise and support of Charles V.[1]

In 1535, Paul III., the very same Paul III. who, when a
Cardinal, in all the debates at the Court of Rome, had un-
swervingly advocated the King's suit for a divorce, and
maintained the justice of his demands ; and who, even after
the sentence against Henry was pronounced at Rome,
urged the reconsideration of the fatal step,[2]—this same
Paul III. issued a Bull of Deposition of Henry VIII., curs-
ing and anathematising him and his posterity, absolving
all his subjects from their allegiance,—a document which the
King of France declared to be a most impudent production, and that the Pope's " impotent threats could not only
do no good, but would make him the laughing-stock of
the world."[3]   So little was the Pope's " impotent threat "
estimated by the English ecclesiastics, that the bishops
then in England, nineteen in number, and twenty-five
doctors of divinity and law, signed a declaration against

[1] David Lewis, in his " Reformation Settlement," p. 30, note, says :—" The
Papal judgment affirming the validity of the King's marriage with Catherine
was given at Rome on the 23d March 1534, or a year after the decision of the
English Church against it, and a week before the rejection of the Papal supremacy and jurisdiction by Convocation, which could not then have heard of the
sentence passed at Rome."

[2] See the facts stated by Mr Froude, " History of England," vol. ii. p. 332.
London, 1858.

[3] " State Papers," vol. viii. p. 628, quoted by Froude.   It must not be left
unnoticed that the actual publication and issue of this Bull has been denied.
Dr Lingard denies that there is any evidence to show that the Bull of Excommunication was published ; and the Rev. Richard Watson Dixon, in his " History of the Church of England," vol. ii. p. 97, London, 1881, throws great
doubts on its authenticity, stating that Sanders was the first, in 1588, who
gives a summary of the Bull, and he states that he is unable to discover where
Burnet obtained the text he prints.   Froude, on the other hand, seems to
have no doubt of its actual publication.

the Pope's pretensions and his assumed ecclesiastical jurisdiction, which concluded with the following remarkable
words :—" The people ought to be instructed that Christ
did expressly forbid the Apostles or their successors to take
to themselves the power of the sword or the authority of
kings ; and that if the Bishop of Rome, or any other
bishop, assumed any such power, he was a tyrant and
usurper of other men's rights, and a subverter of the
Kingdom of Christ."[1]   The House of Lords passed a Bill
ratifying the marriage of Henry and Anne Boleyn, and
settled the succession on their issue.

It was in May 1537 that Anne was accused and found
guilty of adultery, to which we shall have again to refer.
Paul III. attempted to take advantage of the circumstance of Anne's misdemeanour.   He hoped Henry would
have relented, and return to his allegiance.   He sent
again for Sir Gregory Cassalis, and renewed the former
negotiations.   He expressed his satisfaction that God had
delivered the King from his unhappy connexion ; he
assured the King's ambassador that he waited only for the
most trifling intimation of a desire for reunion to send a
Nuncio to England to compose all differences, and to grant
everything which the King could wish.   He hinted that a
union with Henry would make them arbiters of Europe,
and that they could thus dictate their own terms to the
Emperor and Francis I.   In the contemplation of this
" holy alliance " he conveniently forgot the " Clementine
League," and carefully glossed over the formidable Brief of
Dispensation as a mere official form, which there had been
no thought of enforcing, reminding Cassalis that from the
first he had been a constant friend of Henry, urging (when

---

[1] Quoted by Burnet, " History of the Reformation," fol. i. b. iii., vol. i. p.
399.   Nares' edit., 1830.

himself a cardinal) on his predecessor and on the Emperor Charles to sanction the divorce, and only from external pressure "seeming to consent to extreme measures, which were never intended to be enforced." [1]

Henry VIII. had emancipated himself from the thraldom of the Papacy. He had braved the supposed danger ; he had felt the extent of Papal wrath, and the anathemas passed by him as the idle winds—

> " His curses and his blessings
> Touch me alike ; they are breath I not believe in."
> " Henry VIII.," Act ii., Scene ii.

Henry saw no reason to retract his steps, and therefore remained firm to his purpose.

Such is the simple and true history of this transaction. The Pope of Rome, from motives of expediency, gave his sanction to an illegal union between Henry and Catherine. He gave his written sanction also for a divorce, of the same Henry from Catherine, but from fear of the consequences he withheld the formal Bull of confirmation. He dreaded his old enemy the Emperor Charles V., Catherine's nephew. He temporised with both monarchs ; he was, in fact, " between the hammer and the anvil ; " and finally, he paid the penalty of his vacillating conduct ! Henry very properly freed himself, according to the established law of the land, from the trammels of a worldly, time-serving Bishop. He reasserted the dignity of the crown of England, and its independence of a foreign Priest.

Cranmer's share in these transactions (to which we shall have presently to refer more particularly), save as Archbishop, was no greater than any other ecclesiastic or noble in the land.

[1] See Letter of Sir Gregory Cassalis to Henry VIII., Cotton MS. Vitel., b. xiv. fol. 215.

APPENDIX TO CHAPTER IV.

Note to p. 50.

IT has been asserted, on the faith of a manuscript in the British Museum, "Cotton MSS., Vespas., B. 5," that Cranmer acted with a perfect knowledge of the alleged fact, that Henry had had illicit intercourse either with Anne or with her sister Mary, and that therefore criminal intimacy with some members of the Boleyn family formed no obstacle, in his opinion, to the marriage with Anne Boleyn.

The charge was made by the Rev. Dr Littledale, in his Lecture on " Ritualistic Innovations," Lond., 1868, p. 38, and which I challenged at the time of its publication. Dr Littledale states that " Cranmer was fully aware that, whatever the merits of the marriage question as between Henry and Katharine might be, there was one obstacle, if not two, fatal to the legality of a union with Anne Boleyn. Even if Anne were not betrothed (some say actually married) to Lord Percy, at *any rate Henry had seduced her sister, Mary Boleyn,* a fact which the law of that day righteously held to create a relationship between the parties which made such a marriage as Henry planned incestuous. Cranmer drew up a treatise to prove that the obstacle was insignificant." And in a note he adds—" The case is even blacker if Henry was, as is alleged, the seducer of Anne's mother, Lady Boleyn, also. The King denied this, but it is very significant that Cranmer, in the infamous document mentioned (Cotton MSS., Brit. Mus., Vespas. B. 5), actually provides for this abominable contingency, and accounts it of no moment."

The passage relied on is found in p. 81 of the MS. :—

" Hence, neither the Roman Pontiff, nor the whole Church together, can convert into a relation by birth and marriage any one who is not naturally such, nor divest of those characters one who, by God and nature, is thus constituted ; rights of this kind being rights of blood and nature, and not susceptible of change and variation by human expedients. With respect, however, to the affinity founded on ecclesiastical sanction only, the case is different, whether it has arisen from illicit intercourse *with the sister, daughter, or mother of a wife;* for unquestionably, by no means whatever, does it impede by natural and divine law, but by human law only, the contraction of a marriage, and by no means does it dissolve it when contracted."

" Hinc, nec Romanus Pontifex neque tota simul ecclesia verum cognatum et affinem efficere possunt, qui non est, nec illum destituere qui a Deo, et naturâ constitutus est, cum jura hujusmodi, jura sangui-

E

nis et naturæ sunt, quæ humanâ ope mutari variarique nequeunt. De eâ vero affinitate, quæ sanctione ecclesiasticâ solum inventa est, secus ; *sive cum uxoris, sorore aut filiâ, seu matre, ex illegitimo coitu, fuerit orta,* quæ proculdubio naturali et divino jure, nullo quovis modo impedit, sed humano solum, ne matrimonium contrahatur, et contractum dissolvit."

In the first place, there is no evidence that Cranmer ever wrote this treatise ; it bears no signature nor date, and is a fair copy of some other document. After having carefully studied the context, I am thoroughly satisfied that the writer had no such intention in his mind as imputed to him. This is evident on the face of it. Incest, that is, marriage within the prohibited relationship, he says, is contrary to the law of God and of the Church, but affinity contracted by carnal connexion is created solely by human institution of the Church. This disobedience the writer, whoever he may have been, tells us the Roman Pontiff can easily relax by the grant of a dispensation (and Popes had repeatedly acted in this manner), but that neither the Roman Pontiff nor the whole Church together, can make a man a true relation by blood or marrriage who is not so, nor unmake him who by God and nature has been so constituted, since rights of this kind are rights of blood and nature which no human power can change or vary. In the case of that affinity, however, he adds, which has been invented by ecclesiastical institutions, it is otherwise. We, then, have several hypothetical cases suggested of the very worst sort, the " Division " being the fifth of a series of twelve propositions, where it is pointed out that, *as the teaching of the Roman Church,* the marriage in such cases is not in the slightest degree invalidated ; and he sums up the whole with the formality of Euclid : " Quorum doctrine undequaque manifestum," etc. From the doctrine of these authorities, it is evident on every ground, etc., that such marriages are not invalid. Now, who are the authorities cited ! It is not the Reformer Cranmer (at that time he was a firm adherent of the Roman Church) who is supposed to be laying down the law, but popes, divines, and schoolmen, members of the unreformed Church and the Canon Law of the Roman Church, whose words are cited. That the writer was stating hypothetical cases, and not in any way applying them to any one in particular, becomes more evident when we find him including in his list " *the daughter of a wife,*" which not even the most malignant opponent could assert had anything whatever to do with the case alleged against Henry and the Boleyn family. The anonymous and unknown author was evidently a learned canonist who discussed, as a thesis, wholly apocryphal cases relating to the law of marriage, but does not appear to have had before him the special case of Henry at all. The insinuation that Anne was the daughter, by Henry, of Lady Boleyn can never be sustained. It is true, as I have already remarked, that Sanders quotes an Act passed in 1536, referred to in the *Guardian*, "ordering every man who had married the sister of a former mistress to separate from her, forbidding all such marriages in future ;" and on this erroneous interpretation of the Act it has been concluded that this Act was passed in consequence of *Mary* Boleyn having been previously Henry's mistress. The charge, however, forces upon us the accusation against Pope Alexander VI., that Lucretia was at the same time his daughter, wife, and daughter-in-law.[1] (See ante *note*, pp. 40, 41.)

Were the above document omitted to be noticed, I might be charged with avoiding an alleged "conclusive evidence against Cranmer." The reader must exercise his own judgment on the facts before him.

---

[1] Pontanus in Bray's "Histoire," tom. iv. p. 280. Hague, 1732. "Alexandri filia, nupta, nurus."

CHAPTER V.

CRANMER'S SECOND MARRIAGE AS A PRIEST.

WE have mentioned that Cranmer was commissioned by the King to proceed to Rome to defend his opinions, as maintained in his book, and to obtain the views of the various learned bodies abroad on the question of the proposed divorce. He first went to Rome, as one of an Embassy, with the Earl of Wiltshire, as also in various parts of Italy, where he remained for some time. This journey was undertaken in the year 1530. At Rome Cranmer presented the Pope with a copy of his book, and offered to maintain his views by public discussion, which offer was, as we have seen, either evaded or refused.

At Rome, like Luther, on his visit to that city, Cranmer witnessed many things which opened his eyes to the real character of the Papacy, then in a most degraded and corrupt state.

Pope Clement, desirous to conciliate Cranmer, conferred on him the title of "Grand Penitentiary of England," which appears to have been a mere sinecure.

The King, in acknowledgment of Cranmer's services, besides an ecclesiastical preferment, appointed him, in January 1532 (new style), Ambassador to the Court of the Emperor Charles V.[1] Cranmer was also employed in

---

[1] Here I may be permitted to add a few observations. Mr Friedman, in his late work on "Anne Boleyn," has taken occasion, whenever he has had to refer to Cranmer, to add some depreciatory epithet. At this very period, without giving a single example or proof for his assertions, he thus describes

negotiations respecting the trade between England and the Low Countries, and the contingent to be furnished by the King towards the war with the Turks, against whom a crusade was then being organised. He was also occupied on other foreign affairs, in which he furnished Henry with much curious intelligence and useful information.

On a second mission, Cranmer proceeded through Germany, in 1531, to confer with the leading German Reformers. One of the principal persons in the Imperial Court, Cornelius Agrippa, was convinced by Cranmer's arguments. The Emperor was so displeased with the conduct of Agrippa that he was placed in confinement. The Reformers, at this time, had formed the League of Smalcald in their own defence against the exactions and encroachments of Papal power; but Cranmer found the Protestant Universities less favourable to his theories as to the divorce. We have already referred to the opinions attributed to Luther. The Emperor bestowed benefices and other preferments on those who opposed the King's project. There is no evidence of the alleged wholesale bribery which is said to have taken place. The accounts of Henry's Ambassadors show that the payments did not

Cranmer—"then in his 43rd year, rather learned, of ready wit, a good controversialist, and withal elegant, graceful, and insinuating, *an admirable deceiver, he possessed the talent of representing the most infamous deeds in the finest words*" (vol. i. p. 176, 1884). He declares him to be "a most useful tool of Cromwell and Henry," that "he had given ample proofs at the Court of Charles V. of his deceit" (p. 178), and that he "had a consummate talent for dissembling" (p. 244). True, Mr Friedman quotes Eustache Capius' Letters to the Emperor Charles V. for his authority, but as Capius was the Emperor's Ambassador, in fact spy, at this time, watching the interests of Charles, in all the acts of the King and his advisers to the prejudice of his aunt, Queen Catherine, it would have been more satisfactory had Mr Friedman relied on better authority than an enemy, and stated a few facts to support his assertions, which he does not; and further, the documents referred to are not accessible in England. Capius himself was not over scrupulous in his own conduct.

extend beyond official fees. These probably were excessive, and gave occasion for this charge of bribery.

In 1532 we find Cranmer at Nuremberg, where Osiander
officiated as the chief Minister of the Reformed Church. Osiander is represented to have been a pious and learned man.
He agreed with Cranmer on the question of the divorce.
These interviews with Osiander resulted in an intimacy
which led to the marriage of Cranmer with this Minister's
niece. It was impossible for Cranmer, in his protracted
sojourn among the Reformers, not to have imbibed many
of their notions, which he subsequently developed.

This second marriage of Cranmer, as a priest, has drawn
down upon him unmeasured abuse. He has been deliberately charged with *perjury*, on the erroneous supposition that a priest of Rome subscribes an oath to maintain
perpetual celibacy. William Cobbett goes so far, in addition to the charge of perjury, to assert twice that this
second marriage took place while his first wife was alive![1]

The celibacy of the priesthood is matter of discipline,
not of doctrine, and "therefore it may be changed, as in
the alterations of times and circumstances it has seemed,
or shall seem, good to our eccleslastical rulers."[2] Monks
and friars are compelled to take the vow of chastity, which
would include celibacy, but a priest of Rome takes neither
vows of chastity nor celibacy. Cranmer, when charged
with having entered into the state of matrimony, admitted
the fact, but at the same time affirmed that "it was better
for him to have his own, than do like other priests,
holding and keeping other men's wives."

During the preceding reign it had been decided by the
courts of law in England that the marriage of a priest was

---

[1] " History of the Protestant Reformation," &c., §§ 104 and 251.
[2] " Faith of Catholics," 1846, vol. iii. p. 228.

voidable, but not void, and, consequently, that his issue
born in wedlock was entitled to inherit. But such marriages were not reconcilable with the Canon Law of the
Church of Rome. But that Canon Law, as binding in
England, had been, so far as it conflicted with the Common
Law, abrogated by the statute of 20 Henry III. c. 9, though
apparently in active force when Henry ascended the throne.
Bishop Skelton admitted on his death-bed that he was a
married man. " We know," writes Dean Hook, " from
public documents, many of the clergy were married men."[1]
And he cites a letter written by Erasmus to Archbishop
Warham, the immediate predecessor of Cranmer in the
See of Canterbury, wherein he alludes to Warham's " sweet
wife and his most dear children."[2] The objection now
taken is, that a priest (a widower) was not allowed to marry
a second time. But as there is no Scriptural prohibition,
Anglicans were not bound by any such local regulations.

While in Germany, Cranmer received the royal command
to return to England to be created Archbishop of Canterbury ; a preferment, as is alleged, reluctantly accepted by
him.[3] His mission in Germany not being completed, he
sent his wife to England, and delayed his own departure.
William Cobbett did not hesitate to revive the absurd story
which he borrowed from Sander, that "his German frow"
was sent to England in a chest—a tub—" bored with holes
in it to give her air," which was upset by the sailors, to
their great merriment. Strype refers to the circumstance
as follows :—

[1] " Lives of the Archbishops," vol. vi. pp. 232 and 318.
[2] " Benevale cum dulcissima conjugali, liberisque dulcissimis." — Eras.,
" Oper.," iii., 1695.
[3] " Expected or not, the Primacy was forced on him. Cranmer's conduct
was certainly consistent with his profession that he did not desire, as he had not
expected, the dangerous promotion."—" Encl. Brit.," 9th edit., " Cranmer."

"The silly story comes through too many hands before it came to Parsons or Sander to make it credible. Cranmer's son tells it to his wife, nobody knows when ; she, when a widow, tells it to a gentleman, nobody knows when ; and they tell it to Parsons, nobody knows when ! No place, person, or time mentioned ; and so all the faith of this matter lies upon a woman's evidence, and hers upon *those two honest men*, Parsons and Sander."[1]

If Cranmer's detractors are not ashamed of their champions, we can only add that nothing, in the estimation of honest men, could possibly be so damaging to their credit than that they should select as their advocates and patrons the secular priest, the "lying" SANDER, the Jesuit PARSONS, and WILLIAM COBBETT, the reputed author of the "History of the Protestant Reformation."

We may here note that after the famous—or rather infamous—"Six Articles Act," to be presently referred to, was passed, one of which articles imposed the penalty of death as a felon, without the benefit of clergy, on those who continued to declare that the clergy might marry, and which Act was cruelly enforced, Cranmer was compelled to submit to this unnatural law. It is not true, as sometimes alleged, that he at any time *secretly* kept his wife in the Palace at Lambeth. He was compelled, in consequence of this enactment, to send her away, and he put her again under the care of her parents.

The charge of perjury against Cranmer on account of his marriage opens up the entire history and question of the compulsory celibacy of the clergy.

It was not until the eleventh century (A.D. 1084) that the right of marriage was taken away from the priests in the Western Church by an arbitrary decree of Gregory VII.[2] As yet, however, it was an order affecting discipline, and not a binding dogma of the Roman Church; it was never

---

[1] "Memorials," b. iii. c. xxxviii. p. 461. London, 1694.
[2] "Pol. Vergil, De Rer. Invent.," lib. v. cap. iv. p. 313. Amst. 1671.

made a doctrine of the Church.   This, as a fact, is evident
from the order issued by Innocent III. at the fourth Lateran
Council, A.D. 1215.   The fourteenth canon, "Of the Incon-
tinence of the Clergy," says :—"But those who, according
to the custom of their country, have not put away the marriage union, if they have fallen let them be punished more
heavily, since *it was in their power to use lawful marriage*,"[1]
thus clearly showing that celibacy was not then even the
law of the Church.   It was not until A.D. 1563, at the
twenty-fourth session of the Council of Trent, that the
Church of Rome legislated upon the subject.   The ninth
canon pronounces anathema against those who say that
priests, or regulars *who have solemnly professed* chastity,
are able to contract marriage, or, being contracted, that it
is valid.   It will be observed that this law affects those
only who had taken the vow of chastity.   This law was
passed several years after Cranmer had been made Archbishop.   Cranmer never made that vow ; and it was *after*
his second marriage that he was appointed, by the Pope
himself, an Archbishop in the Roman Church.

In an historical point of view there is no vestige of a
prohibition to marry found in the first three hundred years
after the Apostolic age.   In 325, at the first General
Council (Nice), an attempt was made to impose this yoke
on the priesthood, but the proposal was rejected.

Marriage came from God, and was His earliest institution.   The very first page of the Bible declares, "It is not
good for man to be alone." (Gen. ii. 18, Douay version.)
This state was appointed to man before his fall, and while
his affections were pure and unsullied.

Enoch, Noah, Abraham, Moses, Samuel, Ezekiel (the
prophet of the Most High), were married men.

[1] Lab. et Coss., "Concil.," tom. xi. col. 168.   Paris, 1671.

The priests under the Jewish law were married, even the High Priest himself. (Lev. xxi. 13.)

Our Lord selected married men for His Apostles.

The early Fathers say the great majority of the Apostles were married, *e.g.* :—

Ignatius, who lived at the latter end of the first century, in his Epistle to the Philadelphians, wrote :—"Such as were Abraham, and Isaac, and Jacob, and Joseph, and Isaiah, and the other prophets ; and Peter, and *Paul*, and the rest of the Apostles, which were married." [1]

Ambrose says, "All the Apostles, with the exception of St John and St Paul, were married men." [2]

Scripture refers to Peter's wife on two occasions.—Matt. viii. 14 ; 1 Cor. ix. 5.

Eusebius describes a touching interview between Peter and his wife, and says, that St Peter and Philip begat children. [3] The Evangelist Philip had four daughters. St Luke was a married man. St Paul did not think the married state inconsistent with the office of a bishop. [4] Indeed Bellarmine admits that there is no precept whatever in Scripture for celibacy. [5]

But while the Church of Rome declares marriage to be a sacrament instituted by Christ, which confers a grace, they would deny that grace and sacrament to a priest, under the pretence that such a sacrament would be incon-

---

[1] " . . . Sicut Petrus et *Paulus* et reliqui Apostoli, qui nuptiis fuerunt sociate."—" Isaaici Vossii.," Amstel., 1646, pp. 177-8. See James' " Corruption of the Fathers," p. 127, Cox's edition, 1843.

[2] Amb., " Opera," col. 1961. Paris, 1549.

[3] Euseb., "Hist.," iii. 30. p. 124. Cantab., 1720.

[4] 1 Tim. iii. 2-4 ; Titus i. 5, 6 ; 1 Tim. iii. 12 (and see verse 11 in reply to the Douay note) ; and also see 1 Cor. vii. 2 ; Heb. xiii. 4 ; 1 Tim. iv. 3 ; 1 Cor. ix. 5 ; 1 Cor vii. 9.

[5] " In tota scriptura nullum tale extat præceptum."—Bellarm. "de Cler.,'' lib. i. c. 18. tom. i. p. 113. Colen., 1615.

sistent with the holy state of priesthood! The result has been most lamentable.

As a matter of discipline :—

The 5th (so-called) Apostolic Canon says, "A bishop, priest, or deacon shall not put away his wife under pretence of religion. If he sends her away, let him be separated from the communion ; and if he persevere, let him be deposed."

The Council of Gangra says, "If any one thinks that a married priest cannot, because of his marriage, exercise his ministry, and abstains on that account from communion with the Church, let him be accursed" (A.D. 380).[1]

The Trullan Council, A.D. 692, ordained that whoever, in spite of the Apostolic Canons, should dare to prohibit commerce or living with a lawful wife, should be excommunicated, and this applied to priests as well as laity.

The seventh Canon of the Second Lateran Council, A.D. 1139, is in direct contradiction to the above, wherein it is declared, "We command that no one hear the masses of those whom he may know to be married."[2]

The Decretum of Gratian, a book received in the Roman Church as the Canon Law, gives the names of seven Popes, from A.D. 411 to 641, who were sons of priests : Popes Hosius, Boniface, Felix, Agapetus, Theodorus, Silverius, and Gelasius ; this last Pope was the son of a bishop.[3] He observed on this fact: "These Pontiffs born of priests are not to be understood as born of fornication, but of legitimate marriages, which were everywhere lawful to priests before the prohibition came ;[4] and in the same sentence it is admitted that in the Eastern Church to this day priests are permitted to be married.

[1] Lab. et Coss., "Concil.," tom. ii. col. 419. Paris, 1671.
[2] *Ibid.*, tom. x cols. 999 and 1012. Paris, 1671.
[3] "Decret., Dist." 56, c. 2. [4] *Ibid.*, 56, c. 13.

The English clergy, up to the eleventh century, were generally married. The monasteries in England, except Glastonbury and Abingdon, were colleges for married priests.

In the time of Chichely, Archbishop of Canterbury, 1413-1441, married clergy still exercised ecclesiastical jurisdiction. St Patrick of Ireland states in his Confessions, that his father was a deacon, and grandfather a priest. It is notorious that the office of successor of Patrick at Armagh, went for 200 years, A.D. 926-1129, in one family.

It was, therefore, a modern innovation and imposition of the Church of Rome to establish so unnatural a custom as that of compelling the celibacy of the clergy. And what reason was given by the Doctors of Trent for passing this law ? Cardinal de Capri said, " that married priests would turn their affections to love their wives and children, and they would be drawn away from their dependence on the Pope." [1]

When members of the unreformed Church censure Cranmer for having married as a priest, they exhibit a lamentable ignorance of the history of their own Church. Up to, and previous to the passing of, the " Six Articles Act," under Henry VIII., the marriage of priests was a common occurrence, and this was under the direct sanction of a decree of a General Council and the authority of a Pope, specially extending to priests of this country. Pope Alexander III. did not hesitate to allow the Bishop of Hereford, in England, to have a multitude of married men to hold livings in his diocese. The licence of Pope Alexander III. is considered of sufficient importance to be recorded in their book of Canon Law, the " Corpus Juris Canonici ;" it appears even in the last Leipzic edition

---

[1] Paolo Sarpi., "Hist. Con. Trid.," tom. ii. p. 254. Amsterdam, 1731.

of 1839. In the second volume, column 441, is recorded the words of Alexander : —

"Truly, concerning the clergy of the inferior orders, who being appointed in the married state, have long since held ecclesiastical benefices, by the concession of your predecessors, of which they cannot be deprived without a great struggle and much shedding of blood, we think that we must give this answer to your shrewdness, that because the nation and the people there are barbarous, and *there is a multitude in question*, you may suffer them *under dissimulation* to keep the ecclesiastical benefices they have so long held."

In the face of these authorities, recognised as such in the days of Cranmer, it is difficult to appreciate the objection to his marriage as a priest. The decree of the Trent Council, as noted above, was passed after Cranmer's death.

CHAPTER VI.

THE consideration of Cranmer's conduct in taking his archi-episcopal oath of allegiance to the Pope, at the same time making a reservation of his allegiance under another oath to his Sovereign, is reserved for consideration in a separate chapter. "Casuists may suggest divers expedients and salvos, but an honest man has only one method of taking an oath."[1] Such, no doubt, is the view which may be taken of Cranmer's conduct by every right-minded member of the Reformed Churches who values the sacredness of an oath. But a censure coming from members of the unreformed Church amounts, as will be presently shown, to an act of inconsistency most palpable, since the practice was universally adopted ; otherwise bishops could subject themselves to the penalties of præmunire. Both Mr Charles Butler and Dr Lingard severely censure Cranmer for this alleged act of duplicity. But Dr Lingard erroneously states that his " protest " was secretly made.

The two oaths are palpably contradictory. The arch-

---

[1] " Encyclopædia Britannica," eighth edit., p. 482. Title, " Cranmer." Such was the opinion of the editor of the eighth edition. In the ninth edition, however, this extreme view of Cranmer's conduct seems to be considerably modified, where we read—" The morality of this course has been much canvassed, though it seems really to involve nothing more than an express declaration of what the two oaths implied. It was the course that would readily suggest itself to a man of timid nature who wished to secure himself against such a fate as Wolsey's. It showed weakness, but it added nothing to whatever immorality there might be in successively taking two incompatible oaths."

bishop's oath to the Pope requires him to swear that he will be faithful and obedient "to St Peter," "to the Holy Roman Church," and to his " Lord the Pope," and to the rights, honours, privileges, authorities of the Church of Rome, and of the Pope and his successors. The oath proceeds to assert that—

" I will cause to be conserved, defended, augmented, and promoted. I shall not be, in counsel, treaty, or any act, in which anything shall be imagined against him or the Church of Rome, their rights, seats, honours, or powers. And if I know any such to be moved or compassed, I shall resist it to my power, and as soon as I can I shall advertise him, or such as may give him knowledge. *Heretics, schismatics, and rebels to our Holy Father and his successors, I shall fight against and persecute (persequar et impugnato) to my power.*—So God help me, and the Holy Evangelists."

The oath taken by the bishop to the King was as follows :—

" I, ——, Bishop of ——, utterly renounce, and clearly forsake, all such clauses, words, sentences, and grants which I have, or shall have, hereafter, of the Pope's Holiness, of and for the Bishopric of ——, that in anywise hath been, is, or hereafter may be, hurtful or prejudicial to your Highness, your heirs, dignity, privilege, or estate royal. And also I do swear, that I shall be faithful and true, and faith and truth I shall bear to you, my Sovereign Lord, and to you and your heirs ——, and to live and die for you and yours against all people. And —— your councils I shall keep and hold, *acknowledging myself to hold my Bishopric of you only*, beseeching you of restitution of the temporalities of the same ; pronouncing as before, that I shall be a faithful, true, and obedient subject of your Highness, heirs and successors, during my life ; and the services and other things due to your Highness for the restitution of the temporalities of the said Bishopric, I shall truly do and obediently perform. So God help me, and all saints."

It will be thus seen that the obligations embraced in each declaration are incompatible.

It would be a hard and thankless task, according to our present notions of morality, to attempt to justify Cranmer in submitting to the ordeal of being made an Archbishop under the stipulations required by the head of his Church, and at the same time nullifying the essence of his pledge of allegiance to the Pope by renouncing it in favour of his sovereign in things spiritual.

There is a remarkable passage in the Letter addressed by Cranmer to Queen Mary while a prisoner at Oxford, in September 1555.[1] The Bishop of Gloucester was the presiding judge on his trial. As Cranmer's reasons alleged for his refusing to accept that bishop as his judge, the first was that the bishops themselves had sworn never to consent to the Pope's jurisdiction within this realm, on taking the oath of allegiance to the King, and contrary to that oath he (Dr Brooks) now sat in judgment under the authority of the Pope.   Cranmer continues :—

"The second perjury was, that he took his bishopric both of the Queen's Majesty and of the Pope, making to each of them a solemn oath : which oaths be so contrary, that the one must needs be perjured. And furthermore, in swearing to the Pope to maintain his laws, decrees, constitutions, ordinances, reservations, and provisions, he declareth himself an enemy to the imperial crown, and to the laws and state of this realm : whereby he declared himself not worthy to sit as a judge within this realm ; and for these considerations I refused to take him as my judge."

Surely this statement is inconsistent and contradictory, or Cranmer's memory must have been very defective.

There is another curious circumstance disclosed in the " Letters of Cranmer " on this subject,[2] also written to the Queen while in prison at Oxford in September 1555, on information conveyed to him by the Queen's Proctor, Dr Martin, that the Queen herself *had taken two contradictory oaths on her coronation.*   The letter is as follows :—

" I learned by Doctor Martin that at that day of your Majesty's coronation you took an oath of obedience to the Pope of Rome, and at the same time you took another oath to this realm, to maintain the laws, liberties, and customs of the same.   And if your Majesty did

[1] See Jenkyns' "Remains," vol. i. letter No. ccxcix. Oxford, 1833.
[2] *Ibid.*, Letter ccc. To Queen Mary. Vol. i. p. 383.

make an oath to the Pope, I think it was according to the other oaths which he useth to minister to Princes ; which is, to be obedient to him, to defend his person, to maintain his authority, honour, laws, lands, and privileges. And if it be so (which I know not but by report), then I beseech your Majesty to look upon your oath made to the Crown and realm, and to expend and weigh the two oaths together, to see how they do agree, and then to do as your Grace's conscience shall give you : for I am surely persuaded that willingly your Majesty will not offend, nor do against your conscience for no thing. But I fear me that there be contradictions in your oaths, and that those which should have informed your Grace thoroughly, did not their duties therein. And if your Majesty ponder the two oaths diligently, I think you shall perceive you were deceived ; and then your Highness may use the matter as God shall put in your heart."

All that can be said in favour of Cranmer is that *previous* to taking the oath he consulted lawyers and acted on their advice, and that he declared to the King that he could receive the archbishopric only from his Majesty himself as supreme Governor of the Church of England, and not at the hands of the Pope, whose authority within the realm he denied. Before taking the Papal oath he *publicly* declared the limitations by which he secured himself in his allegiance to the King, and his determination to reform the Church against a power which would neither admit the supremacy of the former, nor the necessity of alteration in the latter.

It is alleged that this protest was taken in secret, what Dr Lingard designated as " the theological *legerdemain of a secret protest.*" There was, however, no secrecy in the matter.[1] By this " protest " itself Cranmer declared that he *made the same publicly,* " that whereas, on his consecra-

---

[1] The original Latin of Cranmer's Protestation is in Cranmer's Register, Lambeth Library, Reg. fol. 4, and is reproduced in Strype's "Cranmer," Appendix No. v. The words of the protest are as follows :— " In Dei nomine Amen. Coram vobis autentica persona, et testibus fide dignis, his presentibus, Ego Thomas in Cant. Archiep. electus dico, allego, et in hiis scriptis *palam*, *publicè*, et *expresse* protestor," &c.

tion, he is obliged to take the oath to the Pope *for form's sake*," he had no intention to oblige himself by the said oath, which should seem contrary to the law of God, to his King or country, or to the laws and prerogatives of the same, and that he did not intend to oblige himself to the oath, so as to disable himself freely to speak, consult, and consent in matters concerning the reformation of the Christian religion, the government of the Church of England, or the prerogatives of the crown; and everywhere to execute and reform those things which he should think fit to be reformed in the Church of England. Subject to the above, and his allegiance to his King, he would take the oath. This protest was taken in the presence of the Royal Prothonotary, of two Doctors of Law, of one of the Royal Chaplains, and of the official Principal of the Court of Canterbury, in the *chapter house at Westminster*, and not, as alleged, in "an upper chamber." This protest was, at his request, attested by witnesses; and on taking his Episcopal oath, he declared that he took the same subject to his written protest. On receiving the Pallium at the altar he repeated his protest.

That Cranmer was sincere in this protest that he derived his authority from the King, is confirmed by the fact, that having acted under a commission from Henry VIII., he considered his authority was on that King's death at an end, and applied to Edward VI. for its renewal.[1]

But was Cranmer singular in this proceeding? In one sense he was, for his protest was made *before* taking the Episcopal oath, whereas Archbishop Warham, who had taken a similar oath to the Pope, *subsequently* took the same second oath of allegiance to the King. Gardyner, Bishop of Winchester, in the face of his oath, published

[1] Jenkyns' "Remains," i. xxxiv. Oxford, 1833.

his memorable work, " De Verâ Obedientiâ,"[1] not only in direct violation of his oath to the Pope, but he wrote an elaborate argument, in the same work, in defence of that violation, on the ground that no unlawful engagements could be binding, however solemnly incurred. Fox, Bishop of Hereford, also wrote a book to the same effect, entitled, " De verâ differentiâ Regine Potestates et Ecclesiasticæ." Every Bishop under Henry, save Fisher, voluntarily took the same oath of allegiance. Had Cranmer not taken the oath of allegiance he would have subjected himself to the penalties of *Præmunire* and *Provisors* under subsisting Acts of Parliament passed in essentially Papal times.

Bishop Bonner, when Ambassador at the Court of Rome, in an assembly of Cardinals strongly insisted on the King's independence of the Pope in matters ecclesiastical, but for this declaration he was glad to save his life by flight. Strype, in his " Life of Cranmer,"[2] gives the oath of allegiance taken by Bishop Bonner at his consecration :—

" Ye shall never consent, nor agree, that the Bishop of Rome shall practise, exercise, or have, any manner of authority, jurisdiction, or power within this realm, or any other of the King's dominions ; but ye shall resist the same at all times to the uttermost of your power ; and from henceforth ye shall accept, repute, and take the King's Majesty to be the only supreme head of the Church of England."

And yet one never hears these Bishops called to account for taking two contradictory oaths, but Cranmer alone is to be branded as a perjurer !

Cranmer, for maintaining his opinion, is, it seems, to be condemned ; but for Gardyner, Bishop of Winchester, Dr Lingard has the excuse, " he acted through fear of displea-

---

[1] See Lord Herbert's " History of Henry VIII.," pp. 389-390. Edit. 1649.
[2] Fol. edit., p. 87.

sure"—stimulated by fear, "*as was thought.*" Thus we
have the two leading Prelates of the Roman Church giving
an example to their brethren, and to the whole kingdom ;
and the obsequious Bonner, Bishop of London, concludes
his "address to the reader" with observing, in his Preface
to Gardyner's book :— ·

"If thou at any time heretofore have doubted either of true obedience, or of the King's marriage or title, or of the Bishop of Rome's
false pretended supremacy :—having read over this Oration (which,
if thou favour the truth, and hate the tyranny of the Bishop of Rome,
and his devilish fraudulent falsehood, shall doubtless wonderfully content thee), throw down thine error, and acknowledge the truth now
freely offered thee at length."[1]

But Dr Lingard adds, that Gardyner "consented, in
order to avoid the royal displeasure, to renounce the Papal
Supremacy." Let us see how Gardyner showed his fear.
He writes :—

"The title of Supreme head of the Church of England is granted to
the King by free and common consent in the open Court of Parliament :
wherein there is *no newly-invented matter* sought : only their will
was to have the power, pertaining to a prince of God's law, to be the
more clearly expressed, with a fit term to express it by, namely, for
this purpose, to withdraw that vain opinion out of the common people's
head, which the false pretended power of the Bishop of Rome had, for
the space of certain years, blinded them withal, to the great impeach-
ment of the King's authority."

Dr Lingard has not the slightest justification for his
apology for Gardyner's opinions freely expressed. While,
therefore, he thus lets off Gardyner, he does not hesitate to
speak of Cranmer as a *fanatic*, and not a man of learning.
The Doctor's anger is raised because Cranmer is said to
have declared the Pope was the Antichrist of the Apocalypse. He says :—

"Cranmer, as the first in dignity, gave the example to his brethren,
and zealously maintained from the pulpit, *what his learning or fana-*

[1] Quoted by Todd, "Vindication of Cranmer," p. 64, 1827, from M.
Wood's Transl. of Bp. Gardyner's "Oratio," &c., and of Bonner's Preface.

ticism had lately discovered, that the Pontiff was the *Antichrist* of the Apocalypse ; an assertion which then filled the Catholic with horror, but at the present day excites nothing but contempt and ridicule."

Cranmer was not singular in his alleged *fanaticism.* Wicliffe, a century before, made and promulgated the same discovery. The Poets Chaucer and Dante were of the same opinion. In the beginning of the sixteenth century, the title was so often applied to the Papal power, that Julius II. forbade the clergy even to speak of the coming of Antichrist ; whose coming, by the way, had been long before predicted by Pope Gregory I., in that person who should assume the title of " Universal Bishop," which the Pope, second in succession to Gregory, actually did assume, and which title is retained by Popes up to the present day !

On the 31st March 1534 the Convocation of Bishops asserted the Royal Supremacy before even the subject had been submitted to Parliament. They declared that "the Pope of Rome had no greater jurisdiction, in this kingdom of England, conferred on him by God, in holy Scripture, than any other foreign Bishop." The proclamation of the King's Supremacy was issued on the 24th May 1530, and had been published by the authority of Archbishop Warham, who asserted that it was " the King's right above the Pope."

The Pope's Canon Law did not respect the validity of an oath taken to the prejudice of the Pope's usurped rights in this country.

This Canon Law asserted that :—

" Princes' laws, if they be against the canons and decrees of the Bishop of Rome, be of no force nor strength." " It appertaineth to the Bishop of Rome to judge, which oaths ought to be kept and which not." " He [the Pope] may absolve subjects from their oaths of fidelity, and absolve from other oaths that ought to be kept."

And oaths taken contrary to the interests of the Roman Church are accounted as perjuries.

Being educated in such a school, Cranmer and the other Bishops of his day adopted the same principle, but applied it to their own case, and they had as much legal right to do so as had the Pope. We say nothing of the morality of either party. The King, by right accustomed, and, according to the law of England, was held as supreme in Church and State. Any oath taken by Englishmen against the prerogatives of the Crown was illegal, and amounted to treason. It was only turning the tables on the Pope, and the Kings of England had as much right to enact their own laws in their own country as had the Pope of Rome over that section of the Church he claimed to rule. Popes had no respect for oaths as such. The statute 20 Henry III. c. 9, passed in the year 1236, declared that the Pope's Canon Law had no place in England, except so far as the King or Parliament permitted, or contrary to the common law of the country.

Nevertheless, it is impossible to justify contradictory oaths. To every unprejudiced member of the Reformed Church, Cranmer's conduct must receive its condemnation. But such a proceeding is highly inconsistent when advanced by members of the Roman Communion, since we find all the English Bishops, save Fisher, Bishop of Rochester, were equally culpable, and so long as the deliberate statements expressed in their books of so-called " Moral Theology " remain unrebuked or unrepudiated. In these books we find amphibiology and mental reservation in taking certain oaths permitted, when such oaths are deemed hurtful to the interests of the Roman Church.[1]

[1] Liguori, a canonised Saint of the Roman Church, lays it down as an accepted principle of his Church :—" It is a certain and common opinion

In England, the only consistent Bishop was Fisher. He was "Papist" first, and "Englishman" after, and was in consequence adjudged a traitor to his King and country. But what was the position of the Bishops of Ireland? The history of those Bishops in respect of their oaths is remarkable in the history of the Roman Church in Ireland at that period. My observations will be limited to those Bishops only who were respectively appointed by Henry VIII. and Edward VI., who having taken, as to Henry's Bishops, the oath of allegiance to the Pope, retained their Sees under Mary, and admitted the allegiance of the Bishop of Rome, and survived her reign, and those who were appointed by Mary, taking the oath of allegiance to the Pope, *all* of whom again renounced the Pope, and took the oath of allegiance to Elizabeth in matters spiritual as well as temporal, in November 1558, and accepted the Reformation at her hands,[1] repudiating their oaths to the Pope.

amongst all divines, that for a just cause it is lawful to use equivocation in the propounded modes, and to confirm it (equivocation) with an oath."—Tom. ii. p. 316, *et seq.*, No. 151, *de jure.* Mechlin edition, 1845. Again: "A promise made without such a mind [that is, without intention to keep the oath] is not, indeed, a promise, but simply proposed; therefore the promise being evanescent, the oath is also such, and is considered as made without the mind of swearing, which certainly, as we have seen, is null and void."—*Ibid.*, p. 330.

[1] For authorities the reader is referred to—

1. Camden's "Annals of Elizabeth," p. 17. London, 1635.

2. Leland's "History of Ireland," second edit., 1848, c. xii. p. 208.

3. Robert King's "Primer of the Church History of Ireland," third edit., Appendix xxiv. p. 1208. Dublin, 1851.

4. Second volume of "Tracts of the Irish Archæological Society," p. 134.

5. Thomas More, "History of Ireland," vol. iv. pp. 21-2, edit. 1845.

6. Dr O'Conor [Roman priest], "Historical Address," part ii. p. 275. Buckingham, 1812; and see Letter ii. p. xxxviii. "Columbanus ad Hibernos."

7. Cox's "History of Ireland," pp. 273-4. London, 1689.

8. Dr Reed's "History of the Presbyterian Church in Ireland," pp. 22, 27, vol. i., edit. 1834.

9. Dr Murray's "Ecclesiastical History of Ireland," second edit., 1848, c. xii.

It was in May 1536 the Irish Parliament, on the suggestion of Brown, Archbishop of Dublin, who gave the first vote, that the Royal Supremacy of Henry was acknowledged, and the Pope's authority over the Irish Church was solemnly renounced, and the Oath of Supremacy of the King in matters spiritual as well as temporal was freely taken by the Irish Bishops, Priests, and Nobles.

In the year 1537 (28 Henry VIII.) several Acts of Parliament were passed, both in England and Ireland, by which the Bishops were ordered to abjure allegiance to the Pope, and accept the authority of the Crown in all ecclesiastical matters. As affecting Ireland, the Act 28 Henry VIII. c. 5 authorised the King, his heirs and successors, to be the only supreme head on earth of the whole Church of Ireland. By the Irish Act, cap. 8, it was enacted that the King, his heirs and successors, should ever afterwards have the sole authority to appoint Archbishops and Bishops. By cap. 13, those who maintained and defended the authority and jurisdiction of the Bishop of Rome should, on conviction, be deemed guilty of *præmunire*, as enacted by Act 16 Richard II. (A.D. 1403) ; and this Act further required that the Oath of Supremacy of the King in all matters ecclesiastical, and the renunciation of all authority or jurisdiction of the Bishop of Rome, should be taken. All civil officers and ecclesiastical ministers, and all persons spiritual and temporal, of whatever degree, should, before acceptance of office, take the Oath of Supremacy ; and their refusal to do so was constituted an act of high treason. This Oath of Supremacy of the Crown was freely taken by every Irish

10. Froude's "History of England," vol. ii. p. 88. 1883.

11. *The Tablet*, 10th August 1868, a Roman Catholic newspaper, quoting *Dublin Review*, a Roman Catholic monthly. .

12. Harrington's "Narrative in proof of the uninterrupted Consecrational Descent of the Bishops of the Church of Ireland," &c. London, 1869.

Archbishop and Bishop, notwithstanding their previous oath to the Pope, on appointment to their Sees, as also by the leading laity on the passing of these Acts.

The eight Bishops who had taken the Oath of Supremacy under Henry VIII., and who had survived the reigns of Edward and Mary, and continued to hold their Sees under Elizabeth, were—

1. Hugh O'Cervellan, Bishop of Clogher, Prov. Armagh.

2. Eugene Magenner, Bishop of Down and Conor, Province Armagh.

3. Cornelius O'Cahan, Bishop of Raphoe, Prov. Armagh.

4. Alexander Devereux, Bishop of Ferns, Prov. Dublin.

5. Christopher Bodkin, Archbishop of Tuam.

6. Roland de Burgh, Bishop of Clonfert, Prov. Tuam.

7. Eugene O'Flanagen, Bishop of Achonry, Prov. Tuam.

8. Wm. O'Shaughnessy, Bp. of Kimacdaregh, Prov. Tuam.

Henry VIII. died 28th January 1547, and was succeeded by Edward VI. All the above-named Bishops who took the Oath of Supremacy under Henry continued to hold their Sees under Edward. Edward, in addition, appointed nine Bishops, who continued to hold their Sees under Mary and Elizabeth, taking the same oaths, viz.—

1. Thomas ——, Bishop of Derry, Province Armagh.

2. Arthur Magennis, Bishop of Dromore, Prov. Armagh.

3. J—— Brady, Bishop of Kilmore, Province Armagh.

4. James Fitzmaurice, Bishop of Ardfert, Prov. Cashel.

5. Raymond De Burgh, Bishop of Emly, Province Cashel.

6. John O'Henelan, Bishop of Kilfornora, Prov. Cashel.

7. Patrick Walsh, Bishop of Waterford, Province Cashel.

8. Roland de Burgh, Bishop of Elphin, Province Tuam.

9. Redman Gallagher, Bishop of Killala, Province Tuam.

Edward VI. died 6th July 1553, and was succeeded by Mary.

For three years after the death of Edward, the Irish Bishops continued to submit to the authority of the Crown of England. By Act of Parliament, 4 Mary c. 8 (1556), all the statutes of Henry VIII. requiring all to abjure the Pope's authority were repealed. From that date, and during the reign of Mary, the Pope's authority was revived. The whole of the above seventeen Bishops, appointed by Henry and Edward, repudiated their oaths of allegiance in matters ecclesiastical to the Crown of England, and, in conformity with the statutes of Mary, reverted back to the authority of the Pope. The twelve Bishops who were appointed by Mary, who had taken the oath to the Pope, and the eight survivors appointed by Henry, and the nine appointed by Edward, who survived the reign of Mary, all conformed under Elizabeth (save two) and took the oath of allegiance to Elizabeth. These two who refused were Walsh of Meath, and Leverous of Kildare, who were deposed. The names of the twelve Bishops appointed by Mary were :—

1. Patrick M'Mahon, Bishop of Ardagh, Prov. Armagh.
2. Peter Wale, Bishop of Clonmaronore, Prov. Armagh.
3. Wm. Walsh, Bishop of Meath, Province Armagh.
4. Roland Baron, Archbishop of Cashel.
5. Roger Skiddie, Bp. of Cork and Cloyne, Prov. Cashel.
6. Terence O'Brien, Bishop of Kildare, Province Cashel.
7. Hugh Lees, Bishop of Limerick, Province Cashel.
8. O'Hirley, Bishop of Ross, Province Cashel.
9. Hugh Curwin, Archbishop of Dublin.
10. Thomas Leverous, Bishop of Kildare, Prov. Dublin.
11. John Thormey, Bishop of Ossory, Province Dublin.
12. Thomas O'Fehel, Bishop of Leighlen, Province Dublin.

The Archbishopric of Armagh was vacant.

On the accession of Elizabeth the authority of the Pope

was again abolished by the Act 2 Elizabeth, c. 1 and 2 (1560). The ancient jurisdiction over the Estate Ecclesiastical and Spiritual was restored to the Crown, revoking the Acts passed in the reign of Mary, and the Acts of Henry VIII. were revived. The Oath of Supremacy to the Crown of England was re-enacted, requiring the abjuration of the Pope's authority to be taken by every Archbishop and Bishop, and all other ministers of religion, which, as stated, was readily taken in Ireland by all the Bishops then holding Sees, save Walsh and Leverous. Swearing, un-swearing, and re-swearing as times required.

As to England, when Elizabeth came to the throne, although the leading reforming Bishops, Cranmer, Ridley, Latimer, Hooper, and a noble army of martyrs, had suffered at the stake, during the reign of Mary, the ecclesiastical body, as well as those in educational and other establishments, amounting to about nine thousand four hundred, all, except about two hundred, took the oath of allegiance to the Queen, renouncing the authority of the Pope, the Mass, the dogma of Transubstantiation (on account of which so many had been sacrificed during the reign of Mary), the use of images in public worship, and other Romish practices. They acknowledged Elizabeth as Supreme Governor of the Church of England, and adopted the English Reformed Liturgy. No attempt has been made to refute or explain away this astounding fact, of the wholesale conversion in England of the Roman Priesthood, but desperate efforts are made to vindicate the Irish Bishops from the supposed odium of a similar scandal brought about under similar circumstances.

The example in Ireland of the Irish Bishops in 1560 was followed by almost the entire body of the Irish Priests. They retained their respective Sees, benefices, titles, emoluments, and endowments. The Irish Royal Supremacy Act was passed not only by the "Lords Spiritual and Temporal," but also by the "Commons" of Ireland.

The first decided step to throw off the allegiance to the Pope was taken in England under Henry in 1532. The manner in which this change was hailed by the clergy was freely expressed in an address to the King by the Provincial Synod of the Province of Canterbury; "in other words, by what was virtually the Church of England by representation:"—

"We, your most humble subjects, daily orators and beadsmen of your clergy of England, having our special trust and confidence in your most excellent wisdom, your princely goodness, and fervent zeal in the promotion of God's honour and Christian religion, and also in your learning, far exceeding in our judgment the learning of all other kings and princes that we have read of; and, doubting nothing but that the same shall still continue and increase in your Majesty, first do offer and promise in *verbo sacerdotii* here unto your Highness, submitting ourselves humbly to the same, that *we will never from henceforth enact, put in use, promulge, or execute any new canons, or constitutions provincial, or any other new ordinances, provincial or synodal, in our convocations, or synod, in time coming,* which convocation is, always hath been, and must be assembled only by your high commandment of writ; only your Highness, by your royal assent, shall license us to assemble our convocation, and to make, promulge, and execute such constitutions and ordinances as shall be made in the same, and thereto give your royal assent and authority."[1]

In the face of these facts, we can better appreciate the conduct of Cranmer as being entirely consistent with "the genius" of the times in which he lived, although a recent writer on this subject says that Cranmer acted as if the "laws of God, of virtue, and of honour had become obsolete." The history of the representatives of the

[1] Wilkins' "Concilia," iii. 754, ex regist. Warham. Quoted by the Rev. R. W. Dixon, "History of the Church of England," vol. i. p. 110. London, 1878.

Papal Church in this country, it would seem, confirms that view. They were all Papists.

Le Bas, in his "Life of Cranmer," in comparing Cranmer's conduct with that of the other Bishops, justly observes :—

"The distinction between Cranmer's conduct and that of many other of Henry's dignitaries and prelates is evidently this : they, in spite of their oaths to the Pope, supported innovations morally hostile to his authority; while Cranmer refused to shelter himself under any *secret* reservation ; and declared distinctly and openly, and solemnly, at his consecration, the exact sense in which he understood the customary engagement to the Bishop of Rome. By this proceeding, he placed his own rectitude in honourable contrast with the servile duplicity of his brethren. And the utmost that can possibly be said to his disparagement is, that he *might* have followed a still *more excellent way*, by declaring to the King his inflexible resolution to reject the Primacy, if the Bishop of Rome was to have any concern in his investment with it."

This is the most that can be said for Cranmer in his vindication—if a vindication. But the Reformed Church is not responsible for Cranmer's conduct ; though, humanly speaking, the Reformed Church ultimately reaped the benefit of Cranmer's subsequent conduct and actions.

CHAPTER VII.

THE FATE OF ANNE BOLEYN; HENRY'S MARRIAGE
WITH JANE SEYMOUR, ANNE OF CLEVES, CATHERINE
HOWARD, AND CATHERINE PARR; AND CRANMER'S
ALLEGED PARTICIPATION IN THESE ACTS.

WE have now arrived at the period when Cranmer was created Archbishop of Canterbury, the seventieth in that See, and the last English Archbishop who received the " Pall " from Rome. He received the *Pallium*,[1] the insignia of his office, on the 2d March, and was consecrated 30th March 1533 at the hands of the Bishops of London, Exeter, and St Asaph; Archbishop Warham having died 22d August 1532.

While in Germany, as detailed in a former Chapter, Cranmer, most unexpectedly, received the King's command to return to England, to be raised to the Primacy.

---

[1] The *Pallium*, or *Pall*, is a "sacred" garment, specially manufactured for the Pope, and is obtained from the wool of two lambs slain on the eve of St Agnes. " This symbol of the plenitude of ecclesiastical power is deposited on the tombs of St Peter and St Paul, where it is left all night. It is afterwards, when duly consecrated with great ceremony, laid aside by the sub-deacon for those for whom it is designed. The modern *pallium* is a short white cloak, ornamented with a red cross, which encircles the neck and shoulder, and falls down the back. These *Palls* are purchased from the Pope at a very considerable sum; and no archbishop can perform the duties of his office before receiving this garment, nor is it legitimate to use that of his predecessor," ("Encyclopædia Britannica," 8th Edit., title "Pallium," p. 220). According to Mathew Paris, in the days of Henry I., the Bishop of York paid £10,000 for his *Pall*, although Pope Gregory I. said: "I forbid giving any thing for the *Pallium*." " Pro ordinatione, vero, *vel pallio*, sue charitis atque pastello, eundem qui ordinandus, vel ordinatus est, omnino aliquid dare prohibeo," ("Lab. et Coss.," tom. v. Epist. Greg., Papæ I., lib. iv., ep. xliv., col. 1199. Paris, 1671.

It is not improbable that he owed his elevation to his con-
sistant advocacy in promoting the divorce from Catherine.
Cranmer's detractors, on the other hand, assert that the
selection was made of a pliant instrument, and one who
could be made a ready tool in the hands of Henry and
Crumwell. Be this as it may (for it is a mere conjecture),
the command took him by surprise, and he showed great
reluctance in accepting the preferment. He delayed his
return for some four or five months, with a hope that the
King might change his mind.

But even in this it is asserted that the "interregnum was
not unusual in appointing a successor." That may be,
but nominated successors "seldom wait four or five months
before they accept office." We have Cranmer's own declaration made in his final trial before the Papal Commissioners
at Oxford. He said :—

"I protest before you all, never man came more unwillingly to a
Bishopric than I did to this ; insomuch that when King Henry did
send for me, that I should come over, I prolonged my journey full
seven weeks at the least, thinking that he would be forgetful of me in
the mean time." [1]

Cranmer may possibly have been apprehensive that his
marriage might have created some unpleasantness, but as
that marriage was not a secret transaction, he having sent
his wife to England before his arrival here, the Pope no
doubt had cognisance of the fact, but that fact did not
raise any objection in the Pope's mind in confirming the
King's nomination.

The appointment gave dire offence to Gardyner, then
Bishop of Winchester, who, for his strenuous support of
the King's Supremacy, considered himself entitled to the

[1] Notwithstanding this statement, Mr Friedman, in his late work, "Anne
Boleyn" (vol. i. p. 178. 1884), asserts that "Cranmer gladly accepted the
office of Archbishop."

preferment.   For ever after he was the bitter enemy of Cranmer.

The first public duty forced on the Primate was the declaration of divorce from Catherine, which had been so long agitated.

The King had been privately married to Anne Boleyn, 25th January 1532.

There is conclusive evidence that the marriage took place without Cranmer's knowledge.   This is established by his Letter to his friend Archdeacon Hawkins, wherein he says—

" It hath been reported, throughout a great part of the realm, that I married her, which was plainly false.   For I myself knew not thereof a fortnight after it was done ; and many other things be also reported of me which be mere lies and tales."[1]

According to Eustache Capius, the ambassador of the Emperor Charles V. in England, the ceremony was performed by an Augustinian friar, who was afterwards rewarded by the King making him General of the Mendicant Friars.[2]   According to Lord Herbert, Dr Rowland Lee performed the ceremony.

The formal divorce not having taken place, the King was in the anomalous position of having two wives ; a position, if we are to credit Gregory Cassalis, actually sanctioned by the Pope.   Cranmer, appreciating this complication and the scandal thereby created, desiring to ascertain the King's pleasure, wrote to the King that he was ready to discharge " his office and duty as supreme judge in causes spiritual."   To this the King replied in grandiloquent terms, and appealed to his conscience, and that he would do nothing but according to God's justice in the

[1] Jenkyns' " Remains," vol. i. p. 31.   Oxford, 1833.
[2] Letter from Capius to Charles V., 28th January 1535, quoted by Mr Fried an.   The letter may be genuine, but little reliance can be placed on this decided partisan.

cause.[1] This little episode is, of course, set down by Dr Lingard and others as an "hypocritical farce." But how is it that Gardyner, Bishop of Winchester, and Bonner, Bishop of London, do not come in for a share of the condemnation ? Bonner, in his preface to Gardyner's book, writes—

"In this oration, *De Verâ Obedientiâ*—that is, concerning true obedience,—he (Gardyner) speaketh of the King's marriage, which by the ripe judgment, authority, and privilege of the most and principal universities of the world, and then with the consent of the whole Church of England, he contracted with the most dear and most noble lady, Queen Anne : after that, touching the King's title as pertaining to the supreme head of the Church of England : lastly of all, of the false, pretended supremacy of the Bishop of Rome in the realm of England, most justly abrogated."[2]

Neither Bonner nor Gardyner is introduced in the pages of Dr Lingard with any ridicule or reprehension as to the conduct of either in regard to the divorce. On 3d April 1533, Convocation gave its solemn decision in favour of the King for a divorce. It is generally admitted that the King's cause was supported by a large majority of the nobles, bishops, abbots, judges, and secular priests. Bishop Tunstall declared the sentence to be lawful. The Convocation of York, under the influence of Archbishop Lee, agreed with Canterbury that it was a lawful and just action to divorce Queen Catherine.

On the 10th May 1533 a Court was held at Dunstable, near Ampthill, where Queen Catherine was then residing. She refused to appear before the Court on being summoned. Cranmer presided at this Court in his capacity of Primate, assisted by Bishops Gardyner and Bonner. The decision of the Court was unanimous, and Cranmer, as President, is said to have given judgment. The words of this judgment

---

[1] See the Letter given by Collier, vol. ii., Rec. No. 24, p. 15, edit. 1714.
[2] See Michael Wood's translation of Gardyner's " De Verâ Obedientiâ," quoted by Todd in his " Vindication of Cranmer," p. 55. London, 1826.

G

have been variously given ; but whatever form was adopted, it is said that this judgment was drawn up by the lawyers of the Crown.

On the 12th April the King's marriage had been publicly solemnised, and on the 23d May Cranmer confirmed the union by a judicial sentence, given at Lambeth; and Anne, with great splendour and pomp, was crowned Queen. In the year following (1534) an Act of Parliament was passed declaring the validity of the marriage, and that the issue of that marriage was lawful.

Elizabeth, the daughter of Queen Anne Boleyn, was born 7th September 1533. Cranmer stood as godfather. The Dowager-Duchess of Norfolk and the Dowager-Marchioness of Dorset stood as godmothers.

With reference to the divorce, there can be no ground for doubt that Cranmer acted from the conscientious belief that the first marriage was illegal. He had privately maintained that opinion before he had any idea that he would be called upon to take an active part in the proceedings. That Cranmer was subsequently aware of the King's ultimate intentions towards Anne Boleyn, we can scarcely doubt. But he had no control over the King's will or affections ; nor, indeed, maintaining his own opinions could he urge any valid objection to the second marriage.

The divorce and subsequent marriage taking place without the sanction of the Pope, the King ignoring —as he had a right to do—the Pope's jurisdiction in England, and appealing from his authority to a general Council, set the Vatican in a ferment.

The form of appeal was drawn up, and presented by Bonner, Bishop of London, in person, to the Pope. This interview took place 13th November 1533. The Pope was furious, but he considered it prudent to limit his action by pronouncing that the whole proceedings in England, from the beginning to the end, were utterly void, and that the King had exposed himself to the penalty of excommunication, which was threatened to be put in force, unless he submitted to the dictates of the Pope. By the intervention of Francis I., King of France, a message was conveyed to the King, that, if he submitted to the Pope's authority, matters might be amicably adjusted. It is clear that the Pope had no care for the justice or morality of the case, if he were only allowed to adjudicate in the matter, as Popes had already done in many similar cases. Ecclesiastical morality in those days, from the highest to the lowest officials, was very lax. But it seems unjust that the wrath of the members of the unreformed Church of the present day should be concentrated on Cranmer. It was, however, unfortunate for the Primate that further complications ensued, which have laid him open to the severe censure of his numerous detractors.

The proposal through the King of France resulted in negotiations with Pope Paul III.—the same Paul who, when Cardinal, had advocated the divorce. These proceedings were arrested by the accident of the delay of the King's envoy on his journey to Rome, which was taken advantage of by the Emperor Charles V. On the 24th March 1534, the Pope's Consistory declared that the marriage with Catherine was good and valid, and that the sentence of excommunication should issue against the King. What right, it may be asked, had the Pope to interfere? The rupture between England and Rome was now complete.

Cranmer had now to put his Episcopal authority in force, which he did under the direct command of the King.

Various priests, "Papalings," from their pulpits, vehemently condemned the conduct of the King, and otherwise slandered the Queen, calling them Ahab and Jezebel. Those priests in his diocese he interdicted from preaching, an order also enforced by the Bishops of London, Winchester, and Lincoln, in their respective dioceses.

We now come to the next complication in which the Archbishop was involved, and for which he has also been severely censured. The matter had reference to proceedings previous, and subsequent, to the trial and execution of Anne Boleyn.

Various versions of this transaction are given, and especially whether Anne Boleyn was really guilty of the charge of adultery. The King is also accused of having connived at the crime. Some go so far as to say that he was aided and abetted by Cranmer. So many contradictory statements have been made, that it is difficult to arrive at the truth. But Cranmer's alleged connivance of the Queen's disgrace is a malicious falsehood.

It has been alleged that so early as January 1535 suspicions had been raised in the King's mind as to Anne's chastity.[1] In April 1536 the Council, acting on information they allege to have received, which implicated the Queen, issued a special commission on the 24th of that month, comprising the Lord Chancellor, the judges, and the leading noblemen of the realm. It was on the 1st of May 1536 that a tournament was held at Greenwich. At this *fête* the Queen, not aware of the suspicions raised against her, gave (as is also alleged) certain tokens of partiality for her "paramour." This was witnessed by the King himself. Suspicions were now brought home to the King. Anne and her (alleged) paramours, Seaton and

---

[1] It may be noted here that Catherine died 7th January 1536.

Morris, were arrested on the 2d May 1536. Though she persisted in declaring her innocence, Seaton made such a confession, that carried with it, in the estimation of the Court, proof of guilt. The King is said to have twice offered her pardon if she would confess her guilt.[1] It was scarcely likely that she would comply with such a request. On the contrary, she persisted in her declaration of innocence to the last.

That Cranmer was in any sense a party to these proceedings does not appear, but it is certain that on the 3d May he wrote a letter to the King, interceding on behalf of the Queen. The very terms of this letter precludes us from supposing there had been any previous collusion between the King and Cranmer. The letter runs as follows :—[2]

" . . . And if it be true that is reported of the Queen's Grace, if men had a right estimation of things, they should not esteem any part of your Grace's honour to be touched thereby, but her honour only to be clearly disparaged. And I am in such perplexity, that my mind is clean amazed : for I never had better opinion in woman, than I had in her; which maketh me to think, *that she should not be culpable.* And again, I think your Royal Highness would not have gone so far, except she had surely been culpable. Now I think that your Grace best knoweth, that next unto your Grace I was most bound unto her of all creatures living. Wherefore, I most humbly beseech your Grace to suffer me in that, which both God's law, nature, and also her kindness, leadeth me unto ; that is, that I may with your Grace's favour wish

---

[1] It is said that Anne made some confession to Cranmer, with the hope that her life would be spared; and, in anticipation of her release, she had proposed to live at Antwerp ; but if she made any such confession, it has never been revealed. It has been most maliciously and shamefully suggested that Cranmer bribed Anne, in the Confessional, by offer of her pardon if she confessed her guilt, but there is not one scrap of evidence to support this slander. According to the testimony of Alexander Ales, in his long and interesting letter to Queen Elizabeth, dated 1st September 1559, it was Anne herself who sent for Cranmer to visit her in her prison. (See Stevenson's "Calendar of State Papers. Foreign. Elizabeth," 1559, p. 527).

[2] Jenkyns' "Remains," vol. i. pp. 164-5. Oxford University Press, 1833. "Cranmer's Works," P.S. ii. 323.

and pray for her, that she may declare herself inculpable and innocent."

This is scarcely the letter of one conniving with the King to prove the Queen guilty !

.There is a remarkable postscript to this letter, which places Cranmer's alleged participation in these transactions in a proper light, which is as follows :—

"After I had written unto your Grace, my Lord Chancellor, my Lord of Oxford, my Lord of Sussex, and my Lord Chamberlain of your Grace's purse, sent for me to come unto the Star Chamber, and there declare unto me such things as your Grace's pleasure was they should make me privy unto. For the which I am most bounden unto your Grace. And what communication we had together, I doubt not but they will make the true report thereof unto your Grace. I am exceedingly sorry that such faults can be proved by the Queen, as I heard of their relation."

A Commission was issued for the trial of the Queen, consisting of the highest lay officials of the realm, including the Lord Chancellor, the Queen's own uncle ; the Duke of Norfolk ; and the Earl of Wiltshire (Sir Thomas Boleyn), the Queen's father.[1]   A true bill was found against her by the Grand Jury of Middlesex, and by the Grand Jury of Kent, and the Petty Jury (12th May 1536) also found her guilty.   It was the Duke of Norfolk who gave sentence that Anne was to be burned or beheaded, at the King's pleasure.   In these transactions Cranmer took no part whatever.   If the sentence was unjust, then the Chancellor and judges, and the long array of illustrious persons named on the Commission, and three juries, were guilty of murder. It is alleged that all the actors in this sad affair proceeded under fear and coercion of the King.   For the reputation of Anne, it is to be hoped that it was so, but this would say little for the morality of the times.   Cranmer, on account of his known sympathies for the Queen, was during these

___

[1] Some writers deny that the uncle and father were on the Commission.   Mr Froude records it as an undoubted fact.

proceedings ordered not to quit his residence at Lambeth. He, however, had an interview with the Queen, while in prison, but what took place has never transpired. The King was not satisfied to let matters remain on the footing of this verdict, but he must have a formal declaration that his marriage was void from the commencement; and for this purpose Cranmer was summoned by the King to hold a Consistory at Lambeth. This mandate must have gone hard with the Archbishop, but obey he must the royal command. His only alternative was to resign the office of Primate. The duty of condemning, as void, that which he himself had previously held to be legal, was manifestly inconsistent, if we set aside the charge of adultery. But Cranmer did not act alone, either in the initiatory or final proceedings, with regard to the matrimonial affairs between Henry and Anne. His opinions and actions were shared by nearly all the leading Ecclesiastics and Nobles of the period. It is therefore unjust to select Cranmer—who, by reason of the accident of his office, had to preside at the final meeting which took place on the 14th May 1536—for vituperation and condemnation as a ready tool to carry out the wicked devices of his Sovereign. The last scene is thus described by the Rev. Richard Watson Dixon :[1]—

" At the hour of nine, May 17th, the barges of the assessors, proctors, and other assistants in the pageant of justice, arrived at Lambeth stairs. The assessors of Cranmer were the Lord Chancellor Audley; the Duke of Suffolk; the Earl of Oxford; the Earl of Sussex; the Lord Sandys; Secretary and Vice-Gerent Crumwell; Sir William Fitzwilliams; the Comptroller of the Royal Household, Paulet; Doctor Tregonwell; Doctor Oliver of Oxford; Gwent, the Dean of Arches; Archdeacon Bonner; the active Councillor, Archdeacon and Doctor Bedyl; the active Archdeacon and Doctor Layton; and the active Doctor Legh. The

[1] " History of the Church of England from the Abolition of the Roman Jurisdiction," vol. i. p. 389. 1878.

King's Proctor was Doctor Richard Sampson, Deacon of the Chapel Royal, a man whose zeal in the King's business was more conspicuous about this time than his ability ; and for the Queen appeared Doctors Wotton and Barbour. Witnesses and notaries were in attendance. The Archbishop led the way into the crypt of Lambeth ; and in that sepulchral chamber the cause was pleaded, witnesses were heard, the sentence was pronounced, within the space of two hours. The Archbishop declared that, having first invoked the name of Christ, having God alone before his eyes, having carefully examined the whole process, in that case with the help of counsel learned in the law, he found the marriage consummated between the King and the most Serene Lady Anne to be, and always to have been, null and void, without strength or effect, of no force or moment, and to be held a thing of nought, invalid, vain, and empty."

The sentence of divorce was confirmed by Act of Parliament, 23 Henry VIII. c. 7, and was subscribed by Convocation.[1] If the marriage itself was void *ab initio*, then the sentence of *death* for treason was unjust.

It is by no means certain that Cranmer, in fact, delivered that judgment; for, according to Sharon Turner and other writers, that duty fell on Crumwell. In any case, we must conclude that, as President, Cranmer delivered the judgment of the Court according to the decision—right or wrong—come to by the meeting. He could not have done otherwise ; the same judgment would have been delivered had Gardyner or Bonner been Archbishop.

Cranmer was in no way responsible for Anne's last tragic fate.

The unhappy Queen, and her alleged paramour, were beheaded. She protested her innocence to the last, undergoing her sentence with a coolness and fortitude becoming such a protestation.

In a letter written by Alexander Ales to Queen Elizabeth, in which he enters into many interesting details with regard to these events, he relates a visit he made on the

---

[1] Wilkins' "Concil.," vol. iii. p. 864, cited by Dixon.

day of execution of Anne, to the Archbishop at the Lambeth Palace. Ales appears to intimate that Cranmer was not aware that the execution was to take place that day ; he records Cranmer's words in conveying this information : —"'She who has been Queen of England upon earth, will to-day become a Queen in Heaven,' so great was his grief that he could say nothing more, and then he burst into tears."[1]

Cranmer had no power to arrest the execution, nor was he responsible for the cold-blooded conduct of the King in marrying Jane Seymour within three days after the execution of the Queen.

If we can judge from popular feeling, Cranmer's participation in these unhappy transactions seems to have given dire offence, particularly with the womenkind, so much so that it was necessary to protect his person with an armed escort when he appeared to perform his public duties.[2]

It does not appear that Cranmer has been made responsible for any other of Henry's matrimonial complications, though even this is attempted. A few observations, however, on this subject may not be out of place in our consideration of the " Times of Cranmer." Resistance to the King's wishes, in these matrimonial arrangements, never seems to have entered the imagination of any of the Ecclesiastics, or Nobles, or Commoners ; nor does it seem

[1] Stevenson's " Calendar of State Papers. Foreign. Elizabeth," 1559, p. 528.

[2] The anger of the populace may have been directed against the spiritual court system of playing fast and loose with the marriage bond. Cranmer, as the embodiment of that system, received the righteous condemnation of the *vox populi*, or "secular" conscience, uncontaminated by the "spiritual" system of "distinctions." Every woman felt that after such a long union with Catherine, and on secret charges as in the case of Anne, any one of themselves might be in like evil case.

to have occurred to any of them that there was anything disgraceful or iniquitous in the proceeding.

The marriage with Jane Seymour was one of affection on both sides. She died shortly after giving birth to a son, afterwards Edward VI. This event caused great and unfeigned grief to the King, and had he been left to his own inclination he would not have married again. He repeatedly declared his intention to remain a widower. In the three years that intervened between the death of Queen Jane and the King's next marriage, the most unscrupulous of his detractors have found no act, or indiscretion, on which to fix, or can call in question his morality. But the vindication of Henry is not our present task.

Edward, the infant son of Jane Seymour, the heir apparent to the throne, was weak and sickly, and, although extraordinary precautions were taken for his safety, it was not believed that he would long survive. So early as November 1537 the Privy Council represented to the King the necessity of his undertaking a fresh marriage while the state of his health left a hope that he might again be a father. It is most certain that the King suffered deeply on account of the loss of Jane, and he shunned the pressing proposals now attempted to be forced on him for yet another marriage. The united judgment of the Privy Council urged the necessity of it,[1] on account of the youth and sickly constitution of Edward.

Mary, the daughter of Catherine, had been, as we have seen, declared illegitimate; and, as was then considered, could be no legal successor to the throne of England. During the trial of Anne circumstances transpired, invented or real, which gave rise to grave doubts as to the validity of the second marriage, and therefore as to the legitimacy of

---

[1] "State Papers," vol. viii. p. 2.

Elizabeth ; among other reasons the supposed existence of a previous contract of marriage entered into by Anne ; the fact of which was, however, never established. In the estimation of all "good Catholics," even at the present day, the marriage with Anne is considered void, and Elizabeth illegitimate, notwithstanding the subsequent promise of the Pope to legalise the marriage, and declare Elizabeth legitimate, if she would accept the Reformation at his hands ! The mere rumour created great consternation [1] throughout the country, as Elizabeth in that case also could not inherit the crown, which was thus supposed to be left open to King James of Scotland, then at open enmity against England. The King was pressed on all sides to marry again, his Prime Minister, Crumwell, being most active in his importunities, and for which he ultimately suffered. The feelings and actions of the King have been freely described by religious opponents. It is to be regretted that religious rancour and the morbid delight in "sensational stories" should induce otherwise gifted writers to distort history merely to give a zest to their romances, and it is a lamentable fact that history is too often learnt from romancers. Happily the Reformation, or the reformed, are in no way responsible for Henry's matrimonial complications. There is no proof that Henry acted otherwise than with becoming dignity in all these subsequent trying occasions. This remark may create a smile, but it is not the less true.

To these remarks Mr Froude adds the following just reflections :—

" Persons who are acquainted with the true history of Henry's later marriages are not surprised at their unfortunate consequences, yet

[1] If the Act of 1536 declaring that marriages with the sister of a former mistress to be illegal and void was directed to the alleged fact that Mary Boleyn was Henry's mistress, then, indeed, there was cause for anxiety.

smile at the interpretation which popular tradition has assigned to his conduct. Popular tradition is a less safe guide through difficult passages of history than the words of statesmen who were actors upon the stage, and were concerned personally in the conduct of the events which they describe."

Three years had passed since the death of Queen Jane Seymour; the King's health was on the wane, and the country had to look only to the sickly Edward as a successor to the crown, or to a civil war if he died. In May 1539, ANNE, DUCHESS OF CLEVES was suggested as a fit person to bring forward, and a favourable opportunity to cement a connection with the Protestants. Crumwell, the King's Prime Minister, urged the alliance, and Holbein's art, as a painter, was enlisted to impart charms where none existed. Her portrait was forwarded to the King. There is no evidence that Cranmer had any hand in this transaction. It is impossible here to enter on the complications of European politics which suggested the Duchess of Cleves to the King, in preference to the Duchess of Milan, who was also proposed. This unhappy marriage was forced on Henry. Anne arrived in England in December 1539. The King's word was compromised to the union— it must take place. He went to meet his future Queen at Rochester. The King, at first sight, was disappointed if not disgusted; he was "discouraged and amazed;" he retired hastily to Greenwich, anxious to escape the projected union, the thought of which was revolting to him. He had been deceived, and now he was to be forced into a marriage repugnant to his feelings.

We must here pause to censure Henry VIII., not on the trite accusation of his supposed vice,[1] but because he per-

---

[1] "Those who insist that Henry was a licentious person must explain how it was that neither in the three years which had elapsed since the death of Jane Seymour, nor during the more trying period which followed, do we hear a word of mistresses, intrigues, or questionable or criminal connexions of any kind.

ANNE OF CLEVES. 109

mitted himself to be drawn into an alliance which he had
so soon after to repudiate. Having engaged in such an
alliance, he was bound to abide the consequences. Nevertheless it was, as Mr Froude quaintly observes, "a cruel for-
tune which imposed on Henry VIII., in addition to his
other burdens, the labour, to him so arduous, of finding
heirs to strengthen his succession." The matter was too far
gone for him to retreat. The future Queen had arrived at
Rochester. After his interview with the Duchess, her appearance and manner being anything but prepossessing, he
said, "I have been ill-treated. If it were not that she is
come so far into England, and for fear of making a ruffle in
the world, and driving her brother into the Emperor and
French King's hand, now living together, I would never
have her. But now it is too far gone, wherefore I am sorry."
His sentiments were not disguised or hidden from the
Duchess of Cleves. He said openly :—"If it were not to
satisfy the world and my realm, I would not do that which
I must do this day for no one earthly thing." She herself
would not accept the hint ; she showed throughout a cold,
heartless indifference, not very encouraging to Henry.

The marriage took place, but, according to Strype, was
never consummated.[1]

The mistresses of princes are usually visible when they exist ; the mistresses, for
instance, of Francis I., of Charles V., of James of Scotland (the contemporaries of Henry). There is a difficulty in this which should be admitted, if it
cannot be explained."—*Note by Froude.*

[1] Strype's "Memorials," vol. ii. p. 462 ; and see "State Papers," vol. viii.
p. 404. There is a circumstance affecting this statement by Strype which cannot be fairly passed over without some notice. Dean Hook, in his "Lives of
the Archbishops," vol. vii. p. 75, 1868, says :—"The King delaying to put
away his wife, the Archbishop was required to conduct the repudiation of that
injured and insulted woman " ; and in a note adds : "Perhaps there is not in
Ecclesiastical History a viler document than that on which he assigned his
reasons for seeking the divorcement." This lax mode of writing has given rise
to the supposition that the document in some way implicated Cranmer. There
is not, so far as my anxious researches can prove, the slightest evidence of the

Stowe tells us that from the day of the King's marriage " he was weary of his life."

In July 1540 a National Synod of the two Convocations sat jointly as one assembly to investigate the whole matter, over which Bishop Gardyner presided. The deliberation was assisted by nearly two hundred clergy, and ecclesiastical lawyers were cited to their assistance. They delivered their unanimous judgment in favour of the divorce. They pronounced the marriage null and void, and that each party would be free to marry again, on the following grounds :—

1. That Anne of Cleves was pre-contracted to the Prince of Lorraine.

2. That the King, having espoused her against his will, had not given an *inward* consent to his marriage, which he had never completed.

3. That the whole nation had a great interest in the

existence of any such document. The Dean does not intimate where that document is to be seen, or its nature, or by whom it is written, or how he makes out that it had anything to do with "Ecclesiastical History," or with Cranmer. Miss Strickland refers also to *a* document in the same vague and unsatisfactory terms. Neither does she give any reference. A recent writer, Mr S. H. Burke, twice intimates, in his " Characters of the Tudor Dynasty," that it was a letter written by Henry VIII. to Cranmer, containing a gross allusion, and on that gratuitous assertion he unfairly charges that Cranmer must have had as corrupt a mind as the King's to have been in a position to receive such a letter from him. Mr Burke likewise gives no authority or reference, and on personal application by me, he was unable to do so ! After several weeks' search at the British Museum, and at the Rolls Office, Fetter Lane, with the kind assistance of the officials, no such letter or document can be found. There is, however, a letter from Crumwell to Henry VIII. (Cotton Lib., Otho., c. x.), and set out in Pocock's vol. iv. of " Chronological Index of Records," 1540, part i. book iii. p. 425, in which Crumwell narrates some details, the acts of Henry, which are said by him (Crumwell) to have governed the King's subsequent conduct, and he then quotes the King's words, " I have left her as good a maiden as I found her," which may be taken from the context in two senses. It may possibly be to this letter that Dean Hook refers, and that Mr Burke has gladly transferred the scandal to Cranmer. But how even this letter can affect " Ecclesiastical History," I cannot discover.

King having issue, which Henry saw he could never have by his Queen.

This judgment for a divorce was signed by two Archbishops, seventeen Bishops, and one hundred and thirty-nine Clergy on July 9, and was confirmed by Act of Parliament by a unanimous vote on 13th July 1540. The decision (though it would be rejected by every Protestant communion) was strictly according to the Canon Law, upon which the Court of Rome would have readily acted had it been consulted under other circumstances. If precedent could justify this decision, there are many cases in which a divorce has been granted by the Court of Rome on slighter pretext. But then our Romish brethren would object that, in this case, a necessary ingredient was wanting to *sanctify* the act—the sanction of the Pope! In such cases they are bound to believe that the Pope can, by his independent will, make that lawful which in the sight of God and man is unlawful.

The decision, however unjust, was in strict conformity with the principles and practice of the Roman Church. On the first head a pre-betrothal was deemed a fatal flaw, and the Queen herself, in an unguarded moment—smarting under the shameful treatment which she was suffering —admitted her pre-engagement. The second plea has been recognised quite lately in the case of the divorce of Lady Hamilton from the Prince of Monaco. In 1880 a Committee of Cardinals pronounced her marriage, contracted in 1869, and with issue, null and void, on the ground of *inward* consent, on her part, being wanting, although her external compliance with the rite was not questioned; and she was subsequently re-married to another.[1] The third reason is one on which Popes have

[1] See Dr Littledale's "Plain Reasons against Joining the Church of Rome,"

repeatedly acted. The French Prelates found no difficulty in the case of Napoleon, when, on the same plea, he separated from Josephine.

While it must be freely admitted that such a divorce could in no way exculpate Henry in a moral or religious point of view, though the act itself was countenanced by the entire bench of Bishops, and of the Clergy, and the Lords and Commons, politically and of necessity no other course could have been taken. But no criminal desire to get rid of one wife to marry another can, in this case, be imputed to the King; and the attempt to cast blame on Cranmer, as the expression of Dean Hook would imply, apart from the governing body of the nation, is a manifest injustice. The Queen expressed her satisfaction with the arrangement, and wrote to her relations requesting them also to acquiesce. She remained in England a pensioner, and was well provided for. She survived Edward and Mary, and was present at the Coronation of Elizabeth.[1]

S.P.C.K., 1884, p. 22. The theory of intention being in the *recipient* of a sacrament is not *doctrinal*. On the administration of a sacrament in the Roman Church—and marriage is *now* (though not in the days of Henry) declared to be a sacrament—to give validity to the rite, there must of necessity be a right *intention on the part of the officiating priest* (Concil. Trid. Sess., vii. c. xi., "De Sacr. in Genere"). Indeed this *intention* of the priest to perform a valid sacrament is so strict, that in their Sacrament of Penance, in which confession to a priest is a necessary part, the penitent is directed to carefully seek for a priest who should *be serious in the performance of his office, and not absolve in a joke,* if the penitent values his own salvation (Sess. xiv. c. vi., "De Pœnetentiâ"). Some doctors, however, state that the *intention* of the contracting parties is the *matter* of this sacrament. If so, then the want of *intention* in either would vitiate the sacrament !

[1] In order, as it appears to me, to bring Cranmer into disrepute with regard to the sacredness of the marriage contract, the Rev. Nicholas Pocock, the editor of Bishop Burnet's "History of the Reformation," and who appears to take every occasion to vilify Cranmer, accuses the Primate, Ridley, and others, of having sanctioned the alleged illegal marriage of the Marquis of Northampton to Elizabeth, the daughter of Lord Cobham, his wife being still alive ; but he omits to state that the Marquis of Northampton had been legally divorced from his wife for adultery. Cuthbert Tunstall was one of

Catherine Howard.—Three years were lost to the nation since the death of Jane Seymour, and Henry's health was sinking, and the chances of James of Scotland increasing. The same motives which impelled the Council to hurry on the King to marry the Duchess of Cleves now induced the King to select another wife—Catherine Howard—who promised to be a fit and loving partner. Had he been actuated by any other desire than to secure the succession and satisfy the fears and hopes of the nation, there was no necessity, on his part, to hazard the perils and inconveniencies of yet another wife.

Henry married Catherine Howard in August 1540. They lived happily until October 1541. He desired prayers and thanksgivings to be offered up for the happy union. But the King had scarcely returned from a journey from the North, when the bitter and sad intelligence was made known to him that his wife had been unchaste previous to the marriage. This communication had been made to Cranmer by one Lascelles, on second-hand authority. Cranmer deemed it his duty to communicate the information to the King.[1] The question, of course, suggests itself, Was Cranmer either bound or justified in interfering in the matter? Here morality, duty, and "chivalry" come into collision! The King rejected the announcement as a vile calumny, but, unhappily, the charge proved to be too true, and was confirmed. Sub-

the delegates who decided the second marriage to be valid. Both Gardyner and Bonner were most active in granting dispensations in cases of divorce. It is strange, therefore, that all this "hue-and-cry" should be turned on Cranmer.

[1] "When he was made cognisant of the charges against Catherine Howard, his duty to communicate them to the King was obvious, though painful, and his choice of the time and manner of his fulfilling it was both delicate to his royal master and considerate to the accused."—"Encycl. Brit.," 9th edit., "Cranmer," p. 550.

H

sequently the Queen herself confessed her guilt. It was an act of high treason; it affected the succession to the throne, as to the legitimacy of the issue. This led to further discoveries, which placed her guilt, even after marriage, as was alleged, beyond doubt. Henry combated the evidence, and shielded the Queen as long as he could. He received the condolence and compassion of all his subjects. The Queen pleaded guilty to the crime on the first charge, but most positively denied the charge of adultery.[1] Henry was moved to tears, and would gladly have found an excuse to save his Queen; but it could not be. She and the partners in her guilt were executed for high treason, on a Bill of Attainder, 12th February 1542. Cranmer laboured earnestly in her behalf, but in vain. On the Council which condemned the Queen were Lord Hereford and Lord Southampton.

Catherine Parr.—Henry lastly married Catherine Parr, with whom he lived in perfect happiness from 1542 till 1547, when she was left a widow. Stephen Gardyner, Bishop of Winchester, performed the marriage ceremony.

Truly we may say that Henry's was a "domestic life unparalleled in English history"; but were the subject suitable for discussion, we might prove that licentiousness was not, at this time at least, one of Henry's vices. Enough has been said to satisfy most minds, that had this been Henry's ruling vice, as usually asserted, he would not have encumbered himself with wives, as he had done, but followed the example of contemporary monarchs, and even that of Popes. An unhappy train of circumstances—a fatality, as it were—blighted his matrimonial alliances, and

---

[1] See Lord Herbert's "Life of Henry VIII.," p. 534. Her confession was made to the Archbishop, the Lord Chancellor, the Duke of Norfolk, and the Bishop of Winchester. See Note *t*, Jenkyns' "Remains," vol. i. p. 308. Oxford, 1833.

each one, except that with Anne of Cleves, can receive, if not a satisfactory, at least a reasonable solution; but the fact of Henry having married six wives in succession, under the circumstances, is in itself no justification for his condemnation, much less a cause of accusation against his morality, and certainly can in no way affect the character of Cranmer, or the cause of the Reformation which followed these events. It can be of no advantage to the cause of the Reformation either to justify or extenuate Henry where he is to be blamed ; and it is no part of the subject now in hand ; but inasmuch as the fame of Cranmer has, by his detractors, been made dependent on Henry's conduct, it is a duty to divest the subject of that sectarian phase which has been imparted to all the events of his reign, in order to damage or prejudice Cranmer's character and the Protestant Reformation in this country. The Reformation was undoubtedly greatly accelerated by Henry's defiance of Papal thunders, and the bold front he assumed to break the galling yoke under which this country suffered. With the Papal party, supremacy of the Pope is "the sum and substance of Christianity,"[1] while, in fact, *dominion* and *power* are the real objects sought to be gained. Having not only stopped the supplies, as will be presently shown, but also having cut the Pope adrift, and proved to him that the barque could sail without his pilotage, the first and great step to freedom was taken by Henry ; the rest soon followed. Hence the

---

[1] "De qua re agitur, cum de Primatu Potificis agitur ?—brevissime dicam, de summa rei Christianæ."—Bellarmine. "Disp. in Lib. de Prim. Pont." In Præfat. sec. 2 tom. i. p. 189. Colon, 1615. M. de Maistre, a modern lay writer, in his book "Du Pape," informs his readers that "without the Sovereign Pontiff there is no true Christianity."—"Christianity entirely depends on the Pope." "Without the Pope the divine institution, Christianity, loses its force, its divine character, and converting power." Vol. i. pp. xxii.-xxxviii., vol. ii. p. 153. Second edit. Paris, 1821.

bitter attacks against Cranmer, his alleged principal adviser. In the estimation of those who comprehend the
nature and genius of the Reformation, which immediately
followed this important separation from the "spiritual"
rule of the Pope, the actions and motives of Henry, his
vices or otherwise, detract nothing from the justice of, or
the necessity for, such a Reformation. But with the prejudiced and ignorant it appears to be different; they
are too often staggered with the objection raised—"How
can that system be of God, or hope to obtain a blessing,
which originated with a Henry VIII., a revengeful, cruel
tyrant, who severed himself from the 'Catholic Church' in
order that he might, without 'let or hindrance,' gratify his
propensities, and establish a religion and hierarchy of his
own?" This they allege to be the polluted source or
origin of the Established Church in this country!—in fact,
of the Reformation, Henry being the head of the one and
pioneer of the other! And this leads us to our next division of our history. But it must ever be borne in mind
that Henry lived and died a thorough Roman Catholic *in
doctrine*, though not a "Papist." He changed nothing in
the faith of the Roman Church in this country. Indeed,
we do not see that even the charge of schism can be
rightly maintained. The law of the Christian Church, as
then acknowledged, was laid down in the Justinian code.
All believers in the doctrine of the Trinity were entitled to
the name of Catholic. Title i. of the first book is as
follows :—

" We order that all who follow this rule (that is, who believe in
the Deity of the Father, Son, and Holy Spirit, in their co-equal
Majesty and triune Godhead, according to apostolic teaching and
Gospel doctrine) shall adopt the name of Catholic Christian."

The only Creeds recognised in the Church were the

Nicene, Apostles', and (so-called) Athanasian. It was not until long after this period, namely, in 1564, that the Church of Rome by her Council of Trent formulated a code of Doctrine to be received under penalty of anathema. And it was only in December of the same year that the Pope took upon himself to add a fourth, a distinct and independent Creed on the Christian Church. The supremacy was no doctrine, but a usurpation, in this country. If the separation was a "schism," it was a *political* and social revolution effected by Acts of Parliament, and in no way a reformation in religion.

With regard to Cranmer's alleged participation in the acts of Henry in separating England from the Church of Rome, we cannot do better than quote the words of Ridley in his review of Phillip's "Life of Cardinal Pole"[1] :—

"The Reformation builds on a rock, removing the hay and stubble, the perishing materials heaped on it by Popes, to secure our Church a firmer establishment on Christ the foundation. Cranmer we look upon but as an instrument raised by God to clear away the rubbish ; and whatever his personal frailties or infirmities may have been, for Christ has appointed men, not angels, for the work of His ministry here, the *doctrines* of the Gospel by him restored are not the less pure, nor the corruptions he pointed out less abominable ; and the better use we make of that blessing which he, by his labour among us, procured for us, we shall esteem him the more highly in love for his work's sake, whatever his faults were in other respects."

[1] P. 287. Dublin, 1766.

CHAPTER VIII.

HERESY, as popularly interpreted, is a negation or depart-
ing from, or unauthorised addition to the orthodox theological belief as professed by the dominant sect of the day;
Schism, an open revolt from ecclesiastical authority as
wielded by such dominant sect. The question of *heresy* is
one of opinion ; that of *schism* one of fact. No religious
community or church—heathen or Christian, Jewish or
Gentile—has been so conspicuously, so frequently, divided
by internal factions, tumults, and rent by schisms, as
exhibited in the history of the Church of Rome. At the
period at which our history now arrives *schism* was rife in
this country, but the charge of *heresy* was reserved for a
later period. The schism led to the emancipation of the
Church in England from the control of the Bishop of Rome,
and Cranmer is credited as being "the principal motor of
England's change of ecclesiastical dominion." The charge
of schism lies therefore principally at his door. Indeed,
in the opinion of most of Cranmer's detractors, all the
actions of Henry (for good or evil, according to the religious
bias of parties) have been attributed to Cranmer as his
alleged principal and confidential adviser and pliant tool.

Du Pin, the Roman Catholic ecclesiastical historian,
furnishes a few practical observations on "Schism," the
principal charge brought against Henry and Cranmer.

He writes [1] :—

"When Churches or Bishops break mutually peace, there may be a doubt which is in schism, and which ought to be held separated from the communion of the whole Church. Some persons believe they can easily reply to this difficulty by saying that those should be reputed schismatics, and excommunicated, who were separated from the communion of the Roman Church and Bishops. As for me, while I doubt not that the authority of the Bishop of Rome, who is the Primate of the Church, and therefore the centre of unity, has always been very great, I am nevertheless obliged to abandon the opinion of those who say that all those who are separated from the Roman See have always been reputed schismatics, and ought now to be considered such."

The then Bishop of Durham, in a letter addressed to Cardinal Pole, maintained that "the separation from the Pope is not separation from the unity of the Church ; the head of the Church is Christ."

Cranmer, on the very first occasion when consulted on the question of the divorce from Catherine, maintained that the Church of England, as a National Church, was not dependent on Rome, and that our ecclesiastical courts should be independent of the Roman Court. From time immemorial England had possessed independent ecclesiastical courts, and the Pope had no right to interfere in proceedings in England. Such were Cranmer's views. Gardyner had previously declared his opinion that the Church should *not* be under the control of the Pope, and that, while he held to the doctrines of Rome, he maintained the supremacy of the King. Indeed, it is said he had done more to undermine the authority of the Roman Church in England than any one of her avowed enemies. Archbishop Warham maintained the same principle in common with every bishop (save Fisher, Bishop of Rochester), and they were supported by the nobles of the land and by both Houses of Parliament.

[1] "De Antiqua. Eccl. Disciplina," p. 256. Paris, 1686.

Neither Cranmer nor any other of the Bishops established any new theory. There is no necessity to support the claim of "divine right of kings," or to draw any argument from the Jewish dispensation, when kings ruled over the Church as well as State, though such was the discipline of the Christian Church for many centuries from the date of the conversion of Constantine. We need only appeal to the admitted law and custom of this country; and in this view of the subject it is our purpose to take a brief sketch of the origin of the Pope's jurisdiction in this country, and the justification of Henry, of Cranmer, and of his other Bishops and Parliament, for reasserting the ancient rights of the Crown of England.

In considering this subject, we are naturally brought back to Austin's mission to England, with his forty followers, at the beginning of the seventh century. There was then a regularly-constituted Christian and Episcopal Church in the British Isles, which had subsisted for many centuries previous to this mission.

Our heathen Saxon invaders, who located themselves in the east, principally in Kent, had driven the Christian inhabitants to the west, where at Bangor they established a monastery. When Austin arrived he found encouragement in King Ethelbert, who, though heathen, was married to a Christian Queen. Austin's interview with the British clergy, and his attempt to subjugate them to the rule of the Bishop of Rome (Gregory I.), their resistance, and the subsequent massacre of some twelve hundred priests and monks, are matters of history.

Austin fixed his abode at Canterbury. Gregory subsequently appointed him Bishop, and the See of Canterbury was thus founded, Austin as first Bishop. He and his successors continued in communion with the Bishop of Rome, whose usurped authority took firmer hold as time advanced. Collier, in his "Ecclesiastical History,"[1] correctly describes the relative position of the two Christian communions at this period :—

"It is evident that the British Christians had the spiritual sovereignty within themselves, were under no superintendency, nor used to apply to the See of Rome to pay their homage to the Pope's supremacy, to get their metropolitans consecrated, or receive directions for discipline or government from thence ; and, which is more, neither were they declared schismatics for want of this deference and application."

King Alfred ruled supreme, independent of the Bishop of Rome, and appointed his own Bishops.

The haughty and ambitious Hildebrand (Gregory VII.) had succeeded in domineering over the greater part of Western Christendom. William the Conqueror, though he extended his conquest under the auspices of that Pope, and had established himself as King of England, at once asserted his independence of a foreign power. "I never paid," he said to the Bishop of Rome, "nor will I pay you homage ; because I neither paid it myself, nor do I find my predecessors paid it to your predecessors,"[2] declaring at the same time that none of the Bishops of his realm should obey the mandates of the Bishop of Rome. He permitted, however, the Pope to pick up his pence in England, with which modicum of *spiritual* gain he was fain obliged to be content. William's successor, Rufus, in like manner prohibited all appeals to Rome, as "unheard of in the kingdom, and altogether contrary to its usages." He and his father both retained the sole power in themselves of investing Bishops.

Ever watchful to gain an advantage where the weakness of others gave him the opportunity, the Pope found no

[1] B. ii. cent. vii. vol. i. p. 80, fol. edit. 1708.
See the authorities cited by Hume, c. iv. an. 1076.

difficulty in working on the fears of Henry I. and King John, over whom he obtained a complete mastery, and with it an unconstitutional and usurped jurisdiction over the realm. The successors of John knew how to regain their own ; the very excess of assumption created a re-action. Edward I. passed several statutes to restrain the encroachments of Rome. He passed an Act (25 Ed. I. c. i.) declaring that Bishoprics, Benefices, Abbeys, being endowed by the King and people of England, of right belonged to them, and that presentments and collections of fines and fees had been usurped and given to aliens, and the pre-rogatives of the Crown disinherited, and the objects of the endowments perverted. This Act declared, "that these oppressions should not be suffered in any manner." This was an exercise of the prerogatives of the Crown ; Rome, nevertheless, clung like a horse-leech to the patient, and was sucking the life-blood out of him. It is said that the revenue derived by the Pope out of England exceeded the King's revenue. Edward III. also tried his hand by an Act, wherein he recapitulated the abuses, declaring himself bound by his oath to see the laws kept, and did, " with the assent of all the great men and commonalty of the realm, ordain that the free elections, presentments, and collections of benefices, should stand in the right of the Crown or of any of his subjects, *as they had formerly enjoyed them*, not-withstanding any provisions from Rome." This was called the " Statute of Provisions," which forbade attempts of the Pope to present to benefices in England. This Act (25 Ed. III. c. 6) declared :—

"That the Holy Church was founded in the state of Prelacy in the Kingdom of England by the King and his progenitors, and the Earls, Barons, and Nobles of this kingdom, and their ancestors, for them-selves and for their people, conformably to the law of God."

This was also strictly in conformity with the ecclesiastical

custom of the early Christian Church.   The appointment
of all Bishops and the Convocation of Councils were
centred in a layman ; they were the exclusive prerogatives
of Emperors and Kings, who were the supreme heads of the
Church.   Those who lay on Henry the charge of schism
for transferring the supreme power or jurisdiction over the
Church from clerical to lay hands, must account for this
Act of Edward III., and show it to be contrary to the
recognised ecclesiastical law of Europe since the days of
the first Christian Emperor Constantine, until usurped by
the Bishop of Rome at the beginning of the eleventh
century.   Edward passed another Act, forbidding appeals
and suits beyond seas, "in things the cognisance whereof
pertaineth to the King's court"; both these statutes were
subsequently confirmed by the 38 Ed. III. c. i.   These,
however, proving ineffectual to repress the evil, Richard II.
(3 Rich. II. c. iii.) confirmed, and ordered to be put in
execution, with additional powers, the previous statutes ;
and in the seventh year of his reign he passed another
Act, prohibiting aliens holding benefices, etc., without the
King's licence, and the King bound himself not to grant
licences for foreigners ; and by the 12 Richard II. c. xv.
incumbents were prohibited from obtaining a confirmation
of their titles from Rome, and all causes relating to presentments, etc., were to be tried in England ; those who
obtained their foreign appointments were called "provisors."
By 16 Richard II. c. v. it was solemnly declared that the
Crown of England was, and had been, and should be, free
from subjection to the Bishop of Rome : the lay Lords and
Commons resolved to die in defence of the rights of the
Crown against the Pope, and the spiritual Lords declared
themselves bound to the King by their allegiance.   By
this Act it was declared that whosoever contravened this

law of the land was to be put out of the protection of the
King, and his goods were to be forfeited, and his person
imprisoned. The writ that was to be prescribed on such
occasions commenced with the words, " Præmunire facias,"
hence the statute was called the "Statute of Præmunire." [1]

The Pope, however, was still at work, and the Cistercian
monks procured Bulls of Dispensation from Rome ; whereupon Henry IV. passed an Act (2 Henry IV. c. iv.)
declaring "those Bulls to be of no force ; and if any did
put them in execution, or procured other such Bulls, they
were to be proceeded against, upon the Statute against
provisors ; " and by the 7 Henry IV. c. 8, any licences
which had been granted by the King for the executing
any of the Pope's Bulls, were declared to be of no force
to prejudice any incumbent in his right. The perseverance of Rome in her usurpations required a confirmation
of all former Acts ; [2] and Henry V. [3] again declared the
Pope's Bulls and licences to be void.

Thus we perceive Henry VIII. reasserted the former
prerogatives of the Crown of England, which had been
lost, or stood in abeyance, in consequence of the weakness
or superstitions of intervening monarchs. It is evident,
therefore, that Henry, by severing from the jurisdiction
of the Pope, was only asserting the legitimate right of the
Crown ; and, in fact, was not in schism, so far as the
" Catholic Church " was concerned.

We cannot pass over this part of our subject without
making a few observations on the supremacy in ecclesiastical matters which now became vested in the reigning
Sovereign over this country. This has been "a stumbling-

---

[1] This is still the law of this country, and all the appointments of Romish
bishops are illegal, and they are subject to the penalties of this Act.
    [2] 17 Henry IV. c. xviii.   [3] 4 Henry V. c. iv.

block and cause of offence" to many who do not rightly understand it, and has been misrepresented by others. When the Parliament of England abrogated the spiritual rule of the Pope in this country, and the headship in spiritual as in temporal matters reverted back to the Crown, Henry neither took the office nor exercised the functions of a Bishop, but, as was due to his position, and as "fountain of honour," all nominations and investitures were made through him, and by his authority all matters were governed ; but, as it was explained and agreed to by the Bishops, "so far only as was permitted by the law of Christ."[1] In 1536 Convocation passed the following resolution :—

"That they intended not to do or speak anything which might be unpleasant to the King, whom they acknowledged their supreme head, and whose commands they were resolved to obey ; renouncing the Pope's authority, with all his laws and inventions now extinguished and abolished, and addicting themselves to Almighty God and His laws, and unto the King and the laws made within his realms."[2]

An important document was issued at the time when Henry assumed his new functions, explanatory of the title conferred on him, and to avoid misconception. By this the people were informed that :—

"The King's grace hath no new authority given whereby that he is recognise as supreme head of the Church of England ; for in that recognition is included only that he have such power as to a King of right appertaineth by the law of God ; and not that he should take any spiritual power from spiritual ministers that is given to them by the Gospel. So that these words, that the King is supreme head of the Church, serve rather to declare and make open to the world that the King hath power to suppress all such extorted powers, as well of the Bishop of Rome as of any other within this realm, whereby his subjects might be grieved ; and to correct and remove all things whereby any unquietness might arise amongst the people, rather than

[1] "Quantum per legem Christi licet supernum caput." See Collier's "Eccl. Hist.," vol. ii. pt. ii. b. i. p. 62. London, 1714.
[2] *Ibid.*, vol. ii. p. 119.

to prove that he should pretend thereby to take any powers from the successors of the Apostles."[1]

The document then refers to the former Acts passed in this reign to curtail the abuses and exactions of the Court of Rome and its Bishop, and states that such Acts had been passed with the express reservation that no article of religion should be thereby affected or changed, and it protests that no such object was intended.

The adoption of the new title by the King must, therefore, be understood as assumed with the above qualification.

When Queen Mary ascended the throne, an Act was passed renewing in her, as a female, all the titles and prerogatives of the late King; and she retained the title of " Supreme Head of the Church of England and Ireland " for nearly a year after her accession.[2] But when Queen Elizabeth came to the throne, in order to avoid giving offence by a misconception of terms, the title " Supreme Head " was removed, and "only Supreme Governor of the Realm," substituted (1 Eliz. c. 1). This is the only title our rulers have since assumed; and the oath of supremacy was altered accordingly.

" The Queen," said Bishop Jewell, " is not willing to be styled in speech or in writing, the *head* of the English Church; for she says that that dignity has been given to Christ alone, and is not suitable for any mortal."[3] An admonition was likewise issued by the Ministers of Elizabeth, in order to warn the people against malicious misrepresentations which had been spread abroad, that the Queen

---

[1] Quoted by Froude from the "Rolls House MSS.," vol. ii. p. 347. London, 1856.

[2] " See " Despatches of Noailles " (the French Ambassador in England), 23d April 1554, par Vertot. vol. iii. p. 175. Leyden, 1763.

[3] " Zurich Letters." First series. Ep. xiv. ad Bulling. May 22, 1559. Camb., 1842.

challenged authority or power of ministry of Divine service in the Church—

"For certainly Her Majesty neither doth, nor ever will, challenge any other authority than that challenged and lately used by the King, Henry VIII., and King Edward VI., which is, *and was of ancient time*, due to the imperial Crown of this realm,—that is, under God, to have the sovereignty and rule over all manner of persons born within these her realms, dominions, or countries, of what estate, either ecclesiastical or temporal, soever they be, so as no other foreign Power shall, or ought to, have any supremacy over them."[1]

It will be thus seen how completely within the Constitution of this country Cranmer acted, in first submitting his allegiance to his Sovereign in preference to that of a foreign potentate.

The declaration of the Church of England is now clearly expressed in her 37th Article :—

" The Queen's Majesty hath the chief power in the realm of England, and other her dominions, unto whom the chief government of this realm, whether they be ecclesiastical or civil, in all causes doth appertain, and is not, nor ought to be, subject to any foreign jurisdiction.

" Where we attribute to the Queen's Majesty the chief government, by which titles we understand the minds of some slanderous folks to be offended, we give not to our Princes the ministering either of God's Word or of the Sacraments, the which thing the injunctions also lately set forth by Elizabeth, Queen, do most plainly testify ; but that only prerogative which we see to have been given always to all godly Princes in Holy Scriptures by God Himself; that is, that they should rule all estates and degrees committed to their charge by God, whether they be ecclesiastical or temporal, and restrain with the *civil* sword the stubborn and evil doers.

" THE BISHOP OF ROME HATH NO JURISDICTION IN THIS REALM OF ENGLAND ! "

The Oath of Supremacy was abolished in the first year of the reign of William and Mary, so that the royal authority in ecclesiastical matters rests solely on the declaration of the Church as expressed in her " Articles " as above

[1] " Wilkins' " Concilia," vol. iv. p. 188. London, 1737.

quoted, and to which every clergyman of the Church of England must subscribe.[1]

The prerogative vested in the Crown of England was exercised by, and acknowledged to belong to, all Christian princes within their own dominions, until voluntarily relinquished by special Concordats with the Pope. The Emperor of Austria, under the Imperial Constitution of 16th January 1783,[2] held in principle the same spiritual authority. All Bishops were appointed by the Emperor ; all ecclesiastical statutes and ordinances were first submitted to the State for approval before publication, extending not only to rescripts in regulations of discipline, but to those which are dogmatical, including Bulls, Briefs, &c., of the Pope, and also Indults for celebration of any new festival or act of devotion. All pastoral or circular letters of Bishops were, in like manner, to be submitted to the Emperor, and no excommunications could have effect without his permission. Austria, notwithstanding, was not declared to be in schism. And yet Henry VIII. is accused of being schismatical for reserving to himself these same privileges ! He was far in advance of his times. It is notorious that the Gallican Church enjoyed all these liberties, and was jealous of her rights. In Spain, the patronage of all ecclesiastical benefices is primarily in the King, and he presents to all Episcopal Sees. Papal Bulls are first submitted for the *Regium Exequatur*, and, if necessary, to the King's Advocate. By the edict of Charles III., published in 1761, and again in 1762, all Bulls, Briefs, &c., must be submitted to the civil tribunals under pains and penalties. On a Roman Catholic episcopacy being founded in Russia by

---

[1] This fact may perhaps account for the great desire evinced by a certain class of our clergy to do away with our " Articles of Religion," for with it the civil authority over the Church would vanish also !

[2] See " Catholicism in Austria," pp. 120-128. London, 1827.

Catherine II., the Pope admitted her supremacy. She reserved to herself the right of nomination of all Bishops, and the Pope submitted to institute on her nomination.[1] It is in England alone that the parcelling out of the country into new ecclesiastical dioceses, with the appointment of Bishops, by a foreign potentate, without permission of the civil government, is tolerated,—a process clearly illegal, as well by the law of the Roman Church, which prescribes that there can be no two Bishops in one diocese, as also by the law of this realm, which vests all authority of appointing territorial Bishops in the Queen. This right of the Crown of England has been allowed to be overridden by the Pope.

To represent Henry, therefore, as assuming any peculiar prerogatives, or introducing a new order of things, or forming a new sect or community, is a manifest perversion of the truth ; and to censure Cranmer for taking the oath of allegiance to the Crown of England, is only an attempt to re-establish, as a right, the usurpation of the Bishop of Rome over this country.

To *reform* is to correct abuses. To say Henry was a Reformer in this respect, is true ; but the religion of the country was left untouched. Henry first judiciously pared down numerous existing abuses in the Church in this country, practised under the direction of the Pope, as we shall presently see, and eventually the country was con-

---

[1] See "Report from the Select Committee appointed to report the nature and substance of the laws and ordinances existing in foreign States, representing the regulation of their Roman Catholic subjects in ecclesiastical matters, and their intercourse with the See of Rome, or any foreign ecclesiastical jurisdiction;" ordered to be printed by the House of Commons, 25th June 1816. This Report shows that, notwithstanding the virtual abrogation of the Pope's spiritual jurisdiction in this country, even at the present day the British Empire is the only one in Europe now open to the laws of the Papacy. See Mac-Ghee's "Laws of the Papacy." London, 1841.

tented to be relieved of the spiritual supervision of the
Pope, and was quite willing to accept Henry in that capacity. It is this dissolution of partnership with the Pope,
the bringing back the English Church to her original discipline and independence, that is called a *schism*.

It is a matter for grave consideration, and difficult of
explanation by Roman Catholics, how it was that all the
Bishops under Henry's reign, both in England and Ireland
(save Fisher of Rochester), took the Oath of Supremacy ;
and that when Queen Elizabeth came to the throne, after
the short and cruel reign of Mary, out of nine thousand
four hundred ecclesiastics in England, who were professed
members of the unreformed Roman Church, all but about
two hundred quietly, orderly, and without compulsion, not
only transferred their allegiance to the Queen, but retained
their livings, and (as before observed) adopted the English
Liturgy and form of worship in the same churches in
which they had before celebrated Mass ! The same wholesale revolution took place in Ireland. The importance and
magnitude of this fact cannot be exaggerated. As testified by Watson (a Priest of the Roman Church, who himself lived at the time [1]), and other secular Priests of the
day, Roman Catholics of England, in the first twelve
years of Elizabeth's reign, lived in perfect peace and har-
mony; and they testify that they might have continued to
do so, had it not been for the treasons and rebellions stirred
up by the Jesuits and their party against the Queen and
her Government. Notwithstanding these notorious facts,
confirmed by Rapin,[2] Foulis,[3] and even by their Annalist,

[1] "Important Considerations ; or, a Vindication of Queen Elizabeth from
the Charge of an Unjust Severity towards her Roman Catholic subjects, by
Roman Catholics themselves," &c., printed in 1601, pp. 39 and 40. See "History and Authenticity of this Book," proved in reprint by the Rev. Joseph
Mendham. London, 1831.

[2] See Tindal's "Rapin," vol. ix. pp. 6, 39. Edit. 1729.

[3] "History of Romish Treasons," pp. 420-428. Edit. 1671.

Bzovius.[1] Cobbett, in his unhappy production, miscalled " History of the Protestant Reformation " (Letter IX.), has the audacity to assert, that Elizabeth " crammed Cranmer's creed down the throats of her people;" "having pulled down the altars, set up the tables," that she "ousted the Catholic Priests and worship, and put up in their stead a set of hungry, beggarly creatures, the very scum of earth, with Cranmer's Prayer Book amended in their hands," and that she compelled them "to acknowledge the Queen's supremacy in spiritual matters, to renounce the Pope and the Catholic religion ; or, in other words, to become apostate." This veracious historian further tells us, that the Pope declared Elizabeth illegitimate, and "could not acknowledge her hereditary right." But this last statement is only partly true ; for the Pope offered not only to confirm her title to the throne of England, but admit the Reformed Liturgy,. if she would only submit to, or acknowledge his authority,[2] but she refused to comply with his terms, as did her father before her. Elizabeth came to the throne in November 1558. It was not until February 1570—twelve years after—that Pius V. issued his Bull of Excommunication against her ; and on this followed all the plottings an1 intrigues of the Jesuits to foster rebellion, and even the compassing of her life by secret emissaries, who had first made their confession, obtained absolution for the contemplated crime, and then pledged themselves to assassinate the Queen.[3]

It was not the renouncing of the Roman religion, it was

[1] " De Rom. Pont.," cap. xlvi. p. 621. Edit. Antv., 1601.
[2] See Sharon Turner's " Modern History of England," vol. iv. p. 165, *et seq*. 1835.
[3] The case of Parry is an instance reported in the " State Trials," Cobbett's edition, An. 1584, No. 60, vol. i. col. 1105. And see Strype, " Annals of Elizabeth," vol. v. pt. i. c. xxi. p. 361. Oxford, 1824. And Camden's " Annals," bk. iii. p. 274. London, 1635.

not the alleged sin of heresy, or even effecting the Reformation, which brought down the wrath of the Pope; it was
the emancipation from Papal authority; it was, as in the
case of Henry, the declaration of the independence of this
country of the Pope—the disowning priestly rule, and
abolishing Papal exactions—that gave offence.

Previous to the complications attending Henry's divorce
from Catherine, and the Pope's unwarrantable interference,
the liberties of this country were subjected to the rule of
a priesthood, deriving their "Orders" from Rome. They
were, in fact, the Pope's subjects, to carry out his ambitious
designs; and, in order to appreciate the political and social
reforms carried out by Henry and his Parliament, with the
sanction of the English Episcopate, it will be necessary to
enter on a few particulars.

Innocent III. (A.D. 1200) declared himself to be "the
Vicegerent of the true God," and to profess a divine
judgment, that he could change the nature of things and
make new laws, and dispense with holy laws, and "convert
righteousness into unrighteousness by converting and
changing ordinances."[1]

Pope Boniface (A.D. 1294) "declared, *defined*, and pronounced that it was altogether necessary for the salvation
of every human creature, that he should be subject to
the Roman Pontiff."[2]

---

[1] Decret. D. Greg., "De Magistate et Obedientia," tit. 33, p. 424. Edit.
Taurini, 1621.

[2] *Ibid.*, lib. i., "De Translatione Episcop.," tit. ix. And see "Corp. Juris
Can.," tom. ii. p. 1159. Edit. Lips., 1839. Bishop Fessler, who acted as
Secretary-General at the late Vatican Council of 1870, declares this to be an
accepted *Article of the Roman Faith*, by virtue of the decree on Infallibility,
being an *ex-cathedrâ* definition. "The True and False Infallibility of the
Popes," 2d edit., p. 67. London, 1875. And Cardinal Manning, in his
"Vatican Decrees," says that this decree has retrospective action, and was an
infallible utterance.

Popes not only claimed but actually exercised in this country the power of deposing and excommunicating monarchs, and giving away their lands, and of placing whole nations under interdict. When Henry came to the throne the Pope claimed to put in force the Canon Law in England, notwithstanding the statute of Henry III., which had limited its authority in this country. The following are a few extracts from the Canon Law, relating to oaths of allegiance :—

" The Roman Pontiff absolves from the oath of allegiance, when he deposes any from their dignity." [1]

" The pontifical authority absolves from the oath of allegiance." [2]

" The same is done *frequently* by the holy Church, when it releases *soldiers* from the obligation of their oaths." [3]

" Oaths of allegiance to excommunicate persons are void." [3]

" No one owes allegiance to any excommunicate persons before they are reconciled to the Holy See." [3]

" No oaths are to be kept if they are against the interest of the Church of Rome." [3]

" Oaths which are against the interests of the Church are not to be called oaths, but perjuries." [4]

" We declare that you are not bound by your oath of allegiance to your prince, but that you may resist freely even your prince himself, in defence of the rights and honours of the Church, and even of your own private advantage." [5]

" The kingly power is subject to the pontifical, and is bound to obey it." [6]

" Whoever resists this power resists the ordinance of God." [7]

Cranmer undertook to examine this Canon Law. He made a collection of the passages to submit to the king. Cranmer also pointed out the following extraordinary passage, to which special attention is drawn :—

[1] " Decret.," pars ii. c. xv. Q. vi. p. 647. Edit. 1839. Leipsic.
[2] *Ibid.*, p. 648.
[3] *Ibid.*, " Extrav. Commun.," lib. i. tit. viii. vol. ii. p. 1159.
[4] *Ibid.*, " Decret. Greg. IX.," lib. ii. tit. xxiv. cap. xxvii. vol. ii. p. 358.
[5] *Ibid.*, cap. xxxiv. p. 360.
[6] *Ibid.*, " Decret. Greg. IX.," lib. i. tit. xxxiii. cap. vi. vol. ii. p. 190.
[7] See the whole collection set out in Jenkyns' " Remains," vol. ii. pp. 1-10. Oxford, 1833.

"The Bishop of Rome may be judged of none but of God only ; for although he neither regard his own salvation nor no man's else, but draw down with himself innumerable people by heaps into hell ; yet may no mortal man in this world presume to reprehend him ; for as much as he is called God, he may be judged by no man ; for God may be judged by no man."[1]

Such were the laws and prerogatives claimed by the Pope to be exercised over every English subject, until Henry VIII. threw off his spiritual rule over this country. It is the Papal law Cardinal Wiseman desired so earnestly to bring back into England, when substituting a Hierarchy for the Vicars Apostolic, such as existed in this country previous to 1850.

These laws—the Canon Law of the Roman Church—still remain unrepealed by her. It is the law to which all Roman Catholics are subject at the present day. Can any Englishman who is bound by this Canon Law consider himself a loyal subject of the Queen of England, and does not the very recital of the law, to which Henry was called upon to submit, present sufficient justification, if none other existed, for the step he, under the advice, as is alleged, of Cranmer, took in order to free this country from its operation, which could alone be done by depriving the Pope of his "spiritual" jurisdiction?

But the matter did not rest with the supreme ruler of the Church of Rome ; each priest, in his district, assumed powers superior to those of the secular rulers. The clergy asserted a complete immunity from the administration of secular justice. They were only amenable to "the Church," and the courts of the king could not call them personally to account for any enormity. Whatever crimes they might perpetrate, whatever disorders they might commit,

[1] This passage still remains in the present editions of Rome's Canon Law (Decret l. part i. Dist. 40. sec. 6).

whatever evil example they might set before the community, they could laugh to scorn the powers of national
law, so long as they enjoyed the Papal favour. Not only
were they thus secure in their own persons, but they were
the guardians of all the villains in the land, for every
church, with a certain space around it, was a sanctuary of
refuge, and if the thief, the murderer, or any other criminal
could get within the line of protection, the officers of justice
were set at nought, and thus the priests became the standing obstacle to right, and the safeguard of the grossest
iniquity. Our Henry VII. presented petitions to the Pope
to do away with this nuisance, but without success. The
statute 1 Henry VII. c. iv. was passed to punish lewd
Priests and Monks. Most of these escaped ruffians, unable
to return to society, became Monks ! Before this period the
Courts had no power to punish Priests, though convicted
of adultery or incest. In his first Parliament, Henry VII.
made another step in advance to mitigate the evil by
lessening the privileges of the clergy; he enacted (A.D.
1487) that all clerks convicted of felony should be branded
on the hand : this did not prove a sufficient restraint ; and
it was further enacted that all murderers and robbers
should be denied the benefit of clergy. But the Lords
(governed by priestly influence) specially exempted from
the operation of this law all such as were within " Holy
Orders" of Bishop, Priest, or Deacon. Priests considered
their liberties were in danger, and protested, declaring that
their privileges were invaded ; and through their influence
the statute was not revived by the fifth Parliament. The
Abbot of Winchelcomb declared, in a sermon delivered at
Paul's Cross, that the Act was "contrary to the law of God,
and to the liberties of the ' Holy Church,' and that all who
assented to it, as well spiritual as temporal persons, had, by so

doing, incurred the censures of the Church!" The subject created a great disturbance both in and out of the House.

Further, the country was overrun with Monasteries and other ecclesiastical establishments of great wealth. The Monks held in their hands the greater part of the wealth of the country derived from land, possessing also costly treasures in gold, silver, and precious stones. The wealth was derived principally from death-bed bequests, depriving the legitimate descendants of their rights. The Statute of Mortmain was specially passed to check this acquisition of land by monastic establishments, but the cunning of the Priests devised methods for evading the law.[1] They toiled not, but they reaped a plenteous harvest. The number of idle drones who inhabited the Monasteries at the time of their suppression was upwards of fifty thousand, forming about one forty-fifth part of the adult population.[2] They appropriated or possessed, according to Hume, one twentieth part of the land of the whole kingdom. They lived in idleness, without earning a penny, or adding one penny to the wealth or revenue of the country. Every idle man is a loss to the wealth of the country. The spoliations by Henry were not exceptional. William I. took from the Abbey of St Albans all the revenues "which lay between Barnet and London Stone."[3] King John sequestered eighty-one Priories. So early as 1360 the popular voice was raised against the Monasteries. Wycliffe[4]

[1] This law is evaded at the present day by conveying lands to trustees, and by this means also the payment of succession duty is evaded.

[2] See Chalmer's "Estimate of the Comparative Strength of Great Britain," p. 38. See also Gilbert's "Social Effects of the Reformation," and Sir John Sinclair's "History of the Public Revenue," vol. i. p. 184. For an elaborate account of the establishments suppressed, see the Rev. Richard Watson Dixon's "History of the Church of England," vol. ii. p. 11 *et seq.* London, 1881.

[3] Speed's "Chronicles," 3d edit., 1632, b. ix. c. ii. p. 24.

[4] See Froude's "History of England," vol. ii. p. 411. London, 1858.

denounced their existence as intolerable. The good Bishop Grosseteste inveighed against the vices of the Monks ; and Archbishop Morton obtained leave from the Pope to visit the Monasteries, on proof being tendered of the dissipated lives of the inmates. In 1400 the House of Commons petitioned Henry IV. for the secularization of monastic property ; and, to appease the public indignation, more than one hundred Monasteries were suppressed, and their possessions given to the King and his heirs. In 1489, at the instigation of Cardinal Morton, Archbishop of Canterbury, Pope Innocent VIII. directed a general investigation throughout England into the conduct of the regular clergy, with power to correct and punish. The systematic vice and dissipation are described to have been something too shocking to dwell upon. In 1511 another ineffectual attempt was made to apply the moral besom ; and twelve years later Wolsey and Stephen Gardyner tried their hands at a reformation of morals and ecclesiastical abuses, but failed. *Under a Bull from Rome*, dated 10th June 1519, and another, dated April 1527, all the minor Monasteries, and also several of the larger Monasteries, were suppressed.[1] At length, in 1535, Henry VIII. seriously set to work to cleanse the Augean stables. He issued a Commission under Lord Crumwell, with power to liberate all below twenty-one years of age who desired to free themselves from these ecclesiastical prison houses. ·The Commissioners reported, among other things, that many poor wretches, who were above the age indicated, most piteously implored the Commissioners to free them from their incarceration, revolting against these moral charnel-houses.[2]

---

[1] See Rymer's "History," vol. vi. pt. ii. pp. 8-17. Edit. 1745.
[2] See Dr Leigh's Letter to Crumwell, MSS. Cotton. Cleop., E. iv. fol. 229.

Wolsey had reported to the Pope the frightful state of depravity which was brought to light. Mr Froude says of this report :—"If I were to tell the truth, I should have first to warn all modest eyes to close the book, and read no further." The full report of this visitation is lost. Burnet informs us that he had seen an extract from a part of it concerning one hundred and forty-four houses[1] that contained abominations in it equal to any that were in Sodom. In the confessions made by the Prior and Benedictines of St Andrew, in Northampton, "in the most aggravating expressions that could be devised, they acknowledged their past ill life, for which the pit of hell was ready to swallow them up. They confessed that they had neglected the worship of God, lived in idleness, gluttony, and sensuality." The report was called the *Black-book*, hence the origin of the well-known expression ; and when laid before the House there was one universal shout of DOWN WITH THEM. But Henry gave them a chance, and with his own hand, probably assisted by the much maligned Crumwell, prepared a code of regulations for the guidance of all monastic establishments, which was a wonderful production, characterised by strong common-sense, piety, and moderation.

Among other regulations, Henry prescribed that " women, of whatever state or degree," should be wholly excluded from the monasteries ; that the monks of each establishment should all dine together soberly and without excess, with giving thanks to God ; "that the President and his guests should have a separate table," but that, "not even sumptuous and full of delicate and strange dishes, but

---

[1] The reader, who may be curious in such matters, may consult the following MS. documents in the British Museum :—Cotton. Cleopat., E. iv. fols. 114, 120, 131, 137, 161, 249 ; and see also Sir Thomas Audley's Letter to Crumwell, "State Papers," vol. i. p. 450.

honestly furnished with common meats," thus cutting at once to the root of their leading vices. After admonishing them not to encourage "valliant, mighty, and idle beggars and vagabonds, as commonly use to resort about such places," they were enjoined to distribute alms " largely and liberally," in accordance with the directions of the statutes founding the Monastery; that the Monks were to have single beds, and any boy or child was forbidden to associate with the Monks, "other than to help them to mass." No man was allowed to wear the habit of the Order under twenty-four years of age ; that "they entice nor allure no men with suasion and blandyments to take the religion upon them ; *item*, that they shall shew no reliques, or feigned miracles, for increase of lucre,[1] but that they exhort pilgrims and strangers to give that to the poor that they thought to offer to their images or reliques." That men "learned in good and holy letters " be kept in each estab-lishment to teach others, and that every day for the "space of one hour a lesson of Holy Scriptures be kept in the convent, to which all under pain shall resort ; " and that each of the brethren, "after divine service done, read or hear somewhat of the Holy Scriptures, or occupy himself in some such honest and laudable exercise." We then have

[1] "There were few religious houses which were without one or more such objects of devotion [relics], celebrated in the neighbourhood as being efficacious in the cure of disease, or prompt in the aid of childbirth. Besides these, which were the relics proper, there were found in many places miraculous images or figures, some of which not only wrought cures, but gave signs of sensibility to adoration. In them the actions of life were imitated by mechani-cal contrivances ; and the faith of the worshippers in the saint was stimulated by beholding his body move, his eyes wink, his head nod, or his arms expand. Some of these also were brought to London with the rest of the spoil, and exhibited in public to justify the King's proceedings. They, there can be no doubt, were impostures for the sake of gain ; but in condemning them, it may appear to an enlightened age that the whole of the religion of rags and bones was nothing but the invention of rascality playing on folly."—Dixon's " History of the Church of England," vol. ii. p. 48. London, 1881.

special directions as to the decent conduct of public worship.

Had Henry been the headstrong, impetuous tyrant as represented, or had he been actuated by the desire of gain to appropriate to himself and his favourites the wealth of these Monasteries, his forbearance and anxiety to reform these monastic establishments was a strange mode of giving effect to these propensities. But Henry's forbearance was of no avail ; the evil was beyond reformation. The minor Monasteries were, as stated, first suppressed. This warning was not appreciated. Eventually, by a general consent of the nation, Henry VIII. swept away the plague spots from the land, retaining, nevertheless, the Universities and a few leading establishments, exceptions to the general rule. The number of these establishments suppressed has been estimated at three hundred and seventy-six.[1]

It must be borne in mind that Church property, properly so called, was not included in these confiscations. Further, the Supremacy of the Pope operated directly upon the wealth and welfare of this country. Enormous sums were annually carried out of the kingdom to Rome, in the shape of " Peter's-pence," first-fruits, offerings, annates, fees, and more particularly in causes carried to the appellate jurisdiction of Rome. Matthew Paris and the Abbé Fleury give us a sad description of the miseries entailed by this

---

[1] The Rev. Mr Gleig, in his "School Series," before alluded to in pp. 35, 55, gives the following version of the popular tradition of these events :—" There was no reason after this (*i.e.*, the separation from Catherine) for holding further terms with Rome, and Henry, as if he felt his ground to be safe, went on fiercely with the work of change. He got up cases against some convents, and found others made to his hands, and set about a system of wholesale plunder of their estates (A.D. 1534). He put to death all who refused to change their minds as he had changed his, and among others a good man, Sir Thomas More, Lord High Chancellor of England. Yet he gave no freedom of conscience to any one (A.D. 1535)."

system of extortion. The English presented petitions to the Pope to mitigate the evil. Matthew Paris records that [1] :—

" The extortions and abuses becoming so oppressive and unbearable, the nobles appealed to the Papal Court for redress, complaining among other things, that all the best benefices were given to Italians who did not know the language of the country. ' But now behold,' they exclaimed, ' in addition to the aforesaid subsidies, the Italians, whose number is now infinite, are enriched in England by you and your predecessors, who have no consideration for us in churches; leaving the above-mentioned religious persons whom they ought to defend, defenceless, having no cure of souls, but *permitting rapacious wolves to disperse the flock and seize the sheep.*' "

One of their grievances is thus specially referred to :—

" Also it is aggrieved in the general taxes collected and imposed *without* the consent and will of the King, against the appeal and opposition of the King's Commissioners and all England."

Matthew Paris gives us the Pope's answer :—

" The Lord Pope, gathering from the past to trample under foot the poor English, imperiously, and even more imperiously than usual, demanded of the English prelates, that all the beneficed clergy in England who resided on their livings should confer one-third of their livings on the Lord Pope, and that those who did not reside, should grant one-half."

Fleury, in his " Ecclesiastical History," [2] says :—

" England, fatigued and exhausted by Rome's exactions, began to speak and complain like Balaam's ass, overpowered with blows." The same historian further informs us, that the Pope, "annoyed at the firmness with which the Archbishop Serval refused to confer the best benefices of his Church on unworthy and unknown (*indignes et inconnus*) Italians, caused him to be excommunicated by bell, book, and candle, in order to intimidate him by this degrading censure."

England afforded to the Popes a rich prize, a golden harvest ; it was to them, as Innocent IV. testified, " a very garden of delight, an inexhaustible well." [3]

[1] Matthew Paris, " Historia Angliæ," p. 716, &c. Edition 1640.
[2] Lib. lxxii. Nismes, 1779.
[3] Matt. Paris, " Historia Angliæ," p. 705. London, 1640.

Such was the state of things when Henry VIII. came to
the throne of England. He ascended that throne under
the patronage of the Pope of Rome, and shortly afterwards
obtained the title from him of " Defender of the Faith."
He afterwards fell under the ban of his curse and excommunication, not because he had changed his religion, but
because he refused to acknowledge the Pope to have a
supreme power in these realms ;—because he re-asserted
the dignity belonging to the title of " King of England,"
as supreme ruler of this realm ;—because he deprived the
Pope of his opportunity to plunder, and his liberty or
power of working on the feelings and fears of the people of
this country.

Camden, on this separation from the authority of Rome,
remarks : " By means of this alteration of religion, England, as politicians have observed, became, of all the king-
doms of Christendom, the most free, the sceptre being, as
it were, delivered from the forraine servitude of the Bishop
of Rome, and more wealthy than in former ages, an infinite
mass of money being stayed at home, which was wont to
be exported daily to Rome, being incredibly exhausted
from the commonwealth for first-fruits, pardons, appeals,
dispensations, Bulls, and other such like." [1]

Henry VIII. freed this country from Priest-rule and its
consequent and inseparable corruptions, not by any sudden
action or caprice, but by well-considered and well-digested
salutary laws. One of our historians[2] has very aptly observed that the cause which Henry was impelled onwards
to lead was, the cause of human nature, human reason,
human freedom, and human happiness. It was an effort to
rescue England, and consequently mankind, and the mind

[1] Camden's " Elizabeth," b. i. p. 20. London, 1635.
[2] Sharon Turner's " Modern History of England," vol. ii. pp. 355-6.
London, 1835.

and religious worship itself, from sacerdotal despotism ;
to liberate society from the oppressing and debilitating
dominion of dictating and inquisitorial Priests, intruding
both into domestic and civil concerns, interposing themselves between the Creator and his creatures. Though
Henry did not foresee or even contemplate the consequences of his acts, reformation was effected step by step
by carefully weighed Acts of Parliament, all which were
prepared, if not by himself *manually*, certainly under his
dictation and supervision. Cranmer has the reputation of
being the King's adviser ; Cranmer has the discredit of all
Henry's questionable proceedings, why should he not be
credited with those actions which have proved beneficial to
the welfare of the nation ?

.The first step taken by Henry to bring about this great
social Reformation was, to clip the wings of the clergy. In
1529 he mitigated one great abuse, by causing an Act[1] to
be passed by which spiritual persons were debarred from
having pluralities of livings and from taking lands to farm.
The evil of concentration of livings and lands in the hands
of the clergy or Priests was greatly on the increase ; foreign
Priests, nominated by the Pope, enjoyed the fat of the
land, while they held his dispensation to be absentees.
They were engaged in trade, in farming, in tanning, in
brewing, in doing anything but the duties which they were
paid for doing ; while they purchased dispensations for non-
residence at their benefices. In some cases, single Priests
held as many as eight or nine livings.

Henry completely swept away these abuses ; and the
Act declared, that if any person should obtain from the
Court of Rome, or elsewhere, any manner of licence or
dispensation to be non-resident at his cure or benefice,

[1] 21 Henry VIII. c. 13 (1529).

he should be fined.   Here was a bold and prudent step in the proper direction of reform.

In the 24th year of his reign (cap. xii.), an Act was passed for the restraint of all appeals to the *Court of Rome.* The evils resulting from appeals in spiritual and temporal matters became intolerable.   The enormous expense and delays, not to mention the indignity offered to the Courts of Law, the Parliament, and King, arising from this usurpation of power by a foreign prince, affected all branches of society.

The Act declared :—

" From sundry old authentic histories and chronicles, it was manifestly declared and expressed that this realm of England was an empire, and had been so accepted in the world ; governed by one supreme head and King, having the dignity and royal estate of the Imperial Crown of the same, unto whom a body politic, composed of all sorts and degrees of people, divided in terms, and by names of spirituality and temporality, been bounden and owen to bear, next to God, a natural and humble obedience."

And then, after pointing out the evils, delays, expenses, and annoyances resulting from this system of appeals to a foreign Court, it was by this Act further provided, that all causes determinable by spiritual or temporal jurisdiction should be adjudged within the King's authority and jurisdiction *in the realm ;* and it was further enacted, that whosoever procured from the See of Rome any appeals, processes, sentences, &c., should incur the forfeiture of *præmunire,* established by the Act 16 Richard II. c. v.

Impute what motive you will to Henry and his Parliament, and to his adviser Cranmer, there is no person, be he Englishman or foreigner, Protestant or Roman Catholic, who will deny the wisdom, or the absolute necessity of this enactment.

By another Act (cap. xix.), "for the submission of the

clergy and restraint of appeals," it was declared, that the clergy should not enact any constitutions or ordinances without the King's assent; and all Convocations should be assembled only by the King's writ; and all appeals in spiritual matters should be according to the statute last mentioned; in fact, giving, for the first time, an appeal for lack of justice in the Archbishop's Court, to the Crown delegates in Chancery.

By the next statute (cap. xx.), all fees theretofore payable to the Pope of Rome on appointment of Bishops, and for Bulls, Palliums, &c., were cleanly swept away; and it was declared, that no man should be presented by the See of Rome for the dignity of an Archbishop or Bishop, and that annates or first-fruits should not be paid to the same See. This Act was eventually passed on a petition of a Convocation of Bishops and Clergy. The abstraction of these fees from this country robbed the clergy, and that was sufficient to rouse *their* opposition. It deprived them of a portion of their incomes, which was transferred to the Bishop of Rome. It is a fact worthy of remark, that the first active movement towards the separation from Rome originated with the clergy themselves. Their petition to Parliament to remove this tax upon their income concluded:[1]—"May it please your Highness to ordain, in this present Parliament, that the obedience of your Highness and of the people be withdrawn from the See of Rome."

The next reforming Act (25 Henry VIII. c. xxi.) was all-important. After stating that this country had been "greatly decayed and impoverished by intolerable exactions of great sums of money as had been claimed and taken, and continually claimed to be taken, out of this

[1] Strype's "Memorials," vol. i. part ii. p. 258.

K

realm, by the Bishop of Rome and his See, in pensions, causes, Peter's-pence, procurations, first-fruits, suits for provisions, and expedition of Bulls for Archbishoprics and Bishops, and for delegates and rescripts on causes and contentions and appeals, jurisdictions legantine, and also for dispensations, and other infinite sorts of Bulls, breves, and instruments of sundry natures, names, and kinds, in great numbers, heretofore practised and obtained, *otherwise than by the laws and customs of the realm*, the specialities thereof being over long, and large in number," says this enactment, "and too tedious, particularly to describe;" and this simple recital from the Act of Parliament gives us some idea of the extent of scandalous abuses then existing, and "set up by a person," as the Act continues, "abusing and beguiling the King's subjects, pretending and persuading them that he hath power to dispense with all human laws and customs, to the great derogation of the Imperial Crown and authority"—all these were with the united national consent cleared away; and the Act declared that no impositions whatever should be paid to the Bishop of Rome. All abbeys were also relieved from payment of pensions to the See of Rome; nor were they allowed to accept any constitutions from thence, and were prohibited taking oath to the Bishop of Rome. Will any one venture to question the wisdom or necessity of this enactment, or to question the motives of Henry or his advisers, be they Cranmer, Gardyner, or Crumwell?

It must be specially noted that the Act, last above referred to, specially provides that "no Article of the established religion of the Catholic Faith of Christendom" was to be, in consequence, altered.

Then followed the famous Act, 26 Henry VIII. c. i. (1534), declaring, what the "Preamble" of the Act stated *had been already recognised by the clergy of the realm in their Convocations*—that "the King was, and his heirs and successors should be, the only supreme head on earth of the Church of England." The Church of England had been from the commencement, from the planting of the Gospel in this country by the Apostles or their immediate successors, and for eight hundred years, independent of the See of Rome. A submission was first exacted by Austin, the emissary of Pope Gregory I., which was resisted ; but this refusal was closely followed, as predicted by the Pope's emissary, by a ruthless massacre of Bishops, Priests, and Monks at Bangor. The independence of England of the Ecclesiastical control of Rome was asserted by William the Conqueror, William II., Edward III., Richard II., and Henry IV. "The King," said the learned Bracton, Lord Chief-Justice in the reign of Henry III., "is the Vicar and Minister of God in the land, and he himself is under none save only under the Lord."[1] This independence was lost or impaired by the weak and vacillating conduct of some of the intervening kings, and Henry VIII. now only revived a right of independence of himself and of the Church of England. In the following year Pope Paul III., "filling his belly with the east wind,"[2] and applying both hands lustily to his "inflated wind-bag," fulminated his impotent Bull of Deposition against Henry VIII., as a retaliation for his rejection of the Pontifical authority. He excommunicated and deposed Henry, interdicted the nation, and absolved his subjects from their oath of allegiance. He transferred the kingdom to any successful invader, and prohibited all communication with the English monarch. He deprived the King of Christian burial, and consigned

[1] "De Legibus et Consuetudinibus Angliæ," lib. ii. c. viii. sect. 5. fol. 5. London, 1569.　　　　　　　　　　　　[2] Job xv. 2.

the sovereign, and his friends, accomplices, and adherents, to anathemas, maledictions, and everlasting destruction ; and excommunicated, anathematised, cursed, and condemned Henry to eternal damnation. He stigmatised his posterity with illegitimacy and incapacity of succession to the Crown, while he delivered his partisans to slavery. The English clergy he commanded to leave the kingdom, and admonished the nobility to arm in rebellion against the King. He annulled every treaty between Henry and other princes. He enjoined the clergy to publish the excommunication by bell, book, and candle ; and all who opposed his infallibility incurred the indignation of Almighty God and the blessed Apostles Peter and Paul. Henry at once passed an Act, as he had a right to do, declaring all Papal Bulls published in this country void.

Let us pause a moment to consider this step. Of what crimes had Henry, and his Archbishop, who, it is alleged, was always at his elbow as his adviser, been guilty? He had followed the advice given him by the Pope himself, the predecessor of this anathematiser, and had saved " his Holiness " the disagreeable necessity of pronouncing for or against the divorce, by "taking the matter into his own hands." And even the then Pope had himself, when a Cardinal, pleaded Henry's justification, and taken credit for so doing. He had done away with pluralities of livings, and foreign licences permitting a non-resident clergy ; he prohibited appeals to Rome in matters temporal and spiritual ; he abrogated all fees paid to Rome on ecclesiastical appointments ; he prevented the "drain of gold " passing from England to Rome in the shape of Peter's pence, &c. ; and, lastly, he re-asserted the dignity and authority of the King of England as supreme head "on earth " of the Church in his own dominions : in fact, he had the courage to brave the thunders of the Vatican, and to place himself above the prejudices and superstitions of his day, and sense enough to withdraw himself from Papal jurisdiction (being many years in advance of his age), and therefore he was to be excommunicated and damned to all eternity.[1] Henry's Parliament had done little more than what every Roman Catholic country has since accomplished. Henry and his advisers were the pioneers, simply because England was a more suffering victim to Papal rapacity than any other country in Europe. Whatever may have been the *motive* which put in action these important Political and Social reforms, England has reason to be thankful that a Henry VIII. had arisen who had the will and determination to uphold the dignity of his rank as King of England, the independence of his throne, and the courage to sweep from the face of the land the accumulated abuses which were eating its very vitals, and to free England from a servile, galling, oppressive, and degrading clerical despotism. And, above all, it cleared the way for the reforms in the religion of the country initiated by Cranmer, the result of which also freed this country from equally gross abuses and superstitions fostered by the Church of Rome, and which had for a series of years enslaved the minds of the people.

" Libertas : quæ sera, tamen respexit inertem."—VIRGIL.

To complete the chronology of events. The Suspended

---

[1] It is a matter for curious speculation to consider whether Henry was excommunicated for passing these salutary Acts, or because he divorced himself from Catherine and married Anne Boleyn without a Papal Bull. If for the former, then the Pope was actuated by the love of money and temporal power, though, as the so-called Vicar of Christ, his kingdom is supposed to be not of this world : if for the latter, as is asserted by the more zealous advocates of the Papacy, then Paul III. acted contrary to his own expressed convictions as to the legality of Henry's acts.

Bull of Excommunication of 1535 had been published, but not put in force, for what it was worth, until 1538.

In reply to certain foreign objections raised to the course adopted by England, the "Protestation" made in 1537, by the King and his Council, and the clergy, stated the argument as follows :—

"That which the Pope hath usurped against God's law, and extorted by violence, we by good right take from him again. But he and his will say, we give them a primacy. We hear them well; we gave it you indeed. If you have authority as long as our consent giveth it you, and you evermore will make your plea upon our consent, then let it have an end where it began; we consent no longer, your authority must needs be gone." [1]

In 1539 an Act was passed for the dissolution of monasteries, nunneries, and abbeys (31 Henry VIII. c. xiii.). It has been urged that the consequences of this Act deprived the poor of their best friends and supporters; but when rightly considered, the concentration of such enormous wealth in the Monks, created the poverty. Out of the spoils Henry established several new Bishoprics, and retained a portion for the Crown, which was principally applied to meet public expenses; funds being urgently required to put the country in a state of defence, and he divided a portion, as is alleged, among his Courtiers.

It is one of the popular fallacies inseparably attached to these confiscations, that Henry VIII. appropriated to himself all, or a greater part, of the spoils from the sales of the abbey and monastic lands, &c.; and it seems almost hopeless to attempt to turn the current of the generally accepted opinion on this head. It is nevertheless the fact, that the lands were sold at greatly below their value; this was the inevitable consequence of a forced sale. But to each sale a condition was attached, that the purchaser "should maintain

---

[1] See Strype's "Memorials," vol. i. App. No. 72.

hospitality liberally, on a scale to contrast favourably with the careless waste of their predecessors." The exchequer was empty. There was a civil war within, fostered principally by the Pope's militia, and a well-founded fear of invasion from without, by a combination of Italy, France, Spain, and Germany. More than the proceeds of these sales was expended in suppressing the civil war, and in erecting fortifications and defences on the coast. Dover Castle was principally built, and other works of fortifications along the south coast, with a part of the proceeds of the sale by Henry; without this timely aid this country would have been left entirely unprotected. The Scilly Islands, then the refuge of pirates, were also extensively fortified.

If Cranmer, as alleged, gave a willing assent to the act of "spoliation," he dissented from the application of the funds.[1] His recommendation was to erect Colleges and Seminaries throughout the country, and that sound learning and religious education should be fed with a better class of Priests than hitherto existed.[2] But, however the proceeds may have been applied, none can deny either the wisdom of the Act itself, or that wholesome results followed. In this, again, every European nation has followed the example of Henry. France long since did so : Italy has recently followed suit;

[1] "The dissolution of the monasteries was the work of the Minister [Lord Crumwell], not of the Archbishop ; but the latter showed a laudable zeal in trying to secure as much as possible of the confiscated monasteries for the benefit of religion and learning." ("Encycl. Brit.," "Cranmer," 9th edit., p. 550). "He had projected that there should be a provision made in every Cathedral for readers of divinity, and of Greek and Hebrew, and a great number of students to be both exercised in the daily worship of God, and to be trained up in study and devotion ; and thus every Bishop should have had a college of clergymen under his eye, to be preferred according to their merit. But this design miscarried." ("Biographica Brit.," Keppis.)

[2] See Froude's "History of England," vol. iii. p. 255. London, 1858.

and even Catholic Spain has confiscated the chief portion, if not the whole, of her ecclesiastical properties, and appropriated the proceeds to the Crown.   Indeed, she has gone even further than this, for she has passed a law declaring void every will which contains any devise of property for ecclesiastical purposes.

To come nearer home. No one will deny the loyalty of the Irish rebel leaders of the sixteenth century to the Pope of Rome, and their devotion to the Roman religion. Yet they did not hesitate to share in the spoils at the expense of their religion.   In 1541, at a full Irish Parliament, assembled at Dublin, held by St Leger, and at which O'Neil, Desmond, O'Brien, O'Donnell, MacWilliam, and other Irish leaders of the revolt against England were present, and took an active part, an Act was passed confiscating all the property belonging to the (so-called) religious establishments of the country ; and the leading Irish Nobles, without the slightest compunction, divided the spoils among themselves, selling part at merely nominal prices. In order to secure to themselves their newly acquired property, and to enable them to acquire a recognised title, they waived all their former differences and animosities, acknowledged Henry's title as King of Ireland, and consented to submit themselves to the rule of their hereditary enemies, whom they had sworn shortly before to exterminate.[1] Surely our Roman Catholic fellow-countrymen are unjust when they reserve their invectives for Henry VIII. and English Nobles, and forget that the Irish Romanists were equally guilty, but without even the excuse, if such were required, which Henry could advance.

Why should members of the unreformed Church of the

---

[1] "State Papers," vol. iii. pp. 295-6, 334, 392, 399, 463-5, 474 ; quoted by Froude.

present day blame Henry in this so-called act of spoliation ? He was only carrying out the example set by the Pope himself, and followed, as already remarked, by every " Catholic " country in Europe. All the minor monasteries had been already suppressed, and their properties confiscated and appropriated, under no less authority than a Papal Bull,[1] and by the Pope's license, given in 1527, eighteen years after Henry's accession to the throne.

Even previous to this, Cardinal Wolsey, as we have stated, obtained a Bull from Rome, dated 10th June 1519, empowering him to visit all monasteries and all the clergy of England. In the preamble of this document, we find severe reflections against the manners and ignorance of the clergy, who were said, in it, to be delivered over to a reprobate mind; and by another Bull of Pope Clement, dated 3d April 1524, Wolsey was further authorised to suppress several specified monasteries and (so-called) religious houses.[2]

These powers were again revived by the Pope, in November 1528, conferring on Wolsey and Gardyner together the permission to examine the state of the monasteries, and suppress such as they thought fit.

The extinction of the various orders of Monks and Friars, who were a scandal to the Church, and interfered with its discipline, by placing themselves beyond the authority of the diocesan Bishops, was hailed with approbation by the greater portion of the secular clergy. They did not regard the spoliation of the Regulars with an evil eye, and, when the property was on sale, they did not imagine that the purchase of it was sacrilege. This has been an

[1] See Rymer's " History," vol. vi. part ii. pp. 8-17, third edition, folio. Hagæ Comitis. 1745.
[2] See Burnet's " History of the Reformation," p. i. b. i. p. 36, Nares' edit. London, 1830.

after-thought, and we must not approach the conduct of the sixteenth century with a sentiment which only came into vogue at a subsequent period.[1] Surely they were better judges of what was beneficial to the Church than our modern champions of the Papacy.   And it is worthy of note, that Bishop Gardyner himself, whose attachment to Papal doctrines was most conspicuous, busied himself as much as any one in declaiming against (so-called) religious houses, and took occasion, in many of his sermons, to commend the King for suppressing them.[2] If these monasteries were abodes of piety and virtue as well as of wealth and almsgiving, would a whole Parliament—indeed a whole nation—have sacrificed such social blessings at the bidding of a King who had no army at his back, but rested solely for his power to fight Pope or Priests on the good-will of the nation alone ?

If it were lawful for the Pope of his free will and under his assumed power, to sanction or take the lead in permitting the act of spoliation, and, as we shall presently see, confirming in the most solemn manner this act, it was lawful for Henry to follow up the good work and complete the act of confiscation.   This was the last crowning act of Henry's reign towards the great object—REFORMATION.

" Heaven has had a hand in all."—" Henry VIII.," Act ii. scene i.
" Methinks I could cry Amen !"—*Ibid.*, Act. v. scene i.

It now becomes a duty to give the views taken by the most recent writer on the subject, on the Papal side, of these confiscations of monastic properties.[3] He asks, " Who were the accusers of the Monastic Houses?" and in

---

[1] Hook's " Lives of the Archbishops," vol. vii. p. 124.   1868.
[2] See Burnet's History of the Reformation," pt. i. b. iii. vol. i. p. 403. Edit. 1830.
[3] Burke's " Historical Portraits of the Tudor Dynasty," vol. ii. c. iii. 1880.

what manner was Cranmer implicated in these robberies ?
The writer overlooks the fact that the "accusations" were
advanced long before Cranmer's time ; and it is admitted
that Cranmer was not on the Commission. This writer
singles out each Commissioner (every one of them
members of the unreformed church), and professes to bring
home the charge that they were, one and all, most
abandoned characters, that they carried out their duties in
a most savage and cruel manner, particularly in dealing
with convents, and in their conduct towards the nuns and
other female inmates of their establishments ; that their
Reports were a tissue of misrepresentations and perjuries,
and that even the King himself was deceived ! It does not
appear, however, in what manner Cranmer participated
in these alleged immoralities and perjuries. Although
Cranmer was not one of the Commissioners, his crime is
limited to the alleged fact (and this is the gist of the
accusation) that he was in intimate relations with
Crumwell, the King's Prime Minister, who was the
Director-General of the "marauding expeditions." We
are told that Crumwell was the main instigator of the
dissolution of the monasteries, and that he was Cranmer's
intimate friend ; and from this fact we are asked to "judge
how far he [Cranmer] adopted Crumwell's views ;" and that
Crumwell knew how to pick out his "accomplices and
advisers." Crumwell being "the great inquisitor," and, we
are told, that Lord Crumwell and Archbishop Cranmer
carried out their programme by terror and corruption. In
this indirect manner Cranmer is sought to be made
responsible. Selecting John Loudon, Dean of Witinford,
one of the "Inquisitors," a man of "most abandoned
character," though a "bigoted Romanist" and persecutor,
as an example, Mr Burke further states, without any

authority, that this man also "was an agent of Dr
Cranmer," and that "Cranmer deemed it his policy to
keep such men attached to his interests, but nevertheless ,
the Archbishop did not like him." How is one to meet
such reckless and unproved statements, this indirect mode
of attack, granting that the Commissioners were all that
is reported of them ?

The most ready answer to those taking the Papal view
of these transactions, is that the Pope of Rome, by solemn
Bull, confirmed the titles of all the holders of these confiscated properties, granting absolution for the supposed
mortal sin of perpetrating these same sacrileges, and
confirmed all their titles with a solemn Bull of Dispensation. This took place in the reign of Queen Mary, who,
we know, was a devout, sincere, and consistent adherent of
the Papacy. She and her Parliament restored all the rites
and ceremonies of the Roman Church, which had been
abolished under Edward VI. She repealed the Acts of
Henry which abrogated the powers of the Pope, and those
of Edward which abolished Papal rites and ceremonies.
The Pope's power and supremacy was, with the consent of
Parliament, restored, which were accepted on their bended
knees. The Queen, as an earnest, relinquished such of the
confiscated properties as were held by the Crown, but the
"plundered" properties held by lay and clerical owners
were retained by them. Neither the Lords nor Commons
would grant the Pope any rights in this country, until he
confirmed the titles of the proprietors, purchased, or otherwise acquired by them, under Henry's and Edward's
confiscations. The Act of Parliament 1 and 2 Philip and
Mary c. 8, which restored the Pope's power in England,
confirmed the title of the "plunderers," and freed them
from all ecclesiastical censures, and it enacted "that all

holders of Church property should keep it, and that any
person who should attempt to molest or disturb them
therein should be deemed guilty of *præmunire*, and be
punished accordingly." But this was not considered
sufficient, they required the Pope's *dispensation* and *absolution*, to clear them of the supposed mortal sin. On these
terms alone would they admit the re-establishment of the
Pope's authority. The bargain, as Strype has it,[1] was
struck between the Pope and Parliament. Cardinal Pole,
who now was again in favour, as the Pope's Legate,
conducted the negotiations, and in his master's name
ratified that bargain, gave the "plunderers" a dispensation
with plenary absolution, on account of their iniquities,
having obtained a special Bull from Pope Paul IV. to
enable him to act in that behalf.[2] The Roman Catholic
Historian Dodd says, that the Parliament was not satisfied
with the general Bull of Dispensation which had been
issued, but insisted on a special Bull to meet their
peculiar case, which was granted. Lord Petre, the Queen's
Secretary of State, was still more particular, for he obtained
also from Paul IV., in 1555, a special Bull for himself,
confirming his title in particular, and was so careful in the
matter that he got his lands specially designated by name
in the Bull of Dispensation.[3] The present descendants of
the Queen's Secretary of State, though still staunch
adherents of the unreformed Church, have no conscientious
scruples in maintaining their lands thus acquired.

---

[1] "Ecclesiastical Memorials," vol. ii. c. xix. p. 161, 162, An. 1554.
London, 1721.

[2] See Strype as above, vol. iii. p. 159. The Bull of Dispensation is given
in the same volume, p. 60, and in the "Harleian Miscellany,", vol. vii.
p. 267, 280. London, 1811. Wilkins' "Concilia," iv. 102. Heylin's
"Ecclesia Restaurata," p. 141-2, vol. i. Cambridge, 1749. See Dodd's
"History," vol. ii. p. 115. Brussels, 1739.

[3] Strype as above, vol. iii. p. 162.

The confiscations in Henry's reign amounted to Romanists plundering Papists, in which the Reformed Church took no part. And the confiscations under Edward were justified by the Pope's dispensation and precedent.

But this is not all; we have yet Ireland to deal with. The like spoliation, as we have seen, took place in Ireland in 1541, when Ireland was in full revolt against England. And while that country was essentially "Popish," and their devotion to the unreformed religion at that time was most conspicuous, they did not hesitate to share in the spoils at the expense of their religion. And in order to secure themselves in these spoils, they sought the protection of Henry, against whom they had been in revolt, acknowledging his title as King of Ireland.[1] The Pope's Bull of Confirmation, &c., extended to Ireland.

We hear a great deal of the iniquity and injustice of these confiscations, but nothing of the Pope's confirmation.

If truth is the object of investigation into the records of those days, much labour will be spared by the perusal of the "Letters relating to the Suppression of the Monasteries," edited from the Originals in the British Museum by Thomas Wright, Esq., and "Printed for the Camden Society," London, 1843.

The Editor in his Preface says :—

"'I leave these letters to tell their own story. They throw light on the history of a great event, which changed entirely the face of society in our island, an event which I regard as the greatest blessing conferred by Providence upon this country since the first introduction of the Christian religion. I will not at present enter into the history of this revolution, but leave the documents for others to comment upon. I have suppressed nothing, for I believe that they contain nothing

---

[1] See "State Papers," vol. iii. pp. 295-6, 334, 392, 399, 463-5, 474.

which is untrue ; and the worst crimes laid to the charge of the
Monks are but too fully verified by the long chain of historical
evidence reaching, without interruption, from the twelfth to the sixteenth century. Those who have studied in the interior history of
this long period the demoralizing effects of the Popish system of confession and absolution, will find no difficulty in conceiving the facility
with which the inmates of the monasteries, at the time of their dissolution, confessed to vices, from the very name of which our imagination now recoils. These documents are of peculiar importance amid
the religious disputes which at present agitate the world ; and I think
that even the various lists of the confessions of the Monks and Nuns
of the several religious houses, entitled *comperta*, and preserved in
manuscript, ought to be made public. The great cause of the Reformation has been but ill-served by concealing the depravities of the
system which it overthrew."

If, then, we are indebted, even in the slightest degree,
to Cranmer, directly or indirectly, as sought to be charged
against him, for freeing this country from these monastic
institutions, whatever his failings, faults, or motives may
have been, we say again, that we bless him for his work's
sake. But, as a fact, Cranmer was in no way responsible
for these spoliations, any more than he was responsible
for the "massacre of the Pilgrims of Grace," or the " Im-
molation of the Carthusians," also sought to be charged
against him by Mr Burke.[1]

[1] I do not overlook the fact that, in some recent works, it is asserted that the
charges of immorality against the occupiers of these Monastic establishments
are grossly exaggerated. Be it so ; still the confiscations met the approval of
the Bishops and Clergy, indeed of the entire nation, confirmed, as we have
seen, by the Pope. The result of such confiscations proved a lasting benefit to
the country at large, while, on the other hand, *Church property*, properly so
called, remained intact. Every Bishop retained his See and revenue, and
every Priest his Benefice, freed, however, from the "black-mail" imposed by
the Bishop of Rome.

CHAPTER IX.

WE now come to the most painful branch of our subject,
which involves the consideration of persecutions for conscience' sake. In these Cranmer is said to have participated. It is a lamentable fact that the dominant party in
the Christian Church has been for many centuries a
persecuting sect. A peculiar feature in these persecutions
is that the denial of certain theological *dogmas* has been
deemed a crime worthy of a cruel death, while immoralities
and other vices have been considered trivial breaches of religion in comparison with alleged heresy. It was Thomas
Aquinas,—the "Seraphic Doctor,"—a canonised Saint of
the Roman Church, who laid down the proposition :—

"If falsifiers of money, or other malefactors, are justly consigned to
immediate death by secular princes, *much more* do heretics, immediately after they are convicted of heresy, deserve not only to be excommunicated, but also justly to be killed."[1]

Again, Liguori, a recently canonised Saint, whose works
have received the most formal approval of his Church, as
not containing "one word worthy of censure," under the
title, "What is heresy?" writes: "If the accused confess his
crime, the sentence is given: if not, he is to be led to conviction or to torture."[2] Alphonsus à Casteo, another
eminent theologian, says :—

[1] "Secunda Secundæ Partis Summ. Theolog." S. Tho. Aquinatis. Romæ.
1586. Quæst. xi. art. iii. p. 93.
[2] Lig., "Theolog. Moral.," tom. ii. n. 201, lib. iv. Edit. Mechlin, 1845.

" The last punishment of the body of heretics is death, with which we will prove, by God's assistance, heretics ought to be punished. . . . From which words it is abundantly plain that it is not a modern invention, but that it is the ancient opinion of wise Christians that heretics should be burned with fire."[1]

That this is the recognised *law* of the Roman Church is evident from the fact that the Fourth Lateran Council under Innocent III. commanded the extermination of all heretics in the most emphatic manner, and which decree holds its place in Rome's Canon Law at the present day, set out in full as a decree *emanating from a general council*.[2] Devoti, in his " Jus Canonicum" (the book now in use in England, Roman Edition, 1837), in the first volume, p. 379, tells us that every thing contained in the Decretals is *law. Quidquid igitur in iis comprehenditur legem facit.* This *law* has been painfully put in force under the Bull " Unigenitus." Further, Pope Honorius III. issued a Bull for the extermination of heretics. To the like effect was the Bull of Innocent IV. Pope Alexander IV. appointed Inquisitors, and Urban IV. instructed them to exterminate heretics. Pope Clement IV. confirmed the constitutions of Pope Innocent IV. against heretics ; Nicholas III. issued a Bull for their excommunication, and Pope John XXII. for their extermination. Boniface IX. confirmed the exterminating laws of Frederick II. Pope Innocent VIII. decreed the punishment, and Julius II. the anathematising, of heretics. Pope Leo X. condemned, among other (so-called) errors of Luther, his assertion that "the burning of heretics was contrary to the rule of the Holy Spirit ;" and two of Luther's followers were publicly

[1] Alph. à Castro, "De hæret. punitione." Madrid, 1773, cap. xii. pp. 123, 128.
[2] The decretal is headed, " In concilio Generali," vol. ii. p. 758. Edit. Lips., 1839. And see " Coloniæ Munatianæ," Innoc. III., In Concil. Generali, An. 1216. Romæ Concil. Later., p. 240. This edition is to be seen in the Library of the Athenæum Club, Pall Mall.

L

burnt, and no doubt Luther would have shared the same fate had he not been forcibly protected or hidden away. Paul III. issued the noted Bull, "*In Cœna Domini.*" Pope Julius III. issued his Bull against all those who should oppose the Inquisition ; and Paul V. called into exercise *all* the persecuting decrees, Acts of Councils, and Bulls, that had ever been enacted or issued.

I need scarcely weary the reader with a recapitulation of the harrowing details of the merciless persecutions and slaughter of the simple and unoffending Waldenses and Albigenses, the awful massacres in the Netherlands of Protestants by the Duke of Alva, and the formal approval of this act by the Pope ; and the like approval of the massacre on St Bartholomew's day ; and the thousands on thousands of victims of the "holy office" of the INQUISITION, of which the Pope even to the present day is the " Prefecture."

We might cite also the numerous instances of the infliction of the punishment of death, in the most cruel manner, for conscience' sake, in pre-Reformation days, and of the numbers of men, women, and children who expiated their alleged crime of heresy at the stake during the Papal rule in this country, under Mary.   They principally suffered for denying the truth of that " theological enigma " (not of the " Real Presence "), but of the alleged *real corporeal presence*, in the consecrated elements, of " the body, blood, bones, and nerves (*ossa et nervos*), soul and density " of our Lord Jesus Christ ; an entire change of the *substance* of the elements being asserted, passing under the designation of " Transubstantiation."

In strict conformity with the laws of the Roman Church, every Bishop takes the oath :—"All heretics and schismatics, and rebels against the same our Lord (the Pope) and his successors, I will prosecute and attack (*persequar et impugnabo*) to the utmost of my power."[1] And this is the oath which Cranmer himself took on his consecration, imposed on him by his Church,—the Roman Church. Presuming, then, that the charge against Cranmer was true, that he advocated persecutions for conscience' sake, he was then a member of the unreformed Church, and would only be conforming to the law of that Church, and the oath which he subscribed. Surely his condemnation in acting up to that law, so repeatedly enforced by Infallible authority, should not be (if he so acted) brought in judgment against him.

If the Reformers were also persecutors, they acted under no law of the Reformed Church ; and further, all the persecuting laws which disgraced our statute-books were passed in pre-Reformation times, and have since been repealed ; even the, so-called, "penal laws" of Elizabeth's reign, which were enacted to protect the throne from treasons, and the life of the Queen, have also been repealed ; but the Roman ecclesiastical penal laws stand unrepealed, though they cannot be put in force, by reason of her inability to do so. The *spirit* still exists, as has been fully admitted in the successive numbers of the Roman Catholic Monthly, *The Rambler.*[2]

Bishop Milner, in his " End of Religious Controversy," part iii., Letter xlix., advances the following apology for his Church :—

" If Catholic States and Princes have enforced submission to their Church by persecution, they were fully persuaded that there is *a Divine authority in this Church to decide in all controversies in religion,* and that those Christians who refuse to hear her voice when she pronounces upon them are obstinate heretics. But on what grounds can Protestants persecute Christians of any description whatever ? "

[1] " Pontificale Romanum," p. 88. Edit. Paris, 1664.
[2] See January 1854, p. 2, June 1849, and September 1851.

The italics are Bishop Milner's own.

There is truth and reason in this line of argument, for the " unreformed " act on the enforced authority of the head of their Church ; and throwing the responsibility on " Princes " is a mere subterfuge. But " on what grounds can Protestants persecute ? " asks Dr Milner. We answer, on no grounds whatever ; for there is nothing in the religion of Protestants that affords any grounds whatsoever for persecuting others for religion. On this principle, Roman Catholic individuals who persecute are in some degree excusable, *because their religion* is to blame ; but Protestants who persecute are inexcusable, *because their religion* is *blameless in this respect*. We heartily agree with Dr Milner in this.

Before we pass on to the immediate consideration of the specific charges against Cranmer on the score of persecution, let us pause for a moment to record the law of the unreformed Church in England at that period. We shall see that it was in strict conformity with the acknowledged and established custom of the Papacy. In 1539 an Act of Parliament was passed by the King, Lords, and Commons, with the consent of the clergy in Convocation (which, however, Cranmer strongly opposed), called the " Six Articles Act." Those six articles are as follows (31 Henry VIII. c. 14) :—

" 1st. That in the most blessed sacrament of the altar, by the strength and efficacy of Christ's mighty words (it being spoken by the priest) is *present really*, under the form of bread and wine, the natural body and blood of our Saviour Jesus Christ, conceived of the Virgin Mary, and that after the consecration *there remaineth no substance* of bread and wine, nor any other substance but the *substance* of Christ, God and man."

" 2d. That the communion in both kinds is not necessary *ad salutem*, by the law of God, to all persons, and that it is to be believed, and not doubted of, but that in the flesh, under the form of bread, is the very blood, and with the blood, under the form of wine, is the very flesh, as well apart as though they were both together."

" 3d. That Priests, after the order of Priesthood, received as afore, may not marry by the law of God."

"4th. That vows of Chastity, widowhood by man or woman, made to God advisedly, ought to be observed by the law of God."

" 5th. That it is meet and necessary that private masses be continued and admitted in the King's English Church and congregation, as whereby good Christian people, ordering themselves accordingly do receive both godly and goodly consolations and benefits, and it is agreeable to God's law."

" 6th. That auricular confession is expedient and necessary to be retained and continued, used and frequented in the Churches of God."

Every religious sect has a right to form its own code, and the members of the unreformed Church in England had a perfect right to pass such an act to bind themselves, " for (as the act declares) abolishing diversity of opinion in certain articles concerning religion." But what they had no right to do was to attach fearful penalties on all those who did not coincide with the views of the framers of this enactment. For the Act proceeds, in section 5, to declare that all offending against the first article, as to the *change of substance* of the consecrated elements, shall be adjudged *heretics*, and " every such offender and offenders shall therefore have and suffer judgment, execution, and pains of death, BY WAY OF BURNING, without any adjuration, clergy, or sanctuary, and forfeit everything."

Section 6 enacted, that offenders against the other five articles, by preaching or teaching, should be adjudged felons, and suffer PAINS OF DEATH, as in case of felons [that is, by hanging], without any benefit of clergy.

Section 7 enacted, that offenders against the last five articles, by word or writing, were to be adjudged, for the first offence, to forfeit all their property for life ; and for the second offence were to suffer as FELONS BY DEATH.

Section 9 declares, that if any man, which is or hath been a Priest, shall keep company with a wife, he shall suffer as a felon [that is, by death]; whereas (by section 10) if the Priest kept company with any other woman, he only forfeited his goods for life!

If it be pretended that this was only the tyranny of Henry VIII., and not the act or instigation of the unreformed Church, as often asserted, to cover over˙ this iniquitous law, we answer that Henry and his Parliament and Convocation merely followed the example of their predecessors of earlier Roman Catholic times, of a Roman Catholic Prince acting on the solicitation of Roman Catholic Bishops. We refer to the Act 2 Henry IV. c. 15 (A.D. 1400), an act passed to suppress alleged heresies. It recites that a new sect of heretical preachers had arisen, and that the diocesans could not, by their jurisdiction spiritual, sufficiently correct the said false and perverse people without the aid of his Majesty:—

"ON THE PRAYER OF THE PRELATES, it is enacted that none shall preach without license, and any offender against the Act shall be arrested by the diocesan and imprisoned and fined; and any person refusing to adjure, or relapsing, shall be delivered to the Sheriff, who *then, before the people, in an high place go* TO BE BURNT, that such punishment may strike in fear to the minds of others. So that such wicked doctrines, nor its authors, shall be in any wise suffered."

The secular arm is always called on to carry out the atrocious persecuting principles of the rulers of the Church. *Semper eadem* is Rome's motto.

So far from Cranmer being an advocate of persecution,[1] he argued for three days boldly against the passing of the "Six Articles Act," speaking repeatedly against the

---

[1] "If, however, he was a persecutor both in theory and practice, it must be remembered that no one of any party in those days had grasped the principle of religious toleration."—"Encyclopædia Britannica," "Cranmer," 9th edit., p. 551.

measure ; and, when desired by the King to absent himself from the debates, he firmly but respectfully declined to comply, urging among other reasons that penalty of death ought not to be imposed for mere matters of opinion ; and in spite of his remonstrance the Act was forced through Parliament. He also wrote a long treatise against this Act to be submitted to the King, but which appears never to have reached him, having been lost by an accident. Dr Lingard throws discredit on Cranmer's persistent opposition to this Act, and asserts that he was eventually "confounded by the King's godly learning," and this is stated on the faith of a letter among the MSS., "Cleopara, E. v., p. 128," alleged to have been written by one of the Lords present at the debate ; but this does not so appear, nor does the document bear any name. It may and probably was written by some person attached to the Papal cause, from hearsay. The following passage, which Dr Lingard *does not quote*, would seem to carry out this view :—"And also, *news here*, I assure you never Prince showed himself so wise a man—as the King hath done in this parlyment." In fact, Strype properly designates this letter as "a flying report." Lord Herbert, Burnet, Strype, and Collier assert that " Cranmer for three days together in the open assembly opposed these Articles boldly."

It is not the fact, as alleged, that Cranmer subscribed these " Six Articles." The clergy were not required to do so. They were imposed by Act of Parliament, and by that Act the clergy were enjoined *to read* them in their churches once a quarter, but they never were required to subscribe them.[1]

---

[1] I have ventured to question the fact of the " signature." I cannot, however, pass over the following testimony.—It still is a question whether the words of Cranmer are to be taken literally. In a letter addressed by Alexander Ales to Queen Elizabeth, 1st September 1559 (see Stevenson's

Bearing in mind these few leading principles and facts, we have now to examine the charges against the Primate for his responsibility and alleged share in the persecutions of his day.

With reference to these persecutions for conscience' sake, Mr Jenkyns, in his "Remains of Cranmer" (Preface, p. lxxii), remarks that the Archbishop was often compelled by his station to be a party to these proceedings ; and must, therefore, have been present at many of the theological discussions which were occasioned by them. He adds :—

"It may be abundantly proved that Cranmer, though not sufficiently in advance of his times to give up the principle of persecution, was yet continually exerting himself to mitigate its rigour. He usually endeavoured to reason the prisoners into a recantation of their obnoxious tenets, or, at least, into such an explanation of them as might screen them from punishment ; and it is said, that sometimes, in despair of saving their lives by other means, he secretly furthered their escape. Can so much be said in favour of any of Cranmer's contemporaries ? We need not be surprised that he was driven to such expedients, since James V., King of Scotland, about this time, was unable to save one near relation from death, and another from exile, when charged with heresy, and could only avert the danger, from his aunt, by persuading her to recant."

The specific charges are limited to the cases of Fryth, Lambert, Anne Askew, and Joan Boucher. The first three martyrs were burnt during the reign of Henry VIII.

"Callendar of State Papers, Foreign, Elizabeth," 1558-1559, p. 532), he gives an interesting account of his interview with Cranmer, with reference to the passing of the Six Articles Act. He writes :—"Before this law was published, the Bishop of Canterbury sent Lord Pachet from Lambeth to me at London. He directed me to call on the Archbishop early in the morning. When I called upon him, 'Happy man that you are,' said he, 'you can escape ! I wish that I might do the same; truly my See would be no hindrance to me. You must make haste and escape before the island is blocked up, unless *you are willing to sign the decree, as I have, compelled by fear.* I repent of what I have done. And if I had known that my punishment would have been deposition from the Archbishopric (as I hear that my Lord Latimer is deposed), of a truth I would not have subscribed." P. 533.

for their alleged erroneous views on the dogma of " Transubstantiation." Joan Boucher was condemned in the reign of Edward VI. for alleged heresy on the doctrine of the Incarnation.

Cranmer, it has been remarked, was but little in advance of his age on the subject of toleration when the law was to be maintained ; but, whenever he was personally or privately concerned, he evinced a liberal mind and a mild disposition, the more remarkable, as it seemed to be scarcely intelligible to those with whom he was concerned.[1] During the time Warham held the See of Canterbury in 1519, six men and one woman were burned as heretics in Coventry. In 1521, Longland, Bishop of Lincoln, carried out persecutions. We have also the persecution of the Lollards. In 1527 we might record the cruelties practised on poor Bilney, and the persecutions by Tunstal between the years 1527 and 1531. Sir Thomas More was a noted persecutor. Indeed all the Bishops in those days were persecutors on principle, according to their notions. Alexander Ales, in his Letter to Queen Elizabeth, calls Gardyner "a most violent persecutor."[2]

Fryth was the first Englishman after Wicliff who wrote against the received theory of *Transubstantiation.* His celebrated controversy with Sir Thomas More, and his writings on the subject, are supposed to have considerably influenced Cranmer in changing his views with respect to that extravagant dogma. Fryth, with Andrew Hewett, was burned at Smithfield on the 4th July 1533.[3]

[1] Hook's "Lives of the Archbishops," vol. vii. pp. 114-117. 1860.
[2] See Stevenson's "State Papers," "Elizabeth," 1559, p. 526.
[3] Foxe's "Acts and Monuments," vol. ii. p. 309. London, 1641. Burnet, following Hall and Stowe, gives the date as 1534. If we follow the date of Cranmer's letter, 4th June 1533, Foxe's date would appear to be more accurate.

From a letter written by Cranmer to Archdeacon Hawkyns,[1] it is clear that Cranmer was not responsible for this cruel sentence. Fryth being then in prison, the King (Henry VIII.) directed that he should be examined by the Archbishop, the Bishop of London, the Lord Chancellor, and others, as to his alleged heresy. Not being able to convince Fryth, they handed him over to his ordinary, Bonner, the Bishop of London. His examiners were Gardyner, the Lord Chancellor, Lord Suffolk, and the Earl of Wiltshire. Bonner gave sentence against him, who, in turn, handed him over to the secular authorities to be dealt with as a heretic. The words of Cranmer in the letter to the Archdeacon would appear conclusive on this head :—

" Other news have we none notable, but that one Fryth, which was in the Tower in prison, was appointed by the King's grace to be examined before me, my Lord of London, my Lord of Wynchestre, my Lord of Suffolke, my Lord Chancellor, and my Lord of Wylteshere, whose [Fryth's] opinion was so erroneous that we could not dispatch him, but was fain to leave him to the determination of his Ordinary, which is the Bishop of London. His said opinion is of such nature, that he thought it not necessary to be believed as an article of our faith, that there is the very corporal presence of Christ within the host and sacrament of the altar, and holdeth of this point most after Æcolampadius. And surely I myself sent for him three or four times to persuade him to leave that his imagination, but for all that we could do therein, he would not apply to any counsel ; notwithstanding now he is at a final end with all examination, *for my Lord of London hath given sentence and delivered him to the secular power, where he looketh every day to go unto the fire.* And there is also condemned with him one Andrewe, a tailor, of London, for the said self-same opinion."

From the cool and offhand manner in which Cranmer alludes to this fearful sentence of death, we may fairly presume that, had the case been within his jurisdiction, he would have been compelled, by the cruel and exacting law of his Church, to give a like sentence. We of the Re-

[1] See Jenkyns' " Remains of Thomas Cranmer," vol. i. p. 31. Oxford, 1833.

formed Church have a right, and do, condemn Cranmer in this, but it is the height of inconsistency for members of the unreformed Church to join in the "hue and cry" against Cranmer for carrying out, or, as in this case, tacitly acknowledging, a sentence which was in strict conformity with the law of their Church, unrepealed even to the present day. To condemn Cranmer is to condemn their own Church and her cruel laws.

Lambert was another victim of religious intolerance, whose cruel fate is sought to be laid to the responsibility of Cranmer. Dr Lingard, in his "History of England," thus refers to the circumstance :—

"Of all the prosecutions [he does not call it a *persecution*] for heresy, none excited greater interest than that of Lambert, *alias* Nicholson, a clergyman in Priest's orders, and a schoolmaster in London. Nor is it a least remarkable circumstance in his story, that of the three men who brought him to the stake, Taylor, Barnes, and Cranmer, two professed, even then, most certainly later, the very same doctrine as their victim, and all three suffered afterwards the same, or nearly the same, punishment."

For this charge against Cranmer Dr Lingard has not advanced any proof, while he admits that the particulars of Lambert's examination have not been preserved! He appears to have borrowed the charge from Phillips, in his "Life of Cardinal Pole," who asserted that Cranmer had consented to Lambert's and Anne Askew's death; and he is followed in the same line by Dr Milner and Charles Butler, Esq., but none of them give any authority. There is a letter extant from Thomas Dorset,[1] written at the time, mentioning the examinations of Lambert. He says that Lambert was first examined before three Bishops, without naming them. His second examination, he says, was before the Bishop of Worcester, who "was most extreme agaynst hym," and was sent by him with Lambert's articles

[1] MS. Cotton. "Cleop.," E. iv., fol. 110.

to the Lord Chancellor ; and that Lord Norfolk, the Earl
of Essex, and the Countess of " Oxfforthe" wrote to the
Bishop against him.   But Cranmer's name is not mentioned. Lambert, when brought before the Court of the
Archbishop, appealed to the King direct ; the King heard
the appeal, and was by him condemned to the stake.
There is no evidence whatever that Cranmer took any part
in his condemnation. Stone (in his remarks on Phillips'
" Life of Cardinal Pole "), who had investigated all the
evidence that could be adduced on the subject, writes :—

" Fuller acknowledges the consent which Phillips has alleged ; but
I cannot see for what reason, as it is not authenticated by any historian
that I can meet with.   Henry had disputed with Lambert, and ordered
him to be burnt, or retract his opinion ; and Chancellor Wriothesley
prosecuted Askew, and put her on the rack ;—but it nowhere appears
that Cranmer's advice or consent was asked upon either of them."

No fresh evidence on the subject has since come to
light.   It was Crumwell, the Vicar-General, according to
Collier, who delivered judgment on Lambert's case. [1]

The Court held by the King was attended in great state
by Nobles, Peers, and Bishops, among whom was the
Primate.   It appears that each Bishop was assigned a particular point on which to question the wretched man.
When it came to Cranmer's turn to speak, he began by
addressing him as " Brother Lambert," and continued
mildly to lead him on to consider an argument drawn from
the History of St Paul.   Whereupon the impetuous Gardyner, believing that the Archbishop would get the worst
of the argument, interposed, and took up the discussion
with his usual vehemence.   Further than this, Cranmer
took no part in the proceedings.   He was present at this
mock trial with the other Bishops and Nobles, in his official
character.   It was Sampson, Bishop of Chichester, who
opened the proceedings.

[1] See Collier's " Ecclesiastical History," vol. ii. p. 152.

With regard to the fate of *Anne Askew*, Dr Lingard refers to her only in a note, in which he says that she was, after two recantations, condemned to the flames *by Cranmer and other Bishops.* It is as certain that Cranmer had no hand in this matter, as that Anne Askew recanted. Foxe, in his " Acts and Monuments," has preserved her answer to the false surmises of her recantation as follows :—

" I have read the process, which is reported of them that know not the truth, to be my recantation. But, as the Lord liveth, I never meant thing less than to recant. Notwithstanding this, I confess that, in my first troubles, *I was examined by the Bishop of London about the Sacrament.* Yet had they no grant of my mouth but this, that I believed therein, as the Word of God bid me to believe ; *more had they never of me.* Then he made a copy which is now in print, and required me to set thereunto my hand. But I refused it. Then my two sureties did will me in no wise to stick thereat, for it was no great matter, they said. Then, with much ado, at the last I wrote thus :—I, Anne Askew, do believe this, if God's Word do agree to the same, and the true Catholic Church. Then the Bishop, being in great displeasure with me, *because I made doubts in writing,* commended me to prison, where I was a while ; but afterwards, by the means of friends, I came out again. Here is the truth of this matter.—ANNE ASKEW."

Thus, it appears, that the courageous lady did not recant, and it was the Bishop of London, Bonner, who undertook to be her judge. Indeed, in the foreground of all these melancholy proceedings, should stand the relentless persecutors Bonner and Gardyner, and not Cranmer. The name of Cranmer, throughout the narrative of this lady's sufferings, is not once introduced either by Foxe, Lord Herbert, Burnet, Strype, Collier, or Hume.[1] There can be no doubt that the sentence of condemnation was pronounced by Bonner, in whose Register proceedings against her were

---

[1] The Rev. R. W. Dixon, in his " History of the Church of England," vol. ii., 1881, pp. 395-401, goes into minute particulars of this event, naming each particular person before whom she appeared; he does not once name Cranmer.

recorded.   It was Bonner, in company with Mr Rich. who
visited her in person, and attempted by every means, in
"flattering words," to induce her to recant.

Dr Hook seems to go out of his way to extenuate, if not
to apologise for, Bonner.   The verdict of Mr Froude, who,
equally with Dr Hook, aims to combine the impartiality of
the historian with the indifference of a philosophical in-
quirer, is more consonant with the generally received truth.
He has read the "State Papers" in which the suggestions
of this apology are founded by the Dean of Chester, and
yet he maintains that the epithet of "bloody" must ever
be associated with the name of Bonner, and his "brutality
was notorious and unquestionable."   Martyrdom (in Mr
Froude's emphatic language)—

> "Was often but a relief from more barbarous atrocities.   In the sad
> winter months that were approaching (A.D. 1555), the poor men and
> women who, untried and uncondemned, were crowded into Bonner's
> prisons, experienced such miseries as the very dogs could scarcely
> suffer and survive.   They were beaten, they were stoned, they were
> flung into dark foetid dens, where rotting straw was their bed ; their
> feet were fettered in the stocks, and their clothes were their only
> covering, while the wretches who died in prison were flung out into
> fields, where none could bury them."

Why should the Dean have gone out of his way to extenuate such conduct ?

Had Bonner been a reforming Archbishop, such as was
Cranmer, his memory would have been for ever execrated
by the opponents of the Reformation; but, to the end, being
a consistent follower of the (so-called) "ancient creed" of
the Roman Church, he closely adhered to the persecuting
principles of his Church, hence the vials of Papal wrath are
not poured on the head of this blood-thirsty and persecuting Bishop.

We may note here that Archbishop Warham, on the
matter of persecutions, cannot come out with a clean

conscience; and Sir Thomas More, as already observed, was a notorious tyrant and persecutor. Voltaire described More as a superstitious and barbarous persecutor, and that it was for such cruelties he deserved to be put to death, and not for having denied Henry's Supremacy.[1]

In 1538, Crumwell issued a Commission, in the King's name, against the Foreign Anabaptists. This Commission was addressed to the Primate, W. Stokesley; to Sampson, Bishop of Chichester; to eight Archdeacons, and to several others; commanding them to proceed with vigour against all who were infected with the error of the sect. Under this Commission some of these enthusiasts were burnt. Such was the savage law in these pre-Reformation days, to which Cranmer had to conform. He then was not better enlightened, and was certainly no worse, than his Ecclesiastic and Lay associates. With regard to the persecutors under the "Six Articles Act," Cranmer's name does not appear.[2]

With reference to persecutions generally on questions of religious doctrines, we have no reason for doubting that if any such cases had come before Cranmer in his official capacity, he would have considered it his duty to act up to the laws and customs of the Church of which he was then a member. Members of the Reformed Church may, with perfect consistency, condemn Cranmer for any participation in these atrocities, but it is a suicidal act on the part of members of the unreformed Church to join, as I have often repeated, in this "hue and cry" against Cranmer.

[1] "Essay on the Spirit of Nations," cap. cxxxv. vol. iii. p. 205. See vol. xvii., Works. Paris, 1785.

[2] The Rev. R. W. Dixon, in his "History of the Church of England," vol. ii. p. 137, 1881, maintains that the persecutions which took place under this act "were neither instigated by the clergy nor in the main conducted by them, —these were lay persecutions, not clerical." Mr Dixon, however, does not establish this assertion by proofs.

The case of *Joan Boucher*, which occurred in the reign of Edward, stands on a very different footing to the other three already mentioned, although it may be safely asserted that, had she existed in pre-Reformation days, her fate would have been equally sealed, and more promptly carried out.

The accusation against this unhappy woman had no relation to the Sacraments, but she was condemned for denying the Incarnation of Christ; she and Van Paris suffered for the like offence. They were condemned under an unrepealed Act of Parliament (2 Henry IV. c. 15) passed long previous to the Reformation period, and in Papal times when England was essentially "Popish" in doctrines and practices. No Protestant will, it is hoped, attempt to justify Cranmer in the active part he is said to have taken in the transaction. That he urged on Edward to consent to the issue of the fatal mandate, is probably true, but that he guided "poor Edward's shrinking fingers"[1] to sign the death-warrant, is a myth. This piece of scandal has been entirely set at rest by Mr Bruce in his "Biography of Roger Hutchinson," as presently noted.

Foxe seems to intimate that Cranmer persuaded the King to put his hand to the condemnation; Sir John Haywards mentions the alleged violence used by Cranmer in persuading the King. Strype, on the other hand, seeks to exculpate Cranmer, and objects to Hayward's statement as being incorrect.

The entry in the King's journal is as follows :—

"Joan Boucher, otherwise Joan of Kent, was burnt for holding that Christ was not Incarnate of the Virgin Mary; being condemned the year before, but kept in hope of conversion; and the 30 of April the Bishop of London and the Bishop of Ely went to persuade her, but she withstood them, and reviled the preacher that preached at her death."[2]

[1] "Saturday Review," No. 622, vol. xxiv. p. 403.   28th Sept. 1867.
[2] Soame's "History of England," vol. iii. p. 544.   London, 1826.

Ridley was then Bishop of London, and Goodrich (the Lord Chancellor) was Bishop of Ely.

From this extract it has been justly argued that if the King had been importuned by Cranmer, as alleged, to sign the warrant for committing Joan to the flames, something further would have appeared. The following is the entry in the Privy Council Book, 27th April 1550:—

" A warrant to the L. Chancellor to make out a writ to the Sheriff of London for the execution of Joan of Kent, condemned to be burned for certain detestable opinions of heresie."

The persons stated to have been present at the Council on that day were: "The Lord Chauncellor, the Lord High Treasurer, the Lord Great Chamberlaine, the Lord Chamberlaine, the Lord Pagett, the Bishop of Ely, the Threasurer, Mr Comptroller, Master of the Horse, Mr Vice-Chamberlaine, Sir Rauf Sadler, Sir Edward Northe."[1] Cranmer's name does not appear, nor is there any evidence that he was present when the sentence was passed. Joan was executed under the cruel unrepealed law, on a writ *de hæretico comburendo*,—an old and existing Act passed in Romish times,—addressed to the Sheriff of London, on the authority of a warrant signed by the Council, issued from the High Court of Chancery. Mr Bruce further observes :—

" It would have been contrary to constitutional custom for the King to have signed any such document; it is quite clear from the entry quoted that, in point of fact, he did not sign it; and the narrative which the worthy martyrologist was misled into inserting, and Cranmer's difficulty to cause the King 'to put to his hand,' and the tears by which subsequent writers have declared that his submission to the stern pleading of his spiritual father [the Archbishop Cranmer] were accompanied, all vanish."

It would be idle to attempt to palliate or defend Cran-

[1] See Bruce's "Biog. of Roger Hutchinson," prefixed to his works. Parker Society Edition. Cambridge, 1842.

mer for any participation in this miserable piece of bigotry. But, whatever part Cranmer took in the transaction, he acted with others in authority according to law, a cruel Papal law; and even this fact is but a lame excuse to fall back upon. But we do protest against the unfair process adopted by Cranmer's detractors to shift the entire responsibility of this execution on Cranmer, in order to bring him into disrepute, when Cranmer and the others were acting strictly under the law enacted by their own sect.

Again, the allegation that Cranmer was responsible for the persecution of the "Carthusian Monks," and of the "Pilgrims of Grace," advanced by Mr Burke, is utterly without any foundation.

This bit of scandal is taken from Sander, and as to the tortures alleged to be inflicted on them, Bishop Burnet declares the tale to be "a legend":—.

"The English nation knows none of these cruelties, in which the Spanish Inquisitors are very expert. I find by some original letters that the Carthusians who were shut up in their cells lived about a year after this; so if Crumwell [the accusation is not brought against Cranmer, as now sought to be fixed on him] had designed to take away their lives, he wanted no opportunities, but it appears from what More writ in his imprisonment, that Crumwell was not a cruel man, but on the contrary, merciful and gentle. And for the Franciscans, though they had offended the King highly, two of them railing spitefully at him to his face, in his Chapel at Greenwich : yet that was passed over with a reproof; from which it appears that he was not easily provoked against them. So all that relation which he [Sander] gives, being without any authority, must pass for a part of the poem."[1]

The Oath of Allegiance to the King and denial of the supremacy of the Bishop of Rome in this country, was not required by Act of Parliament to be taken by all these persons of foreign importation until 28 Henry VIII. c. x., A.D. 1537. The Carthusian Monks were not compelled to

---

[1] See Pocock's edit. of "Burnet's Hist. of the Prot. Reformation," vol. iv. p. 568. Oxford, 1865.

take this oath, but they publicly called in question the King's authority, and were guilty of high treason. Three Priors and a Monk were committed to the Tower. They had been arraigned at the Guild Hall and tried at Westminster Hall on the 29th April 1535, found guilty, and condemned to undergo the usual punishment of a traitor; and they paid the penalty of their treason; for which Cranmer was in no way directly or indirectly responsible. On the contrary, he had a sincere compassion for them, and this is shown by a letter he addressed to the King's Minister, Crumwell, whose duty, it appears, was to maintain the King's dignity. This letter is dated 30th April 1535, the day after their condemnation. In speaking of these Monks, he writes [1] :—

" It much pitieth me that such men should suffer with so ignorant judgments : and if there be none other offence laid against them but this one, it will be much more for the conversion of all the faulters hereof, after mine opinion, that their consciences may be clearly averted from the same by communications of sincere doctrine, and so they to publish it likewise to the world, than by the justice of the law to suffer in such ignorance. And if it would please the King's Highness to send them to me, I suppose I could do very much in their behalf."

And yet, with this desire of Cranmer to plead on behalf of these *traitors* to their King and country acknowledging a foreign ruler, he is to be credited with the odium of their condemnation merely on the ground,—and none other is alleged,—of the supposed intimacy which is presumed to have existed between the Primate and the Prime Minister !

A recent writer who has revived these accusations could not possibly have overlooked the following account of the alleged persecution of the Carthusian Monks, as recorded by Burnet [2] :—

[1] " Remains " by Jenkyns, vol. i. pp. 134-5, Letter cxlv.
[2] "History of the Reformation," vol. i. pp. 551-2. Pocock's edition. Oxford, 1865.

"The Pope's power over the clergy was so absolute, and their dependence and obedience to him was so implicit; and the Popish clergy had so great an interest in the superstitious multitude, whose conscience they governed, that nothing but a stronger passion could either tame the clergy, or quiet the people. If there had been the least hope of impunity, the last part of Henry's reign would have been one continued rebellion; therefore, to prevent a more profuse effusion of blood, it seemed necessary to execute laws severely in some particular instances.

"There is one calumny that runs on a thread through all the historians of the Popish side, which not a few of our own have ignorantly taken up, that many were put to death for not swearing the King's supremacy. It is an impudent falsehood; for not so much as one person suffered on that account; nor was there any law for any such oath before the Parliament in the twenty-eighth year of the King's reign, when the insufferable Bull of Pope Paul III. engaged him to look a little more to his own safety. Then, indeed, in the oath for maintaining the succession to the Crown, the subjects were required, under the pains of treason, to swear that the King was supreme head of the Church of England; but that was not mentioned in the former oath that was made in the twenty-fifth, and enacted in the twenty-sixth, year of his reign. It cannot but be confessed, that to enact under pain of death that none should deny the King's title, and to proceed upon that against offenders, is a very different thing from forcing them to swear the King to be the supreme head of the Church.

"The first instance of capital punishment was in Easter Term, in the beginning of the twenty-seventh year of Henry's reign (A.D. 1535). Three Priors and a Monk of the Carthusian Order were then indicted of treason, for saying *that the King was not supreme head under Christ of the Church of England.* They were tried in Westminster Hall by a commission of oyer and terminer; they pleaded *Not guilty;* but the jury found them guilty, and judgment was given that they should suffer as traitors. The record mentions no other particulars, but the writers of the Popish side make a splendid recital of the courage and constancy they expressed both in their trial and at their death. It was no difficult thing for men so used to the legend, and the making of fine stories for saints and martyrs of their orders, to dress up their narratives with such pomp, that as their pleading *Not guilty* to the indictment, shows no extraordinary resolution; so that the account that is given by them of Hall, a secular Priest, that died with them, is so false, that there is good reason to suspect all. He is said to have suffered on the same account; but the record of his attainder gives a very different relation of it."

With regard to the "Pilgrims of Grace," they were the leaders of a wide-spread disaffection and revolt among the insurgents of the northern dioceses, in order to re-establish in this country the supremacy of the Pope. Some of these fanatics also suffered for their treason.

Why Cranmer should be made responsible either for the existing laws, or for the enforcement of these laws, how-ever harsh or cruel these laws might have been, is beyond comprehension, except on the unworthy object of making the character of Cranmer as hateful as possible as the acknowledged "Master Builder" of the REFORMATION. The device is weak. True, Cranmer was a unit in the Parliament by virtue of his office, when the protective laws against the usurpations of the Papacy were enacted. It was only a few years back that hanging was the penalty for sheep stealing. It may with equal propriety be said that the then Archbishop of Canterbury, as a unit in the Legislature, was responsible for the enforcement of that law also.

There is yet another case imputed to Cranmer,—the attainder, in 1529, of Seymour, the brother of the Protec-tor, and Lord High Admiral of England. It is needless to enter into details of the acts of this profligate. Being condemned, Cranmer set his hand to the warrant, *with the other members of the Council.* Ecclesiastics in those days escaped the odium of the direct charge of persecution, by availing themselves of the pitiful subterfuge of handing over the delinquent to the civil tribunal to carry out the punishment they had adjudicated. Cranmer did not avail himself of this subterfuge, but joined his colleagues in signing the warrant, hence the odium attached to the act. But the real question would be, whether Seymour deserved his fate? That was a question unanimously decided in the affirmative by the Council, of which Cranmer was one.

All Cranmer's unbiassed biographers represent him as being kind, benevolent, amiable, and forgiving, and in no way given to a desire to persecute for conscience' sake. We have numerous instances recorded by Le Bas in his exhaustive " Life of Cranmer." His hospitality and charity were bounded only by his means, and these were often unduly stretched. At his own expense he established an hospital and appointed surgeons to · receive the poor wounded soldiers from France. According to the account given by his secretary, Morice, his domestic and private life was in all respects as became a Prelate of the Church ; his habits regular, abstemious : and laborious in his studies, and patient and conscientious in the discharge of his public episcopal duties. We cannot ignore Cranmer's sincerity when he gave his persistent opposition to the passing of the " Six Articles Act." When it was being mercilessly put in force he earnestly pleaded for the relief of the prisoners arrested under that Act.

Of course it is stated that Cranmer opposed the passing of this Act, as it would necessitate putting away his wife. That may have been one of his motives, but we dare venture to assert, no unprejudiced member of the unreformed Church of the present day would seek to justify the passing of such an Act of Parliament. Then why attribute unworthy motives in Cranmer's opposition to it ? He succeeded, later on, in considerably modifying the terms of the Act, and ultimately, during Edward's reign, effecting its repeal. Elizabeth's (so-called) penal laws were passed to suppress *treason* against the Crown. This " Six Articles Act " was to coerce men's conscience. We hear vehement denunciations levelled against Elizabeth for passing her laws for repression of rebellions and treasons, but none by members of the unreformed Church against Henry and his advisers Gardyner and Bonner, for passing and enforcing such a cruel law to coerce men's conscience.

Witness also Cranmer's generous bearing towards the treacherous conduct of Drs Thornton and Barber, who combined with Gardyner to bring Cranmer into disgrace with the King,—men to whom he had himself given preferment. On discovery of the plot, he forgave them, and interceded on their behalf with the King, dismissing them only from his service. Cranmer's forgiveness of injuries was so notorious that it became a byword : " Do my Lord of Canterbury an ill turn, and you make him your friend." That he was no bigot, is exemplified by the counsel he gave to Edward, with respect to the Princess Mary, who persisted in her rejection of the Revised Liturgy, and her use of the Mass, and through his instrumentality the Princess was exempted from all further molestation.[1]

Cranmer's generous feelings were also excited in favour of Sir Thomas More and Bishop Fisher, who persistently refused, as persons holding public offices, to take the oath of submission to the King. He pleaded for More and Fisher, even after he had failed to persuade them to admit the royal supremacy. The fate of Sir Thomas More and of the Venerable Fisher, Bishop of Rochester, were important events in this period of our history, and have been very much misrepresented. Cranmer was in no way responsible for their cruel fate. They are esteemed as Martyrs ! A few observations on the other side of the question may not be considered out of place. We have not to defend the Church of the Reformation for the execution of either More or Fisher, for it was not the

[1] See Strype's " Eccl. Mem.," vol. iv. c. i. Anno 1551.

Reformed Church of England that was committed to this
act. Nor have we to justify the act. We do not attempt
to justify it. They were put to death under the laws
enacted by a Roman Catholic King. *Treason*, and not
religion, was the crime of which they were accused, convicted, and executed, under a law passed by a Parliament
composed exclusively of members holding the Roman
Catholic faith, and unanimously confirmed .by the Bishops
in Convocation, who were exclusively of the same religious
persuasion. They both were consistent, uncompromising
adherents of the Papacy, and persecutors. Sir Thomas
More, when in power, enforced on others his own opinions
on matters of religion without even a shadow of mercy. He
was a relentless persecutor ; he enforced and even strained
the law, by every means, fair or foul, to impose what he
called orthodoxy on the people, and in his capacity of
Chancellor exercised his powers beyond their due limits.[1]
More, on his own authority, committed Phillips to the
Tower unconvicted, where he languished for three years,
on the unproved charge of his having used unorthodox
expressions on Transubstantiation, Purgatory, Pilgrimages,
and Confession. Phillips at length appealed to the King,
as supreme head of the Church, through the Commons,
and obtained his liberty.

Again, More most illegally and unwarrantably committed the "poor bedeman," John Field, to the Fleet for
two years, on a private examination by himself of the
accused, in violation of the laws of the land, and shamefully
ill-treated him ; and, on his obtaining his liberty, he was
again imprisoned by More without trial. With More,
heresy (so-called) was a crime deserving of death; and

---

[1] Mr Friedman, in his late work on "Anne Boleyn," 1848, vol. ii. p. 88,
boldly asserts that "there is not a tittle of evidence that More was guilty of
the cruelties imputed to him."

when the seals were intrusted to his hands, Smithfield fires recommenced, the offences being principally a denial of Transubstantiation, or an accusation of the lewdness of Priests.   Abjuration   or   death was More's remedy for heresy.   Poor James Bainham, after suffering the " black-hole " of the Bishop of London, was carried to the private house of Sir Thomas More, where for two nights he was chained to a post and whipped, and subsequently imprisoned and tortured ; More himself superintending the application of the rack.   Bainham was ultimately burnt as a relapsed heretic by order of More.   At the stake he solemnly laid his death expressly to the credit of Sir Thomas More, whom he called his accuser and judge.   The accusation against him was, "that he had said Thomas à Becket was a murderer.   That he (Bainham) had spoken contemptuously of praying to Saints, and saying that the Sacrament of the altar was only Christ's mystical body, and that His body was not chewed with the teeth but received in faith."

But why dwell on such scenes !   This was a sample of many similar cases.   More was pitiless in condemning what he deemed a crime.   What reason had he to exclaim against similar acts of others practised on himself, when, with equal sincerity, they were visited on him.   Political necessity and national safety dictated the latter course, but mere religious bigotry and intolerance the former. Bishop Fisher was never pressed to acknowledge the King's supremacy in ecclesiastical matters, but for denying it, and speaking against it ; for had he kept his opinion to himself he would not have been questioned.   But denying the King's titles, of which his being supreme head was one, was adjudged by the law treason ; so he was tried for speaking against it, and not for his refusal to acknowledge it.[1]

[1] See Pocock's edition of Burnet's " History of the Protestant Reformation," vol. iv. p. 568.   Oxford, 1815.

Burnet further says that Fisher was a "remorseless persecutor of heretics, so that the rigour of the law, under
which he fell, was the same measure that he had measured
out to others."

Sir Thomas More and Bishop Fisher countenanced and
encouraged the mad impostor, "the Nun of Kent," who
inflamed men's minds with her prophecies against the
King, and who, but for a strong arm, would have raised a
rebellion in the land in favour of the Pope. She gave
colour to her supposed divine mission by forged miracles,
to which she subsequently pleaded guilty. In the Bill
of Attainder against the Nun of Kent and her accomplices, More and Fisher were declared guilty of "mis-
prision of treason." They, holding important public offices,
in direct opposition to the law of the country, denied
the King's supremacy, and otherwise impeached his
title. And further, Fisher wrote and published a book
impugning the validity of the King's marriage.[1] This
declaration of "misprisions and treason" was for a warning
only, and the King's Prime Minister, Crumwell, intimated
that the King would accept their apologies. More was
pardoned on the charge of his complicity with the Nun of
Kent, on an evasive explanation which was accepted ; but
Fisher was obstinate, and even undertook to justify himself.
He still continued to foster the conspiracy against the
King. He was again urged to apologise, but he again
refused, and there was nothing left but to pass the Bill for
his Attainder (6th March 1534). The Nun was executed
for treason, but Fisher, in spite of himself, was still
unpunished. In March 1534, the Bill was passed declaring
the marriage with Catherine invalid, and the marriage with
Anne was confirmed. It was declared that whosoever

[1] MS. Cotton. Lib., Cleop. E. iv. p. 160.

impugned by word or deed the legitimacy of the issue of that marriage would be guilty of treason, and a Commission was appointed to take the examination of persons who were suspected, or would not submit to the Act. This course became necessary, for it was at this time that news of the Pope's decision against the marriage arrived in England, the Convocation had declared the Pope's authority abolished ; and the Bull of Excommunication against Henry which followed absolved all his subjects from their oath of allegiance to the King, inviting them to rebel against him. A Commission sat to receive the oaths of allegiance of all classes holding offices under the Crown, ecclesiastical and lay. Fisher and More were now required to conform to the law ; and why not ? All the other Bishops and officers of the Crown readily took it. The oath [1] was read to them and they refused to take it ; they

[1] The following is the oath that was offered to be administered to More :— "Ye shall swear to bear faith, truth, and obedience alonely to the King's Majesty, and to his heirs of his body of his most dear and entirely beloved wife Queen Anne begotten, and to be begotten. And further to the heirs of our Sovereign Lord, according to the. limitation in the Statute made for surety of his succession in the crown of this realm mentioned and contained, and not to any other within this realm, nor foreign authority or potentate. And in case any oath be made, or hath been made, by you to any person or persons, that then you do repute the same as vain and annihilate. And that to your cunning, wit, and uttermost of your power, without guile, fraud, or other undue means, ye shall observe, keep, maintain, and defend the said act of succession, and all the whole effects and contents thereof ; and all other acts and statutes made in confirmation or for execution of the same, or of anything therein contained. And this ye shall do against all manner of persons, of what estate, dignity, degree, or condition soever they be ; and in no wise to do or attempt, nor to your power suffer to be done or attempted, directly or indirectly, any thing or things, privily or appartly, to the let, hindrance, damage, or derogation thereof, or of any part of the same, by any manner of means, or for any manner of pretence. So help you God, and all saints, and the holy evangelists."

The oath tendered to *ecclesiastical* bodies generally seems to have been a little different. There is still existing the oath taken by the Priors of the Dominican convents of Langley Regis, of Dunstable, of the Franciscan convents of Ailesbury and De-Mare, the Carmellites of Hecking, of the Prioress of the Dominican nuns of Deptford, in the name of themselves and of

were thereupon told, as was the fact, that they were the first to refuse it. They were allowed time for reflection, but they still refused. Cranmer, then Archbishop, and Crumwell, the King's Minister, made every endeavour to save them. Indeed, not only did Cranmer and Crumwell urge them to take the oath of Supremacy of the King, but we have also the fact that the Chancellor Audley, Lord Suffolk, and Bishops Gardyner, Bonner, and Tunstal, did the like. It was the *preamble* of the act which so offended Fisher and More. Cranmer proposed even that they should be allowed to be sworn to the Act of the King's succession, and not to the preamble of the Act, thereby allowing them to accept the King's supremacy, " de facto " and not " de jure." They were both deeply affected in their interviews with them. More and Fisher were then committed to the keeping of the Abbot of Westminster. They were again examined, and, persisting in their refusal, they were sent to the Tower. Fisher and More refused to do what the Bishops and clergy throughout the realm had all the brethren, and made under the respective seals of their convents. After renewing their allegiance to the King, and swearing to the lawfulness of the marriage of Queen Anne, and to be true to the issue thereof, and that they should always acknowledge the King as head of the Church of England, and that the Bishop of Rome had no more power than any other bishop had in his own diocese, and that they should submit to all the King's laws notwithstand-ing the Pope's censure to the contrary, they further declare that in their sermons they should not pervert the Scriptures, but preach Christ and His Gospel sincerely, according to the Scriptures and the traditions of orthodox and Catholic doctors ; and in their prayers, that they should pray first for the King, as supreme head of the Church of England, then for the Queen and her issue, then for the Archbishop of Canterbury and the other ranks of the clergy. Under the signatures is added a declaration that the oath is taken freely and without compulsion. This document bears date the 4th May, 1534.—(See Burnet's "History of the Reformation," vol. iv. Records, b. ii. pt. ii. No. 50.)

It is evident that the great bulk of the ecclesiastical orders were at this time quite glad to free themselves of Papal rule and Papal exactions. It was not until the dissolution of the monasteries was being carried out that an opposition was got up by the ejected monks, &c.

readily consented to do, and who did not thereby consider that they were acting against their conscience. The whole country gladly submitted to the new dispensation, and were happy in their release from Papal tyranny and Papal rule, the clergy being released from onerous pecuniary exactions, the laity from intolerant priestly despotism. Some few desperate "Papists," who openly and deliberately persisted in their disloyalty and treason, were executed. To release such noted men as Fisher and More would have been an injustice to those who suffered. It became absolutely necessary to enforce the Act of Submission; any hesitation on the part of the Parliament would have lost the advantage gained by the nation, and have thrown them back under the power of the Pope. It was now a question who was to rule in England,—the King or the Pope. There was, nevertheless, every desire to spare Fisher and More. Fisher, in June, 1535, actually wrote a letter to the King questioning his supremacy. Even this the King offered to overlook if he did not publish it; but Bishop Fisher persisted in promulgating his views.

It must be noted that the two illustrious prisoners were not treated as criminals; they were allowed their own attendants, and to correspond with and see their friends: yet even here they did not desist in defaming and slandering the King. They were even engaged, while in confinement, in schemes of rebellion;[1] and consequently, in May 1535, they were again called upon for their submission to the King. A deputation from the Council waited upon them, but they still refused to take the oath. Their trial was delayed to give them a further chance of escape; but the Pope (Paul III.) at this very time (21st May 1535) most injudiciously, perhaps purposely to insult the King,

[1] "State Papers," vol. vii. p. 635. Quoted by Froude.

conferred on Fisher the foreign title of Cardinal, which contravened the law of the land, and encroached on the King's just prerogative. This hastened the action of the Council. Being once again in vain called upon to submit, Fisher was, on the 17th June, tried in the Court of the King's Bench before the Chancellor Audley ; and the High Commissioners, Lords Crumwell and Sufford, were on that Commission. Cranmer was not on that Commission. The jury found Fisher guilty of *treason*, in attempting to deprive the King of his title and dignity, and was condemned accordingly. On the 22d June, he was beheaded as a traitor on Tower Hill. All the actors in this drama were members of the unreformed Church. The crime of this murder is at *their* door.

It must be admitted by all, that it was a sad spectacle indeed, and one which almost makes us shed tears, to see an old man, already on the verge of the grave, tottering to the scaffold, to lay his head on the block, renouncing the few years—perhaps days—left to him, for a "principle," the admission or rejection of which could neither affect his own eternal salvation, nor the good of Him for whom he sacrificed himself. The only consolation we have—if it be a consolation at all—is, that Fisher died an easy and no ignominious death. He carries with him the sympathies of all. But why is not the same sympathy extended to CRANMER, RIDLEY, LATIMER, HOOPER, and the noble host of martyrs of the Reformation ? They suffered a cruel death. They, too, were sacrificed—not for a "principle," but for rejecting a comparatively modern theological speculation, imposed by the Roman Church for belief as an Article of Faith, on pain of death by fire, but the rejection of which was a case of *conscience*, and could not affect other than the individual himself.

Before dismissing this part of the subject, I cannot refrain from quoting a striking passage from the writings of a Roman Catholic layman, Mr Pugin, on the fate of Bishop Fisher, and the responsibility of the execution. It were well if all Roman Catholic writers could afford to be as truthful as Mr Pugin :[1]—

" It is a fearful and terrible example of a Catholic nation betrayed by a corrupted Catholic hierarchy. . . . It was in a solemn convocation, when England's churchmen were assembled, a reverend array of Bishops, Abbots, and dignitaries. . . . Yet the fear of the tyrant, and the dread of losing a few remaining years of wealth and dignity, so far prevailed, that they sacrificed the liberty of the English Church at one blow. . . . One venerable Prelate, aged in years, and worn with fasting and discipline, alone protests against this sinful surrender ; his remonstrance is unsupported by his colleagues, and he is speedily brought to trial and execution. His accusers are Catholics, his judges are Catholics, his jury are Catholics, his executioner is a Catholic, and the bells are ringing for high mass in the steeples of St Paul's as the aged Bishop ascends the scaffold and receives the martyr's crown. And yet how do modern Catholics ignorantly charge the death of this great and good man on the Protestant system, which was not even broached at the time ! All the terrible executions of this dreadful reign were perpetrated before even the externals of the old religion were altered or its essential doctrines denied."

More's fate soon followed. On the 7th May he was examined. On the 26th June a true bill was found against him. On the 1st July he was brought to the bar. His treason was established. In vain he was again urged to submit ; and thereupon the jury found a verdict of guilty, and he was beheaded as a traitor. He was judged by his equals. The jury that convicted him were all members of the Roman Church, and were not actuated by any sectarian views.

We cannot, in the present state of society, measure the

1 " Earnest Address on the Establishment of the Hierarchy," by the late Mr Pugin, p. 2. Dolman, 1851.

justice or injustice of an Act of Parliament which brought these eminent personages to the block. We now hang in cases of murder : this in a future generation may be deemed barbarous. Only a few years ago we hanged for, comparatively speaking, most trivial offences. Queen Mary, of unhappy memory, seconded, perhaps instigated, by her ecclesiastical advisers, for they in fact ruled, brought to the stake and burnt alive many hundreds for refusing to admit an arbitrary theological proposition, that the consecrated wafer was converted (transubstantiated was the term invented to designate this new doctrine) into the body and blood, bones and sinews, soul and divinity, of our Lord and Saviour Jesus Christ, and chewed by the recipient, and was the same very God who was born of the Virgin Mary, and suffered on the cross, the elements, bread and wine, ceasing to exist ; this alleged wonderful change taking place after a manner they themselves could not at all explain. And they inflicted the same punishment upon those who denied that the Pope ought to have supreme ecclesiastical jurisdiction in this country ; while, in the previous reign of Henry, the fate of decapitation (a more merciful sentence, at all events) awaited those who asserted that the Pope had, or ought to have, any such ecclesiastical or spiritual jurisdiction in this country over the King. Hundreds suffered under Mary's laws.

A martyr to any cause excites our sympathy and commiseration ; and to sacrifice life to maintain a principle, however erroneous we may think it, is an act of heroism which, with many, covers the guilt which provokes the blow. In Fisher we find the martyr sacrificing himself to maintain a principle. He considered himself bound by his ecclesiastical vows, and was firm and consistent to the end, and for this we are now informed that he is to be canonised, that is, declared a saint in heaven! The Church of Rome has been a long time discovering the fact, if it be a fact! He was persistent in maintaining and spreading those opinions, which he, in his conscience, was bound to do; but this, and his refusal to submit himself to the laws of his country, amounted to treason; and in addition he incurred the penalty of præmunere, under an unrepealed law, when those who enacted this law were all members of the Roman Church. He knew the fate that awaited him, and the penalty he would have to pay. But as to More, we are constrained to view his punishment in another light. While in power he put in action with relentless fury the laws which enabled him to torture and burn those who did not receive an abstract doctrine as a point of faith, and those who *denied* the authority of a foreign Prince, which was called "heresy." The day of retribution came round, when he forfeited his own life for *maintaining* that same authority, which was declared to be "high treason." More may be accounted a martyr by some; but with him the honour was certainly shared by those he himself persecuted. He was himself a victim of retributive justice. More's case is the more conspicuous from his high position and brilliant accomplishments. But it must be remembered that these very qualities, and his position, would have rendered an evasion of the law in his favour more dangerous to the State. We lament the necessity which gave occasion for such violent measures, but the blame should primarily rest on him who sought to maintain a usurped power in this country, which, as we have seen, was so grossly abused.

The fate of Bishop Fisher naturally suggests a comparison with that of Cranmer. The circumstances are characteristic of the age they lived in. Henry and Fisher were

N

both zealous " defenders of the Faith " of the unreformed Church, but Fisher was " Roman " *first* and " Englishman " *after*. He set at defiance the laws of his country by denying Henry's right to rule over the Church in England, —according to the ancient law of the land. He would only acknowledge a foreign ruler ; he suffered, therefore, as a " traitor " to his country. Rightly or wrongly, it was the law of England. His death was neither degrading nor painful. Cranmer, on the other hand, was a true and loyal subject to his King and country. He refused to acknowledge the authority of a foreign Priestly despot, but following his conscientious convictions, in matters of religion, he was adjudged a *heretic, and to suffer death by fire*. His accusers could not put in force the cruel sentence, until they had received the confirmation and decree of the Pope, and on his mandate Cranmer suffered degradation and the torments of the stake ! Thus Henry was primarily responsible for the beheading of Fisher ; the Pope for the cruel tortures inflicted on Cranmer. Fisher was offered his pardon (and there can be no doubt it would have been confirmed) if he had consented to acknowledge the King's Supremacy in Church as well as State in his own country. Cranmer signed his recantation on the promise of liberty ; that promise was shamefully repudiated. Fisher is to be canonised as a saint in heaven for his alleged martyrdom, a traitor to his King and country, while Cranmer does not even receive a sign of commiseration.[1]

[1] See Appendix B.

CHAPTER X.

DURING the latter part of the reign of Henry, Cranmer retired from public life, occupying himself in literary pursuits, which marked the progress of his views tending to the ultimate development of Reformation principles. It was probably on account of these views becoming apparent that he became the victim of secret conspiracies to supplant him from his office and bring him into trouble.

So early as 1537, after the fall of Anne Boleyn, the Papal party became most active, and particularly in enforcing their ancient rites and customs. While these matters were under discussion by Convocation, the King communicated to them his determination that all things should be abolished that could not be supported by Scripture. Cranmer strongly supported this view, and urged the more general knowledge of the Scriptures. The result was, that in 1537 a series of doctrinal articles were sanctioned by the clergy and published with royal authority, in a work entitled " The Institution of the Christian Man," known also under the title of the " Bishop's Book." Though not wholly carrying out the ultimate views of the Reformers, it contained much of the doctrines laid down in the Confession of Augsburg and in the writings of Lutheran divines, particularly in their leading doctrine of Justification. This work still contained many errors imputed to the unreformed Church. On this book Strype observes :—

"We find many Popish errors here, mixed with evangelical truths; which must either be attributed to the defectiveness of our Prelates' knowledge as yet in true religion, or as being the principles and opinions of the King, or both. Let not any be offended herewith, but let him rather take notice what a great deal of gospel doctrine here came to light, and not only so, but was owned and propounded by authority, to be believed and practised. The sun of truth was now but rising, and breaking through the thick mists of that idolatry, superstition, and ignorance which had so long prevailed, and was not yet advanced to its meridian brightness."

The form of administration of the "Lord's Supper," called the "Mass," and the doctrines involved in that administration, were retained, which resulted in the persecution of Lambert and others.

In August of the same year, Cranmer witnessed the fulfilment of his longing desire, namely, the issue of a new and revised translation of the Bible in English, under his own patronage. Coverdale's version had been issued in October 1535, sanctioned by Royal authority. In 1536, an order was issued by Crumwell that the entire Bible in Latin and English should be provided for every church, and laid in the choir for the more easy perusal by the people. This translation was strongly opposed by Gardyner and the anti-reformation party, alleging as a reason that this translation contained many faults; but to the enquiry of the King whether it contained any heresies, Gardyner could give no satisfactory reply. "Then, in God's name (said the King), let it be issued among our people." Cranmer's joy was unbounded on the issue of the new translation, and for which the Royal authority was obtained. Every Curate was ordered to possess an English Bible, and every Abbey should have six. The copies set up in St Paul's and other churches brought together crowds eagerly listening to those who undertook to read aloud the sacred writings. Only fifteen hundred copies of this edition being printed the demand could not be supplied.   This was remedied by the issue in 1539 of another revised edition, going by the title of "Cranmer's Great Bible." Cranmer's Preface contained many excellent and practical suggestions.[1]   In proportion as the popularity of this edition increased, so was the opposition raised by the anti-reformers.   It is a re-markable fact, with reference to the issue of the Scriptures in our native tongue, that Tindal, the first translator, Rogers, the editor of the first edition, and Cranmer, the great patron and supporter of their work, forfeited their lives in the great cause they had at heart!

Cranmer soon became an object of the envy, jealousy, and malice of the opponents of progress, and numerous com-plaints were conveyed to King Henry; and Crumwell himself was getting out of favour with the King, in conse-quence of the part he took in the Anne of Cleves compli-cation.   He was also accused of heresy, treason, etc., being an active agent for progress and reform.   He was proceeded against on Bill of Attainder, on charges more or less true; he was forsaken by all his friends, except Cran-mer, but whose advocacy was of no avail.[2]   Crumwell was

[1] The six later issues of 1540 and 1541 all have Cranmer's Preface. Two of these, of November 1540 and November 1541, bear also on the title-page the names of Tunstall and of Heath, who are said to have "overseen and perused the Translation at the command of the King's Highness."

[2] There is only a portion of Cranmer's Letter to the King on this occasion preserved. The Letter proceeds thus :—"I heard yesterday in your Grace's Council that he (Crumwell) is a traitor, yet who cannot be sorrowful and amazed that he should be a traitor against your Majesty; he whose surety was only by your Majesty; he who loved your Majesty, as I ever thought, no less than God; he who always so set forward whatsoever was your Majesty's will and pleasure; he that cared for no man's displeasure to serve your Majesty; he that was such a servant in my judgment, in wisdom, diligence, faithfulness, and experience, as no prince in this realm ever had; he that was so vigilant to preserve your Majesty from all treasons, that few could be so secretly con-ceived, but he detected the same in the beginning? I loved him as my friend, for so I took him to be; but I chiefly loved him for the love which I thought I saw him bear ever towards your Grace singularly above all other. But now

beheaded 28th July 1540. He was a reformer, in one sense, of abuses, but whether actuated by Evangelical principles is doubtful. Bishop Fox had passed to another world, Latimer and Shaxton had been deprived of their Bishoprics, and imprisoned under the "Six Articles Act." Cranmer now stood alone. While Crumwell was in prison Cranmer was sought to be included in a Commission to revise the "Articles of Religion." He refused to assent to the proposed alterations, but he succeeded in obtaining a modification of the Penalties of the "Six Articles Act."

In 1540 we find Cranmer engaged in reforming the ecclesiastical foundation in Canterbury, and in establishing a Grammar School. The Commissioners sought to limit the entrance to this school to the sons of the gentry, but Cranmer insisted on the establishment being equally for the benefit of the poor, for whom he successfully pleaded.

The following is an extract from a speech delivered by Cranmer on the occasion, to the objection that—

"The children of husbandmen are meeter for the plough or to be artificers, than to occupy the place of the learned sort. Let none be put to school but gentlemen's sons."

To this Cranmer replied :—

"Poor men's children are many times endued with more singular gifts of nature, which are also the gifts of God ; they are often more diligent to apply their study than the gentleman's son, delicately educated. Is the ploughman's son, or the poor man's son, unworthy to receive the gifts of the Holy Ghost ? Are we to appoint them to be employed according to our fancy, not according to the gifts of Almighty God ? To shut the bountiful grace of the Holy Ghost in a corner, and attempt to build thereon our fancies, is to build the tower of Babel. None of us all here, but had our beginning from a low and base parentage. All gentlemen, for the most part, ascend to their estate through learning."

if he be a traitor, I am sorry that ever I loved him or trusted him, and I am very glad that his treason is discovered in time, but yet again I am very sorrowful ; for who shall your Grace trust hereafter if you might not trust him ?" &c.—Jenkyns' "Remains," Letter cclviii. vol. i. p. 298.

It had been answered that the most part of the nobility were made by feats of arms. "As though," replied the Primate, "the noble captain was always unfurnished of good learning ! If the gentleman's son be apt, let him be admitted : if not, let the poor man's child, that is apt, enter his room." Had Cranmer lived in these days he would have been a strong advocate for Board Schools.

Cranmer was now also actively engaged in causing various superstitious relics to be removed from churches in his Diocese ; and the suppression of superstitious customs, such as creeping to the cross, etc. ; and he succeeded in passing a law intended to check the luxurious life of some among the clergy. In 1541 he was engaged in correcting disorders which prevailed in All Souls' College, Oxford.

In 1542 the Romanising influence still predominated in Convocation. They objected to the English Version of the Bible, then in use, and sought to prevent its appearance in Churches, under the pretence of a desire of introducing an improved version. Gardyner was foremost in this scheme, suggesting that many words could not be properly rendered, and should therefore be left untranslated.[1] Cranmer, however, defeated this scheme, by obtaining the King's direction that the new version should be entrusted to the Universities. In addition, Cranmer now urged the revision of the "Service Book," and to divest images of saints of their ornaments. The invocation of saints had been already removed from the Litany. And he now urged the necessity of having the offices of devotion in the English language ; but in this he did not succeed until the year 1546, that book being known as "Henry VIII.'s Primer," which, although a great improve-

[1] This is one of the characteristics of the original translation, issued by the College at Rheims.

ment, still contained some addresses to the Virgin Mary. In 1544 Cranmer wrote to the King, proposing the introduction of congregational singing.

From the year 1543 onwards, the contest was still protracted, and the anti-reforming party so far succeeded in their views, that Tindal's version was prohibited, and other versions were only allowed to be read under certain restrictions. None were to read the Bible aloud, without licence from the King or the Ordinary. Noblemen and gentlemen might cause the Bible to be read to their families and servants, and householders might read it to themselves privately. But all women, except those of the families of the nobility and gentry, and all artificers, labourers, or servants, with all persons of the lower class, were strictly *prohibited* from perusing the Scriptures. This prohibition continued until the end of Henry's reign. This led to the publication by the anti-reforming party of an amended Exposition of Faith, containing more advanced Romish doctrines than "The Bishop's Book," entitled "A necessary Doctrine of Erudition for any Christian Man." Gardyner, commending this book on its adoption, wrote that "the King's majesty hath, by the inspiration of the Holy Ghost, composed all matters of religion;" while Cranmer, on the other hand, wrote annotations upon the "Necessary Doctrine," refuting some of the errors according to his views, and setting out the truth as he then conceived it. Thus it appears that the battle of the Reformation was now well begun.

Cranmer's proceedings in all these matters gave dire offence to the Papal party, and Gardyner was the leading spirit to create strife and foster conspiracies against the Archbishop, who now found himself in a sea of troubles. The clergy at Canterbury were instigated to sow seeds of dissension. Three men were burnt alive at Windsor for alleged heresy. A scheme was set on foot to implicate the leading reforming persons of rank, even including the Queen, Catherine Parr, who was a supporter of the Reformation, but Gardyner's emissary was waylaid, his compromising documents seized, and the scheme failed. Cranmer was now sought to be impeached; the Articles and Depositions were presented to the King. These papers the King placed in the hands of Cranmer himself, which took the Bishop by surprise, and he thereupon requested the King to appoint a Commission to investigate the charges. The King was so confident in the innocence of Cranmer, that, in complying with this request, he nominated Cranmer himself for one, and overruled his objections, observing that, if there was any truth in the charges, he would be honest enough to acknowledge them. Dr Leigh and Dr Rowland Taylor were sent for, who examined into the question, and Gardyner's further plot was exposed. Two others, Dr Thornton and Dr Barber (already mentioned), both of whom had received favours at the hands of Cranmer, were discovered to be implicated in this scheme. On Cranmer reproaching them for their baseness, they fell on their knees to ask his pardon. Acting in his usual spirit of clemency, Cranmer forgave them.[1]

This scheme being frustrated, another was set on foot, undertaken by the zealous Romanist, John Gostwick, a Member of Parliament, who charged Cranmer in "The House" with preaching heresy in his sermons. The King was so incensed at this fresh attack on Cranmer, that he

---

[1] "It illustrates a favourable trait in the Archbishop's character that he forgave all the conspirators, though he might doubtless have secured their punishment through his influence with the King. He was, as his Secretary, Morice, testifies, 'a man that delighted not in revenge.'"—"Encycl. Brit.," 9th Edit. "Cranmer."

compelled Gostwick to sue for pardon, and to acknowledge his fault to Cranmer.

Another remarkable instance of Henry's kindly inter-ference on behalf of Cranmer is thus recorded by a late biographer. The Romanists in the Privy Council besought the King to give them leave to examine the charges against Cranmer, and to commit him to the Tower if they found occasion, assuring the King if that were done many would come forward against him with just accusations who were now afraid to do so. Henry discerned their purpose, but consented that Cranmer should be called before the Council on the day following, and gave them leave to commit him to the Tower if they saw sufficient cause.

At midnight the King sent for the Archbishop to tell him what had passed. He thanked his Majesty for the previous notice, and expressed his willingness to be con-mitted to the Tower, if he might afterwards be fairly heard. Henry stood amazed at his simplicity, and told him that, when once in prison, three or four false knaves would easily be found to witness against him. Henry then directed Cranmer to request the Council to confront his accusers with him, and, if they refused to do this, he was to produce a ring, which the King then gave him, by which they would know that the affair was revoked from them for the Royal determination.

The following morning, Cranmer was summoned to at-tend the Council at eight o'clock, but was kept waiting in the ante-room among the attendants nearly an hour. Dr Butts, the King's physician, informed Henry of this new promotion of the Archbishop to be a serving-man. " It is well enough," replied Henry, " I shall talk with them by-and-by." At length Cranmer was admitted. The Councillors told him that a complaint was made, that he, and others by his permission, had infected the realm with heresy, and therefore it was the King's pleasure that he should be committed to the Tower for trial. Cranmer reasoned with them, and urged that his accusers might be brought forward ; but, finding this was refused, he produced the King's ring. At the sight of it, they rose and went to the King, fearful of the consequences of their conduct. Henry gave them that reception which he was accustomed to give to those with whom he was seriously displeased ; saying, he perceived well how the world went among them, and commanded them to lay aside their malice towards the Primate. This was the last attempt against Cranmer while Henry lived. The King possessed much discernment. Referring to a change in Cranmer's armorial bearings, from three cranes to three pelicans, he told him to be ready, like the pelican, to shed his blood for his spiritual children who were brought up in the faith of Christ, adding, " You are likely to be tasted at length if you persist in your tackling."

There is yet another plot against Cranmer to be noticed. Sir Thomas Seymour spoke against him to the King, accusing him of niggardly conduct, and a design to amass wealth for his children by adopting a penurious and improper style of living.[1] Henry took no notice of this complaint till some days after, when he sent Sir Thomas to Lambeth with a message, at the Archbishop's dinner hour. Seymour now found how widely different the case in reality was from what he had stated, and saw that ample provision was made for the household and for visitors, as well as a liberal supply for the poor, while all was conducted with propriety. On his return Henry sternly in-

---

[1] According to a letter Cranmer wrote on this subject, he stated that in consequence of the large expenditure he was obliged to make by virtue of his office, and paying for everything double their price, he was, in fact, better off when he was a student at Cambridge.

quired, " Dined you not with my Lord ? " Seymour perceived the King's meaning, and, kneeling down, entreated
pardon for having made a false report.   The King rebuked
him severely, saying, that he saw through their devices,
and knew that their desire was to be allowed to participate
in the Bishop's lands, as they had done in the estates of
the monasteries ; but in this they should be disappointed,
and as for Cranmer, he well knew that the Archbishop injured himself by his liberality and hospitality.   Besides
keeping a proper order in his household, suited to his station, Cranmer always had several strangers staying with
him, particularly foreigners distinguished for their learning ;
among these were Martin Bucer, Paulus Fergius, Peter
Martyr, and Bernardine Ochinus ; being desirous, by his
intercourse with them, to promote their spiritual welfare,
and also to forward the great work of the Reformation.

. Thus Cranmer retained the confidence and affection of
Henry until the King's death.   On his death-bed the King
sent for the Archbishop, who ministered to him in his last
moments.   His last act was to press the hand of his
faithful servant.

Henry died a confirmed believer in every doctrine of
the Roman Church as then accepted as such.

Henry VIII. died 28th January 1547, and was succeeded
by his son EDWARD, then ten years old, under a Protec-
torate.   At the funeral of the deceased Monarch the leading part was taken by Gardyner, Bishop of Winchester.
He headed the Bishops and Priests, who prayed and
chanted round the royal hearse in the chapel of the Palace
at Windsor.   He, as Prelate of the Garter, received the
car-borne corpse.   On the day of the interment he stood at
the high altar, and was the chief celebrant of the Mass,

while Cranmer sat with the rest of the Bishops on the Bench.[1]

On EDWARD being proclaimed King, the Archbishop was placed at the head of the Regency, acting with sixteen others, under the will of Henry. On Somerset was conferred the title and power of Lord Protector, now Earl of Hereford. Cranmer's first step was to recognise his dependence on the authority of the Crown, by taking out a licence from the King for the discharge of his duties as Metropolitan, and he required all his suffragans to do the same.

Cranmer was no great politician. His energies were directed to the carrying out the Reformation, which only required opportunity for developing. This, to a great extent, he effected, despite the many opposing elements, and the stormy conflict of parties, each seeking to promote individual interests. Gardyner was one of the greatest opponents in endeavouring to thwart Cranmer in his reforming progress.

Leaving the political events of this short but eventful reign, we have only to consider the progress of the Reformation under the guidance of the Archbishop. On his advice a Royal Commission was formed, with power to visit the entire Church throughout the country, which, for this purpose, was divided into six districts. The Commissioners were to report the state of religion, and to carry into effect the enactments of Parliament for the Reformation then fairly set on foot. The articles and injunctions for these visitors (who were accompanied by selected preachers of ability) show the wisdom and care of those entrusted to carry out this important work. The result

[1] Dixon's " History of the Church," ii. 42. Edit. 1881.

exhibited the miserable state of corruption and superstition that prevailed throughout the country. The clergy were in a sad state of ignorance, utterly incapable of instructing the people by sermons. To remedy this, Cranmer devised the plan of preparing a series of "Homilies" to be read from the pulpits. He showed the example by himself preparing the Homily on "Salvation." A glorious work. When we now peruse these magnificent compositions, we cannot but express our surprise that the compilers, at this early stage of the Reformation, had such clear and decided views on the various innovations in doctrines and practices, the accumulations of some centuries. Gardyner's concurrence in this work was requested, but he gave it his most strenuous opposition, declaring that no innovation in religious matters should be made during the King's minority. By reason of Gardyner's obtrusive conduct in opposing the Reformation, he was confined in the Tower as a state prisoner during the King's reign. Poynet was appointed Bishop of Winchester in his place; a more disreputable appointment could not have been made. Bonner was also committed to the Tower; he, however, recanted and was released from prison. He was subsequently deprived of his See, and in his place Ridley was, by translation, appointed Bishop of London.

We have here again to note the partial manner in which Dr Lingard, in an offhand manner, refers to Gardyner's imprisonment. He demanded a legal trial, whereupon the Council appointed a Commission to take his examination. This Commission consisted of the Primate, the Bishops of London, Ely, and Lincoln, Sir William Petre, Judge Hales, and two Masters in Chancery. The proceedings occupied twenty-two Sessions, from 15th December 1550 to 14th February 1551, when the Commission—not simply Cranmer, as often stated—pronounced him contumacious, and his Bishopric void.   On this Dr Lingard observes :— " *Cranmer* cut short the proceedings, and pronounced Gardyner contumacious." [1] He makes no allusion to the numerous Sessions, and his observations would lead us to suppose that, by Cranmer's arbitrary interference, Gardyner had not a fair hearing.   No opportunity seems to be lost in order to make Cranmer *personally* responsible for acts done in conjunction with others, who appear to escape obloquy.   Had the case been reversed, under Papal rule such a contumacious *heretic* would have been consigned to the flames.   Gardyner and Bonner, however, afterwards had a full opportunity of avenging themselves in the fires of Smithfield, in the reign of Mary, and on Cranmer personally.   The apologists of Mary exculpate her of these crimes.   She must, therefore, have acted under the guidance of these two leading ecclesiastics, staunch adherents of Papal dogmas.

Through Cranmer's influence the " Six Articles Act " was repealed.   He also obtained from Convocation, though not without some opposition, a vote that all such customs theretofore had or used, which forbade marriage of the clergy, should be utterly void and of none effect.   A majority of forty-three voted in the affirmative, thirty-two against.   Many of this minority " entered into the Holy State of matrimony when the marriage of Priests became legal."   " Their concubines, probably, insisted on marriage when marriage was allowable." [2]   An Act was introduced into Parliament ultimately declaring the legality of such marriages.   On this the Archbishop

---

[1] " History of England," vol. vii. p. 87.

[2] Strype, 156 ; Wilkins, iv. 16 ; Collier, n. 226, quoted by Dean Hooke.

sent for his wife, and he and his children[1] were again permitted the holy privilege of man bestowed by God in Paradise.

"The controversies of the day hinged on the doctrine of the Eucharist." From a mere commemoration, as originally practised by the early Christians, "the Lord's Supper" was in course of time converted into a *sacrifice*, on the assumption that on the consecration of the elements of bread and wine they were converted respectively into the *substance* of the same body of Christ (including His blood), *soul and divinity*, as was crucified, and for the denial of this alleged conversion many were brought to the stake as heretics.   Before a change was made in the service, certain queries were prepared and addressed to the Bishops on the subject, which were discussed in Convocation on 20th November 1547 by the Lower House, and on the same day a proclamation was issued that the Sacrament was to be received in both kinds,[2] which was ratified by Parliament, and the Mass Service was abolished, with its alleged propitiatory character, and for which our simple and beautiful Communion Service was eventually substituted.

The dogma of Transubstantiation, the actual substantial change of the consecrated bread and wine into the very body, blood, bones, nerves, soul, and divinity of the Lord Jesus Christ, at the bidding of a Priest, was the great theological question of the day strenuously opposed by the Reformers.

---

[1] Cranmer's family consisted of two daughters—Ann, who died in her father's lifetime, and Margaret, who survived him ; and a son, whom he named after himself, Thomas.

[2] It is a fact worth recording, that at the Council of Claremont, held November 1095 A.D., under Pope Urban II., assisted by thirteen Archbishops, two hundred and fifty Bishops and Abbots, by the 28th canon, it was directed that all who communicated should receive the body and blood of Christ under both kinds, unless there be necessity to the contrary.—Labb et Coss., "Concil. Gen.," tom. x. col. 506. Paris, 1671.

It was one not of an empty speculation, it involved the personal safety of every individual in the realm.   To question the theory was a cruel death.   And it cannot be too deeply impressed on the reader that it was in fact for the refusal to accept this theological enigma that so many poor wretches were brought to the stake and burned alive.

Cranmer appears to have been awakened to a new light on the subject by Dr Ridley's persuasion, and by reading the Treatise of Rabanus Maurus, a writer of the ninth century, who powerfully combatted and exposed the theory of a substantial change in the elements, when, for the first time, it was seriously advanced.   Cranmer does not seem to have grasped the entire truth at once, which passed through him by a filtering process.[1]   Cranmer eventually published a discourse on the Sacrament, " a work abounding with irresistible argumentation, as well as impressive eloquence, with sincere piety and profound learning."

Bishop Gardyner, while a prisoner in the Tower, attacked Cranmer's discourse on the Sacrament almost immediately after its publication; which attack, according to Strype, was printed in France under the title "An explication and assertion of the true Catholic Faith touching the most Blessed Sacrament of the Altar, with confutation of a

---

[1] Fox, in his "Acts and Monuments," says :—

"During the time of King Henry VIII., until the entering of King Edward, it seemeth that Cranmer was scarcely yet thoroughly persuaded in the right knowledge of the Sacrament, or at least was not yet fully ripened in the same, wherein shortly after, being more groundedly confirmed by conference with Bishop Ridley, in process of time did so profit in riper knowledge that at last he took upon himself the defence of that whole doctrine, that is, to refute and throw down, first, the corporeal presence; secondly, the fantastical Transubstantiation; thirdly, the idolatrous adoration; fourthly, the false error of the Papists, that wicked men do eat the natural body of Christ; and lastly, the blasphemous Sacrifice of the Mass.   Whereupon, in conclusion, he wrote five books for the public instruction of the Church of England; which instruction yet to this day standeth, and is received in this Church of England."

book written against the same, 1551," but under an assumed name. There was another reply written by Dr Smith, then of Louvain, a miserable renegade who changed his religion three or four times as it suited his purpose. They both charged Cranmer with inconsistency by reminding him that he had been a " Papist, then a Lutheran, and lastly a Zuinglian " in his Sacramental profession.

The Archbishop was not long in replying to these two attacks, confronting as well the " crafty and sophistical cavillation of Gardyner, and such assertions in Smith's ' Puny Book ' as seemed anything worth the answering." This answer was first printed in 1551,—again in 1552, and was again reprinted in 1580, such was the popularity of the work, and the interest created. In his reply to Dr Smith, Cranmer thus wrote :—

" This I confess of myself, that not long before I wrote the said catechism, I was in that error of the real presence, as I was many years past in divers other errors, as of transubstantiation, of the sacrifice propitiatory of the priests in the mass, of pilgrimages, purgatory, pardons, and many other superstitions and errors that came from Rome, being brought up from youth in them, and housled therein for lack of good instruction from my youth, the outrageous floods of papistical errors at that time overflowing the world. For the which, and other mine offences in youth, I do daily pray unto God for mercy and pardon, saying, Good Lord, remember not mine ignorances and offences of my youth.

" But after it had pleased God to show unto me by His holy word a more perfect knowledge of his Son Jesus Christ, from time to time, as I grew in knowledge of him, by little and little, I put away my former ignorance. And as God of his mercy gave me light, so through his grace I opened mine eyes to receive it, and did not wilfully repugn unto God and remain in darkness. And I trust in God's mercy and pardon for my former errors, because I erred but of frailness and ignorance. And now I may say of myself as St. Paul said, When I was like a babe or child in the knowledge of Christ, I spake like a child, and understood like a child, but now that I am come to man's estate, and growing in Christ through his grace and mercy, I have put away that childishness."[1]

[1] Cranmer's " Remains," by Jenkyns, vol. iii. pp. 13, 14.

In reply to Gardyner, he said :—

" It is lawful and commendable for a man to learn and embrace the truth. As for me, I am not, I grant, of that nature that the Papists for most part be who study to devise all shameful shifts, rather than they will forsake any error, wherewith they were infected in their youth."

Cranmer's theory was summed up in the work in question with the following passage :—

" As our regeneration in Christ by Baptism is *spiritual*, even so our eating and drinking is a *spiritual* feeding, which kind of regeneration and feeding requireth no *real* and *corporeal* presence of Christ, but only his presence in spirit, in grace, and effectual operation."

And again as to the alleged change of *substance*, he thus expressed himself :—

" The *substance* of the bread and wine, as they affirm, be clean gone. And so there remaineth whiteness, but nothing is white; there remaineth colours, but nothing is coloured therewith ; there remaineth roundness, but nothing is round ; and there is bigness, but nothing is big ; there is sweetness, without any sweet thing ; breaking, without anything broken ; division, without anything being divided ; and so, other qualities and quantities without anything to receive them. *And this doctrine they teach us as a necessary article of faith.*" [1]

Cranmer might have added, " on pain of being burnt alive."

The rejection of the dogma of Transubstantiation, and adoration of the Host, naturally carried away with it the alleged propitiatory character of the Mass and Masses for the dead. The new service-book was brought into public use in the fall of the year 1548. It was grounded upon the Liturgies of the primitive church, omitting most of the Romish additions, adopting the phraseology of the Scriptures.

The order abolishing all Romish books of devotion, and for the punishment of those who interfered in the full use of the " Service-Book " was signed by Cranmer, Chancellor

[1] See " Remains," Jenkyns, vol. ii. pp. 309-404. Oxford, 1832.

Lord Rich, and by four others of the Council, and which Ordinance was confirmed by Act of Parliament (3 and 4 Ed. IV. cap. x.).

The King's "Primer" of 1545 was not suppressed, except that the passages relating to the invocation of saints were directed to be blotted out. The same Act directed the abolition of all images in churches except those that formed parts of tombs or monuments. The new formulary of Ordination expunged the five inferior orders of the ministry, Readers, Subdeacons, Exorcists, Acolyths, and Door-keepers. In addition, the Ordinance abolished, among other ceremonies, gestures, rites, &c., the use of gloves and sandals, of mitre, ring, and crozier, anointing with chrism, and substituted the old form "Receive ye the Holy Ghost, &c.," in the act of Ordination of Priests, in the place of pre-senting the Cup and Paten.[1]   Such, then, are some of the sweeping reforms in the Church effected under the super-vision and direction of Cranmer. The several changes came into operation 1st April 1646.

In 1550 Hooper was appointed Bishop of Gloucester, when an altercation took place as to the adoption of the re-cognised "priestly vestments." Hooper opposed the use of all such vestments, being more in advance than Cranmer. At Cranmer's door is laid the charge of having caused the imprisonment of Hooper for his resistance to the law in this respect. To this Strype, ever ready to excuse Cran-mer, says :—

"Neither was Cranmer any other ways instrumental to Hooper's imprisonment, than by doing that which was expected from him, namely, giving a true account of his unsuccessful dealing with him."

[1] This latter custom was established by the Council of Florence, 1439, when the old form of consecration by laying on of hands was abandoned, and this altered form is now in use at the present day in the Romish Church. The re-introduction of the old *form* of laying on of hands in ordination in the Church of England was not added until the year 1646.

It was in this year that Cranmer published his great
work, entitled "Defence of the true Catholic Doctrine of
the Sacrament of the body and blood of our Saviour
Christ," before alluded to, and which evoked the attacks
of Gardyner and Smith. This work had a great influence
in converting many to reformed views concerning the
Sacrament.

A separate chapter is dedicated to the writings of Cranmer; it is therefore only necessary here to mention the
part he took in forwarding the Reformation.

In 1552 the Articles of Religion were now published by
authority. Cranmer subsequently admitted, when examined before the Commissioners, that he was the author
of them. They did not essentially differ from the XXXIX.
Articles as now accepted. Cranmer's Articles were principally compiled from the Augsburg Confession of Faith,
and particularly that prepared in 1551 by the Protestants,
to be laid before the Council of Trent. The first, second,
and twenty-third, and parts of the twenty-fifth, twenty-
sixth, and thirty-fourth, are certainly taken from that
source.

During Edward's reign, under the influence of Cranmer,
the total removal of images from Churches took place
under the order of the Courts of Law in 1548; in the
same year the reformed Prayer Book was sanctioned by
"Act of Uniformity"; the elevation of the consecrated
elements, and their worship, were forbidden; and for stone
altars were substituted tables.

In April 1552, sanctioned by the Act of Uniformity,
changes were made in the Service. The following were
the omissions directed to be made:—Introits; the expression commonly called "The Mass"; the word "Altar";
the mixing of water with wine; the invocation of the Holy

Ghost on the elements; the sign of the cross on the consecration of the elements; the "Agnus Dei" sung during
Communion; the allusion to the angels as bearing up our
prayers to the heavenly tribunal; prayer for the departed
in the prayer for the whole Church, and in the burial
service; the option as to auricular confession; the reservation of the consecrated elements for the sick; the rubric
as to the use of vestments, cope, albe, etc.; the benedic-
tion of water in the baptismal service; chrism, or anointing in baptisms, and the visitation of the sick; chrism, or
the white robe in baptism; the Holy Communion at
funerals.

The following *additions* were made :—

"The sentences, exhortation, confession, and absolution
at the beginning of Morning and Evening Prayer; a
rubric allowing the communion table to stand in the body
of the church; the commandments and responses in the
Communion Service; a new exhortation to the negligent
in the Communion Service, by Peter Martyr; the words
'*militant here on earth*' in the title of the prayer for 'the
whole state of Christ's Church'; the declaration against
corporeal presence, appended by order of Council to
Communion Service."

The following *changes* were also made :—

"The Service appointed to be said where the people
could best hear; common bread in the Holy Communion
instead of wafer bread; the words that 'we receive these
thy creatures of bread and wine, may be partakers of his
most blessed body and blood,' instead of that 'they may
be unto us the body and blood of thy most dearly beloved
Son, Jesus Christ.'"[1]

[1] See Dr Blakeney's "Handbook on the Liturgy of the Church of
England," pp. 29, 30. London, 1884.

Such, then, were the principal alterations under the judicious guidance of Cranmer. Further alterations were made under Elizabeth, purging the Service from the last relics of Romanism.

That there could be nothing offensive or heterodox in even the subsequently revised Service, or that thereby the Church of England apostatised from the Christian faith, or could be adjudged heretical, we have the testimony of the Pope himself, who offered to legalise the reformed Liturgy of Elizabeth if she would accept it at his hands. Lord Coke, in his charge at the Norwich Assizes, 4th August 1606, stated that he had often heard from Queen Elizabeth that Pius IV. had offered to accept the Book of Common Prayer; and that he had also frequently conferred with noblemen of the highest rank in the State who had seen and read the Pope's letter to that effect.

But further than this. The Reformation itself, so nobly begun by Edward and completed by Elizabeth, also practically received the sanction of the Pope—on terms, however, which Elizabeth refused to accept. Pope Paul, finding that Elizabeth was firm and determined to hold her own against his usurpation, offered to her to let things remain as they were, provided she would acknowledge his Primacy, and accept the Reformation from him.[1]

His successor, Pius IV., proffered the same conditions to the Queen by letter, written 5th May 1560, wherein he offered to comply with all her requests to the utmost of his power, provided she would allow of his Primacy.[2] He addressed the Queen as " our most dear Daughter in Christ,

[1] See Sir Roger Twysden s "Vindication of the Church of England," p. 148, London, 1657, and Cambridge, 1847, p. 177.

[2] The Latin letter is included in Dr Cardwell's documentary " Annals of the Reformed Church of England," Oxford, 1839, vol. i. p. 233; and see Sir Roger Twysden, as above.

Elizabeth, Queen of England," expressing his great desire
" to take care of her salvation, and to provide as well for
her honour as the establishment of her kingdom." These
"velvet paws" had, however, "claws," which soon made
their appearance. For not complying with the Pope's
modest request, he solemnly damned Elizabeth, his "dear
Daughter in Christ," to all eternity with bell, book, and
candle; much in the same terms as contained in the Bull
anathematising her father.

Under the above circumstances, it does appear rather
hard and contradictory that Cranmer should have been
charged with the crime of heresy, and burnt alive,—the same
sentence the Pope passed on Elizabeth, but as he could
not execute it in this world, he relegated that process to
the next !

The latter part of the reign of Edward was signalised
by political intrigues, resulting in the execution of
Somerset, and the ambitious claims put forward by Northumberland on behalf of Lady Jane Grey. Whether
Somerset deserved his sad fall and fate are matters for
history. Cranmer was foremost in the defence of Somerset.
His letter to the Nobles engaged in the proceedings against
the Protector induced them for a time to falter in their
determination. At the same time, he did not hesitate to
remonstrate with Northumberland on the vices and pro-
fanity of his supporters. But we have yet to learn why
Cranmer should be made responsible for the acts of
Somerset or Northumberland.

With reference to Lady Dudley, more commonly known
as Lady Jane Grey, when the legal instruments for settling the crown upon this unfortunate Lady were completed,
Cranmer, as one of the Council, was called upon to sign it.

He at first refused to do so, alleging his oath to the King ; he, however, ultimately consented on the urgent request of Edward, then almost dying, backed by the assurance of the highest legal authorities of the land.   He was the last to put his signature to it, and after the cautious Cecil had himself signed.   The document, altering the succession of the crown in favour of Jane Grey, is dated 21st June 1553. It is the part Cranmer took in signing this document that formed one of the subsequent charges against him of " high treason," and, by his modern assailants, of perjury.

During Edward's reign a new code was being prepared but never completed, entitled " Reformatio Legum Ecclesiasticarum."   On the preparation of this code, Cranmer, as President of the Commission, was assisted by Prelates, divines, and lawyers, in all numbering thirty-two.   Among these we find Thomas Goodrich, Bishop of Ely ; Richard Cox, Almoner of the King ; William May ; Rowland Taylor of Hadleigh ; John Lucas ; Richard Goodrich, and Peter Martyr.   Had it passed into law, it would have been so far an improvement on the Papal system, that the punishment of death was not awarded for heresy ; but they appear, unhappily, to have incorporated in their proposed system the provisions of the Act of Parliament passed in essentially " Popish " times, that death should be awarded to those who " denied the fundamental doctrines of Christianity, the Catholic faith, the doctrine of the blessed Trinity." And in this we perceive the old leaven of hereditary persecuting spirit still operating.   Members of the unreformed Church should, of all persons, be the last to condemn this suggested code on the ground of its severity.

On this document, Dr Lingard, in relating the persecutions under Mary, observes :—

" Fortunately for the professors of the ancient faith, Edward died before the code of ecclesiastical laws, *supplied by Cranmer*, had obtained the sanction of the Legislature : by the accession of Mary. The power of the sword passed from the hands of one religious party to those of the other; and within a short time Cranmer and his associates perished in the flames which they had prepared to kindle for their opponents." [1]

Independent of the gross misrepresentation conveyed by the above extracts, that Romanists would have been *burnt* as *heretics* had the law come into force, Cranmer and his associates are to be condemned for a *supposed intention* which might never have been sanctioned by Parliament, and certainly was not included in the proposed code of laws, and we are to acquit Romanists for the real act, to whom "the power of the sword" had been claimed to be transferred, as if they have not all along wielded that sword with fearful cruelty on alleged heretics. It was no doubt Dr Lingard's hope to persuade his readers, that persecutors were equally busy on both sides, and that Cranmer and his associates led the way to the atrocities of Mary or that of her agents.   Mr Charles Butler charitably adds, "Mary did no more than execute against Cranmer and his associates the punishments to which he had wished Mary and her associates to be exposed to their projected persecutions." Mary's tools wanted no example to be set before them, they had ample precedent and authority, without seeking shelter under the wings of the Reformers. They acted on an hereditary prescription of six hundred years ; and, judging from the condemnation of Cranmer, by his late biographers, for even mentioning in a letter to a friend, as the news of the day, in an offhand manner (as we have seen), the condemnation of Fryth to the flames, as exhibiting in Cranmer a frightful depravity, they appear jealous that any one else, out of their own communion

---

[1] " History of England," vol. vii. p. 258.

should indulge in the questionable luxury of roasting a few heretics. Cranmer is justly condemned for this exhibition of levity, in so important a transaction as burning a heretic, but they have not one tear to shed, or one sympathising regret for the cruel fate of Cranmer, when, even after he had been betrayed by promises of pardon into recantations of his alleged heresy, he was notwithstanding burnt alive. No! Cranmer, they tell us, only suffered by the same fires he would have himself kindled. Such is the force of religious prejudice.

During Edward's reign "plundering" of monastic properties was continued with greater recklessness than in the preceding reign; the parties of the court dividing the spoils. Cranmer and the leading Reformers protested against the work of destruction. The Primate expressed his anxiety that the revenues thus derived should be dedicated to the advancement of learning and religion.[1] In fact Cranmer actually surrendered to the King, under the Act of Parliament, "twelve good manors of the See of Canterbury;" and he conveyed to him the parks and splendid residences of the Archbishop at Oxford, at Knowles and at Mayfield.

The vandalism of the times cannot be justified on any grounds, except on the excuse that they followed the example of their predecessors. Martin Bucer, in a letter to the Marquis of Dorset, exclaimed :—

"It has been well said that no one ever grew rich by pillage of private or public property. What sense of God can that man have who hopes that permanent wealth can be built up by the hands of sacrilege? If the drones must be driven out of the hive, why should wasps and hornets be let in, to gorge themselves on its stores?"[2]

[1] See p. 291 of the 4th vol. of his "Remains," Jenkyns' Edition, Oxford, 1833, and note b, and his letter addressed to Crumwell, dated 29 Nov. 1539.
[2] Quoted by Le Bas. "Life of Cranmer," vol. ii. p. 261. 1833.

Latimer also raised his voice against the sacrileges ; in the presence of the King he is reported to have said :

"Thus much I say unto you Magistrates—if ye will not maintain schools and universities, ye shall have a brutality."

Such was their barbarity, that valuable books were destroyed, which "were guilty of no other superstition but red letters on their fronts or titles." These proceedings form the blackest page in the history of early (so-called) Reformers, and the subsequent "white-washing" by the Absolution of the Pope in confirming the titles of the plunderers, is but a sorry justification. The clerical Leaders of the Reformation strongly inveighed against these outrages.

It is true that these marauders had the example before them of their unreformed predecessors of the previous reign, both in England and Ireland, and that they were actuated by a violent reaction consequent on the exposure of the frauds and vices of the inmates of the various ecclesiastical establishments ; but that would not justify vandalism. If the vandalism of some of these so-called Reformers exemplified their enthusiasm for their newly acquired religion, their conduct will bear favourable comparison with the unreformed, who considered that they were doing God service in torturing, burning, and otherwise extirpating those who happened to differ from them on questions of abstract dogmas, miscalled religion.[1]

Edward died 6th July 1553. With the death of Edward Cranmer's public career was suddenly brought to a close, and his further schemes of reform arrested. While the

---

[1] The Rev. R. W. Dixon, in his " History of the Church of England," vol. ii. p. 71 *et seq.*, 1881, sets forth the vandalism of the unreformed under Henry VIII. in the destruction of all the shrines, monuments, and painted windows relating to Thomas à Becket ; and on p. 206 their general vandalism on edifices, books, MSS. &c.

majority of Edward's Bishops and Clergy recanted and again accepted the Pope's spiritual jurisdiction, Cranmer, Ridley, Latimer, and Hooper consistently refused. True, the progress of the Reformation had been abruptly checked, but the seeds had been sown. Henry had weeded the garden, Edward sowed the seed, Mary harrowed the ground and fertilised it with the blood of martyrs, and Elizabeth reaped a glorious harvest! "Under which we have enjoyed more liberty, we have acquired more glory, we possess more character and power, than hitherto has befallen the lot of any other country on the globe."[1]

P.S.—There is a remarkable confirmation of the observation made by Cranmer (*ante*, p. 211, first paragraph), in our own times, found in the March number, 1857, of the Roman Catholic Monthly, *The Rambler*, under the title of "Literary Cookery." The main object of the Article appears to be to lecture Roman Catholic controversialists on the necessity of cultivating the virtues of openness and truth-telling, acknowledging that they are at present too liable to the charge of "shirking of difficulties, cooking of figures, cobbling history, philosophy, and science," to meet their purpose. *The Rambler* then makes the following startling acknowledgment :—" See how unfair we Roman Catholic writers often are—how we keep back the strong points of our opponents, and put forward, in our own behalf, arguments which will not bear to be carefully examined ; how we think ourselves bound to show that there is not a jot or scrap of truth in any of the enemies of the Catholics ; that all who oppose us, or contend with us, are both morally reprobate and intellectually impotent." Coming from a *Roman Catholic Periodical*, this I consider a remarkable confirmation of Cranmer's charge against Romanists of his day, which is not the less true now than at that time. This I have conclusively proved in my "Reply" (Shaw & Co., London, 1887) to "Catholic Belief," a recent work in its sixth edition, confidently recommended by Cardinal Manning.

[1] Speech of Sir Robert Peel in the House of Commons, 9th May 1817.

CHAPTER XI.

CRANMER'S FALL AND MARTYRDOM.

IT is not my intention to dwell on the harrowing scenes which took place during the short reign of Queen Mary. She was a devout "Papist," and, no doubt, acted under the firm conviction that she was doing God's service. She and her advisers were faithfully and zealously carrying out the Papal system of enforcing their religious belief, in accordance with the recognised principles of the unreformed Church. Whether the Queen was personally responsible, or her Bishops, for the burnings of so-called "heretics," the adherents of the Roman Church do not seem to be agreed. An anxious desire is exhibited to shield the Queen ; while Charles Butler, Esq.,[1] says :—

"There appears to be reason to think that Mary's Bishops in general did not promote the persecutions. Little blame seems imputable to Cardinal Pole, or Bishop Tunstal ; more is chargeable to Gardyner ; the greatest part of the odium fell on Bonner. Dr Lingard suggests some observations which, he thinks, render it very probable that neither Bishops Gardyner nor Bonner were quite so guilty as they have been represented."

That the burnings took place under Papal rule is admitted. Who, then, was responsible ? Mary strictly conformed to the spirit of the times. We have only to deal with the cruel fate of Cranmer. There can be no doubt that for this the Pope of Rome was ultimately. responsible. Cranmer was tried by a Papal Commission, and was excommunicated by a Papal Consistory. The

[1] "Book of the Roman Catholic Church," p. 207. London, 1825.

Papal Commission deprived the Primate of his office as Archbishop, and the Pope confirmed the sentence of death.

Cranmer, we have seen, signed the instrument settling the succession on Lady Dudley—(Lady Jane Grey.)[1] It does not appear that Cranmer took any part in placing her on the throne. Her triumph was but of short duration. Cranmer, Lady Jane, her husband, and two of the other sons of the Duke of Northumberland, were tried on the 13th November 1553, at the Guild Hall, and found guilty of high treason, which judgment was confirmed by Act of Parliament. Why Cecil and the others who signed the same document, were not likewise prosecuted, does not appear. Sir John Cheke obtained the Queen's pardon. Lady Jane Grey paid the penalty by death on the block, as a traitor, without any mercy being shewn to her. Queen Elizabeth has been branded as a cruel tyrant for having consented, after a long delay, to the execution of Mary, Queen of Scots, who had notoriously fostered dangerous rebellions ; she had even assumed the royal arms of England. With these facts clearly established, Elizabeth has been the subject of bitter attacks, while the execution of this unfortunate lady is scarcely censured.

With regard to the Document of Succession, we find a long letter, written by Cranmer, while in prison, to the Queen, endeavouring to exculpate himself from the charge of *treason*, on the ground principally that he signed it after protesting against the Act, that he signed it with great reluctance, and on the urgent importunity of the Council and of Edward himself. He implored the Queen to

---

[1] Lady Jane Grey was daughter of the Duke of Suffolk, and grand-daughter of Mary, the sister of Henry VIII. She married Lord Guildford Dudley, the fourth son of the Duke of Northumberland. Presuming Mary and Elizabeth were illegitimate, Lady Dudley would have been next in right of succession to the throne of England.

pardon him for this act of treason, which he stated only carried out "the sentence of the judges, and other his learned council in the laws of this realm."[1]   His pleading was of no avail, but he was reserved for a more serious charge—in the estimation of the Roman Church—that of heresy.   Cranmer, it must be observed, was then in no way concerned to repel the charge of heresy.   He appeared alone anxious, as a loyal subject, not to suffer as a traitor to his Sovereign.

The first act of the Archbishop under Mary was to deny a charge of having performed Solemn Mass for the repose of the soul of Henry, according to Romish rites, in order to secure the favour of the Queen.   He prepared a document denying the truth of the rumour.   It was Dr Thornton, in fact, who performed the service at Canterbury Cathedral, and Day at Westminster Abbey.   A copy of this statement fell into the hands of Scory, then Bishop of Rochester.   Multiplied copies were extensively circulated.   When charged with having written this document, the Primate did not repudiate it, but only expressed his regret that it had prematurely appeared, as it had been his intention to issue a more perfect document.

With reference to this charge, the Archbishop's denial was headed :—

"A declaration of the Rev. Father in God, Thomas Cranmer, Archbishop of Canterbury, the untrue and slanderous report of some, which have reported that he should set up Mass at Canterbury, at the first coming of the Queen to her reign, 1553."

In this document we find the following passage, and it is quoted here simply because the accusation is repeated even at the present day as proof of Cranmer's alleged inconsistent conduct :—

---

[1] Cranmer's "Remains," by Jenkyns, vol. i. p. 360, Letter ccxcv.

" And as for offering myself to say Mass before the Queen's Highness, or in any other place, I never did, as her Grace knoweth well.
But if her Grace will give me leave, I shall be ready to prove against
all that will say to the contrary ; and that the Communion Book set
forth by the most innocent and godly Prince King Edward VI., in his
high Court of Parliament, is conformable to the order which our
Saviour Christ did both observe and command to be observed, and
which His Apostles and His primitive Church used many years ;
whereas the Mass in many things not only hath no foundation in
Christ, His Apostles, nor the primitive Church, but also is manifest
contrary to the same, and containeth many horrible blasphemies in
it." [1]

It may be mentioned that the Sarum Office, which was
identical in all essential points with the Roman ritual, had
been restored by Act of Parliament in 1553. The Sarum
Office had been in use in the last year of the reign of
Henry VIII. Cranmer never, as has been alleged,
acquiesced in the re-introduction of that ritual.[2]

Cranmer now saw that his doom was sealed. He set
about at once to put his house in order. His steward was
directed to discharge all outstanding debts, which, when

[1] "Memorials of Cranmer," Strype, p. 437.   Oxford, 1812.
[2] It was the Rev. Nicholas Pocock, the editor of Burnett's " History of the
Reformation," who said that Cranmer " was contented to celebrate the office of
the Mass at the very time when he believed it to be idolatrous and blasphemous." The fact being that from the gradual change in his views which
commenced in 1546, Cranmer left no stone unturned to get rid of every known
accretion which then obscured and defiled the Lord's Supper. Thus, even before the repeal of the bloody Act of the " Six Articles," he procured the abolition of the " scaring bell," which gave occasion to the "idolatry" to the
vulgar ; and this was followed by the order of 1548 forbidding any elevation ;
and this again by the " first Prayer-Book," from which every expression which
implied a Real Presence and proper Sacrifice had been carefully weeded out.
(See Eascourt's "Dogmatic Teaching of the Book of Common Prayer,"p. 40.)
Mr Pocock, after the manner of all " Ritualistic " Priests, never omits to abuse
Cranmer when an opportunity offers. Mr Pocock is an advanced member of
that school, and his opinions must be accepted with caution. (1.) He is a
Member of the English Church Union. (2.) He signed the Petition for
Licensed Confessors. (3.) He signed the Petition to Convocation in favour of
Popish vestments. (4.) He signed the Petition for the toleration of extreme
ritual. (5.) And he signed the remonstrance against the Purchase Judgment.

P

effected, his mind was set at rest, and he was now prepared to meet the worst. He was summoned before the
Queen's Commissioners to deliver an inventory of all his
goods. It appears that the original intention was only to
deprive the Archbishop of his See, and to prohibit him
from interfering in matters of religion, since all the others
who had signed the Succession document had been dis-
charged; but evil counsels prevailed. He gave advice to
others to escape the coming persecution he clearly foresaw,
but refused to act on the advice of friends tendered to him
to the same effect. He had ample opportunities of escape.
The charge against him for treason was, either originally
withdrawn, or considered to be merged into the greater
crime of heresy. He was arrested in September 1553, and
sent to the Tower, and from thence to Oxford, with Ridley
and Latimer. Here he was confronted, and put under
examination, on the 12th September; and, after some
tedious disputations with Dr Weston and others, members
of both Universities, he was adjudged a heretic, and committed to "Bocardo"[1] or common jail.

It was between two or three years before the Pope's
authority was again re-established in England, but subsequently all Acts of Parliament passed by Henry VIII., on
that subject, were repealed; and until then there was no law
under which Cranmer could be legally adjudged as an
Ecclesiastic, hence his long and tedious incarceration. It
was not until September 1555, after two years of suffering,
that Cranmer was again brought up to judgment, before Dr
Brooks, Bishop of Gloucester, as President, acting as the
Pope's sub-legate, and a Royal Commission. On appearing before this tribunal, he bowed respectfully to the

---

[1] " Bocardo is a stinking, filthy prison for drunkards, and harlots, and the
vilest sort of people."—" Coverdale," quoted by Le Bas.

Royal Commission, but refused to recognise the Pope's representative.

In a letter addressed to the Queen at this time he bitterly complained of being judged by this foreign tribunal. He wrote :—

"It cannot but grieve the heart of any natural subject to be accused of the King and Queen of his own realm, and especially before an outward judge, or by authority coming from any person out of this realm, where the King and Queen, as if they were subjects within their own realm, shall complain and require justice at a stranger's hands against their own subject, being already condemned to death by their own laws. As though the King and Queen could not do or have justice within their own realms against their own subjects, but they must seek it at a stranger's hands in a strange land ; the like whereof, I think, was never seen."[1]

By this tribunal Cranmer was charged with treason, for having signed the instrument for settling the crown on Lady Jane Grey (Lady Dudley), heresy for his works and public teaching, and adultery for having married as a Priest. It is needless to repeat here Cranmer's defence, as given by Fox, Strype, and by all of his subsequent biographers. As to the charge of heresy, his argument may be summed up in the words of the Apostle Paul :—" the way which they call heresy, so worship I the God of my fathers, believing all things which are written in the law and the prophets." "The Bishop of Rome (he added) treadeth under foot God's laws and the King's."[2] As to the charge of adultery, objecting that he was, as a Priest, married, and that his children were "bondsmen," he per-

---

[1] "Cranmer's Remains," Jenkyns, vol. i. pp. 369-370.

[2] A late writer, a member of the unreformed Church, thus curtly sums up Cranmer's defence (the italics are as in the original) :—"The substance of Cranmer's elaborate reply was to the effect, that at no time did he believe in the principles of the Catholic Church, *although he had repeatedly sworn to those principles with the most open solemnity, and sent men and women to the stake for not maintaining them.*" (J. Hodges, Soho Square.) A statement so utterly devoid of truth that it is surprising that the writer should have had the effrontery to offer it to the public as a historical fact.

tinently asked whether the children of unmarried Priests
were to be placed on the same level with his own honest
issue.   There was no law in England to restrain the
marriage of Priests.   As to denying the Pope's Supremacy,
with which he was also charged, he retorted by referring
to the fact that he only followed the example of his predecessor, Archbishop Warham, as also all the authorities
of the University of Oxford, specially naming his judge,
Dr Brooks, himself, who directly preferred the above
charge against Cranmer.   They sought to fix on him the
acknowledgment that the King was supreme head of the
Church.   His ready reply was that Christ was the head of
the Church—" the King was the head of the people of
England, as well Ecclesiastical and temporal, and not of
the Church."[1]

In his letter "to the Lords of the Council," 23d April
1554,"[2] referring to his examination, he wrote :—

"But concerning myself, I can report that I never knew or heard
of a more confused disputation in all my life.   For, albeit, there was
one appointed to dispute against me, yet every man spake his mind,
and brought forth what to him liked without order.   And such haste
was made that no answer could be suffered to be given fully to any
argument before another brought a new argument.   The means to
resolve the truth had been to have suffered us to answer fully to all
that they should say, and then they again to answer to all that we
could say.   But why they would not answer us, what other cause can
there be but that either they feared the matter, that they were not able
to answer us, or else (as by their haste might well appear) they came
not to speak the truth but to condemn us in post haste before the
truth might be thoroughly tried and heard.   For in all haste we
[Cranmer, Ridley, and Latimer] were all condemned of heresy."

If the "principles of the Catholic Church" consisted in

---

[1] This is much the same sentiment as expressed by Archbishop Warham,
who said that he recognised the King "as the supreme protector, the only
supreme governor, and, so far as Christ permits, the supreme head of the
English Church and clergy."

[2] "Cranmer's Remains," Jenkyns, vol. i. p. 363, No. ccxcvii.

the assumption of the Pope's supremacy in this country, and the power of a Priest to create his GOD out of bread, then Cranmer was justly found guilty of heresy, but not otherwise.

Cranmer's appeal to be heard by a General Council was peremptorily refused, whereupon he was relegated to prison. He was then cited to appear at Rome within a given time ; but being a close prisoner he was unable to appear in answer to the citation, and was in consequence condemned as "contumacious." In his letter to the Queen, from his prison, Cranmer wrote :—

" As for mine appearance at Rome, if your Majesty will give me leave I will appear there ; and I trust that God shall put in my mouth to defend his truth there as well as here. But I refer it wholly to your Majesty's pleasure."[1]

The duty of passing sentence on Cranmer was intrusted to Bonner, his bitter and implacable enemy. The sentence of death at the stake was pronounced 14th February 1556.

Throughout these proceedings Bonner acted towards the Primate in a most brutal and cowardly manner, subjecting him to every possible personal indignity. The writ of execution arrived at Oxford a day or two after its date, 24th February. Had this sentence been at once carried out, as in the cases of Latimer and Ridley, who had been executed some months before, though all these were tried at the same time, in all probability the crowning act of humiliation of Cranmer's retractation would not have taken place. For, up to the present time, having publicly and boldly maintained his reformed principles, and his repudiation of the authority of the Pope, whom he still, before his judges, declared to be Anti-christ, he must have known that his doom was the STAKE. Up to this time he showed no signs of fear of death. He was again sent to his filthy prison, but

[1] " Cranmer's Remains," Jenkyns, vol. i. p. 384, No. ccc.

his execution did not take place until the 21st March following!

Apprehension of evil is often more fraught with woe than the evil itself; and Cranmer was now, and had been, exposed to every kind of temptation which could assail the weakness of human nature. His was no quick and easy passage from condemnation to execution. He was close upon three years a prisoner, and throughout all that long period was subject to every sort of moral and physical torment by which his judgment might be perverted, his bodily frame exhausted, his will subdued. He was exposed for a greater part of the time to the trial of solitary confinement. He was alternately assailed with threats and with promises of a restoration to his high position. Were these no temptations, to put before an old and enfeebled man, to escape the horrors of the fiery ordeal he would otherwise suffer? The prospect was held out to him with the promise of his life, that he might live many years and yet enjoy dignity or ease or both; but of course Cranmer ought to have known that one of the cardinal virtues of the Papacy was, that no faith need be kept with heretics. He was closeted day after day with learned controversialists, appealed to by the recollection of his own earlier sentiments, and entreated to yield to the suggestions of his own kindly nature. He was for a time made a guest of Dr Marshall at the Deanery of Christ-Church, where he was at times pampered and cajoled, and flattered with fair promises, that nothing more was required of him by the Queen than his submission, and from comparative luxury was sent back again to his filthy prison and solitary confinement.

When the occupant of his cell in Bocardo prison at Oxford, he was witness to the prolonged sufferings of his beloved Chaplain, Bishop Ridley, and saw him led to

execution ; and who can tell the effects of such a spectacle
on a mind, left for days to its own isolated and self-concen-
trated contemplations? He was denied all literary relaxation. In his letter to the Queen he wrote :—

" Furthermore, I am kept here from company of learned men, from
books, from counsel, from pen and ink, saving at this time (September
1555), to write to your Majesty, which all were necessary for a man
being in my case."[1]

Clothed in all the symbolic raiments of his high office,
in Alb, Rochet, and Cope ; invested with Mitre, Ring,
Crozier, and Pallium ;—not, as of old, fashioned from costly
taffetas, and ornamented with rich jewels, but now in
mockery made of coarsest canvas, and other rude materials,—he was successively deprived of each, and was led
back to prison with the threadbare gown of a yeoman
bedel thrown over his shoulders, and a townsman's greasy
cap forced upon his head.

Was there under the exterior calmness of his bearing,
no mental pain in this cruel and heartless treatment to one
whose former pomp and greatness was of such an exalted
and glorious description? It were in vain, however, to
deny the fact. The good Archbishop, to whose gradually
maturing perceptions of sacred truth and right judgment,
to a great extent, we owe, under Providence, the great
boon of the Reformation, did ultimately succumb, through
the weakness of human nature, to the manifold intricacies
of his position and his sufferings. Cranmer, under
promise of freedom, signed his recantation on the 16th
February 1556, within two days after his condemnation to
the stake !

Cranmer fell ! and undoubtedly great was the fall.

The delay in pronouncing the inevitable sentence of
death arose from the fact, as stated, that, until the laws of

[1] " Cranmer's Remains," Jenkyns, vol. i. p. 383, Letter ccc.

Henry were repealed, the Pope would have had no jurisdiction in this country. The Pope of Rome ratified the whole proceedings, and at his door lies the ultimate responsibility. In fact, the Pope's authorised representatives were Cranmer's judges. The Pope issued his mandate for Cranmer's degradation, and he confirmed the sentence of death !

And here Dr Lingard, the Roman Catholic Historian, calmly sitting in his study, indited the following passage in reference to this transaction :—

"Cranmer had not the fortitude to look death in the face. To save his life he feigned himself a convert to the established creed,[1] openly condemned his past delinquency ; and stifling the remorse of his conscience in seven [?] successive instruments adjured the faith which he had taught, and approved of that which he had opposed."[2]

Not a syllable do we find here related of the subtlety, and even indignities, with which the fortitude of the Archbishop had been assailed, and subdued ; nor the manner in which the instruments of adjuration were procured (with promises of freedom), and in which they appeared ! " Had not the fortitude to look death in the face ! " Say, rather, the fortitude to contemplate the lingering and excruciating torments of the stake ! " It is not for us, who are placed beyond the reach of such fiery trials, to condemn the weakness for which he made the atonement."

It was the learned Priest Erasmus, contemporary of Cranmer, who made the open and candid confession, that he had " no inclination to die for the truth. Every man

---

[1] The only "established Creeds" of the Roman Church, at that time, were the Nicene, Apostles, and Athanasian Creeds. These three Creeds Cranmer maintained, and never questioned. Neither Transubstantiation, nor the Supremacy of the Pope—the two principal protests of Cranmer—formed any part of the Creed of the Roman Church. The Present—so-called—Pian Creed, was not formulated until the year 1564. This lax way of writing is unpardonable in a historian.

[2] "History of England," vol. vii. p. 274. London, 1823-31.

has not the courage requisite to make a martyr ; and I am afraid, if I were put to the trial, I should imitate St Peter," and thus he wrote to the Dean of St Paul's.

The following is the description given by Strype, in his " Ecclesiastical Memorials," of the transaction :—

" Other historians speak of the Archbishop's recantation, which he made upon the incessant solicitations and temptations of the Popish zealots at Oxford. Which unworthy compliance he was at last pre-vailed upon to submit to, partly by the flattery and terror suggested to him, and partly by the hardships of his own straight imprisonment. Our writers mention only one recantation ; and *that* Foxe hath set down, wherein they follow him. But this is but an imperfect relation of this good man's frailty. I shall therefore endeavour to set down this piece of history more distinctly. There were several recanting writings, to which he had subscribed, one after the other ; for after the unhappy Prelate, by over-persuasion, wrote one paper with his sub-scription set to it, which he thought to pen so favourably and dexter-ously for himself, that he might evade both the danger from the stake, and the danger of his conscience too, *that* would not serve, but *an-other* was required, as explanatory of that. And when he had com-plied with that, yet either because writ briefly or too ambiguously, neither would that serve, but on a *third*, fuller and more expressive than the former. Nor could he scape so : but still a *fourth* and a *fifth* paper of recantation were demanded of him to be more large and particular. Nay ; and lastly a *sixth*, which was very prolix, con-taining an acknowledgment of all the forsaken and detested errors and superstitions of Rome, an abhorrence of his own books, and a vilify-ing of himself as a persecutor, a blasphemer, and a mischief-maker ; nay, and as the wickedest wretch that lived. And this was not all ; but after they had thus humbled and mortified the miserable man with recantations, subscriptions, submissions, and adjurations, *putting words into his mouth which his heart abhorred;* by all this drudgery they would not permit him to redeem his unhappy life ; but pre-pared him a renunciatory oration to pronounce publicly in St Mary's Church (Oxford) immediately before he was led forth to burn-ing. But here he gave his enemies, insatiable in their reproaches of him, a notable disappointment. They verily thought that when they had brought him thus far, he would still have said as they would have him. But herein their politics failed them ; and by this last stretch of the cord all was undone, which they with so much art and labour had effected before. For the reverend man began, indeed, his speech according to their appointment and pleasure, but in the process of it, at that very cue, when he was to own the Pope and his superstitions, and to revoke his own book and doctrine of the Sacrament (which was to be brought in by this preface, that one thing above all the rest troubled his conscience beyond all that he ever did in his life), he, on the contrary, to the great astonishment and vexation, made that preface serve to his revocation and abhorrence of his former extorted subscriptions, and to his free owning and standing to his book wrote against Transubstantiation, and the owning the evangelical doctrines he had before taught."

On this passage Dr Wordsworth remarks[1]:—

"Notwithstanding all the researches of the historians, it cannot, I think, be denied, that this part of Cranmer's story is involved in great obscurity and uncertainty. That Cranmer made a submission and retractation, cannot be denied ; but I own, I know not how to reconcile six submissions, and the nature of them, their dates, &c., with other circumstances of the narrative. We are not told the period at which he was removed to the lodgings of the Dean of Christ Church, and plied with the several topics and acts of seduction, enumerated by Foxe. But let it be observed, that the 14th of February was the day of his degradation, at which time surely the Archbishop's behaviour gave no warnings of his lamentable fall : and yet the *fourth* submission, as published by Bonner (and it would seem that they are ranged chronologically), is dated the 16th of the same month, only two days after. There are other very suspicious circumstances accompanying Bonner's publication. But the above remark, I think, is alone sufficient to show, that this part of the narrative requires further elucidation."[2]

Jenkyns does not seem to place much reliance on these alleged recantations. He writes :—

"Immediately after this Appeal, or perhaps simultaneously with it, begins the story of his Recantations. These, even if they were better authenticated than they have yet been, could scarcely claim a place in the present publication. Still less can they do so, when surrounded, as they are, with doubt and difficulty."[3]

If, as Dr Hook is inclined to think, Cranmer made this (public) statement in the belief that his life would be

---

[1] "Ecclesiastical Biography," vol. iii. p. 591. London, 1839.

[2] Camerarius, in his "Life of Melancthon," seems to suspect the genuineness of these submissions.—"Vita P. Mel.," p. 340. Edit. 1655. Forged recantations were not infrequent. Some few examples are given in an Appendix to this Chapter.

[3] "Remains," vol. i. p. cxvii. Oxford, 1833.

spared if he persisted in his recantation, he seems all but entitled to the crown of martyrdom. If, as Macaulay maintains, he made it after learning that he was to die in any case, and that a lie would therefore serve him as little as the truth, then, as Macaulay says, he was no more a martyr than Dr Dodd. The question is important, but there are no materials for settling it definitively.[1]

It is a well - known physical fact, supported by the highest men of science, that the effect on an individual subjected to long mental strain and bodily suffering, is that the intellect becomes weakened and the judgment impaired. Such was the state of Cranmer after his three years' incarceration. Mr S. H. Burke, a member of the unreformed Church, in his " History of the Tudor Dynasty," thus describes Cranmer's appearance at the time :—

" Cranmer appeared weak and feeble. It is stated that the gaoler would not grant him a seat, so he had to lean upon a staff. His condition at this moment was a disgrace to the authorities, who subsequently shifted the censure from one to another. His clothes were nearly threadbare, and those who remembered the strong and active Prelate of a few years before, could scarcely have recognised him now. His jaws were drawn in ; his piercing eyes had become glossy and sunk ; the pleasant countenance had changed to the woe-attenuated aspect of despair ; his long beard white as snow ; his head bald ; and his whole appearance that of a man in the condition of uttermost distress ; so that his ' veriest enemies seemed moved to pity '—for the moment."[2]

[1] " Encyclopædia Britannica," 9th edition.   " Cranmer," p. 551.

[2] The following remarkable statement was made by the present Archbishop of York, in the Upper House of York Convocation, on 23d April 1885, as to the conduct of the late Archbishop of Canterbury, Dr Tait, with reference to the retirement of the Rev. Mr Mackonochie, from St Alban's, and his subsequent appointment to St Peter's, London Docks, as reported in the *English Churchman* (30th April), p. 213, col. 2 :—" There were times when a man was sinking out of this life, when his bodily and mental faculties were disturbed, and his judgment wavered and faltered. That being so, he distrusted the rumours which he heard from time to time of this or that eminent person having recanted upon his death-bed the opinions of his earlier life—that he had joined the Church of Rome, for instance, or some other Communion. It was neither just, kind, nor charitable to sit in judgment upon, and compare with the whole of his previous life, what a man had said in his dying moments."

With his mind thus enfeebled by his sufferings, Cranmer was an easy prey to his persecutors, and readily succumbed to their intrigues.

When once the loss of self-respect was incurred, Cranmer, if these several recantations were genuine, appears to have been reckless in his abject misery, and only sought for a season, by submission, to conciliate his ruthless persecutors. It is now of little concern whether he signed one, two, three, or six such recantations. Great as was the fall, still greater was its speedy reparation, by his noble and dauntless bearing in facing the horrible death prepared for him, by his indignant confession of his fault, and his public recantation, by his deep contrition, by his open exposure of his offending right hand which betrayed his weakness.

Let us pause for a moment to consider of what Cranmer was guilty to merit the excruciating torments of the stake.

√ I. He was declared *contumacious* for not appearing at Rome at the command of the Pope. Cranmer was not a subject of the Pope, that he should be commanded; besides, being a close prisoner, he was unable to do so; accordingly the Pope deprived him of his clerical rank and excommunicated him. Under no law of this country had the Pope jurisdiction over an English subject, ecclesiastically or otherwise.[1]

[1] "The Bishop of Rome was incompetent to take cognizance of the cause of an English metropolitan, inasmuch as any exercise of his jurisdiction in England was contrary to the decrees of the Œcumenical Synods of Nice and Ephesus, which, as I have already shown, were in full force at this time. Archbishop Cranmer, therefore, was not bound to submit to any such citation. This sentence was doubly null, as being based on gross injustice, and as being issued by an incompetent authority; for the Bishop of Rome had no jurisdiction over our Churches, and he was also incompetent to judge in the cause." —Palmer's "Apostolical Jurisdiction and Succession of the Episcopacy of the British Church Vindicated," p. 239. London, 1840.

2. The charge of *treason*. If for denying the Supremacy of the Bishop of Rome over the King, then Cranmer's judges were all equally guilty, especially Gardyner, Bonner, and Dr Brooks. The Pope's Supremacy was no doctrine of the Roman Church. It has only been made so since passing the Vatican decree of 1870; the Supremacy and Infallibility are now for the first time incorporated in the Creed of Pope Pius IV. In his examination before Dr Brooks, he denied that he accepted his office as Archbishop at the Pope's hands, "which he neither would nor could do, for that His Highness was the only Supreme Governor of this Church of England, as well in causes ecclesiastical as temporal : and that the full right and duration of all manner of Bishoprics and Benefices, as well of any other temporal dignities and promotions, appertained to his Grace and not to any foreign authority, whatsoever it was."[1] If for having signed the Memorandum of Succession in favour of Lady Jane Grey, then the entire Council, including the cautious Cecil, were equally guilty, but not one of them was proceeded against. Further, the penalty for treason was the axe, a more merciful death, as in the cases of More, Fisher, Lady Jane Grey, and Mary Queen of Scots, and not the stake. Heresy, in the Church of Rome, is accounted a greater sin than treason, theft, or murder!

3. We are reduced to the single charge of alleged *heresy*, for which, according to the cruel law of the Roman Church, the punishment is death by *fire*, as in the cases of Ridley, Latimer, Hooper, and an army of martyrs. Under what law, moral or divine, does the Church of Rome take upon herself to define what is heretical, and then burn the alleged heretic? Cranmer had a right to hold and

[1] Jenkyns' " Remains," vol. iv. p. 115. Oxford, 1833.

teach his religious views during the reign of Edward, and to continue to maintain them. After the death of Edward he obtruded his opinions on no one. He acted strictly and constitutionally according to the laws of his country. And when under examination for heresy he boldly maintained his opinions. Heap what railing accusations they may against Cranmer, as the alleged servile and unscrupulous tool of Henry, in all this monarch's questionable transactions, such accusations will not in the slightest degree justify Rome's cruel persecution of Cranmer, or remove the stigma which will ever attach to her final barbarous act. Nor will the laborious attempts, otherwise to blacken the character of Cranmer, divert the current of indignation against Papal persecutions, or be pleaded as an objection to the Reformation, of which he was "the Master Builder."

The scene at St Mary's Church, Oxford, on the occasion of Cranmer's repudiation of his retractations, was by all accounts a most impressive one, which even brought tears into the eyes of many of his former associates then present; while, on the other hand, the result struck amazement and confusion among his persecutors. The last act of humiliation was exacted from him by a public retractation, confirming what he had privately done in writings also prepared for him to subscribe.[1] After an oration delivered by Dr Cole, Cranmer was led up to a platform erected for the purpose, in order that he should make the expected *public* retractation. After offering a silent prayer, he then rehearsed a general prayer for his Queen, his country, and for himself, when he proceeded in the following terms, as recorded by an eye-witness:—

---

[1] This, no doubt, formed what Dr Lingard sets down as the *seventh* recantation.

"And now forasmuch as I am come to the last end of my life, whereupon hangeth all my life passed, and my life to come, either to live with my Saviour Christ in heaven in joy, or else to be in pain for ever with wicked devils in hell ; and I see before mine eyes presently either heaven ready to receive me, or hell to swallow me up ; I shall therefore declare unto you my very faith, how I believe, without colour or dissimulation. For now is no time to dissemble, whatsoever I have written in time past.

" First, ' I believe in God the Father Almighty, Maker of heaven and earth,' &c., &c ; and every article of the Catholic faith, every word and sentence taught by our Saviour Christ, His Apostles, and Prophets in the Old and New Testament.

" And now I come to the great thing that troubleth my conscience more than any other thing that ever I said or did in my life : and that is the setting abroad of writings contrary to the truth which here now I renounce, and refuse, as things written with my hand contrary to the truth, which I writ for fear of death and to save my life, if it might be ; *and that is all such bills, which I have written or signed with mine own hand, since my degradation,* wherein I have written many things untrue. And forasmuch as my hand offended in writing contrary to my heart, therefore my hand shall first be punished. For if I may come to the fire, it shall be first burned. And as for the Pope, I refuse him, as Christ's enemy and Anti-Christ, with all his false doctrine."

Such a speech took every one by surprise, and greatly exasperated the Romish faction. Lord Williams reminded the Prelate of his former recantation and dissembling. He replied :—" Alas ! my Lord, I have been a man that all my life loved plainness, and never dissembled till now against the truth, which I am most sorry for ; " and he added, " that for the Sacraments he believed, as he had taught in his book against the Bishop of Winchester (Gardyner)." And here, says the Chronicler, personally present at these proceedings, " he was suffered to speak no more." He was then led to execution.

" Coming to the stake with a cheerful countenance and willing mind, he put off his garments with haste. Fire being now put to him, he stretched out his right hand, and thrust it into the flame, and held it there a good space before the fire came to any other part of his body, where his hand was seen of every man sensibly burning; crying with a loud voice, 'this hand hath offended.'"[1]

"As soon as the fire got up, he soon succumbed, never stirring or crying all the while. His patience in the torment, his courage in dying, if it had been taken either for the glory of God, the wealth of his country, or the testimony of truth, as it was for a pernicious error, and subversion of religion, I could worthily have commended the example, and matched it with the fame of any Father of ancient time."

Such was the testimony of an adversary of the Reformation.

To go back a little in our history. The two venerable Martyrs, Ridley and Latimer, had both been brought before the same Commission on the charge of heresy. The contempt with which Ridley held the Pope was shown by a significant act. He stood uncovered, but when he heard the Pope's name mentioned he put on his cap. Being ordered to remove it, he refused, protesting against the authority of the Pope in this country, and he resisted the attempts of the officer of the Court to uncover him. He maintained his noble bearing to the end. He was adjudged "an obstinate and incurable heretic," and condemned to the flames. The aged Latimer, then in his eighty-second year, worn out and withered, dressed in tattered garments, half blind and deaf, and almost toothless, was the miserable object on whom these inhuman wretches wreaked their vengeance. He was in like manner consigned to the

---

[1] Strype gives an account of the expense incurred in the burning of Cranmer, taken from the Harleian MSS. They are as follows:—

"Item, chardges layd out and paide for the burninge of Cranmer as followethe:—

				s.	d.
First, for a C of wood fagots	.	.	.	vj^s *i.e.*,	6 0
Item, halfe a hundrethe of furze faggots	.	iij^s iiij^d	,,	3	4
Item, for ye carriage of y^{em}	.	.	.	viij^d ,,	0 8
Item, p^d to ij laborers	.	.	.	.	xvj^d " ,,	1 4

11 4

From this we are to gather that the county had to pay 11s. 4d. as the average cost of burning a heretic.

flames; but their ultimate doom also awaited the fiat of the equally ruthless Pope. This poor creature still had the force and dauntless courage of a true martyr. He and Ridley were tethered together at the same stake, and when the faggot was lighted at Ridley's feet, Latimer cheered his fellow-sufferer in the ever memorable and emphatic words :—

"Be of good cheer, Master Ridley, and play the man. WE SHALL THIS DAY LIGHT SUCH A CANDLE BY GOD'S GRACE IN ENGLAND, AS I TRUST SHALL NEVER BE PUT OUT."

Their fate took place early in October 1555.[1]

There is no need to enter into further details of this cruel persecution of Cranmer,—the story has become familiar to every one,—save to record the date of Cranmer's martyrdom—21st March 1556—after close on three years' imprisonment, and eighteen months after his public disputations with his accusers, and about five months after the martyrdom of Ridley and Latimer.

Cranmer has been branded as a coward, a renegade and hypocrite, because, when threatened with an agonising death, he, in a moment of weakness, was induced to renounce the reformed faith; an act which, as we have seen, he almost immediately after bitterly repented of, and testified his abhorrence at the stake by the well-known action which even Voltaire has panegyrised as being more intrepid and magnanimous than that of the ancient

---

[1] Mr Burke, in his recent work before alluded to, seeks to cast the entire blame of these fearful cruelties on Bonner, Bishop of London. One can scarcely repress a smile when we read :—"The action of Bonner was utterly unbecoming the *dignity of a Church founded in gentleness, consideration, and mercy!*" (The "Tudor Dynasty," vol. iii. p. 27.) But perhaps Mr Burke was *not* alluding to his own Church, when he referred to these characteristics.

Q

Roman. Cranmer did not take warning from the case of John Huss, when he arrived at Constance, and whose safe conduct had been guaranteed, with immunity from harm, a pledge his accusers basely forfeited. Will any member of the unreformed Church dare assert that, under such frightful circumstances, Cranmer's sin was greater than that of his accusers, who put him to tortures for conscience' sake? Let them answer that question! We read from the pens of the same parties, indignant vituperations heaped on Henry VIII. for sacrificing, by a comparatively easy death—for high treason—Fisher and More; but are silent when the Pope inflicts torture of the most cruel kind, for alleged heresy! But Cranmer's momentary apostacy furnished rather a dangerous triumph to the advocates of the Church of Rome, so long as the case of the Popes Marcellinus and Liberius stand on record. Cranmer, emaciated and feeble, under the fear of terrible torture, abandoned—be it so—the reformed faith, but professing still to hold all the fundamental doctrines of Christianity, Pope Marcellinus, under the fear of death, but in the strength of manhood, abandoned God and sacrificed to idols. And Pope Liberius, to escape the tedium of banishment, subscribed to the Arian heresy, and is, notwithstanding, enrolled among the Saints of the Roman Church!

Peter, himself, under less trying circumstances thrice denied his Lord. He even began to curse and swear, saying that he knew not the man, Christ, although he had shortly before protested that he would rather die than forsake his Master! His repentance was in tears of bitterness. The Church of Rome has accepted that act of penance, and has placed him on the highest pedestal of honour, according to her estimation, as her alleged first

Bishop and a Saint.   On the other hand, Cranmer was deemed by the same Church worthy of death, while faithfully clinging to his Lord and Master, the same Christ repudiated by Peter; but Cranmer denied the usurped Supremacy of Peter's so-called successor, and refused to accept that theological enigma, passing under the hard word *Transubstantiation:*

"Which profanes the soul and parodies our God."

But Cranmer's repentance and retractation were deemed an aggravation of his alleged crime, as he was committed to the flames! So much for consistency.

No one ought fairly to condemn a man for an isolated act, nor for a single failure, under exceptional circumstances of excruciating trial, practised on a mind enervated by mental anguish, and a body weakened and emaciated by long and solitary confinement.   There were circumstances connected with Cranmer's death, in which the divine strength was shown in his weakness—circumstances which one would have thought would have awakened some feeling of generous admiration in any breast that was capable of feeling it, even among those who differed from his doctrine.

The whole course of life and the final manner of the death, are the real measures by which a character should be estimated.   Judged by this standard, who can cast a stone or justly bring a railing accusation against Cranmer? Has any one of his detractors been ever subjected to the same process of bodily and mental anguish, with the frightful prospect of a cruel death?   Who can impugn his honesty of purpose, integrity of heart, or conscientious discharge of his responsibilities, to the full measure of his knowledge and convictions?   What Milton writes of a hero of old may be writ of Cranmer :—

" Sampson hath quit himself
Like Sampson,and heroicly hath finished
A life heroic, on his enemies
Fully revenged."

Cranmer's persecutors overreached themselves. Had
they been contented to accept the recantations, they would
have left the Archbishop to die broken-hearted, pointed at
by the finger of pitying scorn ; and the Reformation would
have been disgraced in its champion.   True, it is said, that
Cranmer's magnanimity and. contempt of death was only
exhibited when he perceived that his fate was sealed, notwithstanding his recantation.   But whose was the disgrace,
—Cranmer in boldly facing the tortures of the stake, or those
who cowardly cajoled him in the time of his abject depres-
sion, then even almost on the brink of the grave, by false
promises of liberty and restoration of honours, and then to
basely repudiate those promises ?—" Let it, however, be
conceded, that Cranmer's weakness was in all respects as
ignominious as his worst enemies have ever represented it,
still the history of Cranmer's fall must always occupy one
of the darkest pages in the annals of Romish cruelty and
cunning."   His persecutors were tempted by an evil spirit
of revenge, into an act unsanctioned by even their own
bloody laws (for recantation should always secure pardon),
and they gave Cranmer an opportunity of redeeming his
fame, and of writing his name on the roll of Martyrs:—
" Cranmer " (in the eloquent words of Southey) " had retracted ; and the sincerity of his retractation for that sin
was too plain to be denied, too public to be concealed, too
memorable ever to be forgotten.   The agony of his repentance has been heard by thousands, and ten thousands have
witnessed how, when that agony was past, he stood calm
and immovable amid the flames, a patient and willing

holocaust : triumphant, not over his persecutors alone, but over himself, over the mind as well as the body, over fear and weakness as well as death."

"Bound to the stake the martyr smiles at the excruciating pain, and his soul ascends in the lurid flames, chanting hymns of victory."—*Turtle.*

"CRANMER'S MARTYRDOM IS HIS MONUMENT, AND HIS NAME WILL OUTLAST AN EPITAPH OR A SHRINE."—

Strype.

APPENDIX, p. 234.

CRANMER'S ALLEGED RECANTATIONS.

The question that has been suggested is, whether Cranmer signed more than one such document? Fox gives but one; Strype refers to six; Dr Lingard mentions seven. The late learned Dr Wordsworth, in his "Biographical Dictionary," refers to Cranmer's several alleged successive recantations as of doubtful authority. After five alleged recantations, each more complete and emphatic than the preceding one, came the last, a most gross and fulsome libel and abuse of himself; all, if genuine, were exacted from Cranmer in two days, in chronological order. These documents were in the custody of Bishop Bonner, the most malignant and bitter enemy of Cranmer, and were printed and published by him immediately after Cranmer's death, including the recantation prepared for Cranmer to be made in Christ Church, Oxford, *but which he refused to take* when he publicly repudiated his former recantation. It was this last document which constitutes Dr Lingard's *seventh* recantation.

We have no other authority than Bonner for these documents, therefore it is not without reason that Dr Wordsworth should doubt the authenticity of the alleged five successive recantations of Cranmer, and that Fox may have been perfectly correct when he referred to one such document only. It was Bonner, the bitter enemy of Cranmer, and a most bigoted Romanist, who alone vouched for the five subsequent recantations.

In a letter addressed by Thomas Sampson to Henry Bullinger, dated at Strasburg, 6th April 1556, giving other information, he wrote:—"Dr Cranmer was burned at Oxford on the 21st of March. A certain absurd recantation, forged by the Papists, began to be spread abroad during his life time, as if he had made that recantation; but the authors of it themselves recalled it while he was yet living, and he firmly and vehemently denied it. The enemies of God are plotting dreadful and most cruel schemes against England."[1] Sampson here probably refers to the fifth recantation. The continuation of Fabian's "Chronicles," speaking of the burning of the Archbishop in 1556, says: "After he had recanted his *supposed recantations.*"

It has been a frequent practice in the Roman Church to allege recantations of leading or important personages, when no such recantations had taken place. I propose to cite a few authenticated cases.

---

[1] See "Original Letters Relative to the English Reformation," &c. The Parker Society. Cambridge, 1846. The first portion, p. 173. Letter xc.

In the late case of the Rev. R. T. Pope, in his discussion with Father Macguire, unable on the spot to detect the glaring misquotations from the " Fathers," of the latter, subsequently published his learned work, " Roman Misquotations." On his death the Romanists gave out that he had repented and recanted, which was untrue, for at the time of his death he was actually occupied on a new edition of his work, which, but for his untimely death, he would have published.

But the most recent case come to light is that which only lately occurred on the death of the learned M. Littré, the author of the " Dictionary of the French Language." He was what is called an un-believer, a free-thinker ; but ever maintained an unblemished and honourable character. His wife was a zealous Romanist. When in a state of coma, a priest was introduced by the wife, and the last rites of the Church were administered to the dying, but utterly unconscious, man. And this act has been proclaimed as a recantation by M. Littré, and readmission into the Church as a repentant sinner.

We have the case of the illustrious Monclar, who exposed the Jesuits. He died on February 12, 1773. The Jesuits reported that " he died repentant, and had retracted all that he had said, in presence of the Bishop of Apt, who made a minute of that fact." Whereas it was clearly established by Madame de Monclar, the widow, that Monclar had not " retracted a single fact which he had advanced against the Jesuits, or recanted any opinion he had formed," and that " it was altogether untrue that he did so." And the conduct of the Bishop of Apt was thoroughly exposed. (See Poynder's " History of the Jesuits," vol. i. p. 76, London, 1816, who gives all the facts and notarial documents.)

In the case of Anne Askew, the Papists gave out that she had re-canted her alleged heresy, but this she indignantly denied, though placed on the rack, and knowing that her fate was the stake. (See Soame's " History of the Reformation of the Church of England," vol. ii. ch. xii. p. 623, note f, London, 1826 ; and Burnet's " Hist. of the Reform.," vol. i. p. i. bk. iii. p. 538, Pocock's edition.)

The Rev. M. H. G. Buckle, in his Preface to his Translation of Desancti's " Confession : A Doctrinal and Historical Essay," Partridge & Co., 1878 (p. 11), refers to the case of Bernardino Ochino. " I have long recognised," says Ochino, " the truth of the Gospel through God's grace, and although I mounted the pulpit day after day, yet I dared not openly proclaim it ; you may imagine the constant martyr-dom I suffered." (See Benrath's " B. Ochino," p. 89.) Mr Buckle proceeds—" According to the usual custom, the Romanists propa-gated a report that Ochino had recanted in a dangerous illness at Geneva, and been murdered, in consequence, by the followers of Calvin. The truth is, that after being attacked by the plague and losing three of his four children [he having married after he left the Church of Rome], he died at Schlakan in Moravia." (See Benrath's "Life of B. Ochino," ch. ix. p. 298.)   He never recanted.

Pope Clement XIV. issued a Brief for the abolition of the Jesuits. The Jesuits allege that Clement retracted this Brief, whereas Greisinger, in his "History of the Jesuits" (vol. ii. b. vii. ch. i. p. 206, English Translation), proves the contrary.

We have also the pretended recantation of Lord Cobham, refuted. (See Alcock's " English Mediæval Romanism," ch. xii. sec. vi. p. 126 (reprint). London, 1872.) " Being sent back to the Tower, the Ecclesiastical party, wishing to destroy his credit, forged a recantation, which they said he signed ; and which having heard of, he immediately contradicted." (Shobrel's " Persecutions of Popery," vol. i. ch. iv. p. 192. London, 1854. Milman's " Church History," vol. iv. cent. xv. ch. i. p. 185. London, 1824.)

Cellario is said to have also retracted, which is proved to be untrue by Young in his " Life of Paleario," vol. ii. ch. xxiv. p. 552 : *note*. Burnet mentions the case of Thomas Bilney, who untruly was said to have recanted, vol. i. p. 268, Pocock's Edition, 1865.

The pretended recantations of Henry Vors and John Esch are refuted. (See Milner's " Church History," vol. v. ch. ix. cent. xvi. p. 149. London, 1824.)

Luther, appreciating the tricks of Romanists, predicted that he would be charged with recanting on his death-bed. (See Michelet's " Life of Luther," cap. v. p. 206. London, 1872.)

In the abridgment of Gerard Brandt's ' " Reformation in the Low Countries " (vol. i. p. 81, *seq.* London, 1725), the pretended recantation of Angelus Merula (A.D. 1556), the Martyr, is exposed. He maintained that " there is nothing necessary to salvation but what is to be found in the Word of God," &c., &c., and much more in condemnation of Romanism. He was examined before the Inquisition, where they in vain attempted to compel him to recant. A forged recantation was published, which he publicly repudiated. He was executed by order of the Inquisition in June 1557.

I might mention many other similar cases, but I shall conclude this, by citing the case of Palmieri, which we find in Desancti's " Roma Papala," Littera xiv., n. vii., p. 335 (Ferenze, 1817), of which the following is a translation :—" D. Vincenzo Palmieri was one of the theologists in the Synod of Pistoia, and was a man of great learning, especially in ecclesiastical antiquities. He had written a considerable number of books, and in all of them had assailed the Court of Rome as guilty of corrupting the Gospel; but he had done it with such sound arguments, with such strong support from documents, and such logical power, that Rome has never ventured a reply, except by the prohibition of the books, and the persecution of the author. Palmieri lived a peaceful and retired life with his family in Genoa, his native city, but on the approach of death was refused the sacraments, unless he retracted his doctrines. Fully persuaded that he had written in conformity with the truth and dictates of conscience, he would not make the recantation required. That accomplished rogue, Lambruschini, who was afterwards Cardinal, was at that time Archbishop of Genoa. He went himself to Palmieri's bedside, and extracted from him a declaration in which he professed himself a Catholic, and submitted all his writings, as he had always done, to the judgment of the Church. This declaration having been made, my Lord the Archbishop issued in solemn procession from the Cathedral, bearing the host himself to Palmieri. Everyone said that Palmieri had retracted, and the Priests and the Archbishop confirmed the report. Palmieri, who well knew the Jesuits, summoned his nephew, and, in the presence of two witnesses, consigned to them the original duplicate of the declaration given to the Archbishop, and enjoined him to publish it after his death, in the event of the Archbishop publishing a different one. Scarcely had Palmieri breathed his last when the Archbishop published a recantation of Palmieri's, but composed by himself, and the direct opposite of the true one. The nephew published the true declaration, and the Archbishop had to submit to the lie direct, and Palmieri is with the Priests a Jansenist heretic."

Such, then, being the acknowledged practice of the Roman Church in notable cases, it is not a stretch of imagination to attribute to Bonner the responsibility of the publication of five of the six alleged recantations attributed to Cranmer.

CHAPTER XII.

No Biography of Archbishop Cranmer would be complete which should fail to provide a record of the documents written by him during his Episcopate. These have been collected of late years by the Rev. Henry Jenkyns, Prebendary of Durham, and by the promoters of the Parker Society, under the painstaking editorship of the Rev. Edward Cox, Rector of St Helens, Bishopsgate Street, London.

The writings of Cranmer may be conveniently arranged under three divisions—his Letters, his State or Ecclesiastical Papers, and his Printed Books. Their consideration will form the subject matter of this concluding chapter.

SECTION I.

The Letters of Cranmer.

The Letters of Archbishop Cranmer, as contained in the Parker Collection, amount to three hundred and eighteen in number, and extend over a period of twenty-five years. Three only of the whole number (addressed one to Lord Wiltshire, the father of Anne Boleyn, and two to King Henry VIII. about his German embassy) were written previously to his nomination to the Primacy;

so that the whole collection may be regarded as connected with, or resulting from, his high position in the Church and Realm. These Letters are principally addressed to the most exalted personages in the State, to the then Sovereigns (whose reigns coincided with the government of the Church by Cranmer), to Sir William Cecil, and, most frequently, to the Lord Crumwell, the Vicar-General of King Henry. They often reveal important secrets of diplomacy, or state facts nowhere else recorded in history. For examples, the publication of a defence of Queen Catherine's marriage by Cardinal Pole, the conduct of Catherine Howard in her imprisonment in the Tower, the attempt of the Duchess of Cleves to regain her position as the wife and Queen of Henry VIII. They condescend also to the most trivial matters, the provision of venison for the Archiepiscopal household, the recommendation of some English hounds from the English Court to Louis the Elector Palatine, "who doth much esteem the pastime of hunting with great greyhounds, and specially with great mastiffs, which in those parts be had in great price and value;" and the gossip about a Prebendary being neither a learner nor a teacher, but a good " viander."

Several letters are urgent appeals to Lord Crumwell to find places for his domestics, preferments for deserving clergy, or provision for learned foreigners, participants of the Primate's hospitality; and the Archbishop scruples not to make his poverty the reason for his requests, asserting in one letter, " by cause I have many to provide for, and little to provide them of." And in another, addressed to Sir William Cecil :—

" That as for the saying of S. Paul, 'Qui volunt ditescere incidunt in tentationem,' I fear it not half so much as I do stark beggary. For I took not half so much care for my living, when I was a scholar of Cambridge, as I do at this present. For although I have now much more revenue, yet I have much more to do withal, and have more care to live now as an Archbishop than I had at that time to live as a Scholar."

In his correspondence, Archbishop Cranmer gives a veritable insight into the circumstances of the times. For instance, he complains to Crumwell, in Letter No. 198 of the series, of "having found the people of my diocese very obstinately given to observe and keep with solemnity the holidays lately abrogated, and that the people were partly animated thereto by their curates."[1] He testifies to the reality of Calais being at that time a part of the realm of England by the exercise of authority over the clergy there ; he shows the means by which the sale of the newly-translated Scriptures was promoted by a compulsory restriction of the printers to ten shillings as the price of a Bible. Another batch of Letters addressed to the learned foreigners, Bucer, Bullinger, Osiander, Fagius, Peter Martyr, and Philip Melancthon attest his intimacy with the German Protestant Reformers ; and his hopes of find-

---

[1] Before the Reformation the hindrance to trade and agriculture caused by the "holy days," which had become holidays, was so great that the Commons formally complained to the King that—"A great number of holy days now at this present time, with very small devotion, be solemnized and kept through-out this your realm, upon the which many great, abominable, and execrable vices, idle and wanton sports, be used and exercised, which holy days . . . might *be made fewer in number.*"—Froude's "Hist. of England," i. 208. The statement was drafted by Crumwell (see Brewer's "State Papers," v. 468). Accordingly (July 15th, 1536), Convocation "by the King's Highness' authority as supreme head on earth of the Church of England," declared that the number of holy days was—"The occasion of much sloth and idleness, the very nourish of thieves, vagabonds, and divers other unthriftiness and incon-veniences . . . and loss of man's food, many times being clean destroyed through the superstitious observance of the said holy days, in not taking the opportunity of good and serene weather in time of harvest ; but also pernicious to the souls of many men, which being enticed by the licentious vacation and liberty of those holidays, do upon the same *commonly* use and practice more excess, riot, and superfluity than upon any other days."—Stephen's "Eccl. Statutes," p. 333. Strype's "Cranmer," i. 122. See "Church Intelligence," 1885, Feby. 2, p. 19.

ing a common formulary of doctrine which all could accept, while they testify to the great respect and esteem entertained for him, and for his office by the leaders of the German Reformation. These Letters also afford testimony to the personal virtues of the Archbishop, and show the combination in him of a strict fidelity in matters in which principle was involved, and a large toleration when circumstances could in any way justify his moderation. He thus refused to an old servant of the King a Dispensation to marry within the prohibited degree of affinity (see Letter No. 178), and on the other hand proposed that Fisher, Bishop of Rochester, and Sir Thomas More should be allowed to be sworn to the Act of the King's Succession, and not thereby to the Preamble of the Act, allowing them to accept the King's Supremacy as established *de facto* and not *de jure*. There is no reference in his Letters to his wife or children, an omission not to be wondered at ; but there can be no doubt of the strength of his parental and marital affection from the tender sympathy expressed by him for the widow of Bucer in her bereavement, and for his Chaplain and servants in their sicknesses. Three Letters are addressed to his successor, Matthew Parker, but they are all merely appointments for him to preach at St Paul's Cross. This correspondence, as might be expected, gives considerable information about the condition of Cranmer's own Diocese, and sets forth his zeal in the visitation of it, his anxiety for the usefulness and improvement of his Cathedral School, and his proposals for the government of his Chapter, and for the due fulfilment of their duties by the Prebendaries and Preachers. The real value, however, of the correspondence consists in its testimony to the influence which Cranmer had with the King, and in its revelation of the innermost councils of the chief actors in the development, progress, and ultimate successful accomplishment of the English Reformation.

It has been well said that a man's character can best be appreciated by his letters. In these his inner self, his faults and his virtues, his pride, selfishness, or ambition, his disinterestedness, patriotism, and philanthropy are exposed to public view. Archbishop Cranmer will nobly stand the test. His written Letters are the best credentials in the face of friends or of foes, as to his high aims, his purity of purpose, his constant perseverance in the path of duty, his diligent endeavour to ascertain and to maintain the ancient path as marked out by the Holy Scriptures, and by the testimony of the Primitive Church. They make us acquainted with the man, no less than with the Prelate; and while we admire the unfailing tact, the gracious courtesy, the unflinching courage of his convictions, the honesty exhibited in all his negotiations, either as a Statesman or as the Primate, we cannot but give a warm tribute of respect to the simple, true, affectionate, and ever sympathising heart laid bare to us in this lengthened epistolary correspondence.

SECTION II.

Ecclesiastical, or State Papers.

The first effectual step in the Reformation of the Church of England was the acknowledgment by the Convocation of the clergy, and by Parliament of the authority of the Sovereign as in all causes Ecclesiastical or Civil, and over all persons, clerical or lay, within his dominions, Supreme. The Act of Submission, 25 Henry VIII. c. 19, was, however, nothing but the revindication for the Crown of those inherent powers claimed for it by the successive Sovereigns of England, whether of the Norman, Plantagenet, or Tudor Dynasties ; the final act in a long-continued contest between the Tiara and the Throne ; between the Kings of England and the Popes of Rome, carried on through five long centuries with various alternations of success. To quote the words of Dr Hook, "King Henry only claimed the authority and power which had always been inherent in the kingly office, although it had not always been maintained by his ancestors." The Act of Supremacy was the rightful issue of the principles contended for in the Constitutions of Clarendon, the Statutes of Carlisle, the enactments of the Provisors and Præmunires, of the Wycliffian age. It placed the National English Church in its proper position. The Church of England, from the Conquest to the accession of Henry VIII., had its Head out of the kingdom, and it was only natural that where the Head was, there the heart should be also. The best affections of Englishmen were devoted to Rome. On the assertion of the Royal Supremacy by Convocation and Parliament, the Church of England assumed its true position as the National Church, owning no foreign sway, inculcating henceforth no divided and half-hearted allegiance, but seeking with a single eye, the National welfare, and the best happiness of the people. There are no grounds for supposing that either the King or the Primate had laid down in their own minds any definite or preconceived plan for the further alteration of the National Faith. So far as they were concerned, the assertion of the Royal Supremacy was quite independent of any reformation of doctrines. But the new recognition of the Church of England as a National, independent, territorial Church, and as such equally with the Church of Rome a true member of the one Holy Catholic Church, naturally involved further changes and a more effectual adaptation of its organization to its new position. These changes, both in doctrine and in discipline, although unforeseen by the first maintainers and advocates of the Royal Supremacy, were providentially effected by a development, so slowly, gradually, progressively matured, that they involved no violent revolution, no break in the continuity of the English Church, no great alienation of any portion of the people. It will be my purpose to point out the various Ecclesiastical or State Papers, by which the Primate became the honoured instrument of securing to our country that Reformation under which England for three hundred years has taken a prominent position among the nations, and exercised so vast an influence as an arbiter of the world's affairs.

The first document worthy of notice is a speech by Archbishop Cranmer, addressed to the Southern Convocation in 1536. This Convocation was presided over by Lord Crumwell as the King's representative, and not only so, but the President introduced into it, Alexander Alisse, a Scotch Jurist, as his assessor. The chief purpose for which the Convocation had been summoned was to provide a remedy for the dangers of the times. The varied and protracted contentions about the royal Divorce, the relaxation of the authority of the Church of Rome, the general uncertainty and unsettlement in the matters of faith, had induced a keen appetite for religious controversy, and produced an universal spirit of vehement disputation. The Lower House exhibited in this very Convocation a formal complaint, divided into sixty-seven heads, against the new and erroneous doctrines that were commonly preached, taught, and spoken. In addition to these com-

plications, the Northern Dioceses had witnessed in the
" Pilgrims of Grace " a wide-spread disaffection, in which
the insurgents demanded violently the restoration of the
Supremacy of the Pope. Under these grave circumstances
the Archbishop addresses the Convocation, and urges them
to issue, in accordance with the directions of the King,
some authoritative Declaration as to the extension of
the Catholic Faith by the National Church on its separation from the Papacy. Cranmer's speech is worthy of the
grave importance of the occasion. He and his suffragans
were about to propose the First Formulary agreed on by
the Church of England after its separation from the See of
Rome, which proved (it may be observed in passing) the
foundation on which the more copious exposition of
doctrine subsequently set forth during the reign of Henry
VIII. were constituted.[1] The Primate said :—

"It beseemeth not men of learning and gravity to make much
babbling and brawling about bare words, so that we agree in the very
substance and effect of the matters. . . . There be weighty controversies now moved and put forth, not of ceremonies and light
things, but of the true understanding, and of the right difference of
the Law and the Gospel, of the manner and ways how sins be forgiven,
of comforting, doubtful, and wavering consciences, by what means they
may be rectified that they please God, seeing that they feel the strength
of the law accusing them of sin, of the true use of the Sacraments, the
number of them, whether the outward work of them doth justify man,
or whether we receive our justification by faith. . . . These be no
light matters, but even the principal points of our Christian religion."

This speech of Archbishop Cranmer, on the very thres-
hold of the proceedings commenced under his influence

[1] It may be here stated that the subject in dispute turned chiefly upon the
Sacraments. The Bishops of London, York, Lincoln, Bath, Chichester, and
Norwich maintained that the received number of seven should be retained,
while Cranmer and the Bishops of Worcester, Salisbury, Hereford, and Ely
opposed this theory. Alisse, the Scotch jurist, on being invited to give his
opinion, supported Cranmer, whereupon an unseemly altercation took place
between the Bishop of London and Alisse.

R

for the Reformation of the English Church, is most important, it provides the key-note to the whole of his subsequent conduct. It proves the purity of his motives, and the high aim he ever kept in view. It was with the Archbishop no mere contest between the Churches of England and Rome, no question of expediency as to the rejection or retention of established practices. He sought to bring every matter under the dominion of conscience, and to discover, and to declare, what was necessary for the salvation of every single man. No other Churchman or Statesman in the kingdom was known to be animated with the same singleness of purpose, or sought, as he did, as the end of his Church legislation, the welfare of the individual soul.

The result of the Convocation was the issuing the Document known as the "Articles" of 1536; its most exact title is the following :—"Articles devised by the King's Highness Majestie, to 'stablyshe Christian quietnes and unitie among us, and to avid contentious opinion ; which Articles be also approved by the consent and determination of the Hole Clergy of the Realm. Anno MDXXXVI."

Cranmer was intimately concerned in the preparation of this document. Portions of it in his handwriting are yet extant. It may be said to be the most important, being the first document connected with the Reformation. It defines the true position of the English Church as resolved to hold the Catholic Faith, although severed from the Papacy ; and it provided that groundwork of religious belief which remained as the root and foundation of every successive amendment and of every later advance towards the purity and practices of the primitive Christianity.

The contents of these Articles may be thus briefly summarized. The acceptance of the three Creeds (the

Apostles', the Nicene, and the Athanasian) is peremptorily
required, of which the very self-same words are to be kept,
and which are to be explained by the four Holy Councils
of Nice, Constantinople, Ephesus, and Chalcedon. Baptism (and Infant Baptism) is set forth as a Sacrament, by
which men obtain remission of sins, and the grace and
favour of God, according to the saying of Christ, " Whosoever believeth and is baptized shall be saved." Penance
as a Sacrament is retained with various explanations.
The " Sacrament of the Altar" is maintained without
material alteration, and the teaching of Transubstantiation
is fully asserted. " Orders," " Matrimony," " Extreme
Unction," and " Confirmation " find no place as Sacraments. Images are allowed with solemn cautions,
against their superstitious use. The ancient custom of
Palm branches, ashes, holy candles, creeping to the Cross
on Good Friday, sprinkling with Holy Water (to put us in
remembrance of our Baptism, and the Blood of Christ
sprinkled for our redemption upon the Cross), the hallowing
the font, the kissing of the Cross, and other like customs
are allowed, accompanied with the protest—" That none of
these ceremonies have power to remit sin, but only to stir
and lift up our minds to God, by whom only our sins are
forgiven." Prayers for the dead are permitted as a charitable practice, while Purgatory, and the deliverance of
souls by the Bishop of Rome's Pardons, are condemned as
being unsanctioned by Scripture, " or that masses said at
Scala Cœli, or elsewhere, or before any image, might likewise deliver them from pain and send them straight to
heaven." It contains, however, the germ of the future repudiation of Romish teaching, and in many points the
name only of the former doctrine appears to be retained,
its erroneous teaching being mitigated and explained away.

The Articles seem to have failed in their purpose of establishing Christian quietness and unity, or of avoiding contentious opinions. In the following year, the Archbishops, Bishops, Archdeacons, and other learned men consulted further together on the affairs of religion, and set forth another Formulary, entitled " The Institution of a Christian Man." Its design is shown in the words of the Preface :—

" Towards the advancement of God's glory, and the right institution and education of the People in the knowledge of Christian religion, concerning the whole sum of all those things which appertain to the profession of a Christian man, that by the same all errors, doubts, superstitions, and abuses might be suppressed, removed, and utterly done away, to the honour of Almighty God, and to the perfect establishing of the subjects of the King in good unity and concord, and perfect quietness both in their souls and bodies."

The Preface further sets forth the plan or method adopted in the arrangement of the " Institution " :—

" We have, first of all, begun with the Creed, and have declared, by way of Paraphrases, that is a true exposition of the right understanding of every article of the same. And afterwards we have entreatise of the Institution, the virtue and right use of the Seven Sacraments ; and thirdly, we have declared the Ten Commandments, and what is contained in every one of them ; and fourthly, we have shewn the interpretation of the *Pater noster* [the Lord's Prayer], whereunto we have added the declaration of the *Ave Maria;* and to the intent we would omit nothing contained in the Book of Articles, we have also added the Article of Justification and the Article of Purgatory as they be in the said book expressed." [1]

Cranmer had a large hand in the compilation of this Formulary, not only presiding at the conferences of the Bishops, but by writing some at least of the Explanations. This fact is established by Letters from Bishops Latimer and Fox to Lord Crumwell, who gave the credit of it to the Archbishop, to whom (writes Bishop Latimer), if there be anything praiseworthy, *bonna pars laudis oppine juris*

[1] " Formularies of Faith," pp. 25 and 26. Oxford, 1856.

debitur.[1] This book, says Professor Jenkyns, may be truly pronounced one of the most valuable productions of this reign. The Articles of 1536 were its foundation, but they were much enlarged and improved. It was called the "Bishop's Book," as put forth by them, submitting it "to be overseen and corrected" by King Henry, "if your Grace shall find any word or sentence in it meet to be corrected."

Some of the explanations are written with great animation, and contain, in vigorous language, the most Evangelical teaching of the later Prayer Books. The zeal of Cranmer and his purpose of setting forth the mode of access of a sinner to the divine favour, are everywhere discernible in the expositions of the Articles. The difference and distinctions between Baptism and Penance, and the "Sacrament of the Altar," are set forth with greater plainness, while the whole number of the Sacraments is admitted to be seven; and the teaching in regard to Transubstantiation, to Purgatory, Images, Processions, and ceremonies, is identical with that contained in the Articles set forth in the preceding year by the King and Convocation.

It is proper, in this place, to mention another of the writings of Cranmer connected with the Formulary, "The Institution of a Christian Man," and that is the document known as Cranmer's "Annotations." It appears that the King, in the prospect of a republication of this "Institution," had taken pains to revise it, and to attach to it certain remarks from his own pen, and submitted his revisions to the judgment of Cranmer. The task thus imposed on the Archbishop, says Mr Jenkyns,[2] will be

---

[1] See Jenkyns' Preface, " Remains," p. xvii.
[2] Preface to " Remains," vol. i. p. xiv.

readily admitted to have been of a very delicate matter. But those who are strongly impressed with the current accounts of his pliability, will have no difficulty in fore-telling the course pursued by him. They will anticipate that he approved the corrections without hesitation, and accompanied his approbation with many compliments to the King's superior wisdom. Such anticipations, however, will be altogether disappointed. It will be found, on the contrary, that Cranmer criticised both the grammar and the theology of his master with a caustic freedom, which might have given offence to an author of far humbler pre-tensions than a Sovereign, who had entered the lists with Luther, and who prided himself on his titles of " Defender of the Faith " and " Supreme Head " of the National Church. It is true that he softened the severity of his criticisms by an apology for his presumption, in being "so scrupulous, and as it were a pricker of quarrels to his Grace's Book." But even when these excuses have been allowed their full weight, there will still remain enough of boldness to surprise those who have no idea of Henry other than of a dogmatical tyrant, and of Cranmer than as a cowardly timeserver.

The one dominant principle ever present in Cranmer's mind, which lay at the root of all his proceedings, was his intense respect for the authority of the Holy Scriptures. His every plan and purpose was brought to the test of the " Word and the Testimony." He is described by his father-in-law, Osiander, as *literarum sacrarum studiossisimum*, and allowed of nothing which could not be deduced from Scrip-ture, or proved thereby. By the light of the Divine Word he discerned the unlawfulness of the marriage of Henry with the widow of his deceased brother, formed his best defence of the Royal Supremacy, and conducted the fortunes of the English Church to the completeness of its Edwardian Reformation. With such an appreciation of the Holy Scriptures, it was only natural that his earliest efforts should have been directed to the attainment of a correct translation, and of a general circulation of the whole Bible. Immediately after the declaration of the Royal Supremacy, the Archbishop induced the Convocation to Petition the King that the Bible might be translated by some of the learned men of his Highness' nomination. Bishop Coverdale, in the next year, 1535, published an edition of the whole Bible in English, which was mainly a transcript of Tyndal's translation. This edition was never sanctioned for the use of the English Church. The Primate, however, assisted by some Bishops, prepared, in 1537, a Bible in English, "both of a new translation and of a new print," dedicated to the King's Majesty,[1] which appears to have given him much satisfaction. He thus describes it in a Letter to Crumwell :—"And as for the translation, so far as I have read it, I believe it better than any other translation heretofore made." And in the same Letter he asks for the Royal Licence that "the same may be read until such time that the Bishops shall set forth a better translation, which I think will not be till a day after Doomsday." This Bible was ordered, by a Royal injunction, "to be placed in every church for all men to read therein;" and it was printed by the King's printer, to be sold at ten shillings a copy, by Bartelott & Edward, Whitechurch, on the promise of a monopoly of its sale.[2] In June 1540 this edition of the Bible was printed in larger size, and better type, under the immediate superintendence of Cranmer, who prefixed to it a Preface from his own pen. The Preface was far more

[1] Letter clxxxviii. Jenkyns' "Remains," vol. i. p. 196.
[2] *Ibid.*, ccliii. ; p. 289, vol. i.

hortatory than controversial. The Archbishop appears to have preferred to recommend the study of the Holy Scriptures from the authority of others rather than of himself. The greater portion of this Preface consists of two lengthy extracts from the writings of Bishop John Chrysostom, and Gregory Naziansen. The following extract from the Preface is from Cranmer's own pen, and exhibits the same care for the spiritual welfare of the people which, as exhibited by his other works, was a distinguishing feature of his aims and character :—

"Wherefore in few words comprehend the largeness and utility of the Scripture, how it containeth fruitful instruction and erudition for every man. If anything be necessary to be learned of the Holy Scripture we may learn it. If falsehood shall be reproved, thereof we may gather wherewithal. If anything be to be corrected and amended, if there need any exhortation or consolation, of the Scripture we may well learn. In the Scriptures be the fat pastures of the soul ; therein is no venomous meat, no unwholesome thing ; they be the very dainty and pure feeding. He that is ignorant shall find there what he should learn. He that is a perverse sinner shall there find his damnation, to make him tremble for fear. He that laboureth to serve God shall find there his glory, and the promissions of eternal life, exhorting him more diligently to labour. Herein may princes learn how to govern their subjects ; subjects obedience, love, and dread to their princes. Husbands how they should behave them unto their wives, how to educate their children and servants ; and contrary, the wives, children, and servants may know their duty to their husbands, parents, and masters. Here may all manner of persons, men, women, young, old, learned, unlearned, rich, poor, priests, laymen, lords, ladies, officers, tenants, and mean men, virgins, wives, widows, lawyers, merchants, artificers, husbandmen, and all manner of persons of what estate or condition soever they be, may in this book learn all things what they ought to believe, what they ought to do, and what they should not do, as well concerning Almighty God, as also concerning themselves, and all others." [1]

There is yet another important formulary put forth during the reign of Henry VIII., in the preparation of which Cranmer exercised considerable influence, and that

[1] Jenkyns' "Remains," vol. ii. p. 111.

is the "Necessary Doctrine and Education for any Christian man." This work in reality is nothing but an enlarged and corrected edition of the two Formularies which have been already referred to as "The Articles" of 1536, and the "Institution of a Christian man," 1537. The long lapse of the interval of six years between the inception and the ultimate completion of these Formularies, may be without difficulty accounted for from the course of political events. The visit of the German Reformers, Francis Burcard, Vice-Chancellor of the Elector of Saxony ; Gregorie Boyneburgh, a nobleman of Hesse ; and Frederick Mycorius, Superintendent of the Reformed Church of Gotha, in 1558, to England, on the invitation of Henry, with a view to the adaptation of some one Formulary of Faith for the common acceptance of both the German and English Reformers, and the protracted debates resulting from this visit, necessarily prevented, during the time of their residence in this country, any authoritative Declaration of the National Faith. The delay in the preparation of this final Formulary may be further accounted for by the proposed marriage of the King with the Duchess of Cleves, the sister of one of the royal favourers of the German Reformers. In addition to these considerations, the course of events at home might account for the delay. The fall and execution of Crumwell, the family troubles of Henry in the misconduct of his fifth queen, the equal balance of the Reformers and Anti-Reformers, and the warmth of their disputations with his own kingdom, the intermediate restriction exposed on the National Faith by the limitations of the "Six Articles Act," may help to account for the postponement of any mature consideration of Ecclesiastical affairs. The publication of this final Formulary was attended with far more antecedent study and preparation than its two predecessors. Questions relating to the sacraments were addressed to each of the Bishops. Their replies were duly summarised and considered.[1] The King himself condescended to write its Preface, and its various portions were submitted to and approved by Convocation, and it was finally ratified by the acceptance of Parliament. This Formulary, from the King's active superintendence of its preparation, was called the "King's Book," to distinguish it from the "Institution," which was known as the "Bishop's Book."

The contents of this Formulary, considered as a whole, may be described as retrograde in character, and adverse to the views of the advocates of the Reformation of doctrine. The Bishops who were still votaries of the old system, were in the ascendant. The King himself, who had been lately irritated by his discussions with the representatives of the foreign Churches, whom he had invited to his Court, was more disposed than usual to maintain the existing tenets of the Church. Under these influences, a stronger defence of the administration of the "Sacrament of the Altar" under one kind only, the readmission of Orders, Matrimony, Confirmation, and Extreme-Unction into the enumeration of the Sacraments, and the use of Images, are to be found in this Formulary. Cranmer, however, had sufficient influence to secure a qualification of these admissions by the introduction of purer scriptural teaching in the annexed explanations. Thus in the account of the "Sacrament of the Altar" we find the Doctrine of Transubstantiation plainly stated :—
" But in this most high Sacrament of the Altar, the creatures which be taken to the use thereof, as bread and wine, do not remain still in their own substance, but by

---

[1] See "Post," section iii.

virtue of Christ's words in the consecration be changed and turned to the very substance of the body and blood of our Saviour Jesus Christ." Yet in the further explanation of this Sacrament we read, the more Scriptural statement that :—

"Our blessed Saviour did institute this Sacrament as a prominent memorial of His mercy and the wonderful work of our redemption, and a perpetual food and nourishment for our spiritual sustentation in this dangerous passage and travail of this wicked life. It is therefore necessary that in the using, receiving, and beholding of this Sacrament, we have hearty remembrance of our most loving and dear Saviour Jesus Christ,—that is to say, that we think affectionately of His most bitter passion, which He, being the Lord of glory, suffered for us : and to bewail our sins, which were the cause of the said death and passion, calling necessarily for the grace and mercy of God, which most abundantly is obtained by the virtue and merit of the same passion, and thinking that our Lord, which gave Himself in that manner for us, will not forsake us or cast us away, but forgive us, if we truly repent, and will amend and become faithful servants to Him, which so dearly hath bought us, and paid for us neither gold nor silver, as St Peter saith, but His own precious blood."

These words bear internal evidence of having been inspired by Cranmer. They are the very echoes of his sentiments, and are witnesses to the ever prevalent desire of his heart to promote personal piety and individual edification. It is rather surprising to find the warm eulogy of Bishop Burnet expressed towards a Formulary so strongly tinged with extreme Romanist doctrines as is this " Necessary Doctrine and Erudition of a Christian Man." " Here followeth " (says the Bishop, writing of this document) "an explanation of the Creed, full of excellent matter, being a large paraphrase on every Article of the Creed, such services and practical references, that I must acknowledge, after all the practical books we have had, I find great gratification in reading that over and over again. The style is strong, nervous, and well fitted for the weakest capacities." The three final Articles in the Formularies on "Free Will," "Justification," and "Good Works," are exclusively attributed to Cranmer, and his supervision had probably extended over the whole book, as in the minutes of a letter addressed by Henry VIII. to Cranmer, he speaks of this "'Necessary Erudition' as the Archbishop's own book." There can be no doubt but that the Primate, if he had been the sole author of this Formulary, would have moderated many of its statements. He was, however, only one on a Commission, from the members of which an unity of opinion could not be expected. Cranmer, at the date of the publication of the "Necessary Doctrine," still believed in the Corporal Presence in the "Sacrament of the Altar," and having modified the other teachings of this Formulary, as far as his influence went with his suffragans, he acquiesced in it as on the whole a useful and seasonable publication, although on many points the free expression of his own opinions had been impeded and overruled.

Henry VIII., as he approached the end of life, became more devoted to the furtherance of true religion. In the year 1544 he determined to have an English translation of the Litany, and entrusted the work to the hands of Cranmer, who performed the task with so much grace and power, that in the words of the late Dean of Chichester :—

"The Litany we use in the nineteenth century is the translation made from an old Latin Litany of our Church in the sixteenth, and is a lasting testimony to the great ability of Cranmer at a period when the syntax and rhythm of our language was not yet settled." [1]

The Archbishop, in a Letter addressed to the King, [2]

[1] " Lives of the Archbishops," vol. vii. p. 206.
[2] Jenkyns' " Remains," Letter cclxiv.

gives an account of the method pursued by him in the translation. He writes:—

" I was constrained to use more than the liberty of a translator, for in some processions I have altered divers words, in some I have added part, in some taken away part, some I have left out whole, and some processions I have added whole, because I thought that I had better matter for the purpose than was in the procession." And then he adds, with his characteristic desire to promote personal holiness : —" I trust that it will much excitate and stir up the hearts of all men unto devotion and godliness."

The translation of the Litany was followed, in the next year, by that of the whole Primer, a book containing the Lord's Prayer, Creed, Ave Maria, Ten Commandments, seven Penitential Psalms, and the Litany, and several Morning and Evening Prayers ; thus a comprehensive and popular Book of Devotions, both for public and private use, was provided for the people in the vulgar tongue, which helped to prepare the way for the Book of Common Prayer, which became the chief glory of the succeeding reign.

These Ecclesiastical and State Papers of Archbishop Cranmer synchronised by a curious coincidence with the duration of the reign of Henry VIII. The retrospect of the proceedings in which, during the lifetime of his royal Master, he had taken a part, could not fail to secure to him much personal gratification. He had assisted in establishing the Royal Supremacy, had secured the translation of the whole Bible into a tongue understood of the people, had caused various superstitious customs to be abated or abolished, had superintended the preparation of divers Formularies of Faith, which, if not all that he would have desired, yet contained in them the elements of further improvements ; had published in the vulgar tongue manuals of private devotions, as well as a Litany for the public

Services ; and he could look forward with quiet confidence, under the auspices of a new Sovereign, to yet larger triumphs. His share in those future contests and future victories will be attested by his printed works.

SECTION III.

No examination of Cranmer's writing and sentiments would be complete without some observations on his views of the Sacraments of the Church as accepted during Henry's reign. The present developed theory of the Roman Church is essentially sacerdotal. Grace and salvation are declared to be obtained more or less on reception of one or other of the Sacraments of the Church at the hands of the officiating Priest, technically, *ex opere operato*. Cassander, an eminent divine of the Roman Church, seems to fix A.D. 1140 as the date when the number of Sacraments became seven. He stated that he could not find any one before that date to have suggested *seven* as the orthodox number, which he attributes to Peter Lombard,[1] the great " Master of Sentences," and that they even were not then universally accepted as Sacraments, properly so called. The particular number *seven* was suggested at the Council of Florence in 1439, and finally decreed as an article of faith at the seventh Session of the Trent Council in March 1547, to be accepted under pain of Anathema. These seven were stated to be Baptism, Confirmation, the Eucharist (or Lord's Supper), Penance, Extreme Unction, Matrimony, and Orders. It appears, however, according

---

[1] " Non temere quem quam reperies ante Petrum Lombardum, qui certum aliquem et definitum Sacramentorum numerum statuerat: et de his septem non omnia scholastici æquè proprie Sacramenta vocabant.—Cassander, " De numero Sacrament." Art. xiii. p. 951, Paris, 1616 ; and p. 107 " Consult. Lugd.," 1608.

to Peter Lombard (as evidenced by Cassander), as also
Durandus, another eminent divine, and even by the Canon
Law, " Gloss upon Gratian," that no grace is conferred on
the administration of the Sacrament of Matrimony.[1]

In this state of uncertainty, Henry VIII. ordered a
series of sixteen questions on the subject of the Sacraments to be submitted to the Bishops and other learned
divines, and required them to give their opinions in writing.[2]

Cranmer gave elaborate replies to these sixteen searching questions. The following is a short summary of his
opinions on the Sacraments as at that time entertained. He
says, that the Scriptures do not show forth what a sacrament is. The Incarnation of Christ and Matrimony are
called mysteries, rendered *Sacramenta.* " But one *Sacra-
mentum* the Scripture maketh mention of, which is hard
to be revealed fully, and that is *mysterum iniquitatis,* or
mysterum meretricis magnæ et bestiæ." The early writers,
he says, mention many more sacraments than seven, for all
the figures which signified Christ to come, as well as the
figures of thè Old law, and in the New, such as the
Eucharist, Baptism, pasch, the day of the Lord, washing of
feet, the sign of the cross, chrism, order, the imposition of
hands, the Sabbath, oil, milk, honey, water, wine, salt, fire,

[1] " De Matrimonio Petrus Lombardius negavit in eo gratiam conferri."—
Cassand., " Consult.," ut supra, p. 951. Edit. Paris, 1616.
"In hoc sacramento non confertur gratia Spiritûs Sancti, sicut in aliis."—
"Corp. Jur. Can.," vol. i. col. 1607. Lugd. 1671. Causa 1, Q. 1, c. 101,
and 32, Q. 2, c. 13.
" Ipse vero Durandus hoc argumento utitur ; matrimonium non confert
primam gratiam, quæ est ipsa justificatio a peccatis ; neque secundam gratiam,
sive gratiæ incrementum ; nullam igitur gratiam confert."—See " Bellarmine
de Matrim. Sacram.," lib. i. c. v. tom iii. p. 506. Colon., 1616. " Durand,"
fol. cccxviii. Paris, 1508.
[2] These questions and answers are preserved in the Lambeth Library and
British Museum. See Jenkyns' " Remains," vol. ii. p. 98, Oxford, 1833,
who also gives the full texts of the Questions and Cranmer's replies.

&c., &c., are also called sacraments. He sees no reason why the word sacrament should be attributed to seven only, and he never met in the old authors the two words, "seven sacraments" joined together. "It is no doctrine of the Scripture or the old authors." He finds in Scripture the matter, nature, and efficacy of two, only Baptism and the Eucharist. He finds Penance mentioned in Scripture, "whereby sinners, after Baptism, returning wholly to God, be accepted again into God's favour and mercy. But Scripture speaketh not of Penance, as we call it a Sacrament, consisting of three parts, contrition, confession, and satisfaction."[1]

"That the Scripture taketh Penance for a pure conversion of the sinner in heart and mind, and from his sins unto God, making no mention of private confession of all deadly sins to a priest nor of ecclesiastical satisfaction to be enjoined by him."[2]

Matrimony "as a promise of salvation if the Parents bring up their children in the faith, love, and fear of God." "Of the matter, nature, and effect of the other three, that is to say, Confirmation, Order, and Extreme Unction, I read nothing in the Scripture, as they be taken for Sacraments." "In the New Testament, he that is appointed to be a

---

[1] It was the same Peter Lombard who first defined that these three were parts of "Penance." See Neander's "Church History," vol. vii. p. 483. London, Bohn's edit., 1852.

[2] Nothing can be more clear in the teaching of the Roman Church at the present day, than that *perfect* repentance is not necessary in order to obtain the benefit of Absolution in this so-called Sacrament of Penance. It is clearly laid down that, by an imperfect repentance, arising from the fear of punishment, with confession to a Priest, the sinner, whose sins may be however great or however often repeated, can obtain absolution on confession to a Priest. See Delahogue, "Tract de Sacr. Pœnit." Dublin, 1825. "Catechesm ou abrege de Foi," Paris, 1828, p. 25. "On the Commandment," by Liguori, London and Dublin, 1862, pp. 255-6. "Concil. Tred.," Sess. xiv. c. iv. *De Contritione.* "Catechism of the Council of Trent," Donovan's Translation. Dublin, 1829, pp. 271.

Bishop or Priest needeth no consecration by the Scriptures for election,[1] an appointment thereto is sufficient." "A man is not bound, by the authority of this Scripture, to confess his secret deadly sins to a Priest, although he may have him." " Unction for the sick with oil, to remit venial sins, as is now used, is not spoken of in the Scripture, nor in any ancient author."

That Cranmer was not peculiar in his views and opinions on the Sacraments, I propose to give the answers, to some of the principal questions, by the Bishop of Rochester. The replies were as follows :—

" *Q.* How many sacraments there be by the Scriptures?

" *A.* I think that in the Scriptures be innumerable sacraments, for all mysteries, all ceremonies, all the facts of Christ, the whole story of the Jews, and the Revelation of the Apocalypse may be named sacraments.

" *Q.* How many sacraments there be by the ancient authors?

" *A.* I think that in the doctors be found many more sacraments than seven ; namely, the bread of the catechumens, sign of the cross, oil, milk, salt, honey, &c.

" *Q.* Whether the word sacrament be, and ought to be, attributed to seven only? and whether the seven sacraments be found in any of the old authors?

" *A.* I think that the name of a sacrament is and may be attributed to more than seven, and that all the seven sacraments be found in the old authors, though all, peradventure, be not found in one author. But I have not read Penance called by the name of a sacrament in any of them.

" *Q.* Whether the determined number of seven sacraments be a doctrine either of the Scripture or of the old authors, and so to be taught?

" *A.* Albeit, the seven sacraments be, in effect, found both in the Scripture and in the old authors, *and may therefore be so taught*, yet I have not read this precise and determinate number of seven sacraments, neither in the Scripture, nor in the ancient writers."

It was seven years after this that the Church of Rome

---

[1] The word χειροτονέω *cheirotoneo* (Acts xiv. 23), literally means "stretching forth of the hands," used at popular elections by "show of hands;" hence it acquired the secondary meaning of " to appoint by popular election."

stereotyped, as it were, her present Sacramental sacerdotal system.

It will be thus seen that while Cranmer's views were more advanced and precise than those of the Bishop of Rochester, we have here the principles clearly laid down on which the Church of England has acted, untrammelled by the fetters of Roman dogmatism.

Section IV.

The Writings of Cranmer.

The accession of Edward VI. to the throne materially altered the position of affairs. The well-known proclivities of the youthful Sovereign, and the accordant sympathies of his Council of State, encouraged the Archbishop to commence, without delay, those larger schemes of re-construction and re-adjustment, which had been maturing in his mind, and which had been kept in abeyance during the last reign.

It is not within the design of this Chapter to record the steps which led to the publication of successive editions of our "Book of Common Prayer," in the third and fifth years of Edward VI., and by which the independence of the English Church was completed.[1] The history of these stirring events has been already related in the preceding pages. We are confined in this Section to the consideration of the printed works of Cranmer.

The First Book of Homilies, the public reading of

---

[1] "We are not at a loss to account for the superiority of style discoverable in our Liturgy, the masterly performance of Cranmer and his associates, which has always been admired, but seldom successfully imitated, and never equalled; which is full without verbosity, refined without the appearance of refinement, and solemn without the affectation of solemnity."—Sermon I., p. 21. Oxon, 1805. Dr Lawrence's "Bampton Lectures."

which is still enjoined on the clergy by the XXV. Article
of our Church, was the first of these printed works. Three
of these Discourses on "Salvation," "Faith," and "Good
Works," are ascribed, on contemporary evidence, to the
facile pen of the Archbishop. He steadfastly upholds, in
these treatises the doctrine of Justification by Faith only,
but with such perpetual guardianship and intimate connexion with *the fruit of good works* as the necessary result
of a right and accepted Faith, that in his mode of dealing
with the doctrine he is absolved from all the shibbolethic
and party meaning attached to the use of that phrase in
these more modern days. There are certainly no expressions to justify the imputation of the Archbishop being
either a *Solifidian* or an advocate of the Lutheran doctrine
of an imputed righteousness. We should arrive at a more
correct estimate of Cranmer's statements, if we were to say
that the great cardinal purpose of his teaching in these
Homilies was to magnify the Atonement, and the Sacrifice
of our Blessed Lord on the Cross, as the sole meritorious
cause of man's acceptableness, and to declare and establish
the great truth (which he has made the central teaching of
the Service of the administration of the Holy Communion),
that our Blessed Saviour made on the Cross, by His sacrifice
once offered, a full, perfect, and sufficient sacrifice, oblation,
and satisfaction for the sins of the whole world. In confirmation of this estimate of the teaching of these Homilies,
we have the judgment of Bishop Burnet.[1]

Cranmer was not at all concerned in those niceties,
which have so much been inquired into since that time,
about the instrumentality of Faith in Justification; all that
he then considered being that the glory of it might be
ascribed to the death and intercession of Jesus Christ.

[1] "Hist. of the Reformation," Pocock's edit., vol. i. p. 464. 1865.

The care of the rising generation always occupied a predominant place in the thoughts of the Patriot States- man. Cranmer took the schools of the country under his protection, and constantly sought to promote the welfare of the young. For this purpose, shortly after the publica- tion of the First Book of Homilies, he authorised the use of a Catechism translated into English from the Latin version of Justus Jonas.[1] The real author[2] of this Cate- chism, it is believed, was Osiander (whose niece Cranmer married), who had written in German for the students of Nuremberg and Brandenburg.[3] The authorised use of this Catechism was the source of much trouble to the Arch- bishop. It caused him to be suspected of a wish to inculcate Lutheran teaching, and added fuel to the pre- valent dissensions. John Burcher, writing to Bullinger, 29th October 1548,[4] thus speaks of it :—

" The Archbishop of Canterbury, moved no doubt by the advice of Peter Martyr and of some Lutherans, has ordered a Catechism of some Lutheran opinions to be translated and published in our language. This little book has caused no little discord, so that fight- ing has frequently taken place among the common people on account of their diversity of opinion, even during the sermons."

There is no evidence to prove that Cranmer had any hand in the actual translation of this Catechism from Latin into English. All that can really be attributed to him is the Preface, in which the Catechism is dedicated to King

---

[1] Justus Jonas was a great friend and associate of Martin Luther, and held a professorship at Nuremberg. He was the translator of Osiander's Catechism. Some state that it was Justus Jonas the younger.

[2] Blunt's " Annotated Prayer Book," Preface, p. 37. London, 1866.

[3] Dr Burton says it was framed on the model of Luther's Shorter Catechism, A.D. 1529, and its tone is high Lutheran. How Osiander was opposed to the Lutherans, in some points at least, see Whitaker's " Disputation," Parker Society, p. 380. Whitaker was Dean Nowel's nephew.

[4] Original Letters, " English Reformation," ccx., cviii. Parker Society.

Edward VI. This Preface is very short, and contains no doctrinal nor controversial statement. It is a simple unimpassioned academical eulogy on the benefits of learning, and an earnest caution against the mischief of idleness and ignorance.

Another treatise, in which the Primate had a hand, entitled a "Confutation of Unwritten Verities," quickly followed the publication of Justus Jonas' translation of Osiander's Catechism. As in our days, the apologists of the Church of Rome have devised the theory of Development as the defence of the Decree of the Vatican Council, and of other late tenets of Romish doctrines, so in the first part of the sixteenth century the friends of the Papacy pleaded for their teachings the authority of " Unwritten Verities." This weapon of defence was first forged by the ingenuity of Stokesley, the then Bishop of London. The treatise under review is an able refutation of this claim. Some doubts have been expressed as to the entire authorship being rightly attributed to Cranmer. There are good grounds, however, for placing it among his printed works. Cranmer was a persevering and methodical collector of authorities on all the Ecclesiastical questions which formed, in his dangerous days, the matters of disputation ; and the substance, order, and arrangement of the quotations as printed in this instructive volume are in the handwriting of the Archbishop. The purpose of the treatise is to prove from the Holy Scriptures, and from the ancient Fathers, that the Word of God contains all things necessary for salvation, and that neither the writings of the old " Fathers," nor general Councils, nor the oracles of Angels, nor apparitions from the dead, nor customs of Churches, are sufficient to establish doctrines, or to maintain a new Article of Faith. It is, in a word, the counterpart of the Sixth Article of our Church on the sufficiency of Holy Scripture.[1]

We have now arrived at a period of Cranmer's life in which his opinions reached their utmost divergence from the tenets of the Church of Rome. As at an early period of his life he was led, from his knowledge of the history of his own and of other Churches, and from the testimony of ancient Fathers, to repudiate the domination over all Churches and States claimed by the Popes, so he was led at this later period to renounce the extravagant doctrine of Transubstantiation, and, as a consequence of his new convictions, to convert the Mass into a Communion Service. This most important change in his religious sentiments, which really lay at the root of a true doctrinal Reformation, and of a complete separation from the Church of Rome, arose from no sudden impulse, nor from any new or unlooked-for external collision with the Roman See. It was a work of gradual progress, and the result of a deeper acquaintance with the teaching of the Fathers and with the Liturgies of the Primitive Churches. It affords no real ground for the charge of inconsistency occasionally brought as a railing accusation against the Archbishop. He was a learner in a learning age. It was, indeed, his misfortune to live in times in which, what was denominated a new learning, was the characteristic feature, and of which new learning he was himself one of the chief Masters and Directors ;

---

[1] See Article vi.—" Holy Scripture containeth all things necessary to salvation, so that whatsoever is not read therein, nor may be proved thereby, is not to be required of any man, that it should be believed as an Article of the Faith, or be thought requisite or necessary to salvation."

[2] Cranmer gives the account of himself :—" By little and little I put away my former ignorance. And as God of His mercy gave me light, so through His grace I opened mine eyes to receive it, and did not wilfully repugn unto God and remain in darkness."—Jenkyns' Preface to "Cranmer's Remains," vol. i. p. 75. Edit. Oxford, 1833.

and in such an age of transition, trial, and contention, pro-
gression towards clearer views, and an advancing readiness
to stand in the ancient paths, were no sufficient proofs of
either insincerity, vacillation, or inconsistency.   In such a
time in which the foundations of the Civil and Ecclesiastical polity were in a manner laid bare, no man, lay or
cleric, could justly be blamed for a change in his opinions.
In judging of the character of such change, an inquiry
should be directed as to the motive which induced the
change.   If the change can be fairly attributed to a corrupt
or unworthy motive, if it be proved to bring additional
honours, pecuniary advantages, or personal improvement
in social position, we may then legitimately challenge the
conduct of the convert, and charge him with inconsistency,
time serving, or apostacy.   But Archbishop Cranmer was
a gainer in none of these particulars by his change of views,
and no such accusations against him can be substantiated
or maintained.   We have the written evidence of Cranmer
himself as late as 1537-8 to these two facts :—*First*, that
at this date he believed in the *corporeal* presence in "the
Sacrament of the Altar;" and *second*, that he had personally read the ancient authors on the subject.   It were
better to quote the Archbishop's own words.   He thus
writes to Joachim Vadiamus, in the year 1537-8:—

"Wherefore since the Catholic faith, which we hold concerning the
true presence of the body (*de verâ presentiâ corporis*), has been promulgated from the beginning of the Church by such clear and manifest
passages of Scripture, and has likewise been sedulously commended
to the ears of the faithful by the most eminent ecclesiastical writers, do
not go on, I pray you, to desire any further to root up and overthrow
a doctrine so well supported.   Sufficient are the attempts already
made."[1]

If these words, " *De verâ presentiâ corporis*," " concerning
the true presence of the body," prove, as they are sup-

[1] "Cranmer's Remains," vol. i. 195.   Oxford, 1833.

posed to do, the acceptance by the writer, of the doctrine
of Transubstantiation, then it is probable that, shortly after
this time, some modification of these sentiments, and some
change occurred in his opinions. We have, at any rate,
certain facts which seem to point to this conclusion. In
the first place, the Archbishop succeeded so ill, and
became so entangled in his argument with Lambert, in the
great disputation held in the presence of King Henry
VIII. in Westminster House, that the bystanders were
amazed, and that Dr Gardyner, the Bishop of Winchester,
interrupted him, and took up the controversy himself,
which showed the existence of some ambiguity on his
mind on the subject. And the arguments of Fryth must
have also made a great impression upon him. In the
second place, at this very time there was a deputation of
German Reformers in England, on the invitation of the
King and of the Archbishop, for the express purpose of
establishing a common Formulary of Faith, for the joint
adoption of the English Church and of the Reformed
Lutheran Churches, and that it was only on the later
opposition of the King that any difficulty was made on the
question of "the Sacrament of the Altar." And, lastly, in
a Letter written to Lord Crumwell, on the 15th August,
1538, concerning Adam Damplif, a Priest at Calais, who
had a dispute with the Prior, and being called upon for
his defence declared that "he had ever confessed the Body
and Blood of Christ to be present in the Sacrament of the
Altar, and had only confuted the doctrine of Transubstantiation." To which Cranmer adds the remark, "*and
therein I think he taught the truth.*"[1] These three facts
seem to justify the impression that Cranmer had himself
become, shortly after his Letter to Vadianus, a convert to

---

[1] Letter ccxxviii., Jenkyns' "Remains," vol. i. p. 257. Oxford, 1833.

the Lutheran Doctrine of Consubstantiation. This suspicion of the acceptance of Lutheran Doctrine is strengthened by the public sanction of the Lutheran Catechism of Osiander, and of Justus Jonas, to which reference has already been made. The main cause of the eventual surrender both of the Romish and of Lutheran doctrine is to be traced to the influence of Dr H. Ridley, Bishop of London. That distinguished Prelate, about the year 1546, brought to the Primate's notice the famous treatise of Rabanus, or Bertram (also previously noticed), in which he combated the opinions of Paschasius Radbert, who *first* asserted, in the ninth century, the doctrine *of a change of the substance* of the consecrated elements, or Transubstantiation, though that expression was not then invented. This statement is made on the authority of Cranmer himself:—" I grant " (he said, in his examination at Oxford, before Dr Brooks, the Bishop of Worcester), " that then I believed otherwise than I do now ; and so I did, until my Lord of London, Dr Ridley, did confer with me, and, by sundry persuasions and authorities of Doctors, drew me quite from my opinions."[1] Cranmer, with his accustomed conscientiousness, investigated for himself the authorities adduced by Bertram, as is evidenced by his Common Place Book, yet extant, and only after thus satisfying himself of the truth, as held by the early Fathers, did he openly maintain his newly received opinions. We have the authority of Bartholomew Traheron for the date of the first document of this change of views entertained by the Primate. In a Letter addressed to Bullinger, in the month of December 1548, he says :—

"On the 14th December, if I mistake not, a disputation was held at London, concerning the Eucharist, in the presence of almost all the nobility of England. The arguments were sharply contested by the

[1] Jenkyns' " Remains," vol. i. p. 97. Oxford, 1833.

Bishops. The Archbishop of Canterbury, contrary to general expectation, most openly, firmly, and learnedly maintained your opinion upon
the subject. . . . The truth never obtained a more brilliant victory
among us. I perceive that it is all over with Lutheranism, now that
those who were considered its principal and almost only supporters,
have come over to our side."[1]

The best and most certain proofs, however, of the
Primate's perfect renunciation, at this date, both of the
Romish and Lutheran tenets connected with the Sacrament of the "Lord's Supper," is the gift of his great crowning work to the English Church on the completed Book
of Common Prayer. The Archbishop, indeed, could not
possibly have foreseen the amazing benefits he was about
to confer upon the world at large, in thus giving for the
universal use of his countrymen, a National "Service Book,"
which, in its retention of all the treasures of the ancient
Sarum Breviary, and in its conformity with the primitive
truths of the first and purest ages of the Church, would
in after times be a firm bond of union between the Mother
Church of England, and the numerous daughter Churches
multiplied and extended through the divers nations of the
earth. The re-construction of the Prayer Book was accompanied with every possible circumstance that could impart
to it dignity and importance as a national act. It was
prepared by a committee of Bishops and divines assembled
at Windsor,[2] who carried on their deliberations for the space
of two years. Whether it was sanctioned by the two
Convocations is doubtful, but it was formally authorised by
the two Houses of Parliament, confirmed with hearty good-
will by the youthful Sovereign, and specially acknowledged
by the most solemn declaration to have been superintended
by the presence of the "Holy Ghost."[3]

[1] Original Letters, "English Reformation," clii. Parker Society.
[2] Cranmer's Letter, ccxcix., Jenkyns' "Remains," p. 375. Oxford, 1833.
[3] This aid of the "Holy Ghost" is distinctly asserted in the Act contained

The special writings of Cranmer in connexion with the " Book of Common Prayer" were the two "Prefaces "— " Concerning the Services of the Church," and " Of Ceremonials, why some be abolished and some retained." In the first of these Prefaces Cranmer was assisted by the work of Cardinal Quignonez, a Spanish Bishop,[1] who published in 1536 a reformed Roman Breviary, under the permission granted by Leo X., to Zaccharie Ferrerie de Vicenze, Bishop of Guarda, in Portugal. Mr Blunt, in his " Annotated Prayer Book," has printed in double column the corresponding passages of the two Prefaces.[2]

in the " Statutes at Large," 2 and 3 Edwd. VI. c. 1, " An Act for uniformity of Service and administration of the Sacraments throughout the realms," which recites—" And thereupon having as well eye and respect to the most sincere and pure Christian religion taught by the Scriptures, as to the usages in the Primitive Church, should draw and make one convenient and meet order, rite, and fashion of common and open prayer and administration of the Sacraments, to be had and used in his Majesty's realm of England and in Wales, the which at this time by the aid of the Holy Ghost with one uniform and agreement is of them concluded, set forth, and delivered to his Highness, to his great comfort and quietness of mind, in a Book entitled 'The Book of the Common Prayer and Administration of the Sacraments and other rites and ceremonies of the Church after the use of the Church of England.'" The penalties for breach of the Act were heavy : for the first offence, six months' imprisonment, without bail or mainprise ; and for the second, a year's imprisonment and the loss (*ipse facto*) of benefice. The second Prayer Book was declared by another Act of Parliament to be :—" Agreeable to the word of God, and the primitive Church, very comfortable to all good people desirous to live in Christian conversation, and most profitable to the estate of the realm, upon the which the mercy, favour, and blessing of Almighty God is no wise so ready plenteously proved as by common Prayer, due using of the Sacraments, and after preaching of the Gospel, with the devotion of the prayers." 5 and 6 Edwd. VI. c. 1.

[1] For some notice of the History of the Quignon Breviary, the reader is referred to my " History of the Roman Breviary," p. 5. 1880. Messrs W. H. Allen & Co., Waterloo Place, London.

[2] Mr Blunt, in his Preface, p. xx., edit. 1866, says :—" This Reformed Roman Breviary was intended chiefly, if not entirely, for the use of the Clergy and Monks in their private recitations, and its introduction in some places for choir and public use eventually led to its suppression in 1566. No provision was made (as there had been in the English Reformation) for adapting it to the use of the laity. During the whole forty years of its use there is no trace of any attempt to connect the Quignon Breviary with vernacular translations of

The second Preface is entirely the production of Cranmer's pen.   It is the fashion in these days to pay either
none or little attention to these prefatory writings.   They
are regarded as archaic documents, having no reference
to modern times; but if any one will calmly examine this
Second Preface, he will find in it an attestation, in a
singular degree, to the judgment, temper, and mastery of
his times possessed by the Primate.   What moderation he
exhibits in the burning questions of his day!   How
impartially he arbitrates between those who would retain
superstitious usages and those extremists who would dis-
regard all ancient customs!   To the first of these he
says :—"This our excessive multitude of ceremonies was
so great, and many of them so dark, that they did more
confound and darken than declare and set forth Christ's
benefits unto us."   To the second of these he says:—
" Granting some ceremonies convenient to be had surely
when the old may be well used, these they cannot reason-
ably reprove the old only for their age, without bewraying
of their own folly."   What delicacy of reproof, polish of
remonstrance, and courtesy in considering faults and prejudices are here apparent!   What a wonderful degree of
prescience, the highest prerogative of the true Statesman,
either in Church or State, is here manifested, so that the
words and counsels of the Archbishop, after the lapse of
three centuries, are just as suitable to the circumstances of
the times as when they were first written.   How justly and
wisely he combines the vindication of the English Church
to legislate for her own necessities, with the free and
gracious acknowledgment of the like privilege to other

prayers or Scriptures, and although it was undoubtedly an initiatory step in the
same direction as that taken by our own Reformers, yet it was never followed
up nor intended to be followed up: and the object of the Roman Reform
throws out in stronger light that of the English."

Churches!—"In these our doings, we condemn no other nations, nor prescribe anything but to our own people only, for we think it convenient that every country should use such ceremonies as they shall think best to the setting forth of God's honour and glory, and to the reducing the people to a most perfect and godly living, without error or superstition." This Preface,[1] of all his writings, appears the most complete in its testimony to the possession by Cranmer of all the qualities fitting him for the discharge of his responsible but glorious task, as the Primate of a Church desirous of effecting, within itself, a true and judicious National Reformation.

The new book of "Common Prayer," although generally approved, did not secure the entire acceptance of the nation. The ancient system addressing itself to the senses rather than to the understanding or the heart, and insisting more upon outward observances than personal holiness, was well calculated to enchain and captivate the ruder and less educated classes of the peasantry, and naturally the sudden and peremptory abolition of practices and of ceremonies to which they had looked for salvation, exerted among them sentiments of horror and indignation. These feelings of religious disaffection were further increased by the sufferings caused in the rural districts by the lay purchasers of the confiscated monastic lands, who exacted higher rents, and, at the same time, gave less than their former owners in charity to their poorer neighbours. These

---

[1] The short Preface to the Ordination Services is also attributed to Cranmer. This plain and distinct statement of the threefold Christian ministry of Bishop, Priest, and Deacon throws light on the License requested by Cranmer from the two Sovereigns whom he served. It is evident that the request was no denial of the indelible character, or certain grace of Holy Orders, but only a cautionary effort to avoid any possible danger of incurring a Præmunire by securing the license of the Sovereign to exercise within the Realm the rights of his jurisdiction.

popular risings extended through several counties, but the insurrection in Devonshire, aided by the co-operation of some influential gentry, alone assumed formidable proportions. These insurgents addressed a petition to the Privy Council, in which they formulated their grievances under fifteen heads. They complained of the new English Prayer Book, and demanded the restoration of private Masses, of the reservation of the Host, of the continuance of the service in Latin. They further required the re-enactment of the "Six Articles Act," the restitution of the prohibited days of Holiday, and the removal of the old ceremonies of Holy Water, of Ashes, of Palms, of creeping to the Cross, and of processions. It fell to the lot of Cranmer, at the request of the Privy Council, to prepare an answer to these complaints. He exposed the ignorance and folly of the insurgents, and proved to them, in all honesty and plainness of speech, that the various customs, which they had venerated as ancient ceremonies, had been invented in comparatively modern times, and he exposed with admirable effect the unreasonableness of their complaints. His reply, still extant, was, in fact, a Manifesto and Appeal to the Nation, in which he was enabled to place before it a defence and explanation of the new teachings and customs, and to give sufficient reasons for the abolition of the practices and ceremonies which they desired to retain. He was thus enabled materially to assist in the peaceful acceptance of the Book of Common Prayer, and of the religious changes with which that acceptance was necessarily associated.

There is another printed work of the Primate's closely connected with this western insurrection, viz., his "Sermon against Rebellion." "The greatest cause" (he says) "of all these commotions is sin, and under Christian profession unchristian living. But there be certain special causes, of the which some pertain both to the higher and lower sort, as well to the governors as to the common people." The Archbishop then expostulates with the different classes in the State, and concludes with a fervent prayer,[1] which might form a model for all such supplications. This discourse, the only one we have of the Archbishop, is interesting, as it affords valuable contemporary evidence as to the condition of the country at that time. With the omission of these special allusions, the Sermon might be preached with good effect at the present day, if similar painful occasion should arise.

Cranmer, at this time, was in the very hey-day of his career of energy and usefulness. Happy in his enjoyment of domestic life and on the restoration to him of his wife and children, he was also the most influential person in the kingdom, and had entrusted to him a large share in the direction of the affairs of Church and State. Not content, therefore, with the late appeal to the nation in behalf of the new arrangement made, in answer to the grievances of the Devonshire insurgents, he resolved to stand forth as the champion and exponent of the Liturgical and doctrinal changes effected under his sanction in the conduct of the

[1] " O Lord, whose goodness far exceeds our naughtiness, and whose mercy passeth all measure, we confess Thy judgment to be most just, and that we worthily have deserved this rod wherewith Thou hast now beaten us. We have offended the Lord God. We have lived wickedly, we have gone out of the way. We have not heard Thy Prophets which Thou hast sent unto us to teach us Thy word, nor have done as Thou hast commanded us, wherefore we be most worthy to suffer all these plagues. Thou hast done justly, and we be worthy to be confounded. But we provoke unto us Thy goodness; we appeal unto Thy mercy, we humble ourselves, we acknowledge our faults. We turn to Thee, O Lord, with our whole hearts, in praying, fasting, in testimony and sorrowing for our offences. Have mercy upon us; cast us not off according to our deserts, but hear us and deliver us with speed, and call us to Thee according to Thy mercy, that we, with one consent and one mind, may ever glorify Thee, world without end. Amen."

services of the National Church. With this intention he published in 1552 the most important of all his works, and with which his reputation as a Theologian is identified, entitled, "A Defence of the True and Catholic Doctrine of the Sacrament of the Body and Blood of our Saviour Christ." In this Treatise he set forth plainly and sincerely what in his judgment was the true nature and use of the Lord's Supper; and he then enumerates and refutes the four principal errors maintained by the Church of Rome, viz., Transubstantiation[1]:—"The corporeal presence, the eating and drinking of Christ by the wicked, and the Sacrifice of the Mass." "For what availeth it (he asks) to take away beads, pardons, pilgrimages, and such other like Popery, so long as two chief roots remain unpulled up? Whereof so long as they remain will spring again all former impediments of the Lord's harvest and corruption of his flock." He expresses himself as animated by the purest motives, and concludes his Preface with this earnest appeal :—

"And moved by the duty, office, and place, whereunto it hath pleased God to call me, I give warning in His name unto all that profess Christ, that they flee far from Babylon, if they will save their souls, and to beware of that great harlot, that is to say, the pestiferous See of Rome, that she make you not drunk with her pleasant wine. Trust not her sweet promises, nor banquet with her ; for instead of wine she will give you sour dregs, and for meat she will feed you with rank poison. But come to our Redeemer and Saviour Christ, who refresheth all that truly come unto him, be their anguish and heaviness never so great. Give credit unto Him, in whose mouth was never found guile nor untruth. By Him you shall be clearly delivered from all your diseases, of Him you shall have full remission *a pœna et culpa*. He it is that feedeth continually all that belong unto Him with His own flesh that hanged on the cross ; and giveth them drink of the

[1] Preface to Defence, Jenkyns' "Remains," vol. ii. p. 289. The reader is referred to previous remarks on the Doctrine of Transubstantiation, *ante*, p. 209.

blood flowing out of His own side, and maketh to spring within them water that floweth unto everlasting life."[1]

It is not necessary here to further enter at length into the subject-matter of this Treatise, after what has already been submitted to the reader. It may suffice to record in Cranmer's own words the statement of the Romish doctrine of Transubstantiation :—

"First, the Papists say, that in the Supper of the Lord, after the words of consecration (as they call it), there is none other *substance* remaining but the substance of Christ's flesh and blood, so that there remaineth neither bread to be eaten, nor wine to be drunken. And although there be the colour of bread and wine, the savour, the smell, the bigness, the fashion, and all other (as they call them) accidents or qualities and quantities of bread and wine, yet (say they) there is no very bread nor wine, but they be turned into the flesh and blood of Christ. And this conversion they call *transubstantiation*, that is to say, turning of one substance into another substance."[2]

In contradistinction to this, the Archbishop maintains that "although Christ in His human nature substantially, really, corporeally, naturally, and sensibly be present with His Father in heaven, yet sacramentally and spiritually He is here present. For in water, bread, and wine He is present, as in *signs and sacraments.*" It is plain from these extracts that Cranmer was not only led to renounce the doctrine of Transubstantiation, but that he, with equal wisdom, judgment, and appreciation of the Holy Scriptures and of the ancient Church, rejected the Lutheran tenets of Consubstantiation, and of the anti-Sacramental theories of Zuinglius and Œcolampadius. He was contented to maintain a real presence of the body and blood of Christ "verily and indeed, taken and received by the faithful in the Lord's Supper;" but he entirely refused to designate, prescribe, or define, the mode of that presence. He thus at

[1] Preface to Defence, Jenkyns' "Remains," vol. ii. p. 290.
[2] *Ibid.*, vol. ii. p. 290.

T

once maintained the very fulness of the saying of the Divine Founder of this Heavenly Feast: "This is my body, do this in *remembrance of Me*," surrounded it with the fulness of sacramental blessing, attached to its outward sign an inward and spiritual grace, and yet freed the Holy Institution from all the contrariant, narrow, and enforced definitions which have darkened and degraded a ceremony which should be uplifted far beyond the realm of human disputations. The learned Editor of "Cranmer's Remains" is amply justified in his description of this Treatise :— " The result is most satisfactory, for after all that has since been written, it is not easy to point out any tract of the same length against the Romish errors more distinguished for closeness of reasoning, clearness of arrangement, and a searching investigation of the subject."[1]

This vigorous attack met with an equally vigorous defence. Dr Richard Smythe, the Regius Professor of Divinity at Oxford, and Dr Gardyner, Bishop of Winchester, came forward as champions of Romish doctrines, and published replies to the Archbishop's Treatise. To these replies the Archbishop prepared an answer. He reprinted, without curtailment, both Gardyner's book and his own, adding such further explanations as he thought requisite to meet the objections of his opponents. He thus laid the whole case, as it was argued on both sides, fairly before the reader, in the perfect conviction, that the more thoroughly it was examined, the more decisive would be the judgment in his favour. Bishop Gardyner published a second answer to the Archbishop, under the assumed name of Marcus Antonius Constans, to which Cranmer was about to supply a third Treatise, in further confirmation of his arguments, when the controversy was abruptly closed.

[1] Jenkyns' "Preface," vol. i. p. lxxxvi.

The great changes effected by the Reformation, both in Church and State, rendered necessary some re-adjustment and revision of the existing Civil and Ecclesiastical Laws. For this purpose, Cranmer, assisted chiefly by two eminent civilians, Sir John Cheke and Dr Walter Hadden, prepared a Code of Laws, known by the title, " Reformatio Legum."[1] This code was completed too late in the reign of Edward VI. to have become invested with any legal authority. It is, however, a useful and important document, as being an authentic record of the re-adjustment of the laws deemed necessary by those great leaders of the Reformation. It retained, nevertheless, some of the old Popish leaven of persecution for conscience' sake, but restricted "heresy" to the denial of the admitted fundamental principles of Christianity. A prominent feature of this, the last published work on which Cranmer was engaged, is the injunction laid on the Bishops to hold a Synod of their clergy in their respective Dioceses once a year, in the season of Lent. It is evident from this book of Laws that the present personal autocrated rule of the Bishop in his Diocese was never the intention of the great

---

[1] The " Reformatio Legum " was a work of high pretensions; that, probably, on which Cranmer thought his fame would rest. It was distributed into fifty-one "Titles," in imitation of Justinian's celebrated digest of the Roman law; and, in imitation of the addition to the printed copies of the Pandects; an Appendix, *de regulis juris*, was supplied. Very considerable care was taken in the preparation of it: " Atque hoc modo hæ quidem leges sunt, sive eas ecclesiasticas, sive politicas, appellare libeas. Quarum materia ab optimis undique legibus petita videtur, non solum ecclesiasticis, sed civilibus etiam, veterumque Romanorum præcipua antiquitate. Summæ negotii præfuit Tho. Cranmerus, Archpis. Cant., orationis lumen et splendorem addidit Gualterris. Haddonus erit disertus et in hac ipsa juris facultate non imperitus. Quin hæc satis scio an Johan Gheci viri singularis eidem negotio adjutrix adfuerit manus. Quo factum est, ut cultiori stylo concisinatæ sint istæ leges, quam pro commune ceterarum legum more."—" The Reformation of the Ecclesiastical Laws in the Reigns of Henry VIII., Edward VI., and Elizabeth." Edit. Oxford, 1850. Cardwell, p. xxvi., Preface.

Master Builder of the Reformation. His design was that the Church should be governed by a Diocesan Episcopate, by Bishops acting through and by their Synods. Is not some such modification of the Episcopacy the crying need of the Church in these difficult times ? If this proposed re-adjustment of the ecclesiastical and civil law had taken place, many of the vexatious suits of the present day, before the Privy Council, would probably have been obviated, and in that case another link would have been added to the chain of the benefits conferred upon the English Church by the most distinguished in his long line of distinguished Archbishops.

All these active plans and future reforms of Cranmer were arrested in a moment by the premature death of Edward VI. But the work which the great Archbishop had effected remained sure and steadfast as an anchor embedded in the sand, and became strengthened, annealed, and popularised in the eyes and hearts of the Church and nation by the four subsequent years of fiery persecutions in the reign of Queen Mary.

Who can rise from this record of the writings of Cranmer, of which a few examples have been given, at perhaps too great a length, without an increased admiration of his learning, judgment, talents, self-control, marvellous influence, and authority ?

Born of an ancient and gentle lineage, a diligent student at Jesus College, Cambridge, of the classics and the Civil and Canon Law ; brought early in life to the keen appreciation of the value of the Holy Scriptures ; confirmed in his more liberal views by his intercourse with the foreign Reformers, and his near relationship to Osiander ; trained to the manners of the Court, by his position as Ambassador to foreign countries ; of the strictest personal piety, so that not a whisper of defamation could assail his character; free from the rivalries of hostile politicians, by his known absence of personal ambition, by his yielding disposition to " bend the crooked hinges of his knees," and to conciliate the caprices of an arbitrary Sovereign.

" His views were large and liberal beyond his times ; his heart and his purse were open to ability of every description ; nor, although a strenuous advocate of truth, was he ever uncharitably and inflexibly severe towards those who persisted in error, but exercised on all occasions a patience and forbearance which his enemies applauded, but which few of his friends were disposed to imitate." [1]

Slow in forming an opinion, yet, having formed it, possessed, as an honest man, of the courage of his convictions ; blessed with an excellent judgment, a calm [2] and judicial mind, a true statesmanlike prescience, removed equally from a too great dependence on the sentiments of others, or a too persistent obstinacy in asserting his own opinions ; well acquainted with the treasures of the primitive Liturgies, with the works of the ancient Latin and Greek Fathers ; inflamed above his compeers with an ardent desire to promote the spiritual welfare of the people and their growth in personal holiness, ARCHBISHOP CRANMER was, alike by his natural temperament, and long train of antecedent and attendant circumstances, singularly adapted for the great work assigned him. Had he been of a self-willed, ambitious, or haughty temperament, he might, like Calvin, Luther, Knox, or Zuingle, have left the impression of his name on the fabric of the English Church. He was,

[1] Dr Lawrence, " Bampton Lectures," p. 18. Third edition, 1838.

[2] Dr Hook, who is by no means a friendly critic, nor a sympathiser with Cranmer's difficulties, speaks of him as " courteous, calm, and prudent." " Lives of the Archbishops," vol. vii. p. 296.

however, too honest a man, too well instructed a " Master
Builder." He would remove from the coat of his erring
brother the garish lace and unfitting embroidery forbidden
by his Father's will, but he would not, in so doing, use the
violence of his brother Martyrs, and destroy the garment.
He thus threw off the cerecloths of the Papacy, and at the
same time escaped the taint of submission to any of the
controversialists of the day. Enrolling many of the chief
leaders of the German Reformation among his personal
friends, he never allowed his judgment to be warped by
their prejudices, nor to be led astray by their suggestions.
He acted on higher and nobler principles. He was content to reform and to re-construct the National territorial
Church on its existing foundation, to enforce, in their integrity its ancient Creeds ; to retain its old Liturgies, to confirm its traditional customs, to continue to uphold the dignity
of the Episcopacy, to re-establish its earlier privilege of a
vernacular Bible, to uphold its legitimate Convocations,
and to remove nothing which could be proved consonant
with the teachings of Holy Scripture, and with the
preachers of the first ages of the Faith.

Thus, in singleness of heart, and firmness of purpose,
and in perfect simplicity of soul, ARCHBISHOP CRANMER
was the honoured instrument of effecting that Reformation
for the English Church which, free alike from the accre-
tions of Popery, and from the shortcomings of popular
Protestantism, has provided in these days a pure and
apostolic system, suited for the adoption of all National
Churches, and which, amidst all the multiplied hindrances
and imperfections inherent in human institutions, has
raised this Country, during the past three centuries, to its
present foremost position among the nations of the Earth.

APPENDIX.

Note to p. 27.

JOHN FOX, THE MARTYROLOGIST.

We are informed that "the reputation of the secular Priest SANDER for truth is on a par with JOHN FOX!" The notorious slanderer, Sander,[1] is to be placed in the same scales with the learned, pious, and withal humble John Fox, the author of the immortal work best known as "The Book of Martyrs." The juxta-position of the two names, I regret to state, does not originate with Mr S. H. Burke, for he had before him the statement of no less authority than Dr Hook, Dean of Chichester.

From the days of the Jesuit Parsons to those of Dr John Milner, and from Dr Milner to the present time, Fox, who has so graphically and circumstantially recorded the sufferings of the Martyrs of the Reformation, has been branded by members of the unreformed Church as an impostor, a lying historian, a falsifier of documents, and one wholly unworthy of credit. That a historian, dealing with the numerous individual cases in his "Acts and Monuments," should be universally accurate in all his details, would be unreasonable to expect. Have not, to some extent, the like objections been raised to Gibbon, Hume, Alison, Froude? But of Fox it may be fairly asserted, that no historical work will bear stricter scrutiny for the truth of its broad details than his "Book of Martyrs." Allowing all the industry of his assailants during three centuries, there is nothing of any real moment to justify the charge that Fox was a liar, or that he falsified documents. And even if we cancel, from his history, all his statements to which objection is brought, there will be ample material left to convict the Church of Rome of a cruel and persecuting spirit, which alone can account for the malignant hatred exhibited against the author.

It may be briefly stated that all Fox's contemporaries, who could judge of the truth or otherwise of the alleged *facts*, admired and supported him, while his critics lay behind the possibility of knowledge. Again, the Convocation of 1571 required every Prelate and Archdeacon to keep a copy of "the Acts and Monuments," for family reading, in his hall. By an order made by the Court of the Archdeacon of Essex (Sept. 17, 1577), for Thornchurch Parish, "Fox's last Book of Monuments" was directed to be procured, "and chained to the desk in the

---

[1] "The authority of our countryman, Sander, a man so famous for *veracity*, that if Captain Lemuel Gulliver had not supplanted him, we might use the proverbial phrase, *It is as true as if Sander had used it.*"—Joslin, "Additions to Neves' 'Remarks on Phillips,'" p. 563.

Church."[1] It may be safely presumed that those who enacted this knew the *facts* at first hand, and were satisfied of their substantial truth.

Fox was born A.D. 1517. He entered Brazenose College, Oxford, in 1543. He was chosen Fellow of Magdalen College. He was ordained Priest at the hands of Bishop Ridley, in June 1550. In consequence of his making no secret of his Reformation principles, he was compelled to leave his College. He died 18th April 1587 in his seventieth year. Fox thus passed through the stirring times of the reigns of Henry VIII., Edward VI., Mary, and Elizabeth, the periods covered by his History. Fuller, in his "Church History," Book ix. sec. 68. p. 76, London, 1555, of Fox says :—

" There in this age were divided into two ranks. Some, mild and moderate, contented only to enjoy their own conscience. Others, fierce and fiery, to the disturbance of Church and State. Amongst the former, I recount the Principall, Father John Fox (for so Queen Elizabeth termed him), summoned (as I take it) by Arch-Bishop Parker to subscribe, that the generall reputation of his piety might give the greater countenance to conformity. The old man [Fox] produced the New Testament in Greek, 'This (he said) will I subscribe.' But when a subscription to the canons was required of him, he refused it, saying, ' I have nothing in the Church save a Prebend at Salisbury, and much good may it do you if you will take it away from me.' However, such respect did the Bishops (most formerly his fellow-exiles) bear to his age, parts, and pains, that he continued his place till the day of his death ; who, though no friend to the Ceremonies, was otherwise so devout in his carriage, that (as his nearest relation surviving hath informed me) he never entered any Church without expressing solemn reverence therein."

Fuller gives the following as the Epitaph, " as we find it on his Monument in S. Giles, nigh Cripple-gate in London " (Book ix. p. 187) :—

"CHRISTO S. S.

" JOHANNI FOXO Ecclesiæ Anglicanæ Martyrologo fidelissimo, Antiquitatis Historicæ.

" Indagatori sagacissimo, Evangelicæ veretatis propugnatori acerrimo, Thaumaturgo admirabili, qui Martyres Marianos, tanquam Phœnices, ex cineribus redivivos præstitit."

Fox was an accomplished scholar, author of several learned works, and deeply read in the writings of the Greek and Latin Fathers. At an early stage of his career he had taken strong views on doctrinal questions as a Reformer. He had a recognised position in society.

---

[1] See Archdeacon Hale's " Precedents in Criminal Causes," p. 169.

He had been Tutor of Thomas, afterwards Earl of Northumberland, and of Jane, Countess of Westmoreland. From a mass of manuscripts relating to Fox, preserved in the British Museum, we find him in constant communication with Grindal,[1] afterwards Archbishop of Canterbury, and with Aylmer, Bishop of London, from both of whom he received substantial assistance in compiling his great work. These manuscripts show, with reference to his public life, Fox's intimacy with the highest and most respected characters of the day. Among these we find Cecil, Lord Burleigh ; Sir Francis Walsingham, Secretary of State ; the Duke of Bedford ; Sir Frances Drake ; Archbishops Grindal, Parker ; and of Alymer, Bishop of London ; Dr Nowell, Dean of St Paul's ; Pilkington ; Lever ; and with several others of the nobility and clergy. "And I cannot but observe," says Strype, "the esteem and character that Whitgift expressed of this reverend man." "The Archbishop," adds Strype, his great biographer, "was not a man to speak otherwise than as he thought, and he spoke of Fox as of one that he loved and venerated."[2] Bullinger wrote to Fox :—" I am devotedly attached to you on account of your piety and learning, but chiefly for your book on the Martyrs of England."[3] We find him held in great respect by Sir Thomas Gresham and the citizens of London. He was also a favourite of Queen Elizabeth, to whom he dedicated his work; and withal he was neither ambitious nor sought preferment ; he was ever in straitened circumstances. His whole life was one of strict piety and abnegation. And this is the man who has been branded as a *liar*, and a *forger*, and *defacer of documents*, to give colour to his "lying History."

Harding, the Jesuit, in his controversy with Bishop Jewell, called Fox's "Acts and Monuments" "the dunghill of your stinking Martyrs." To this Jewell replied[4] :—

" It pleaseth you, for lack of other evasion, to call the story of the Martyrs a dunghill of lies. But these lies shall remain on record for ever, to testify and to condemn your bloody doings. Ye have impri-

[1] " Many accounts of the acts and disputations, of the sufferings and ends of the godly men under Queen Mary, came from time to time to Grindal's hands ; who had a correspondence with several in England for that end and purpose. And as they came to his hands, he conveyed them to Fox. Nor did he only do this, but he frequently gave Fox his thoughts concerning them, and his instructions and counsels about them ; always showing a most tender regard to truth, nor adopting common reports and relations till more satisfactory evidence came through good hands."—Strype's " Annals."

[2] Strype's Life of Whitgift, ap. Strype's "Annals," 1587, pp. 504, 505, fol. 1728.

[3] " Acts and Mon. of Fox," edit. 1843, pt. i. sect. iv. p. 65.

[4] Works of Bishop Jewell, pp. 27, 28, edit. 1609 ; and see also pt. iii. c. i. div. 3, pp. 315 and 316.

soned your brethren ; ye have stripped them naked ; ye have scourged
them with rods ; ye have burned their hands and arms with flaming
torches ; ye have famished them ; ye have drowned them ; ye have
summoned them, being dead, to appear before you out of their graves ;
ye have ripped up their buried carcasses ; ye have burned them ; ye
have thrown them into the dunghill ; ye took a poor babe, and in the
most cruel and barbarous manner ye threw him into the fire."

Jewell further retorted on Harding :—

" Our wantons and flesh worms, for so it liketh you to call them,
have been contented to forsake fathers, mothers, wives, children, goods,
and livings, and meekly to submit themselves to all the terror of your
cruelties, and to yield their bodies unto the death ; to be starved with
hunger, to be burned with fire, only for the name of the Gospel of
Jesus Christ ; so delicate and flesh worms and wantons are they !
Ye will say, that they died stubbornly in wilful error. Yet, I reckon
not ye will say they died in great pleasure, or carnal liberty. It is a
strange kind of fleshly wantonness, for a man to take up his Cross and
follow Christ. And yet this is the substance of our Gospel."

This is a practical answer to such as assail Fox's " Book of Martyrs."

Fox commenced his " Acts and Monuments " abroad, where he resided to escape the persecutions of Queen Mary's reign, and did not
return until the accession of Elizabeth. While abroad, he received
considerable assistance in his work from Grindal and from others.
And to that extent he was obliged to rely on the faith and character
of his correspondents. In accepting these communications, Strype
observes that Fox exhibited " a most tender regard to truth, and
suspending upon common reports and relations brought over, till more
satisfactory evidence came from good hands." [1] We also find him
assisted by Aylmer, formerly tutor to Lady Jane Grey, and afterwards
Bishop of London, as also by several English divines.

With regard to the work in question, the first edition, being a mere
sketch, was printed at Basle in 1554 ; an enlarged edition was printed
in Latin in 1559.

On his return to England, Fox devoted his energies in verifying
the communications made to him, examining records, and taking ex-
tensive journeys to verify facts. In 1563 he published another edition,
under the title—

"Acts and Monuments of these latter and perilous days, touching

---

[1] " When all this was understood by Mr Foxe, he came himself to Ipswich
to inform himself truly about it. . . . I have set down all this at length, to
show what diligence and care was used that no falsehood might be obtruded
upon the readers, and Foxe and his friends' readiness to correct any mistakes
that might happen."—Strype's " Annals of the Reformation," vol. i. pp
378-380.

matters of the Church ; wherein are comprehended and described the great persecutions and horrible troubles that have been brought and practised by the Romish Prelates, especially in this realm of England and Scotland, from the year of our Lord one thousand, unto the time now present, gathered and collected according to the true copies and writings certificatory, as well as of the parties themselves that suffered,[1] as also out of the Bishops' registers, which were the doers thereof."

We have first on our list the opinion of Strype, who bears testimony of the " infinite pains" Fox took in compiling his facts. He adds [2] :—

" Herein he hath done exquisite service to the Protestant cause, in showing from abundance of ancient books, records, registers, and choice manuscripts, the encroachments of Popes and Papalins, and the stout oppositions, made by learned men, in all ages and in all countries, against them ; and especially under King Henry and Queen Mary, here in England.   Preserving to us the memories of those holy men and women, those Bishops and Divines, together with their histories, acts, sufferings, and their constant deaths, willingly undergone for the sake of Christ and His Gospel, and for refusing to comply with Popish doctrines and superstitions."

Again [3] :—

" Great was the expectation of the book in England before it came abroad.   The Papists then scurrilously styled it 'Fox's Golden Legend.' When it first appeared, there was extraordinary fretting and fuming at it through all quarters of England, and even to Louvain.   They charged it with lies, and said there was much falsehood in it ; but indeed they said this, because they were afraid it should betray their cruelty and their lies."

The Jesuit Parsons alleged, "as we presume" (for such are his words), that Fox mutilated registers and records, otherwise it might have been, he tells us, able to refute his statements ! Strype, however, tells us that [4] :—

" Fox was an indefatigable searcher into old registers, *and left them as he found them*, after he had made his collections and transcriptions out of them, many whereof I have seen and do possess.   And it was his interest that they should remain to be seen by posterity ; therefore we frequently find references thereunto in the margins of his book. Many have diligently compared his books with registers and council books, and have always found him faithful.

[1] One of the most important accusations against Fox is, that he recorded the burning of an individual who survived the alleged ordeal, and lived to contradict the tale, which is probably a fact.   But it is manifestly unjust to apply to this the trite argument, "ex uno disce omnes."

[2] "Annals," vol. i. p. 374-5.   Oxford, 1824.

[3] *Ibid.*, vol. i. p. 375.   [4] *Ibid.*, pp. 376, 377.

"As he hath been found most diligent, so most strictly true and faithful in his transcriptions, and this I myself in part have found."

And, by the way, I may here note that the writer of the article "John Fox," in the Ninth, and last, Edition of the "Encyclopædia Britannica" (p. 503), remarks :—" It (the 'Acts and Monuments') was vigorously attacked by Catholic writers, and its accuracy *in details* has been successfully challenged, even such blunders as credulity, gross over-credulity, having been expended ; but the honourable lives of Fox and his assistants place the work above the charge of wilful falsehood." The writer gives no illustrations of this "over-credulity." It is always safer to travel along a well-worn groove. To attack Fox's book has been even the labour of our ritualistic Clergymen.

Strype goes into particulars to prove how unfounded are several of the charges imputing untruthfulness to Fox ; and, for the most part, the errors are of very slight importance, considering the magnitude of the work. But the disgrace lies in the fact that these refuted charges are being continually repeated as new and original discoveries.

The learned Oldmixon, in his "History of England," during the reigns of Henry VIII. to Queen Elizabeth, including the "History of the Reformation," London 1730, page 336, writes of Fox :—

"The Rev. Father Mr John Fox, the Martyrologist, a grave, learned, and painful Divine, an Exile for religion, who employed his time abroad in writing 'The Acts and Monuments' of that Church, that would hardly receive him into her bosom, and in collecting Materials relating to the Martyrdom of those that suffered for religion in the reigns of Henry VIII. and Queen Mary, all which he published first in Latin, for the benefit of Foreigners, and then in English, for the service of his own Country and the Church of England, in the year 1561. No book ever gave such a mortal wound to Popery as this. It was dedicated to the Queen, and was in such high reputation that it was ordered to be set up in the Churches, where it raised in the People an invincible Scorn and Detestation of that religion that had shed so much innocent Blood."

And he styles him an "excellent and laborious divine."

Camden, in his "Annals of Elizabeth," thus speaks of Fox :—

"Of the members of the learned, died John Foxe of Oxford, who, with an unwearied zeal for truth, compiled, with general approbation, an 'Ecclesiastical History of England, or Martyrology,' first in Latin, and afterwards enlarged in English."

Soame [1] writes as follows :—

"Invariable accuracy is not to be expected in any historical work of such extent ; but it may be truly said of England's venerable martyrologist, that his relations are more than ordinarily worthy of reliance.

[1] "History of the Reformation," vol. iv. pp. 721, 722. London 1828.

His principal object being indeed to leave behind him a vast mass of authentic information relating to those miserable times which it had been his lot to witness; he printed a vast mass of original letters, records of judicial processes, and other documentary evidence. The result of this judicious policy was a work which has highly gratified the friends of Protestantism, and successfully defied its enemies. Numerous attacks have been levelled at the honest chronicles of Romish intolerance, but they have ever fallen harmless from the assailants' hands."

Neale, in his " History of Puritans," bears the following testimony[1]:— " No book ever gave such a mortal wound to Popery as this. It was dedicated to the Queen, and was in such reputation that it was ordered to be set up in Churches, where it raised in the people an invincible horror and detestation of that religion which had shed so much innocent blood."

The accurate and painstaking Benjamin Brook, in his " Lives of the Puritans," writes as follows[2] :— " Several writers have laboured to depreciate the memory of Fox, by insinuating that his history of the Martyrs contained many misrepresentations and falsehoods. Fox and his friends used the utmost diligence and care that no falsehood might be obtruded on the reader, and were ever ready to correct any mistakes that might happen. Though he might be misinformed in several parts of his intelligence, yet these were inconveniences which must attend the compiling of so large a body of modern history as Mr Fox's chiefly was. No man is likely to receive from various hands so large a mass of information, and all.be found perfect truth, and when digested to be found without the least trace of error. What is the weight of all the objections offered in contempt of the Foxean Martyrs, to overthrow so solid and unanswerable a fabric? It is imputed of so many undeniable evidences of Popish barbarities, that its reputation will be unsullied to the last period of time. The Acts and Monuments of the Martyrs have long been, they still remain, and will always continue substantial pillars of the Protestant Church ; of more force than many volumes of bare arguments, to withstand the tide of Popery ; and like a Pharos, should be lighted up in every age, as a warning to all posterity. No book ever gave so deep a wound to the errors, superstitions, and persecutions of Popery, on which account the talents and labours of Fox rendered him a fit object of papal malice and enmity."

The following is from the Preface of Dr Wordsworth's "Ecclesiastical Biograhpy,"[3] whose character as an author and divine stands above suspicion :—

[1] Vol. i. c. iv. p. 124.   London, 1754.
[2] Vol. i. pp. 331-2.   London, 1813.   [3] P. xviii.   London, 1839.

"I am well aware that by the extent to which I have availed myself of Fox's 'Acts and Monuments,' I fall within the range of such censures as that of Dr John Milner, in which he speaks of 'the frequent publica tions of John Fox's lying book of Martyrs, with prints of men, women, and children expiring in flames, the nonsense, inconsistency, and falsehoods of which,' he says, 'he had in part exposed in his Letters to a Prebendary.' I am not ignorant of what has been said also by Dr Milner's predecessors, in the same argument, by Harpsfield, Parsons, and others. But neither his writings nor theirs, *have proved, and it never will be proved, that John Fox is not one of the most faithful and authentic of all historians.* We know too much of the strength of Fox's book, and of the weakness of those of his Romish adversaries, to be further moved by Dr John Milner's censures, than to reject them as grossly exaggerated and almost entirely unsubstantial and groundless. All the many researches and discoveries of later times, in regard to historical documents, by Burnet, Strype, and others, have only contributed to place the general fidelity and truth of Fox's melancholy narrative on a rock which cannot be shaken.—How great then is the effrontery of those writers who attempt to persuade us, that the accounts given us by Fox are forgeries of his own devising."

Le Bas, in his excellent "Life of Cranmer," says[1] :—

"The work of Fox was compiled with unwearied industry from documents and materials of unquestionable authority ; and it was subjected by him to scrupulous revisal, during the remainder of his life ; which was protracted for many years beyond the period of its first appearance."

And he further adds :—

"With regard to the fidelity of Fox, in the use of documents and records, we have the following testimony of Mr Todd,[2] himself an investigator whose accuracy is far above suspicion :—'In the numer-ous researches, which it has often been my duty to make among ancient registers, and other records, the accuracy of Fox, in such as he has applied to his purpose, is indisputable.'"

Professor Smyth, in his "Lectures on Modern History,"[3] thus approvingly refers to the work in question :—

"Fox's 'Book of Martyrs' should be looked at. It is indeed, in itself, a long and dreadful history of the intolerance of the human mind, and, at the same time, of the astonishing constancy of the human min⅃; that is, at once a monument of its lowest debasement and its highest elevation.

[1] Vol. ii. pp. 196-7. London, 1833.
[2] Todd's "History and Critical Introduction to Cranmer's Defence," &c., &c., p. iv. note. London, 1825.
[3] Bohn's edit., 1834, vol. i. p. 289, Lecture x.

The volumes of Fox are also descriptive of the manners and opinions of the different ages through which the author proceeds. The transactions relating to Anne Askew ; the disputations of Lambert before Henry VIII., of Latimer, Ridley, and Cranmer at Oxford ; with the examination and sufferings of these eminent martyrs ; should be thoroughly read, and may serve as specimens of such atrocities, and at first sight such astounding scenes. Fox may be always consulted when the enormities of the Papists are to be sought for."

The Rev. C. Hebert, D.D., thus speaks of Fox :[1]—

" No one can have at all extensively consulted it without coming upon its historical defects, but it was a work compiled with great care, and by the aid of others, so that possibly a better could not, at that time, have been made, and Bishop Grindal compiled materials for part of it ; for none can charge him with fiction or willing exaggeration. His work is, after all, invaluable, and without a rival it has remained to this day."

Froude, in his " History of England,"[2] says : —

" I have already said that whenever Foxe prints documents, instead of relating hearsay, I have found him uniformly trustworthy ; so far, that is to say, as there are means of testing them."

The Rev. Thomas Frognall Dibdin, D.D., contemplated editing Fox's book. On the issue of his prospectus, Mr Southey wrote to him : " Is your edition of the ' Acts and Monuments ' going forward ? I have always intended to take advantage of its appearance for writing a life of John Fox in the Q. R., wherein I might render due honour to a man for whom I have a great veneration." The venerable and learned Dr Rennell, Dean of Winchester, wrote to Dibdin : " I return you my best thanks for your kind communication of your intention of giving a new edition of Fox's ' Martyrs.' I think it is impossible to conceive an undertaking of more importance to the best interests of the Protestant cause ; and that in carrying this design into execution you will have deserved well of your country. To vindicate Fox's veracity, as would be done in the course of your most laudable undertaking, would be to render an essential service to the Church of England."[3]

In the Preface of John Gough Nichol's " Narratives of the Days of the Reformation, chiefly from the MSS. of John Fox,"[4] we read :—

" I deem it perfectly unnecessary to attempt any formal defence of Foxe's honesty and veracity. I believe him to have been truth-seeking, but liable to mistakes, in an age of difficult communication, and perhaps occasionally subjected to intentional misinformation."

[1] "Lord's Supper," vol. ii. p. 475, A.D. 1517. London, 1879.
[2] Vol. vi. p. 334. London, 1860.
[3] " Reminiscences of a Literary Life," part ii. pp. 840-84. London, 1836.
[4] Printed by the Camden Society, 1859, p. 22 et seq.

And in a note is added :—" I am not myself aware of any personal instance of this ; but it is thus stated, and judiciously commented upon by Granger in his ' Biographical History of England ' :—' The same has been said of Foxe which was afterwards said of Burnet, that several persons furnished him with accounts of pretended facts, with a view of ruining the credit of the whole performance. But the author does not stand in need of this apology ; as it was impossible in human nature to avoid many errors in so voluminous a work, a great part of which consists in anecdotes.' " With all its inaccuracies and the prejudices against Fox, the author adds—" The book becomes most valuable as a record of the doings and sufferings, a mirror of the opinions, passions, and manners of the people of England,—for familiar pictures of public and private struggles for conscience' sake, it is probably unequalled in any country or language. It is the Chronicle of the days of the Reformation, the BOOK OF MARTYRS upon which the intense interest of their own and many subsequent generations was concentrated."

Jenkyns, in his Preface to " The Remains of Cranmer," Oxford edition, 1833, continually refers to Fox's book without the slightest hesitation. With reference to the last days of Cranmer, he adds :— " A doubt may perhaps be raised respecting the propriety of inserting in the present publication the copious extracts from Foxe, which describes these closing scenes of Cranmer.—Foxe's report was collected with great diligence, and is probably as accurate as the confused nature of the discussion and the unfairness of those who presided at it allowed." (Preface, p. cxiv.)

Samuel Carlyle,[1] in his Preface to the " Life and Writings of Fox," informs us that on making enquiries of Mr Jenkyns, with reference to the amount of reliance to be placed in Fox's book, he replied :—" I had occasion, in editing ' Cranmer's Remains,' to compare several of the papers produced by Fox with the original documents, and on such comparison I had good reason to be satisfied with the martyrologist's fidelity and accuracy."

The Rev. Richard Watson Dixon, in his recent excellent work, " History of the Church of England," London, 1881, also repeatedly refers to Fox's " Acts and Monuments."

The main question, as appears to me, is the value of the work itself, independent of any question as to the extreme accuracy of all its parts. With these remarkable testimonies before us, from men of acknowledged reputation, I must confess that I was taken by surprise when I read the following in Dean Hook's book, " Lives of the Archbishops "[2] :—

[1] " Church Historians of England," vol. i. p. 166. London, 1870.
[2] Vol. vi. p. 148. Edit. 1868.

" Protestants complain with justice of Sander, who stands in the same relation to the Roman Catholic writers as Fox does to Protestants. Sander, *the purveyor of filthy scandals of the age*, and it is not too much to say that of some he was the author. Of him, it was said, ' he lied, and he knew that he lied.' But they who would throw the stone at Sander [the Dean having himself already hurled a huge brickbat at his head] must not forget the amount of glass of which their own house is composed. For the character of Fox, I will refer not to a Roman Catholic but to the scholar more competent, from his deep researches into the public records, to form an opinion upon the subject :—' Had [Fox] the Martyrologist,' says Professor Brewer, ' been an honest man, his carelessness and credulity would have incapacitated him from being a trustworthy Historian. Unfortunately he was not honest, he tampered with the documents that came [in] to his hands, and freely indulged in those very faults of suppression [and equivocation] for which he condemned his opponents.' "

The reference given by the Dean is incorrect, it should be " Letters and Papers, Foreign and Domestic," Henry VIII., vol. i. p. lxxxv.

The passsge quoted stands in a note *apropos* to nothing, without a single confirmatory example to substantiate the sweeping charge—amounting, at least, to a charge of deliberate fraud. Had such been forthcoming, we probably would have detected the labour of a "Literary resurrectionist" digging up dry bones, long since buried. But Mr Brewer gives no proofs.

In a note to the above extract, the Dean adds :—

" Some years ago I had occasion to consult the Rev. Dr Maitland, the learned Librarian of Lambeth, on the amount of credit I might give to a statement made by Fox. His answer was, ' You may regard Fox as being about as trustworthy as the *Record* Newspaper. You must not believe either, when they speak of an opponent, for though professing Protestantism, they are innocent of Christian Charity. You may accept the documents they print, but certainly not without collation. Fox forgot, if he ever knew, who is the father of lies.' "

And we are to accept this jaunty statement—more uncharitable than any of Fox's alleged lies—as a correct estimate of the value of Fox's " Acts and Monuments," in preference to the deliberate and well-considered observations of Strype, Soames, Neale, Brooke, Dr Wordsworth, Todd, and Le Bas, and the several other learned men above named! Dr Maitland's reference to the *Record* Newspaper sufficiently indicates his prejudiced mind ; and it is scarcely creditable to Dr Hook to retail such an anecdote, probably never intended by the utterer for adoption and reproduction in a serious Biographical history !

On the subject of Dr Maitland's and other attacks on Fox's Book, the reader may profitably consult the Preface to Townsend's Edition, 1843, of "The Acts and Monuments." Also an elaborate and able reply in "Church Historians of England," London, 1870, vol. i. pp. 99 *et seqq.*, in the Chapter entitled, "The Objectors and Objections to the General Authority and veracity of Fox's Acts and Monuments considered," in which the various leading statements of opponents, including Dr Maitland's, are examined. With regard to Dr Maitland, he has admitted quite enough to justify Fox's Book. In his "Reformation in England," p. 575, he gives the number of martyrs of Mary's reign to be 277. "Finding the number, as I took them from Fox, to consider with that which had been long since given, on, I know not what authority, I am induced to hope that my list is not far wrong." And he has arrived at this estimate, he tells us, "after a good deal of trouble has been taken to make it as full and correct as possible."

The reader will also find most important information, and an able defence of Fox's Book, in the first volume, Chapter ii. pp. 73 *et seqq.*, Religious Tract Society. The Introduction and Biographical Preface is written by the Rev. J. Stoughton, D.D.

To conclude this brief notice, I cannot do better than endorse the recommendation of Dr Samuel Waldegrave, Bishop of Carlisle :—

"We should do wisely in the days of Victoria to outvie the Reformers of the sixteenth Century, by placing a copy of the 'Book of Martyrs,' not indeed in every Church, but in every house ; yea, in every hand; and is there not a cause? Rome is labouring with redoubled effort for the subjugation of Britain. She attacks us openly from without, while there are traitors ready to open our gates from within, and the people have forgotten that she is a siren who enchants but to destroy."

APPENDIX B, p. 194.

The executions of the so-called Martyrs during the reigns of Henry VIII., Elizabeth, and James I., are enumerated by names and dates in a book entitled "A Calendar of English Martyrs of the Sixteenth and Seventeeth Centuries" (London, 1876), bearing the "Imprimatur" of Cardinal Manning. These so-called Martyrs were either beheaded or hanged as rebels and traitors, but not one of them for denying any doctrine of the then accepted faith of the Roman Church. The stake was the punishment for heresy. Notwithstanding, we are told in this "Calendar" that they "suffered death for the Catholic faith;" that they were "called upon to shed their blood for Christ's sake." In publishing this list, "It was thought that such a roll of our Martyrs, marking day by day the recurring anniversaries of their victories, would help to keep alive their memory in the minds of English Catholics, and, moreover, suggest the practical devotion of habitually invoking their intercession," and that their example is to be followed should occasion require. Fifty-four of these are said to have recently been "beatified," the first step to canonisation, and two hundred and fifty-one declared "Venerable" (see *Times*, 10th January, and *Weekly Register*, 26th February 1887). Among these stand forth prominently Bishop Fisher and the Chancellor More, the arch-traitor Campion, Garnet, the accomplice of Guy Foxe, and Felton, who defiantly affixed a copy of the Pope's Bull of excommunication on the gate of the Bishop of London's Palace, and the eleven Priests executed in the reign of King James, who pitiously petitioned the Pope for permission to take the oath of allegiance to the King, who refused, and who (according to the opinion even of Dr O'Conor, a Roman Catholic Priest, in his "Historical Narrative of eleven Priests confined in Newgate for not renouncing the Pope's Pretended Paper," Buckingham, 1812) "died in resistance to legitimate authority, and by the instigation of a foreign power." Dr O'Conor deliberately lays the charge of their "murder" on the Pope. See further on this subject the opinions of Bzovius, the [R.C.], "Annalist," "De Rom. Pont.," c. lxiv. p. 621, edit. Antwerp, 1601, and the "Introduction" to the "Memoirs of Gregoria Panzini," Birmingham, 1793, by the Rev. W. Berington, a Roman Catholic Priest.

Turnbull & Spears, Printers, Edinburgh.